Copyright

SLEEP is a work of fiction. Names, characters, and events in this book are fictitious. Any resemblance to actual persons, living or dead, or events, is entirely coincidental and not intended by the author

H Publishing

SLEEP

A Novel

By

Craig Henebury

For my mother, for showing us what love and commitment really mean.

PROLOGUE

A branch hidden in the darkness clawed a scratch upon Amy's pale cheek. Tears streamed down her face, not from the branches and thorns that had tore at her flesh as she raced farther into the wood. The horror of her situation had brought forth the tears, summoning sorrow until Despair appeared and took hold of her. Life had become unbearable.

Exhausted, Amy finally stopped running and slumped to the ground. She looked down into her daughter's eyes. Though she loved the infant dearly, the child was tainted, hers but also *his*.

The pills had dulled her senses but could do nothing to ease her splintered heart. Amy placed the baby on the ground and removed a small knife from the pocket in her white cotton dress. Unravelling the blanket exposed the infant.

"Oh God, why? Didn't I love you?" she shouted. Neither the wood nor God offered a reply.

She removed the knife from the sheath revealing the blade. Light flashed across Amy's face as moonlight reflected off the steel. She held the blade to the child's wrist. The child looked at her mother and started to cry, perhaps sensing the mother's distress. Amy gripped the knife harder and squeezed on the baby's arm. The cries grew louder. Suddenly, Amy let go of the arm, ashamed. Behind the tears, a smile broke as she realised she was unable to hurt the child further.

"I'm so sorry, my sweet little thing, but Mommy has to go. There is a part of you I love with all the pieces of my heart, but your father is a devil, a deceiver and a most vile man. I cannot go on, but I will let God decide for you."

Amy took the blade and drew it across her wrist, then the next. She felt no pain, just a strange warmth in her arms as her life drained away.

CHAPTER 1

Leaving their home, Maggie and Taylor Pritchard walked the side roads heading toward Richmond Nature Park. It was six thirty-five, the warmth of the early morning July sun could already be felt on their faces. The contrasting cool air made the hairs on their exposed arms bristle. Maggie grabbed Taylor's arm, hugging it as she had done on so many occasions. Taylor looked across to see her smiling, her light brown hair appeared to sparkle as rays of sunshine flashed through the curls.

"It's not *that* cold."

"I'm just giving you a hug. You didn't warm me up this morning." Maggie replied. Maggie took a deep breath. "I love this time of day, it's so quiet and the air's still fresh."

"It's your turn to cook breakfast when we get back."

They made their way across Shell Road and entered the west side of the park. Richmond Nature Park is a mass of trees and dirt path trails, interrupted only by structures rising like concrete fingers from the earth to elevate the Ninety-nine expressway.

Maggie had decided on the walk this Saturday morning. Taylor had proposed a cycle route along the Fraser River toward the airport to watch the planes coming in. Maggie had prevailed.

At this time, it was still possible to catch some of the nocturnal wildlife, snooping around the woods for a final few minutes before disappearing off into their hideaways. The birds were wide awake and at their most vocal, as if this were the only time they could hear themselves talk. The trail would take two hours to cover even at the brisk pace they were used to.

The treks gave them an opportunity to catch up on office gossip. Taylor was a computer programmer for an IT consultancy. Five years ago, he had been assigned as part of a larger team to help customise a new CRM system for a bank. Maggie was already working at the bank as a Customer Services Manager and had also been assigned to the eighteen-month project. Customer Relationship Management was all the rage - knowing who your customers are and anticipating what services they might want or perhaps more precisely, what products they are more likely to purchase.

Only two months into the project, Taylor and Maggie had started going out. Just over two years later they were married, and still working on the same project.

As they reached a fork in the walkway an old man dressed in black shorts and a blue nylon vest came running up from behind them. Taylor stepped toward the left of the fork.

As he passed, the old man said, "Used to run that way. Too old for it now though, just the five miles for me. Have a good day now."

"Er, yeah, you too," Taylor replied, "Wow, I hope I'm that keen when I'm that old."

"Come on, no slacking or you won't reach sixty," Maggie said, bounding past him.

It took around thirty minutes for them to reach the Ninety-nine make their way into the east side of the park. The temperature had risen, and the warm air carried the smell of foliage. The park was quiet.

Quiet, until Maggie's scream echoed around the towering trees. She saw a pale hand partially covered by leaves, lying just off to the side of the path.

Taylor stopped and quickly turned to look at Maggie, her hands were held to her face, her mouth agape, her eyes fixed. He looked in the direction she was staring. The body of a young woman lay motionless, eyes open and fixing a stare at the sky above. The body was clothed in a white dress that was soiled, muddied, and bloody. There were deep lacerations on each wrist with bloody lines leading to the ground, the soil now dark and the surrounding leaves red. Taylor looked back at Maggie, tears now escaping her eyes. She turned away and into Taylor's arms as he walked over to her.

Taylor sat Maggie down on the ground.

"Are you okay?" Taylor asked.

"I think I'm gonna be sick. She looks younger than us, may be not even twenty."

"Sit here for a moment, I'll call the police."

Taylor stood up and pulled his cell phone from the back pocket of his jeans. After checking for a connection, he was about to make the call, when heard something, faint but familiar, and totally unexpected. He took a few steps beyond the body of the young woman and peered into a clump of mixed leaves and foliage. A soiled blanket lay on the ground. Another sound.

"Maggie, come here."

Maggie looked up, her sobbing stopped. "What is it?" she said, getting to her feet.

"Come here. There's a baby. It's just lying here."

Maggie got up and took the few steps over to Taylor. Looking down, she saw a baby, not more than a few weeks old, lying on the ground amongst the leaves. The baby looked up, its eyes wide and alert, repeating the gurgle sound it had made earlier. Maggie bent down and carefully picked the baby up. Gently tilting the baby around she checked the infant for any signs of harm.

"It's a beautiful girl…who needs a clean diaper. She's beautiful," Maggie repeated, using the palm of her hand to warm the child's cheek. "She looks healthy, but her cheeks are a bit pale and she's cold. Do you think she's been here long?"

"I've no idea. I guess probably just a few hours," Taylor replied, looking around at the scene.

"Why would a mother take her own life and leave her baby like this?" Maggie said.

Taylor remembered the phone in his hand. As he dialled 911 he said, "You don't know if she was the mother."

* * * *

Maggie sat holding the baby. Taylor kept pacing backwards and forwards, his hand rubbing the back of his head. He glanced again at Maggie and then at the baby. He stopped pacing for a moment and was about to say something, but with both hands now behind his head, he could only puff his cheeks and expel the air in his lungs. Then he heard talking, then footsteps. Taylor held his breath. His relief was audible when he saw that they were medics.

The police arrived moments later, initially only two uniformed officers who soon radioed in and requested more support. Taylor checked his watch, twenty minutes had passed since he had made the call.

Taylor provided his details and confirmation of ID to one of the officers, who asked him if he was okay.

"Yeah, I was just thinking how it might look if someone else came by and, well, saw us like this," he replied. The officer gave a short chuckle before asking for a short statement.

One of the two medics that had arrived at the scene had taken the baby from Maggie. After checks for heart rate, blood pressure, and temperature, he seemed happy with the infant's condition. The second medic and other officer were with the body. Maggie found herself unable to take much of an interest in what they were doing, her thoughts were for the child.

"The poor thing must be hungry," she said to the attending medic. The medic just smiled before taking the child away.

The second medic appeared to be making preparations for the transfer of the body, apparently in agreement with the police officer that they were dealing with a suicide. Maggie watched as an officer, whose hand was now in a clear glove, placed a small knife into a bag labelled *evidence*. Blood from the knife smeared to the inside of the transparent bag and a wave of nausea swept over Maggie.

The officer holding the evidence bag looked across at Maggie and then down at the bag.

"Are you alright?" asked the officer. Maggie just stood and stared at the officer. "Are you alright?" the officer repeated.

"What will happen to the baby?" Maggie eventually replied.

"She'll been taken to the hospital for further checks and to make sure she's alright. Assuming the baby is fine, she will be the responsibility of Child Welfare. They'll want to come up with an ID and run checks for other family members. We've found no ID on the body and somebody will want confirmation that this is the mother. Could be this woman simply abducted the baby. Are you sure you're okay? It must be quite a shock."

"Err…yes, thank you. It is, but I'll be alright, thank you," Maggie replied as Taylor walked over to her.

"This area is about to closed off until it has been thoroughly checked and cleared as a potential crime scene. Would it be okay if we stopped by, perhaps later on, to take a full statement from you both? Fisher Drive correct?"

"Yeah…sure, we don't have any plans," Taylor replied.

"Well we have everything we need, you can go on your way now. Thank you for calling it in, you'd be surprised how many folks would just ignore something like this. Somebody'll probably stop by later. Try to have a good day now," the officer said.

Taylor put his arms around Maggie, then gently rubbing the tops of her arms, he asked, "You sure you'll be okay? I don't need to get pills off these guys or something?"

"No, I'll be fine. It's just so horrible. How could you do that to yourself and leave a baby like that?"

"Come on, let's start walking back. I think I'll skip breakfast though, if you don't mind."

* * * *

The walk back home seemed much shorter than when they had come, although it had in fact taken them twice as long. They speculated on what had happened with the woman and baby, to the circumstances that might have led to a young woman killing herself and a baby seemingly abandoned. They had taken little notice of the houses and roads they had passed while walking back home.

Although the temperature was up, Maggie felt she needed a hot bath, the sight of the body had left her with a chill and feeling unclean. Taylor made them a strong coffee, grabbed a notepad and pen, and went up to the bathroom.

"Can you remember what that old guy looked like?" he asked, making his way into the bathroom and placing the coffee on the side of the bath tub.

"What for? He couldn't have had anything to do with it. He got to the park after us."

"I know but if I mention that we saw someone to the police they'll want a description. Did he have a moustache?"

"Yes, I think so. Black shorts and a blue top that looked more like a vest. He was white with grey hair that looked like it hadn't been brushed in awhile."

"Anything else you think we should note?"

"About the man?" Maggie asked.

"No, I mean anything else until we discovered…until we saw the baby?"

"No, we hadn't seen anyone else. The park was quiet, empty, that's why we like it at that time. It's supposed to be peaceful."

"You okay to go over what we saw?" Taylor asked softly.

"Taylor is this really necessary? They'll ask us all this when they turn up." Maggie replied.

"If she's not the mother or it wasn't a suicide, then there may be something important that we've seen and just not realised. The longer we leave it the more detail we're likely to forget. I saw it on a program once," he said.

Maggie looked at Taylor, he was leaning forward while sitting on the toilet seat. He was tapping the pen against his knee and his left foot on the toilet mat. He had a habit of becoming restless and speak too quickly when under stress. Maggie reached for his hand.

"I don't think I'll be forgetting this morning in a hurry," Maggie said. "We walked under the highway to the east side. We hadn't walked long, taking the red trail, until I saw her hand. It was horrible. I screamed, you turned and then you saw her." Maggie envisioned the body of the woman, and how she might have looked when life was still a resident. "She had a white dress on, cotton and plain, blue eyes and long blond hair, straight," trying to imagine the hair without the leaves and twigs that had become entwined. "She had a scratch on her face. She looked young, pretty, maybe a few years younger than us. She had scratches to her legs and feet. She was wearing just those canvass shoes. A bit strange don't you think? The white cotton dress and plain canvass shoes, who wears that these days?"

"I didn't notice any jewellery, did you?" Taylor asked, scribbling into the notepad.

Maggie thought of the hands and then the neck, and an ear that was partially visible. "Looked like a small silver ring on her right hand, I remember it because it was in a 'V' shape. I don't remember seeing a necklace or earrings. Taylor what will they do with the baby?"

Taylor stopped writing and looked up. "You heard the officer. They need to confirm who the parents are, and if there's any other family. She may have stolen the baby and then topped herself with guilt or something for all we know."

"If the woman was the mother, I doubt she would have done that to herself if there was a loving father back at home," Maggie suggested.

"I'm sure people with loving families can still become depressed," Taylor chided. Maggie stopped washing herself and looked up at Taylor for a moment before resuming washing. Taylor gave it a moment before continuing, "If there isn't a father, she'll have to go to the grandparents or something. Anyway, what is it with the baby?" Taylor immediately recognised from the look on Maggie's face that he had said the wrong thing. "Listen," he said, attempting to make amends, "the baby will be just fine, they'll find out where it belongs and it's certainly better off now than it would have been if we hadn't have found it. Listen," he said as he gently held her shoulders, "we saved a child a today."

* * * *

The knock at the door finally came at just after three in the afternoon. Two uniformed officers, male and female. The female officer took the lead, standing closest to the door.

"Hello, Taylor Pritchard?" she said offering her hand.

"Yeah, please come in." Taylor replied, shaking the officer's hand.

"How are you? A bit of a scare for you both this morning I imagine," she said as she made her way into the living room. "Hi, you must be Maggie. Nice to meet you Maggie, I'm Officer Sullivan and this is my partner Officer Adkin, but don't mind him." Adkin responded with a tight-lipped smile. "We'd just like to go over a few things from this morning, check a few details. Would that be all right?"

"Would you like a coffee?" Taylor asked.

"Yeah, sure. White, one sugar, thanks," said Sullivan.

"Black, no sugar. Thank you," replied Adkin.

Taylor went into the kitchen to brew some fresh coffee. He left the door open so he could hear the conversation in the living room. Sullivan continued to lead the conversation went over the information that had presumably been relayed to her earlier, stopping to ask Maggie the occasional question. Returning to the living room with the coffees, Taylor sat down next to Maggie on the loveseat. Sullivan repeated her routine and questions with him, although this time occasionally throwing in additional detail that Maggie had provided, as if seeking confirmation from Taylor on what Maggie had described earlier.

As Maggie sat listening to Taylor's answers she noticed how Sullivan gave nothing away, provided no information other than what Maggie had given just a few minutes earlier or from their own statements taken at the scene. When Sullivan had finished with her questions she thanked them for their time and got up to leave. Maggie got up quickly and stepped between the officers and the door.

"Sorry, Officer Sullivan, what will happen to the baby?" she asked.

"We need to establish who the parents of the child are. Assuming they're alive or at least one of them is, then the baby will likely be returned. It'll be up to Social Services to decide, they'll be looking after the child until it's placed back with family."

Sullivan moved to the front door with Adkin lagging behind. Before leaving the house Adkin turned to Taylor and handed him a contact card.

"Thanks for your time and the coffee. If you need anything or if you remember anything else, please give us a call."

"Yeah. Thanks," he replied, looking at the officer's card.

As the two officers returned to their car, Maggie took a step out of the front door towards them.

"Officer Sullivan, do you know who in Social Services will be handling the case? Has anyone been assigned yet?"

Sullivan withdrew and opened a notepad from her right top pocket. Flicking through some pages she eventually said, "Bateman, Jenny Bateman from Child Welfare."

* * * *

A week had passed and were it not for a brief report in the local paper, Maggie might have been forgiven for thinking the discovery of the woman and baby had been nothing more than a bad dream, but Maggie could still picture the baby clearly and the feeling she had when holding the baby in her arms. For the past several months she had wanted to discuss having a child with Taylor but she never seemed to find the right time to bring the subject up.

Before they got married Taylor and Maggie had discussed the prospect of having children at some stage. They both wanted a family, but Taylor would always point out how young they were and how they should look to enjoy themselves a bit before being *tied down* with children. They were both paid reasonable salaries but the loss of one income would require a change in the lifestyle they were becoming accustomed to. Taking the available year off work and then putting a child into nursery was something Maggie had considered, but deep down she knew that when they eventually had a child, she would want to be the one looking after it.

Taylor had taken the day off work and was out at Home Depot, after some wood to extend the deck in the back garden. Maggie had been given two weeks compassionate leave. She picked up her tablet and searched *Social Services.*

Picking up her phone, Maggie called Enquiries and asked to be put through to Child Welfare. After navigating numerous options and then waiting what seemed like hours, someone in Child Welfare eventually picked up only to confirm that Jenny Bateman was not currently available. Maggie left her name and number not really sure she knew what she was trying to achieve.

* * * *

By the evening, rain was falling. Taylor had made a start on the decking but his time in the back garden had been cut short by the sudden downpour. He had gone upstairs to change while Maggie was cooking spaghetti, when Maggie's phone rang.

"Hello," Maggie said, answering the phone.

"Hello, is Maggie Pritchard there please?"

"Yes, speaking."

"Hello, I'm Jenny Bateman. Sorry it's a little late. You phoned for me earlier today, I'm returning your call. Is there anything I can do for you?"

"Hi, yes, thank you for returning my call. I don't know if you know but it was my husband and I that discovered the baby in Richmond Park last week. I understand you are handling the case."

"Yes, Mrs. Pritchard, I'm aware of your name. Thank you for notifying the police. How can I help?"

"I just wanted to know if everything is alright with the baby."

"I'm not really supposed to discuss any of the details, Mrs. Pritchard."

"Maggie, please. I realise it's not really got anything to do with me but I can't help feeling a little responsible, having found her and everything."

"Mrs Pritchard, Maggie, it's normal for you to be concerned, especially given the circumstances in which you found the child. I can assure you we will be doing our best to ensure the child is found a suitable and loving home."

Maggie almost dropped the phone. "Sorry? I don't understand. Haven't you been able to trace any family?"

"I'm sorry, I can't really discuss the child's welfare with you. Like I said, we will ensure the child is properly cared for"'

Maggie paused for a moment.

"Is there anything else I can help you with?" Ms. Bateman asked.

"Please Ms Bateman, it's been a week and you said you'd be ensuring the baby is found a suitable home. Does that mean there's no immediate family, no one claiming the baby?"

Now it was Ms. Bateman's turn to pause.

"Maggie, it's only normal for someone to feel a little attached in these situations. You found a child, abandoned, but you are not responsible for the child's welfare. The government provides for these situations, we have child care homes and adoption programmes. Lots of children have had to start life in a similar way, and tragic as it seems, most of the children end up leading very normal and fulfilled lives."

Most of the children, Maggie thought. "Ms. Bateman are we eligible for adopting the baby?"

"Well, yes of course but…"

"Then what is the procedure? How do we get things started?" Maggie asked, not quite believing what she was saying.

Ms Bateman's voice changed to a firmer tone, her English accent somehow providing greater authority. "Maggie, it's far too early to be discussing the possibility of adoption for the child, and as I said, you are obviously feeling some attachment that will pass with time. We have established and well proven procedures for handling these unfortunate situations."

A week later and after a few more phone calls from Maggie, Ms Bateman agreed to talk Maggie through the process of adoption. Taylor was unaware of the calls Maggie had been making. Ms Bateman's attempts to dissuade Maggie had only served to strengthen her determination. At the end of the latest call Ms Bateman proposed a meeting at her office the following Thursday afternoon, for Maggie and Taylor both to attend.

Putting the phone down, Maggie felt a sense of shock and excitement at the same time. What was she going to tell Taylor? She wasn't sure herself of what she was doing let alone how he might react. But her maternal instincts had been engaged - *if a good home couldn't be found for the baby, we would provide one.*

Taylor came down the stairs, a towel wrapped around his waist. Maggie was still sat at the foot of the staircase, her phone in her hand.

"I heard you talking. Who was on the phone?" he asked.

"The lady from Child Welfare called."

"What lady? Why would she call here?" Taylor asked again, now making his way down the stairs.

"Oh, I phoned Child Welfare earlier in the week. I just wanted to make sure the baby was alright," she said, unsure how much she should be revealing.

In unison Taylor's eyebrows raised as his chin lowered. "What did you do that for? Did they tell you anything?"

"Not at first," Maggie said. "They let it slip that they hadn't found any family yet, and I think the woman *was* the mother. We're going to meet Ms Bateman from Child Welfare on Thursday afternoon."

Taylor's expression altered to a frown. "Why would we be going to see Child Welfare?" he asked.

"Because I told them we are interested in adopting the baby."

Taylor's mouth dropped again. He slumped down next to Maggie.

Maggie put her arms around him, "It's okay, it's just an enquiry, it's not as if we're bringing her home tomorrow."

* * * *

Ms Bateman's office was a twelve-by-ten room with a large single desk at one end, a couple of free standing metal filing cabinets, a few plants and pictures that did nothing to brighten the dark and dreary décor. The absence of natural light, or any sort of light, made Taylor feel he was underground.

Ms Bateman was in her late thirties and slightly overweight. Her hair was dark brown, almost black from the colour she had been using to die it. She was tanned and wore more than a modest amount of makeup. She wore a white blouse that was largely concealed by the deep red suit jacket she was wearing. large brown circular earrings dangled from her ears.

"Nice to meet you, I'm Jenny Bateman," she said, bangles jangling from her wrist as she held out her hand to Maggie.

"Hi, Maggie Pritchard, nice to meet you, and this is my husband, Taylor." Maggie responded, politely shaking Ms. Bateman's hand.

Maggie and Taylor sat in two faux-leather chairs that were positioned in front of the desk. Ms Bateman went around to the other side and sat in a large executive-style chair.

Crossing her legs and bridging her fingers, Ms Bateman said, "So, you'd like to discuss the possibility of adopting the baby you found? We've given the baby a temporary name, June Richmond. She would have been born in June and you found her in Richmond Park."

Maggie glanced at Taylor, it was clear he expected her to do the talking.

"Yes. Thank you for seeing us. You said on the phone that the baby, June, would probably be put up for adoption if you remained unsuccessful tracing any family, or if no one comes forward within three months." Ms. Bateman nodded confirmation. "You also said that if Taylor and I wanted too, we have a right to apply for the baby's adoption, just like anyone else. I know you explained a few things to me over the phone but I wondered if you could go over things again for us," looking at Taylor, "just in case I've missed something."

"Certainly. The adoption process starts with the adoption application, that I can provide you with. You should be aware that it will require the disclosure of personal information such as financial standing, medical history, personal habits and preferences, and any religious beliefs. Normally, the applications are forwarded to the child-bearing parents and they, together with support from our trained advisors, make their selection. Clearly in this case that isn't going to be possible, so the province will act as the child-bearing parents in this case."

"Sorry, what exactly does that mean?" Maggie asked.

"Basically, it means I will make a recommendation to the Welfare Board for their approval. In addition to the application," she continued, "an Adoption Home Study will be required. The home study is typically conducted over three meetings, one of which must be at your home. The study will seek to confirm information you have supplied in your application and provide an assessment as to your worthiness and suitability, for the proposed adoption. Again, most adoptions are not specific. People applying to adopt simply express their preferences –

gender, race, etc, this situation is peculiar in that, if I understand things correctly, you are applying specifically to adopt June Richmond?"

"Yes, that's right. I already feel somehow attached and responsible for her, even more so knowing that she seems to be orphaned."

Taylor remained silent. He felt sympathy for the child of course but that didn't mean he was ready to adopt it. He knew he would also like his own children at some point.

"Let me just run through a few basic details. You both work. Maggie you work for a bank, and Taylor you work for an IT Consultancy. You've both been in full employment for over four years. No criminal records. No defaults on any debts or loans. No specific religious beliefs and you both have degree level education."

Maggie was nodding. Taylor found himself nodding as well, but in disbelief at how much she already knew. *How long had they been talking on the phone?*

"Here's the application you will need to complete. Can I suggest you think it over again and make sure you discuss it thoroughly…together? It's vital that you both want the adoption. It's no good at all for the child if one party does not *really* want to do it. Here's my card. I'll be dealing with the case directly due to the unusual circumstances." She stood up and offered her hand again. "Please contact me if you have any further questions. Nice to meet you both."

Maggie and Taylor got up and Maggie shook Ms Bateman's hand again. Taylor managed a polite smile. Just as they were heading out the door, Maggie turned.

"Sorry, Ms Bateman."

"Jenny, please."

"Sorry, Jenny, could you tell us if anyone else will be being put forward for adopting June?"

Jenny Bateman smiled, she had anticipated that question.

"Maggie, June cannot officially be put up for adoption for three months. During that time the police and social services will be trying to establish the baby's background and other family. Notices and bulletins will be put out by the police, the social services and even the Salvation Army in case the child is reported missing by anyone. Only after that can June be made available for adoption." Jenny Bateman took a small step back, "The adoption process rarely operates a waiting list. Prospective parents are matched to children using their expressed preferences and their own individual circumstances. Look, for what its worth, my view is that should we be unsuccessful in locating any family for the child, and should you wish to proceed with the adoption, then subject to you meeting the appropriate criteria, you will be granted first refusal, so to speak – but any final decision will be with the board, as I can only make the recommendation."

On returning to their car Taylor said, "What are we doing here? I mean, are you really serious about this?"

"Yes, I'm serious. There is a baby with no mother, an unknown father, and no obvious family. It's been more than two weeks; if someone was going to claim the baby it would have happened by now. There are no reports of anyone matching their descriptions even missing. Even if someone does turn up later, why the hell didn't they notice they were missing?"

"You can't go adopting a child because the family haven't noticed it missing. And how do we know if we're ready for this?"

"If they find someone, that's fine. If they don't then it's because we were supposed to find her and we are supposed to look after her. Taylor we'll be fine, you'll be fine." Maggie opened the car door and got in.

* * * *

The following months seemed like years to Maggie. She had left it two weeks after their initial meeting with Jenny Bateman before completing the adoption application. She wanted to be certain Taylor was happy to proceed. The first week she tried not to talk about it with him, she wanted to let him think things through for himself. Finally, she booked them a table at Mercers, an upmarket restaurant renowned for fine steaks, where they had indulged themselves occasionally. Maggie wanted a decision. She had prepared herself so that if Taylor wasn't wholly convinced about proceeding, her decision would be to *not* file the application.

Taylor knew why Maggie had booked the table at Mercers. They had to make a decision – either get on with the application or leave it and move on.

He hadn't mentioned it to any of his friends or colleagues at work, but thoughts of the prospect of adopting someone else's baby were never far away. He had tried to imagine what it might be like – reading bedtime stories, playing with soft toys, finding a place in his heart for a total stranger and taking on that most precious responsibility – the development and welfare of a baby, a new soul. He tried to imagine a time when they would have their own children – *if we have a child, how would I find more space in in my heart for it? Would my feelings for our own child displace those I had for baby June?* By the time their booking arrived he had made up his mind.

Although Mercers had a varied menu, Maggie and Taylor could only ever bring themselves to order the steak. Maggie would order hers medium, cooked in a subtle red-wine jus, whereas Taylor would always have his steak medium-well and cooked in its own juices. The meals were accompanied by a selection of fresh seasonal organic vegetables. The main meals were never too large, allowing just sufficient room for customers with larger appetites to try the belt-busting desserts that were available.

"You know why we're here?" Maggie asked.

"Yes. We need to decide what we're going to do." Taylor replied.

"So..?" she urged. "You know what I want to do. I haven't stopped thinking about it. But I only want to do it if you are absolutely sure. You have to be a hundred percent on this."

"Well, I think," he said, taking a sip of wine and savouring the suspense.

"Well...?"

"Maggie, if we apply and then someone comes forward to claim the child or they deem us not suitable, how are you going to feel?" Taylor asked.

"I told you. I'll be pleased if the child has family. Pissed at them but pleased. And why would they think we're not suitable? We'd make good parents. Look, I know applying isn't a guarantee, it's just a first step. So...?" Her impatience was growing.

"I think we should go for it," Taylor grinned.

Maggie almost knocked the bottle of wine off the table as she got up and grabbed Taylor by the sides of his face and planted a huge kiss.

"I love you, Taylor Pritchard." Maggie said, clearly delighted. "Do you know what?"

'What?' he replied.

"Not all computer programmers are geeks."

Taylor laughed.

"Come on, eat up, we have some serious celebrating to do," she said, with a look that Taylor knew meant he was going to be up most of the night.

"Won't you want to complete the application?" he asked.

"You just need to sign it dummy. Finish up."

He finished his steak in record time and they skipped dessert.

* * * *

Ten days after filing their application, they received an acknowledgement letter from Child Welfare. It looked like a standard letter that simply thanked them for their application stating that they would be in touch '*in due course*'.

Despite trying hard not to, they couldn't refrain from having conversations about what they would need to buy, how to decorate the nursery, which bedroom in their three-bedroom townhouse should be the nursery, and what name to choose for June Richmond.

Maggie had phoned Jenny Bateman for a further update. She felt guilty as secretly she hoped that Social Services would be unsuccessful in their search for the child's other family members.

Maggie first broke the news of the application to adopt, to her Mom.

"Hi Mom, is dad with you?" Maggie asked.

"Yes darling, do you want to speak to him? Is everything alright?" her Mom replied.

"Everything is good, it's just that I have something I'd like to share with you both."

"Okay," her mother replied and then, holding the phone away from her mouth, she called out, "Dad! It's Maggie, she has something she'd like to share with us." Returning the handset to her mouth she said, "Go on."

"You know how Taylor and I discovered that baby in the park. Well, I've kept an interest, you know, to see if anyone comes forward to claim the child. Well, it's been awhile now, and Child Welfare are looking at the prospect of adoption. I want to let you know that we have decided to apply, to adopt the baby."

There was silence for a moment before her Mom said, "Well, I think that's a very good thing you are trying to do. You're both adults and able to make up your own minds, but I thought you two wanted children of your own?"

"Yes, we still do Mom, this wouldn't change that. It's just that, well, having discovered the baby and knowing it's without a home, I just feel we were somehow meant to find her. I can't help feeling some responsibility."

"It's awful what has happened, but the child isn't your responsibility darling. You've already been a great help to the child, but I understand what you are saying." Away from the phone she says, "They want to adopt that baby they found."

"I just wanted you to be the first know that we have applied. It's not certain by any means yet but I wanted you and dad to be aware. We won't know more for at least a month while they continue to try and locate any family." Maggie said.

"I think that's wonderful what you are doing Maggie. Of course, it might be better if they were to locate the child's real family but if not, you and Taylor will make wonderful parents. I'm pleased for you both. Your father and I are supportive, you let us know if you need anything at all," her mom replied.

In the background, Maggie heard her mom say 'that they might be grandparents a bit sooner than they had expected'. "Thanks Mom, love you. My love to Dad. See you soon." Maggie said, before ending the call.

Eventually all their family and friends were told of their plans and though all of them seemed genuinely pleased, most advised caution before getting too attached to the idea.

Before the 'search' period had ended Maggie and Taylor received a call from Jenny Bateman. She asked them to come and see her at her office as she had some things she needed to discuss with them, but she wouldn't expand on what those things were. Maggie feared the worst and felt terribly guilty for doing so.

* * * *

"Thank you for coming to see me," Jenny said, as she invited Maggie and Taylor into her office. "Sorry for dragging you out here but I have something I'd like to share with you. It concerns your application to adopt baby June." Seeing the look on Maggie's face, she added, "It's nothing to worry about, but it is something I feel I should make you aware of."

"What is it?" Maggie asked, not attempting to hide the concern in her voice.

"We've been running some tests on baby June. Don't worry, she's perfectly healthy. The tests we've being doing check things like cognitive processes, visual coordination, and her ability to manipulate objects – move things around perhaps place objects inside a box, that sort of thing. The initial tests are simply routine in these situations, however, we chose to run a few more. Well…we are seeing some rather exceptional results. She's seems to possess extraordinary intelligence and spatial awareness."

Maggie and Taylor stole a glance at each other.

"Of course, she is still only a baby," Jenny continued, "and there are no guarantees that what she is displaying will continue, but what she is currently capable of is way beyond what we would consider normal at this very young stage. We only really became of her abilities by chance. One of the carers had placed her on her back amongst a selection of toys."

"What abilities?" Maggie asked.

"When the carer returned to her she noticed that June was trying to sit up. We wouldn't normally expect a child to sit up until they were perhaps several months old. The carer thought she'd have a go at sitting her up, and she managed to stay upright, for a while anyway."

Maggie frowned at Taylor, who turn made a slight shrug of his shoulders.

"I know that probably doesn't sound much and to be honest that isn't what shocked us, but physically she is doing well nonetheless. What really is impressive," she said, pausing as if to give her next statement greater profundity, "is that she had put some of the building blocks that were lying next to her *together*."

Jenny clearly marvelled at this but the meaning was still lost to Maggie and Taylor.

Maggie responded, "I'm sorry I don't really understand. That sounds quite impressive for one so young but I'm not sure how amazed I'm supposed to be."

"Baby June is not yet five months old, yet she is displaying the spatial awareness and some capacities of a two year old. We're convinced that were it not for the obvious relative physical weaknesses, she could complete a number of tests normally not expected until infants are at least eighteen months or perhaps two years old."

They looked at each other again, now recognising that what they had just been told did sound impressive.

"Further tests have revealed she has a very high attention rate, able to show levels of concentration at least three times what we might expect. We also believe she is already showing exceptional communication and understanding skills. We don't know how, but she can point to different coloured blocks when asked, showing she not only understands colour but more importantly, the question being asked, it's this level of comprehension that she displays that we haven't seen before. Again, we wouldn't expect anything like that until much later. She has all the signs of being an exceptional child, a prodigy." Jenny finished.

"I think I understand what you have just told us – baby June appears to be smart, but I'm not entirely sure why it needed an appointment to tell us. I'm sorry if I'm missing something."

"Maggie, Taylor, if baby June continues to show these kinds of skills she is also very likely to require and need a great deal of attention. If she's as smart as we think she will be, she'll be like a sponge requiring a constant flow of water and yet never really becoming wet." Leaning forward, she continued, "You need to understand that she is likely to crave new challenges and constant learning, and may well become frustrated and impatient very quickly if she doesn't get it. Although she is in no way disabled, looking after her could quite easily be just as exhausting. I know, Maggie, you stated that you would be leaving work to look after the baby should your application be successful, but I do want you to consider what I'm telling you and for you to think about this - is this something you really want to commit to? We still have almost a month before baby June will be eligible for adoption, and there are still two more parts of the Home Study to complete, you can still easily pull out if you wish."

Maggie shifted in her seat and looked across at Taylor, then said, "No. We have every intention of completing the application. Thank you for letting us know but we'd like to assure you that giving the baby a great deal of attention is what we fully expect to be doing. And personally, knowing that the child could be some kind of genius makes no difference, we'll give her all the love and care any true parent would."

Jenny smiled and closed a folder that she had open on her desk. "Well that's settled then," she said. Jenny stood and walked over to Maggie, offering her hand. Holding Maggie's hand in both hands, Jenny said, "Thank you again for coming in. We'll talk again soon."

* * * *

The next four weeks passed without any success for the authorities in discovering anything relating to baby June's origins. Notices had been posted across all police stations in the Vancouver region and surrounding areas, and to all social service departments and buildings across the province as well as the corresponding websites. Baby June had been listed with Toronto, Ottawa and Seattle officials, the Salvation Army, and the Missing Persons Bureau, in case any leads might show up there. But nothing.

Jenny Bateman sat with baby June's case file open on her desk. DNA tests had confirmed that it was the mother that had died. Further tests of the dead woman had concluded death was almost certainly self-inflicted and occurred as a result of massive blood loss from the deep cuts applied to each wrist. The hesitation marks and high levels of codeine and ibruprofen, were consistent with suicide. No suicide note was found. Despite a complete set of forensic data, no match was found.

Jenny picked up the phone and dialled.

"Hi Maggie, it's Jenny, the three months are officially up today, baby June is now available for adoption." She paused to give Maggie a moment. "We need to get your Home Study complete, then, all being well, I'll be in a position to put a recommendation in front of the board for their approval."

"Thanks Jenny. Thank you for your support."

"I can share with you that the DNA results confirm that the woman was baby June's mother. The Coroner has deemed it a suicide. Sadly, there has been no identification of the woman. A necklace with a ring attached was found on the body which the police have released to me – seems they no longer have a need to retain it and someone thought it might be good to pass on to the child at some point. You should have it once the adoption is complete, you can decide on whether to pass it on. Anyway, I'll hold on to it for now."

"Oh, okay, well thank you calling and thanks again for your support with all of this," Maggie said, unsure what else to say.

"You are most welcome," Jenny replied, before finishing the call.

* * * *

The final part of the Home Study would be conducted at Maggie and Taylor's. It was being undertaken by an independent assessor contracted to Child Welfare. This provided the Welfare with a level of independence that was designed to improve the decision making process, but ultimately existed to enable the State to share any blame that may arise from poorly matched adoptions. Unfortunately for Maggie and Taylor, it meant that timescales were dictated by the assessor's availability – in this case a further three months due to the Christmas and New Year holidays.

It would be early January before the Home Study would be complete. Maggie had made several calls to Jenny Bateman attempting to speed-up the process but each time she was kicked back with *procedure*. Jenny advised

Maggie that she would just have to be patient, enjoy Christmas and everything will be completed soon. Jenny reminded Maggie, 'a few months is not long compared to the rest of your lives'.

Maggie and Taylor decided to take a holiday over the festive season. They spent Christmas at Disney World. Taylor argued, they were just checking it out for when baby June would be older, but given the amount of fun he seemed to having, Maggie wasn't so sure that he wasn't simply being self-indulgent. Either way, they had a great time and had made a long list of everything they would come back to see with baby June.

On January seventeenth, the assessor arrived for the final part of the Home Study. The assessor introduced herself as Judy. At around five-foot-four she stood a good four inches shorter than Maggie. They made their way into the lounge, where Taylor was already seated, rubbing his palms along his thighs.

After introductions, Judy remained standing and said, "I'd like to start by taking a look around if I may?"

"Sure," Maggie replied, "I assume you have the home questionnaire that we completed?"

"Yes, thank you," Judy replied. "I'll make a start in the kitchen. This way?"

Judy proceeded into the kitchen not waiting for a response. Opening various cupboards and drawers, she started making notes on to a clipboard she was carrying. She opened the fridge and freezer doors and looked around the window frames and the doors to the patio. She then came back into the lounge and crouched to as if to inspect the collection of CDs. After a few more minutes in the lounge, Judy asked if it was okay to go upstairs. After getting

Maggie's consent she made it clear there was no need for Maggie to escort her around the house.

Maggie and Taylor remained seated in the lounge as they tracked the sound of Judy's movements upstairs – floors creaking, wardrobe doors opened then closed.

"Why was she looking in all the cupboards?" Taylor whispered.

"I don't know, there were questions about what sort of food we ate. She must just be checking against the answers we gave." Maggie replied.

"And why is she looking at my CDs?"

"I don't know. Just let her do what she needs to do. And they're not all your CDs." Maggie said.

After a few minutes, Judy returned to the lounge, still writing as she entered and took a seat opposite.

"Okay, everything seems to be in order. Should you be successful you will receive an information kit which will include advice and tips on how to make your home safer for young children." Judy said. "Do you have any questions for me?"

"When can we expect to find out?" Maggie asked.

"My role is simply to provide a detailed report on the conditions within the home. The report is then provided to the board along with the application and the questionnaire, to help them come to a decision. I don't make any recommendations myself. It's usually about a month or so after I have filed my report."

"Do you file the report right away?" Maggie asked.

"Yes. It'll be written up and sent before the end of business tomorrow," Judy replied, pausing to allow for any further questions. Looking at Taylor and then back to Maggie, Judy stood and said, "Thank you again for your application and time today."

After Judy had returned to her car, she paged through her notes before starting the engine. What she had said about not making any recommendations herself had not been entirely honest. She was required to indicate if she considered the home suitable for adoption or not - at the end of her notes she added the word – *Accept*.

A week later, Jenny advised Maggie and Taylor, that she was now in possession of the complete case file for the adoption and that the case would be discussed at the board meeting after next, scheduled for the third week of February. Maggie almost cried with frustration when she was told she would have to wait a few more weeks. Jenny decided it was probably best to advise her now that there may also be a further wait given the circumstances surrounding the adoption. 'There is a possibility the Board will want a second independent review of the family trace work. I'm confident there won't be any problems but you will have to be patient a little longer', she had said.

Maggie and Taylor spent the time waiting for the final decision by decorating the nursery, buying outfits for baby June, and looking again at names. They had agreed they would not be keeping 'June' but were struggling to agree on an alternative. The short list was, Rebecca, Emily, Emma and Jasmine.

The adoption decision was finally made on March eleventh; it had been approved, Maggie and Taylor were to become parents. They celebrated the news with a meal at Mercers, joined this time by Jenny Bateman. A meal at Mercers was not procedure for Jenny, but she had been persuaded by Maggie to join them. She was genuinely thrilled for them and baby June. At the meal, Jenny confirmed that they would now be able to visit and spend time with baby June at the care home. She said it would be April second before they could take baby June home as a final set of checks were needed before leaving the care home. Maggie and Taylor would also need to meet baby June's carer to go over the care she had received to date and provide them with the opportunity to discuss the baby's exceptional behaviour.

"That's it!" Maggie almost shouted.

"That's what?" Taylor replied.

"We'll call her April."

"But she was born in June."

"I know, and it won't be long before she asks why she has a birthday in June but is called April. We'll explain to her that adopting her was so special and important to us, we wanted to forever remember when she became ours – we'll call her April."

Taylor didn't quite follow her logic and wasn't convinced they would need to tell her she was adopted. Still, he liked the sound of April. "Okay, but I get to choose her middle name."

They raised their glasses and Jenny toasted, "Here's to April Pritchard, a truly exceptional child, and her fine new parents. May they enjoy many happy years together."

CHAPTER 2

Parenthood was more difficult than Maggie and Taylor had expected. During the week, Maggie would be the one getting up to April who would wake every three hours or so. She had passed the need to be fed during the night, but it was as though she needed the attention. Although Taylor wasn't the one getting out of bed at night, his sleep was no less interrupted, making his days at work all the more difficult. During weekends Taylor would be the one getting out of bed, allowing Maggie to stay in it. Maggie seemed capable of sleeping through the disruption, which Taylor assumed was a reflection of her exhaustion.

Taylor took two weeks of paid leave and a further four weeks paternal leave following the adoption. That had given him time to learn his basic parenting skills and see first hand that April was indeed different to how he imagined babies should be. Maggie was entitled to leave, a full year minus whatever share Taylor would take.

April was subjected to regular checks every three months, more than usual for an infant. Even before her second birthday, Maggie had begun to think April had become a curiosity, being given increasingly more complex tasks in sessions that had turned from fifteen minutes to thirty minutes, then one hour and now typically two hours. Maggie enjoyed taking April at first but now the tests seemed unnecessary and gratuitous.

At home, Maggie had started to resent the party pieces April would perform when family and friends came to visit. She would build structures from wooden blocks, complete jigsaws, draw shapes and scenes, by the time she was walking she had worked out how to use the games console and TV remotes, and would react to different types of music.

Maggie divided the time she was alone with April between walks, playing, and her education. As April grew her disruptive sleeping habits had not diminished. Maggie and Taylor would take it in turns reading bedtime stories to her until eventually she would nod off. Then April would wake up again a few hours later, wanting attention and another story to be read. They had tried to leave her, ignoring her in the hope she would just fall back to sleep, but she would simply continue to call out or start playing around in her bedroom. After she was able to walk, she very quickly realised she could use things to stand on and open doors. Now she would simply enter Maggie and Taylor's bedroom to wake them up. She was not yet 15 months.

Over the coming months, Maggie had continued to query April's sleeping habits with the welfare officer present at the checks they undertook. She was assured there was nothing to worry about and that many children show this kind of behaviour. She was told it is even more likely given April's obvious intelligence. What none of them had expected was that April's sleeping patterns would become much more complicated.

* * * *

Taylor was watching a film in bed. Maggie had fallen asleep next to him and April had fallen asleep a few hours before, after the story of Hansel and Gretal. The film Taylor was watching was based on a Stephen King novel and starred Jack Nicholson. Taylor turned the film off, too tired to watch it all. He lay there in the dark, thinking of the twin girls from the film that had always managed to spook him - '*come and play,*' he heard them say.

As he lay there, his heart rate slowing and sleep arriving, he thought he heard a voice. He had become accustomed to waking up to noises, but this seemed different. Now, more alert, he lay there still, waiting to see if the noise repeated. He could hear April talking. April had began speaking recognisable words at thirteen months, and by eighteen months she possessed an extensive vocabulary and an understanding of an even greater number of words. As Taylor lay there listening, it was not loud enough that he could make out what she was saying but it was definitely April, her voice a drone, as if she were reciting a chant or incantation.

Taylor thought about waking Maggie but then decided against it, sleep being a precious commodity. He got out of bed, gently opened the bedroom door and walked across the landing to April's bedroom. Her door was closed, but as he came closer to the bedroom he could definitely hear her talking to herself, but in an odd tone, without any emotion. He slowly opened the door.

April was sat up in her bed, her eyes staring at the opposite wall. Her long straight, fair hair and clear blue eyes caught the dim light. She hadn't seemed to notice Taylor enter the room. She continued talking in that monotonous tone.

"You should have been killed, the witch was right to cook you, you shouldn't have been there, you naughty children. What will your mom say? Better get back, she'll give you a good hiding…"

Taylor stood there a moment, not quite believing what he was seeing. He took another step into the room and then stood in front of April. *Nothing*, she just looked right through him as if he wasn't there.

"...perhaps you'll get eaten by the wolf that was after Red Riding Hood. He's still alive you know. His sharp teeth and big mouth will eat you up..."

Taylor waved his arms. "April? April, are you all right?"

"...you'll not be able to hide in the three little pig's home. The homes have been blown down and the little pigs eaten. The house made from brick was burnt down, the pigs were eaten when the big bad..."

Taylor went back to his bedroom. "Maggie, Maggie wake up, you need to come and see this. It's April, I don't know what's happening."

Maggie took a moment to wake. She got up quickly when she saw the concern in Taylor's expression. They returned to April's bedroom.

"...get you in the end. Look at the gingerbread man, he thought he'd got away. Chicken Licken thought the sky was falling down but it was just..."

Maggie went over to April and sitting on the edge of the bed waved a hand just in front of her.

"She's still asleep," Maggie said.

"Still asleep? What do we do?"

"I think it's okay to wake her. I think we should try and wake her."

"I didn't think you were supposed to wake people up from sleep...talking."

"April, April wake up baby. Wake Up!"

Maggie shook April gently as she spoke. Then April stopped talking and finally looked at Maggie. Maggie held her close.

"It's okay, baby, it's okay, it's just a dream, only a dream…shhh…'

April woke up, confused, she started to cry.

* * * *

The following evening after Taylor had arrived home from work, Maggie and Taylor stood in the kitchen, discussing what had happened.

"She was just talking in her sleep," Maggie said.

"Talking in her sleep. Did you *hear* what she was saying?"

"They're stories we've been reading her, jumbled up in her imagination. I guess it's another party piece we're gonna have to get used to."

"Really spooked me. I've never seen anything like that."

"She's fine. She doesn't remember anything about it and we should be careful not to make things worse by scaring her," Maggie replied with a deliberate look at Taylor.

"I just wasn't expecting that. I've got used to her being awake, not asleep or whatever she was. Do you know if we're supposed to wake her up?"

"Yes. I looked it up today."

"What did you search under?" he asked.

"Sleeping disorders. It's not uncommon, especially in children, and they usually grow out of it as they get older. Some people do a lot more than just sit in bed talking; there was one account of someone who went out driving their car while they were still asleep. And besides, it's not like you've never made noises in your sleep."

"Do you think we should mention it to the *freak police*?"

"I wish you wouldn't call them that, April isn't a freak. She's special. She's just a lot smarter than we are, it's not a fault or a problem. And no, I don't think they need to know."

"I didn't mean that April is a freak. She is special, very special. It's just that I know you don't like all the tests they put her through," Taylor replied, moving to Maggie and holding her in his arms.

* * * *

Months had passed since April had first talked in her sleep. Her second and third birthdays had been and gone and Christmas was just a few days away. Maggie and April had spent the days donning their raincoats and rubber boots, playing in the rain and the splattering of occasional snow. April absorbed everything around her, taking an interest in the trees and the birds, and the fish that occupied the many streams and lakes around their home.

Maggie was amazed by April's ability to learn and memorise seemingly everything she was shown. She would watch the leaves falling and clouds moving in the sky as though studying their movement, she would notice the different currents in flowing water, and the subtle variations in colour. Despite her appetite for learning, April would play like any other child, jumping in the puddles and skipping over cracks in the pavement.

The Friday before Christmas had seen rain fall continuously throughout the day. Maggie was expecting Taylor home earlier than usual, as it was his last day at work before his week off for the holiday. She was keen to have a go at tiring April out in an attempt to ensure she could have a long, uninterrupted evening with Taylor. The morning was spent doing some shopping, and in the afternoon they took a long walk around a park. They took umbrellas, but April insisted on running out into the rain, protected only by her pink plastic raincoat. Maggie wondered if April might catch a cold, but as she thought about it she couldn't remember a time when April had ever really been poorly. She decided a nice warm bath for them both would stave off any unwelcome chill. Maggie had planned pasta and cheese for April's dinner before, *hopefully*, she would fall asleep for the night.

Taylor got home as Maggie was serving up the pasta. He headed upstairs to get changed while April tucked into her food. Two hours after finishing her pasta, April went up to bed and fell asleep.

Taylor had started to watch a film when Maggie came into the living room wearing her silk dressing gown and underneath, dark stockings and her designer black underwear. He couldn't resist. They eventually ended up in bed, exhausted, and Taylor had no idea what the film he had started to watch was about.

The night wore on, and rain pattered at the windows. The wind had picked up and shadows cast by leafless trees moved across the curtains in the bedroom. Maggie and Taylor were fast asleep when the door to their room opened.

Taylor slept nearest the door and his body reacted to the creak from the hinges. Unsure why he was awake, he turned over. Facing the door, it took a moment for him to register it was wide open. He pulled the sheets back slightly and began to sit up when he noticed a figure at the end of the bed. Although startled, he assumed it must be April. She stood not much taller than the bed, only her head and shoulders showing. But something didn't look right.

"It's time to go, Daddy. Time to go out, get your things, Daddy."

It was April, but speaking in that flat toneless voice. Taylor twisted and pulled his legs out to the side of the bed, as Maggie stirred.

"Here are your shoes, Daddy. You need to get dressed."

Taylor could see her silhouette, an arm raised and the outline of what looked like a pair of his shoes. Maggie was starting to sit up in bed.

"What is it?" Maggie asked.

"Come on Daddy, we don't want to be late. You need to get dressed."

Looking closer Taylor realised why April looked odd. She was wearing her raincoat. Maggie switched on her bedside lamp. It took a moment for their eyes to adjust but then they saw April standing at the end of the bed, unmoved by the light that now filled the room, wearing her pink raincoat over the top of her Paddington Bear nighty. Maggie got out of bed and went over to her. April was wearing her rubber boots and apparently ready to venture outside.

* * * *

The frequency of April's sleepwalking episodes increased as she got older. The episodes became more complex in nature until eventually one night, shortly after she had turned seven years old, Taylor woke to hear the front door bang. His body had become conditioned to the various different noises April would create during the night, but the sound of the front door caused his heart to race. His body alert, he jumped out of bed. Grabbing his dressing gown, he quickly checked April's bedroom, although not expecting to see her in there. He rushed down the stairs calling Maggie as he went.

At the bottom of the stairs he could see the front door slightly ajar and cool air blew into the entrance hall.

"April!"

A pair of old moccasin shoes lay next to the front door, his slippers. Sliding his feet into them, he made his way outside. He walked to the end of the garden path and looked around. He couldn't see anyone.

"April!"

Silence, just the rustle of windswept leaves on the road and the groan of mature trees that lined the avenue, as they resisted the wind. Taylor looked left down the street and then right. *Then a sound.* He turned in the direction of the sound, and looked again to his left, harder this time. Taylor started to run towards a lamppost about thirty yards from the house. He found April sitting on the side of the curb, dressed in her coat over her pyjamas and sandals on her feet. She was gently rocking, holding her knees to her chest. Taylor picked her up and carried her back to the house. As he approached the front door, Maggie came rushing out.

"It's all right. I've got her. She was just sitting down at the side of the road. She's fine. Still asleep though."

It didn't matter how many times Taylor had seen it, seeing April act so awake and yet be asleep, unsettled him. He noticed he hands trembling after he placed her down on the sofa. Maggie stood with a hand to her mouth. "I'll leave it to you to wake her," Taylor said. Maggie nodded. "I think we should get some advice on what to do," he added. Maggie agreed.

* * * *

Jenny Bateman arrived for her three o'clock appointment. Jenny was now without bangles, her hair shorter and darker as she tried to keep the years from showing. She no longer handled adoptions but had maintained contact and an interest in the Pritchard family, and in April's development in particular. Copies of April's test results had continued to be forwarded to Jenny. Although officially she was no longer entitled to receive the results, she chose not to let the assessors from the University of British Columbia know of the change to her responsibilities.

Maggie had explained April's sleeping disorder on the phone, how long it had been going on, and how the most recent episode had prompted the phone call to her.

Maggie welcomed Jenny into the house with a kiss to the cheek.

"Hi Jenny, thanks for coming. I hope we're not putting you out."

"No, not at all. We haven't talked in a while and I thought it would be good to come out and see you all. Nice house, by the way. I knew you'd moved a short while back, but didn't know the neighbourhood. I can imagine things have been a little worrying for you."

Taylor made coffee, and April was playing in the back garden with her toy table and tea set, and her imaginary friends.

"I've kept up with the results from April's tests. She is a gifted child. You must be very proud of her."

"Yes, although I have to say I'm much happier now that she doesn't have to be subjected to the tests quite so often. Since she turned five the tests have been voluntary. It was then that representatives from the University took over the tests from Welfare Services. I really don't know how to feel about them but while April seems happy enough to do them I'll keep taking her I suppose."

Jenny gave an understanding, tight-lipped smile.

"Maggie," Jenny said, "April's tests show she is unique. Only very rarely does nature grant us people with April's ability. It isn't possible for us to draw any conclusions on how those abilities might also affect their behaviour and how they might perceive the world, there simply aren't enough of them. And it's only recently that society has had the mechanisms in place to even identify them." Shifting forward, she reached out and gently squeezed Maggie's hand. "I really don't think you need to worry about her. I've had a conversation with someone, someone who specialises in this area and he agrees that April will likely grow out of this before puberty. He doesn't recommend the use of any drugs or medicine. He did however suggest something I hadn't considered...how about getting her a pet?"

"A pet? A dog or cat or something?" Maggie asked in surprise.

Taylor brought in the coffees and then returned to the study den to continue with his work from home.

"Yes," Jenny continued, "he suggested that having a pet might stimulate her, give her something else to think about, maybe help her relax. Let it sleep in her room with her."

Maggie sat reflecting for a moment. April had certainly shown an interest in animals, she knew of many different species and she had expressed an interest in how they moved, how they ate, and even how they reproduced. Although April had never asked to own a pet.

"It's just something to consider. I know it's concerning but you really should try not to worry, she *will* grow out of it," Jenny assured her, placing her hand on Maggie's shoulder.

"What about things we should do around the house? Any thoughts?" Maggie asked.

"I don't know. You tell me, is there much you can do? I guess you could try some form of combination lock, or lock the door at night and hide the key somewhere, but I suspect that may unsettle her a bit, make her think she could really harm herself."

She could, Maggie thought.

"How about putting a bell or alarm on the door? I'm sure you'd be able to fix an alarm so that it woke you up should she try to leave the house again."

Maggie forced a smile. "Yeah, that sounds like a good idea and I'll ask her if she'd like a small pet."

That night it was Maggie that was awake most of the night. The food she had eaten was determined not to remain inside her body.

* * * *

The following week Maggie and April visited nine different pet shops and breeders in the surrounding area. Eventually, April adopted a Domestic Short-Haired cat from a BCSPCA shelter in Burnaby. The cat was approximately eight weeks old, back and white with piercing green eyes. She called the kitten 'Noodles', after her favourite food.

On the day they brought Noodles home, Maggie had decided on another gift for April. They placed the cat basket at the foot of April's bedroom, and April placed soft toys for Noodles to jump and pounce on around the house. After settling Noodles into her new home, Maggie sat April down.

"Sweetheart," Maggie began, "I've been meaning to give something to you for some time now. Just wasn't sure of the best time to give it to you. Seems now might be as good a time as any. You know we have had a talk about Daddy and I adopting you. How we love you very much, the same as if you were our very own. How we found you in the park and how Mommy loved you as soon as I saw you. Well, this was also found with you." Maggie unclenched her hand and inside was a silver 'V' shaped ring on a necklace. She offered it to April.

"I believe the ring belonged to your mother, though we can't be sure. It was placed on this necklace. I thought you might want to wear it, keep it with you."

April took the necklace together with ring and held it up, letting the ring rotate as the silver chain unravelled. "It's pretty." April said. "Why do you think it might have belonged to my mother?" she asked.

Maggie shifted a little in her seat. "Baby, when we discovered you that day in the park, you were just a baby. So small, not more than a few weeks old.

Well...your mom was also there. But she had died sweetheart. She was no longer alive when we found you, but you were. You were cold and hungry, but you were alive. I'm so sorry baby, but I've been wanting to give this to you. Your mom was wearing it and I'm sure she'd like you to have it. I just...couldn't find the right time to tell you."

April's gaze moved from the ring to Maggie. "It's okay, Mommy. I think I always knew. I mean, you had told me how that you and Daddy had found me, but I had always wondered how I got there in the first place. If I was going to be abandoned then why there, why so far into the park?" April looked back at the ring. "Was she pretty? My mother." April asked.

"Yes baby, she was. You have her same straight blond hair and blue eyes. We tried to find out more, who she was, where she might have come from, if she had family. The police, all the services, as well as Mommy and Daddy all tried to find out more. But in the end, there was just you and this necklace with the ring on it. We love you so much sweetie, and we will always be here for you. You are our daughter, always will be. I will always be your Mommy. I just thought you might want to have this."

April closed her hand around the necklace and got up from her seat. She squeezed Maggie around the neck as she gently gave her a hug. "I love you too Mommy, " April said, "Thank you."

In the two weeks that had passed since they had brought Noodles home, April had not experienced any further sleep walking episodes. Maggie and Taylor took encouragement, but given that she could go a few months between episodes, it was premature for them to draw any conclusions. It would be several more weeks before they would feel confident that the kitten was making any real difference to April's sleeping.

Those weeks had revealed that Maggie had fallen pregnant. Although not planned, her pregnancy was not entirely a surprise either. Maggie and Taylor had stopped any intervention over a year ago, and were happy to allow nature to take its course.

* * * *

Another month had passed when Maggie and Taylor woke up to the knowledge that April's sleepwalking had not withdrawn, but rather had taken a terrifying turn.

Maggie awoke during the night. She was feeling hot and was sweating. She kicked back the duvet and lay on the bed. As she lay there, she could just make out April talking. Following Jenny's advice, they had fitted a device to the front door that would trigger an alarm in their bedroom should the door be opened while the device was active. Taylor had tested the device several times and was convinced it was working properly. The alarm had not been triggered.

As Maggie lay there straining to listen, she was sure April was in her bedroom. She thought April might be talking to Noodles, but she couldn't distinguish any words that were being spoken.

Maggie got out of bed. Taylor seemed to be deep into his sleep, he didn't make a move as Maggie got up. Standing up, she had to steady herself a moment before moving around the bed and out onto the landing.

April's bedroom door was closed, but as Maggie approached she could now hear what April was saying.

"I wonder what you need this for?"

Maggie paused at the door as she realised April was talking in that flat, lifeless tone that she had come to despise. Maggie opened the door.

Moonlight partially lit the room. The thin curtains at the window were not fully drawn, and what light was blocked by them entered through the gap between them. April was sat crossed legged on the floor, her back to the door, something laying across her lap. Maggie watched as she realised it must be Noodles laying across April's lap, and that something was very wrong.

April's hands seemed to be moving over the kitten, across, and then up and down. She seemed to be inspecting the kitten's tummy. For a moment Maggie thought April was holding food for the cat, as bits fell from her hands. As Maggie turned up the dimmer in April's room, she was not prepared for what she saw.

As the artificial light replaced moonlight and the room came into colour, Maggie saw April sitting in a pool of blood. Air escaped Maggie's lungs as her shock was vocalised. With her right hand covering her mouth, Maggie started walking over to April. Before Maggie had reached her, April turned her head, her expression soulless.

"Hello, Mommy. Look. See what I have done."

Maggie took another step before she saw what April had done. Noodles lay across April's lap, the cat's stomach open, the body walls pushed back exposing the intestine, kidney and heart, but out of place. April held a small kitchen knife in her right hand and, with a table fork she held in her left hand, she was lifting up an internal organ as though performing an autopsy.

Maggie turned away as her stomach ejected its contents. Her legs weakened and she collapsed to her knees on the carpeted floor. Struggling for breath, Maggie cried out, "Taylor! Taylor! April, what have you done?"

April continued with her autopsy of the cat.

Maggie was struggling to regain any kind of composure as Taylor entered the bedroom. His concern for Maggie quickly overrode the shock he felt as he entered the room. He helped Maggie to her feet and then back out to their bedroom. Sitting her back on the bed he quickly returned to April's room. April offered no resistance as Taylor carefully took the kitchen knife out of her hand. He held with disgust the remains of the cat, enough to move the carcass from April's lap. Turning April towards him, he gently shook her speaking her name at the same time. April woke up, at first confused, and then she noticed the blood on the floor and over her pyjamas, and Noodles lying mutilated. She grabbed Taylor and cried.

* * * *

Taylor was concerned the shock from the discovery of the cat might cause Maggie to miscarriage. Scans however confirmed that both mother and baby were fine, physically at least.

They had discussed what had happened with Jenny Bateman, who in turn took them to visit Dr.Bernard Polski, Professor of Neurology at the University of British Columbia. 'Disturbing as the events are, it seems there is little that can be done to help or stop the episodes from occurring. It's when they do these things while they are awake that its time we should worry,' he had said as they were leaving. Maggie had kept one detail to herself, unsure what it might have meant, if anything at all. It was that April had turned to look at her and said, 'Hello, Mommy. Look. See what I have done.'

* * * *

Maggie was finding it difficult to appear unaffected by April's sleepwalking. She had spent all of April's young life correcting any insinuation from people that April's exceptional intellect somehow made her a freak. But as Maggie considered April's occasional but extreme behaviour, she couldn't help thinking there was more to April than she understood.

April would get upset whenever Maggie tried to talk to her about the episodes. April could remember nothing from what had happened. She would wake up confused and disorientated. Although the duration of the disorientation seemed to shorten as April grew older, it had always followed being woken up. She would hold her Mom tight for several minutes, sobbing. Waking to find Noodles dissected on her lap had left April numb; she hadn't spoken a word the following day, she had just cried for most of it. Maggie decided against broaching what had happened, for a few days at least.

April had taken a week off school. She had always treated her friends, the other pupils, and teachers with respect. In turn and for the most part, April was treated as just another student. It had been suggested to Maggie that April attend a 'special' school that was better equipped to cope with someone of her ability. Maggie resisted, preferring April to lead as normal a life as possible. Maggie did have to concede some ground however. April was capable of learning in one month what most children required a whole year to learn. She had started to learn algebra when the remaining smartest children in her grade were still learning their tables. April would have three half-day sessions each week with a specialist support teacher, where she'd be given additional assignments to help satisfy her capacity to learn. Despite access to a specialist teacher and the extra work, Maggie knew keeping her at the school was no doubt holding April back.

While they were out walking one day, Maggie and April pulled up and sat down on a park bench. Maggie asked April what she could remember from the evening before Noodles died.

"We had eaten toast with grated cheese on top. We sat and watched some cartoons together. Daddy got home late. After dinner he went into the den to study. At eight o'clock, I kissed you and Daddy goodnight and went up to bed. Noodles was already in bed. She was all curled up on the end of my bed. I noticed she had been for a pee-pee in her tray. Before getting into bed I stroked her and kissed her goodnight."

Moisture gathered in April's eyes.

"I don't remember dreaming. I woke up and Daddy was holding me, he looked scared. My light was on and I saw blood everywhere. You weren't there.' More tears appeared and April wiped her cheeks. "I looked and saw Noodles, her body just laying there, her tummy was open and I could see inside." Crying, April hugged her Mom. "I'm sorry, Mommy. I don't know what happened. I don't know why I do these things. It's not fair. What is happening to me? I want it to stop Mommy, help me Mommy, please help me."

Maggie started to cry as she held April tight.

"I'm sorry, baby, I'm not sure what to do, but we'll work something out, everything is going to be alright, I promise." Holding April's face she said,

"Perhaps that's why you're so smart, maybe you will discover a cure for all those other kids that suffer like you do."

They rubbed noses and hugged.

* * * *

It was June twenty-fourth, April's eighth birthday. Friends and family had been around to celebrate. Wrapping paper from the many presents she had received lay scattered around the house. Only the eight candles were left of the giant chocolate-sponge cake they had eaten. Grandma and Granddad were the last to leave, having stayed to help clean up.

Everyone was exhausted. Maggie had been busy the entire day preparing food and trying to keep everyone entertained. The weather had been kind and April and her friends were able to spend most of the late afternoon playing on a bouncy castle they had blown up in the back garden. Taylor had gone into work for a meeting in the morning but was back at home to help two hours later. Before ten that evening, they were all sound asleep.

At twenty minutes past three, April sat up and got out of bed. She was dressed only in her pyjama bottoms. Although darkness filled her room, she walked straight to the door and opened it. Her door opened toward her and led onto the landing. The bedroom next to April's was unused. Taylor and Maggie had been decorating it in preparation for the new baby. Baby Scott was due to be born in less than three months.

Nightlights lit the landing and stairs. April walked to Baby Scott's bedroom and opened the door. Standing at the doorway, looking in, she said, "My favourite colour is red. I'll paint your bedroom red." Leaving the door open, April turned and went downstairs. It would be less than two minutes before she returned.

Maggie and Taylor were fast asleep. The night was warm and the duvet on the bed had been folded back. Taylor woke first. Unsure what it was that had woken him, he heard the shuffling of footsteps, close. Turning, he looked to his side of the bed.

"Hello baby. Are you okay?" Taylor said as April climbed on to the bed. He couldn't see her clearly, but he assumed she was about to get into bed with them. Sleeping between Maggie and him was something she had done on a number of occasions before. Whispering he said, "Don't wake Mommy, she's very tired."

"I won't, Daddy. I just need some colour."

Taylor realised from her tone that April wasn't awake. As he went to sit up he saw it too late. April raised the large kitchen knife high with both hands, bringing it back down quickly into Taylor's chest.

Pain seared through his chest, the knife piercing through the skin and between ribs, rupturing his heart. His muscles went into spasm, fixed in a paralysing clench, as his lungs demanded air, but none was forthcoming. For those few seconds, Taylor's mind was trapped inside a body incapable of carrying out any of its tasks. His mind turned to Maggie and their unborn child but only his eyes moved. He saw the knife being raised again. He tried to scream but heard only echoes in his mind. The knife came down again, this time into Maggie's swollen stomach. The dim light vanished from the room; there was only darkness and then *nothing*.

CHAPTER 3

Munroe sat with a broken toothpick between his lips while he stared out of the window. From his desk at the Vancouver Police Department he watched as the congested traffic came to a standstill on Cambie and Sixth. Like the traffic, Munroe's work was backing up and his current case was in danger of grinding to a halt. For the last six months Munroe had been consumed chasing a double homicide, and a third possible victim was now missing. The case was particularly gruesome and not something that the VPD were used to handling. But today Captain Daniels had requested that Munroe go take a look at an apparent double murder by an eight year old girl. 'The break'll do ya good, and take Agland with ya so he can do the paperwork,' the Captain had said. Munroe wondered how that constituted a *break*, but knew better than to ask.

Grabbing a fresh toothpick from the holder on his desk, Munroe picked up his jacket, nodded to Agland, and they headed out. It was eight-o-five in the morning.

Agland had picked up the record of the phone call that had come in at twenty-seven minutes before eight that morning. The caller was apparently an eight year old girl, April Pritchard of Fisher Drive, reporting that both her parents were dead.

"The notes state here that April had killed them in her sleep," Agland said.

"Killed them in *their* sleep," Munroe replied.

"No. Killed them in *her* sleep is what it says," Agland corrected.

"Who made the notes?"

"Summers. She's thorough, doesn't normally make mistakes."

Munroe shrugged. "Perhaps she was asleep. Eight years old..." he said, with a shake of his head.

Turning into Fisher Drive, Munroe and Agland could not have been prepared for the stark contrast between the tranquillity outside and the horror they would find inside the house. The road was lined with clean, well maintained two-story detached homes on large plots. Mature trees ran along each side and the gardens were manicured and filled with colour. BMWs, Mercedes and Lexus SUVs made up most of the cars parked in front of the oversized double garages. Were it not for the two ambulances and three police cars crowding the street, it would have been a perfect morning for the residents of Fisher Drive.

Before entering the house, Munroe took a small container from an inside pocket and took out a fresh toothpick. He replaced it with the toothpick he had been chewing on, a habit he had developed as a teenager to stop him biting his nails. He bent the tip of the used pick before placing it in the container. He put the container back to the pocket. He nodded to the officer posted at the front door and paused to place covers over his shoes. Then Munroe stepped into the foyer.

The foyer was a large open area with a light wooden flooring. A female medic was standing just inside. A staircase faced the entrance and there were doors left and right. Down each side of the staircase hallways led through to more rooms. One of the doors was open and Munroe noticed the kitchen beyond.

Sitting on the bottom step was a young girl with long straight light blond hair. She sat with her knees tucked up to her chest, she was sobbing. She was dressed in what appeared to be a two-piece pyjama set. Her appearance looked odd to Munroe then he understood why. Her pyjama pants, feet, hands and face were covered in blood. She had blood clotting in her hair, but her pyjama top was for the most part clean. The girl was sat with a VPD police jacket around her shoulders. A female officer, Jones, sat with her arm around the young girl. Jones looked up as Munroe and Agland entered.

"Stay here sweetheart. I won't be a minute," Jones whispered to the girl.

Jones got up from the step and walked over to Munroe.

"This is April Pritchard. She's eight years old. It was her birthday yesterday. She's the adopted daughter of one Taylor and Maggie Pritchard, now deceased," she said referring to a small notebook she had taken from a pocket. "What we have so far is only what April has told us. April apparently suffers from somnambulism, sleepwalking. A few months ago she woke up to find she had killed her pet kitten. It seems her condition has escalated. April woke up this morning in her parent's bedroom. She was covered in blood, their blood. Both parents died from multiple stab wounds from a large kitchen knife. She's still in a state of shock, poor kid. We've contacted the grandparents and a rep from Child Welfare is on the way. We've left everything as we found it upstairs. It's quite a sight."

"Did you put her pyjama top on?" asked Munroe.

"Er...no sir. The jacket is mine. She was wearing the pyjama's when we arrived," Jones replied.

"Thanks, Jones. Stay with her will you please? Are forensics on the way?"

"No sir, thought I'd wait for you."

Munroe nodded in acknowledgement. "Would you place a call, get someone out here? Thanks."

"Sir, medics want to take her. I've asked them to wait until the grandparents get here. You okay for her to wait?"

"Yeah, sure. But would you go with them when they arrive? I want a uniform staying with the child."

Munroe and Agland made their way up the stairs, pulling latex gloves from their pockets and stretching them onto their hands. A line of blood spots could be seen on the staircase, not many, and they had likely dropped from the girl as she made her way down the staircase. As they approached the top of the stairs, they could see a trail of blood stains going across the landing between two rooms. A significant amount of blood.

Munroe was first to step into the bedroom he assumed to be the parents', the door already wide open. It was a large room, with large mirrored double wardrobes opposite and across from the door. Along from the wardrobes, a large pine wood chest of drawers stood with a TV on top. About four feet from the edge of the drawers was the corner of the king-sized bed. The trail of blood led across the carpeted floor to the bed and then up onto the bed.

Laying on the bed were two mutilated bodies. The nearest body to the door was a white male, about five foot eleven, with short black hair. There were multiple stab wounds to the chest and stomach, Munroe estimated perhaps as many as ten. One incision was around six inches long as though a knife had been drawn or pulled down the body to create an opening in the stomach.

The second body was female, around five feet seven with light brown shoulder length hair. Again multiple stab wounds to the chest and stomach, but something looked odd, out of place. Munroe shifted for a closer look.

As he moved around to the end of the bed he noticed excessive flaps of skin and tissue. The female had well toned sculptured arms and legs, yet the stomach looked like it belonged to someone much heavier. A purple tube was protruding an inch or so from a large wound in the stomach.

"Oh Lord." Munroe said, closing his eyes. His toothpick fell from his mouth.

"What?" Agland asked. "What is it?"

Munroe continued around to the other side of the bed. Stopping, blood drained from his black round face. His chin dropped to his chest and he closed his eyes again. Agland walked to Munroe and looked down at the side of the bed where Munroe had been looking. Agland's body wretched. Holding his mouth, he turned and left the bedroom.

Munroe opened his eyes again, having wished that when he did he would find that his eyes had been mistaken. They weren't. On the floor next to the bed lay a tiny baby. Face up its eyes closed and umbilical cord severed at about three inches. The baby had a cut across the top of its left arm but was otherwise unharmed. The baby was not however breathing and, from the pale skin, had likely been dead a few hours. He looked at a few of the photos that were on top of the drawers. He stepped over to the windows, looking around the frame and checking to see if he could open any – the faint smell of death already making its presence felt. Opening a window slightly, he took a deep breath of fresh air and closed the window again. He moved into the ensuite and opened the mirrored cabinet above the sink. He opened and then closed both the built-in under-sink cupboards. He moved out of the bathroom and picked up the toothpick that he had dropped, popping it into a jacket pocket.

Leaving the bedroom, Munroe found Agland on the landing, his face wet from cold water he had splashed on it while in the bathroom.

"I think you should see where the trail of blood ends," Agland said.

Munroe walked across the landing, following the trail to the door opposite the parent's bedroom and trying to avoid stepping in the blood. The door was ajar and Munroe opened it wider with a pen he kept in his shirt pocket.

Munroe followed the blood into the room. The room was mostly blue with aeroplanes and balloons painted on the walls. A lampshade with pictures of trains, on it hung from the light in the middle of the room. A cot stood against the far wall. Pools of blood stained the carpet at the sides of two walls. Two walls that were now filled with small handprints, blood smeared as if a child had tried to paint. With another shake of his head, he took a clean toothpick from his shirt pocket, popped it between his teeth. Before leaving the room again, he checked the windows and for any other signs that someone other than the child may have been in the room.

* * * *

Munroe returned to his double homicide case. He had a new lead following a report back on the unusual bite marks that had been lifted from one of the victims. The papers were calling the perpetrator the '*Cannibal Killer*,' not because the victims were cannibals but simply because the perpetrator displayed cannibalistic tendencies and had killed people. Sometimes simple was best for the media; the label stuck. Vancouver is a city of relatively low crime. The few murders that occur each year are usually domestic, drug or gang related. There hadn't been an official serial killer investigation for during the twenty years Munroe had been in the force.

Agland completed the paperwork on the April Pritchard case, though almost all of it was computerised. There was not a great deal that VPD could do on this one. It hadn't taken Agland very long to discover precedent had been established.

In May 1987, Agland read, *a twenty-three year old Toronto man, Kenneth Parks, got up early one morning, got in his car, and drove the fourteen miles to his in-laws home. Once there, he stabbed and killed his mother-in-law whom he unquestionably loved, and attacked his father-in-law, who survived. Parks then drove to the police and told them he thought he may have killed some people. A year later, Parks was acquitted on the grounds that he had not acted of his own volition and was not responsible for his actions. Despite appeals, this view was later upheld by the Supreme Court of Canada. Parks defence also argued that the circumstances that triggered the episode were also very unlikely to occur again, making the recurrence of sleepwalking with aggression extremely remote. Parks walked away free.*

April was a minor, and with April's history and known sleeping disorder, it was unlikely anyone would agree a crime had actually been committed. Agland filed his report, closed the case, and handed it over to Social Services – April would be their responsibility.

* * * *

Jenny Bateman sat in her office, still coming to terms with the deaths of Maggie and Taylor Pritchard. She had been called to the scene shortly after the killings, and later she made the arrangements for April to enter back into the care system. April's grandparents undoubtedly loved her, but couldn't bring themselves to care for a child that had killed their only daughter. Jenny was unsure if it would be possible to keep April outside a secure care system until they were completely convinced she no longer suffered from her sleeping disorder.

Open on the desk in front of her was a copy of the police report. The report stated –

At between two a.m. and three a.m. on June twenty-fifth, April Pritchard left her bedroom and went downstairs to the kitchen. In the kitchen, April took the large eight-inch knife from a block kept next to the sink. Returning upstairs she climbed on to the bed and repeatedly stabbed both victims. Taylor Pritchard, her adopted father, died from a fatal wound to the heart. Maggie Pritchard, her adopted mother, died from massive blood loss as no single wound proved fatal. Maggie Pritchard was twenty-nine weeks pregnant. The baby had been forcefully removed from the womb and officially died from drowning; the umbilical cord having been severed using the kitchen knife and blood loss from the mother blocking airflow.

Having killed her parents and left the baby to die on the bedroom floor, using her hands, April proceeded to carry blood from her parent's injuries across the landing to the nursery room opposite. Still using her hands, April spread the blood across two of the walls.

Evidence suggests that April then slept the remainder of the night on the floor in her parent's bedroom, where she said she awoke at around seven-twenty. At seven-thirty three she placed a nine-one-one call. Officers arrived at the scene at just before eight where they found April sat on the bottom stair. She was crying and covered in blood.

No other foreign or relevant forensic evidence had been discovered and there were no signs of any external or third-party involvement. The police had closed the investigation.

Jenny closed the report. April was now her responsibility.

* * * *

Within a week following the deaths of her parents, April was being transferred to a ward in the psychiatric unit at the University of British Columbia Hospital. The ultra-modern facility would enable April to lead a relatively normal life during the day and be kept secure at night. It did mean that April would no longer be attending school in Richmond. Her education would instead fall under the responsibility of the university. Child Welfare would be maintaining regular contact with April. In the event that the university chose to no longer provide support for April, she would be returned to the care of Child Welfare. When April reached nineteen, the age of majority in the province of British Columbia, assuming she was no longer considered a threat to herself or anyone else, April would become independent and free to make her own choices. Not entirely sure being surrounded by older teenage students was ideal for April, Jenny still felt this represented the best opportunity.

Jenny glanced up at the wall clock, grabbed her jacket and handbag and left to collect April from the Welfare's Children's Care centre.

It was only a ten minute drive to the Children's centre and when she arrived, April was already waiting with two members of staff in the reception area. They loaded two suitcases into the trunk and April jumped onto the back seat. Jenny drove off.

The Pritchard's house would eventually be sold and what was left after paying off the liabilities would be placed in trust for April. April's grandparent's had also made arrangements for additional funds to be paid into the trust at regular intervals, perhaps easing the sense of guilt they were feeling at not assuming responsibility for her.

Driving, Jenny asked, "So, how are you feeling, honey?"

After a pause April replied, "Lonely."

"I'm sorry, April, that all this has happened. You deserve much better, but sometimes life just doesn't seem to turn out the way it should. Sometimes bad things happen and all we can do is try to carry on, try to make the best of a situation." Jenny placed a light hand on April's knee. "I meant what I said to you, this *isn't* your fault, none of it, many people suffer from sleepwalking and the one thing they all have in common is that none of them were really in control of their actions." April remained silent. "The university are looking forward to you staying with them. You'll have plenty of access to things there and they'll be able to help with…make sure you don't have to worry at night."

"Mom used to say I could help others with sleeping disorders, perhaps find a real cure so no one else has to go through what I am going through. So no one else has to lose the ones they love. Perhaps at the university I can study to become a doctor."

"I think you could be anything you want to be. You have some wonderful abilities, April, abilities that most of us can't even get close to. I'd bet that if you became a doctor you'd be the one to cure cancer or some other horrid disease, and many other things. I bet if you went into business you'd be one of the most successful business women ever, or go into politics and sort out the mess that the world seems to be headed for."

"I couldn't get my parents back though."

Jenny removed her hand from April's knee and back onto the steering wheel. She risked a moment of eye contact, "I know, I'm sorry."

The university campus occupies four hundred and fifty hectares of prime woodland, surrounded on three sides by the Pacific Ocean. April had visited the campus a number of times over the years for the many tests she had been subjected to. She never really had the opportunity to look around, it was always 'in and out', and it was always the same building, located near the botanical gardens and stadium. The psychiatry department was located much farther into the campus, down Wesbrook Mall.

As they drove through the campus, April looked out at the huge sports field, and buildings marked 'Gymnasium' and 'Winter Sports Complex'. She saw the signs for the Aquatic Centre and War Memorial. A small smile broke on April's face as she thought back to the time she would go swimming with her Mom, and how her Mom, a few months pregnant, had referred to herself as a whale when they went swimming. Thinking of her mom brought back memories of the moment she had woken up in their bedroom, covered in their blood, their bodies punctured and lifeless. Then she saw the baby, her baby brother that she would never get to play with. Tears began to fall down her cheeks. They approached the campus hospital.

"All right, before we go in, I want you to keep this card. It has my home and cell phone numbers on it. If you need me for anything or just want to talk, you give me a call. I really won't mind, anytime." Handing April a card, Jenny added, "you can also email me. You'll have access to computer equipment and the internet of course."

April wiped the tears from her cheeks and taking the card she opened the car door.

"Welcome to your new home, honey," Jenny said, as she opened the trunk to retrieve April's suitcases. "I hope everything works out for you. Come on, I'll introduce you."

As they made their way across the car park towards the hospital entrance, Jenny could not have imagined that April would be moving again before the following month had ended.

* * * *

The morning of July twenty-first was bright and a warm ocean breeze blew in from the west. April had been swimming with Emily, a medical graduate studying neuro-psychology at the university. Emily had been introduced to April when she was asked to assist with a series of tests that had been arranged for April to undertake. Emily had then asked to take on the role of *guardian* for April, amazed by the results of the initial test, and had become further intrigued on learning of April's sleeping disorder. The second test would be in two hours, and Emily had promised April a burger and fries from the small café near Tower Beach.

Before making their way over to the classroom, Emily and April took a walk along the shoreline toward Point Grey. They sat for a few minutes on the grass.

"I don't believe the university has ever had anyone quite like you, April." Emily said. "I mean, we do get younger students, prodigies or spoilt rich kids that come here sometimes to study math or music or something, but you…you seem to be good at everything. That test the other day was designed to give a baseline, to see if you had a particular proficiency for something." Emily was smiling, "You scored proficient on *everything*."

"Emily, I'm sure there are smarter people around than me." April replied.

"Here April, sit like me," Emily said. April did as instructed and sat crossed-legged with the palms of her hands facing up and resting on her knees. "Now we are just going to breath in slowly and deeply, fill your lungs, hold for a count of five then breath out slowly," Emily continued, performing the actions as she spoke.

After filling her lungs three times, April said, "You do this to relax?"

"Yes. Stress creates physical changes within the body, some are chemically related, where the body reacts by producing more or less of certain chemicals. Other changes include contraction of muscles, tightening of blood vessels, and adjustments to the brain. If you think of your brain like a computer, then I believe stress has the effect of turning the processing up in certain parts of the brain and lowering the processing in other parts. It's designed to power up our flight or fight response, but at the expense of our modern brain – our more complex functions like problem solving and communication. You have a test and you'll need your modern brain. Come on." Emily got up and helped April to her feet, keeping hold of April's hand as they started to walk back.

Walking over to the classroom, April asked, "Is the brain like a computer? I mean, can it be programmed?"

"Yes. For some time now people have used various techniques to place instructions into people." Looking directly at April, Emily said, "Programming them, or trying to at least. Things like hypnosis, mental suggestion, and a bit more recently NLP."

"NLP?" April asked.

"That's nothing you need to worry about," Emily replied, gently squeezing April's hand.

"How would someone know if they are being programmed?" April asked.

"They don't. Well, not if the person doing the programming knew what they were doing, if they were experienced, that is." Emily replied.

"So how does it work?"

"You ask too many questions, young lady. Tell you what, I have a few books back in my room. You can borrow some of those if you really must know about such things."

In the classroom, April was asked to sit at a desk that had a set of papers on it turned face down. Emily took a seat in a corner of the room. As she sat down, April noticed a large container of plastic tubing of various shapes and lengths. Dr. Ulrike Schuster sat at a larger desk at the front of the classroom. She was short with short brown hair and wore tortoise shell glasses. April also noted the white lab coat she was wearing as if to emphasise this was an *experiment*. Dr. Schuster had joined the university from Berlin two years earlier, but this was the first time April had seen her. Checking her stop watch, Dr. Schuster then asked April to take the pieces of tubing from the container on the floor and build a three-dimensional octagon, as quickly as she could.

"What are the papers on the desk for?" April asked.

"Please keep them as they are. They are part three of the test today, if you get that far." Dr. Schuster responded with a hint of impatience. With April still looking at her, Dr. Schuster tapped on her stopwatch.

April never rushed any of her tests and would always allow herself a smile when the assessor would later say how startled and amazed they were by the speed at which she could solve the problems they had placed in front of her. Of course, they assumed she was simply smiling in response to receiving praise.

April counted the number of pieces of tubing and examined the different shapes. Before putting any pieces together, she would visualise the completed shape, seeing it in her mind. She could manipulate the pieces much faster in her mind than she could ever achieve physically. Then, she simply put the pieces together in accordance with the picture she held within her mind.

"Fifty-six seconds, excellent April, thank you. Okay, for the second part I'd like you to open the box on the floor behind you. Inside you'll find twenty-seven small blocks with a number on each face. That's a hundred and sixty individual numbers and a lot of possibilities." Dr. Schuster lowered her chin to look over her glasses, looking to make sure she was being heard. "The objective is to piece the blocks together to create a larger three-dimensional cube, where the value of each row of numbers is equal to sixty-two. A bit like Sudoko, if you have ever done that. You are welcome to use the floor or another desk if you'd prefer. I'll allow ten minutes. Don't worry about completing it, we just want to see how far you can get."

Dr. Schuster's English was heavily accented, and April found her tone condescending. Schuster started her stopwatch but April remained seated at the desk.

"April, did you understand the question? Would you like me to repeat it for you?"

April turned and opened the box, and as she took each block from the box she looked at the number on each side and then placed it on the floor. Having examined each block, she sat for a moment then carefully constructed a larger cube with nine numbers on each face. Dr. Schuster watched perplexed, the stopwatch counting into the fourth minute.

Emily looked at Schuster then across at April, and then to the cube she had constructed. None of the rows appeared to equal the required number.

"April, it is clear that none of the rows have a value of sixty-two. Please at least try and get *some* of the rows correct," Schuster said.

April continued to place the smaller cubes until they formed the larger cube. "They are *all* correct. As you asked," April eventually replied.

"Don't be silly. I can see none of the rows total sixty-two. If you are not going to cooperate, April, I do have better things I could be doing."

"So do I, Dr. Schuster." April replied.

Dr. Schuster stood. "I don't have to stand here and listen to you, little girl. Emily, please return her to her room, her test will have to be rescheduled." Dr. Schuster turned and left the classroom.

"April, what was that all about?" Emily asked.

"I've done as she asked, even though she was rude."

"You go on to your room, I'll tidy up and catch up with you shortly."

April left and headed back towards her room in the psychiatric ward. She had a relatively large private room that was filled with toys and clothes from her home in Richmond. Jenny Bateman had asked her if she wanted to keep anything as the home was going to be put-up for sale. Jenny had arranged for all the items on April's list to be transferred to her room at the university. On the wall she had hung pictures of her mom and dad, and of all three of them together. A laptop computer the university had provided, along with an iPad were on a desk. A TV hung from a bracket in one corner of the room. April lay on her bed and waited for Emily.

Emily dismantled the tubing and returned it to its container. She moved across to the cube that April had put together and examined each face. None of the values of any of the rows on any of the faces came to the correct value. Emily gazed at it a moment. The quickest anyone had completed the puzzle was a little under seven minutes, a Chinese student more than a decade ago. A few other students had completed it in a much longer time. Most students would get as far six of the eighteen rows correct then give up. *April can do better than that*, Emily thought.

She started to pull the blocks apart. She remembered trying the puzzle herself. She had given up after fifteen minutes with eleven rows complete. Emily looked at each block as she slowly pulled them apart. As she placed the first three blocks back into the box she noticed the numbers, they equalled sixty-two. She pulled apart the next row and turned each block around to show the numbers on the inside face – they also equalled sixty-two. Both shocked and excited, Emily continued pulling each row apart in turn, and each row equalled the correct value but facing the *inside*. Emily sat there astonished. April *had* completed the puzzle in a much harder configuration, and in less than five minutes.

* * * *

Three days later, Emily and April had been joined by Albert for lunch. Albert was the night warden. His shift started at one p.m. and finished twelve hours later, and he would often come in early for a bite to eat before starting work. April and Albert had become good friends. April had been helping

Albert with crosswords and puzzles from the newspapers that he always seemed to carry around. Albert taught April how to play different card games and they would both play chess. Playing chess against Albert made April feel like she could tell the future. She quickly came to understand his level of playing and could always predict where he would move. It hadn't taken very long before April had Albert's next several moves figured before Albert did.

As Albert got up to leave, April asked if she could walk back with him, explaining that Emily had lectures to attend in the afternoon so April was on *free-time.*

The door to April's room could only be opened from the outside after nine o'clock in the evening, unless the fire alarm was activated, in which case the mechanism would be disengaged automatically. A camera would come on in her room in order to film her while she slept, but in the few weeks since staying at the university April had not experienced an episode. Often she would just sit in her room in the evenings watching TV, playing computer games, or reading before falling fast asleep.

Part of Albert's responsibility was to watch April's room. He hated the way she was monitored and kept in her room – *an eight year old lab-rat,* he thought. Albert would let April out of her room in the evening if she felt like having some light conversation, beating him at games, or helping him to complete his crosswords. April would place a plastic duck that she kept on top of a chest of drawers onto its side. When Albert noticed the duck was not standing up, he would come along and let her out of the room.

There wasn't much risk involved; the tapes would only be inspected in the event that Albert reported an episode of any kind – which, as April had pointed out, she couldn't have if she was awake. The ward was always quiet with a very few number of patients that had been hand selected by the university to help further research. All had private rooms, though many never stayed at the hospital overnight and even fewer stayed more than just a few days. All received some of the best care available in the country. Sometimes, April would be alone at night in the ward, other than Albert. Because April wasn't technically sick, she had no need for nurse supervision.

As they reached the ward, Albert said he would see April later. His first job was to clean the ward. April offered to help, but when Albert declined her assistance, April said she was going to walk across to the stadium to watch the team practice.

April sat alone in the stands watching the patterns play out on the field below. Patterns designed to create space or remove space, depending on whether the team was attacking or defending. April occasionally sketched her own patterns into a small notebook she carried around. She also noticed how the coach would shout at some of the players, while for others he would place an arm over their shoulder and talk privately to them.

The afternoon had worn on, and practice would be ending shortly for the day. April headed back to the ward. As she approached the building, she saw Dr. Schuster arrive in the car park opposite. She watched as Dr. Schuster parked and got out of the car. She had a number of folders to carry, and seemed in a hurry. April felt her heart rate quicken and became aware of tiny contractions in the muscles in her legs and arms. April glanced behind to see the stadium clock, then continued to watch Schuster as she entered the hospital building. Dr. Schuster had reported April's behaviour in her last test to the Assistant Dean.

April was a guest at the university at their expense, and she knew that this was dependent on her cooperation with their tests. Emily had been called in to the Assistant Dean's office and asked to remind April of the levels of behaviour that were expected from her. He was apparently not amused by Emily's claim that April had in fact completed the problem as Dr. Schuster has requested, and that Dr. Schuster had been *off* with her. The outcome was for April to be retested two days from then.

April fetched a sandwich to eat and some strawberry flavoured milk from a café before heading back to her ward. Although April had money, provision had been made for her to charge items to her room with the costs to be settled by the university. Now she sat in Albert's office, reading while he continued with his routine. At eight-thirty April closed her book and, as Albert returned, she told him she was tired and would be going back to her room to sleep. Returning to her room, she left the duck standing.

At five minutes passed ten that evening April sat up in bed, got out, and walked over to the drawers. She placed the duck on its side and sat back down on the bed. Ten minutes had almost passed when the door to her room opened.

"Everything all right, April?" Albert asked, poking his head around the door.

April stood up from the bed, and with both hands pushed hard and fast against the door. The door slammed against Albert's neck, jarring the cartilages of his larynx. He fell to the floor holding his damaged throat, choking. April left the room, taking care to step over Albert.

Dr. Schuster collected the files that she had used during the lecture and left the hall to return to her car. Placing the files on the roof of the car, she searched for the car keys in her handbag. In the starlit evening, she hadn't seen the long wooden handle as it came crashing down on to her head. Blistering pain shot through her head, her eyes immediately watering. Barely conscious, she turned around and saw April pulling the wooden broom handle back for another strike. Schuster lifted an arm to her face as she was struck again. She felt a bone in her wrist break and pain now shot up her right arm.

As the handle moved back a third time, a hand appeared and grabbed hold of the end preventing it from smashing forward. Albert grabbed April around her chest and pulled her backwards. She offered no resistance and the broom fell to the floor. April's eyes were open and staring, absent. Her look scared him. Dr. Schuster put a hand to the back of her head and felt blood emerging from a cut. She slid down by the side of the car and sat on the tarmacadam. Albert asked if Dr. Shuster was okay before turning April around and calling her name as he tried to wake her. She seemed in shock, but otherwise okay. Eventually, April awoke confused and then after seeing the bruising around Albert's neck and Dr. Schuster with blood on her hands, alarmed April said, "Was that me? Did I do that?" She started to cry.

A report produced by the Security Chief on the campus detailed the attack on Dr. Schuster. The report and April's growing lack of cooperation became the subject of an extraordinary meeting that included the Vice President and several other Senate members at the university. The attack was debated with some Senate members, arguing that April was suffering from an episode coupled with stress from the tests and relationship with Dr. Schuster. Others were less convinced, believing instead that April had somehow planned the attack, knowing she could fall back on her sleep disorder as a possible cause. After two and half hours the meeting concluded that April's tendency toward violence, coupled with her exceptional intelligence and ingenuity, posed a threat to both staff and fellow students– her invitation to stay was revoked.

The university strongly recommended a period of psychiatric treatment under secure conditions. Despite objections lodged by Jenny Bateman and the absence of any precedent, Child Services referred April Pritchard to a minimum six months observation at Ashford Mental Institution, the only hospital in lower British Columbia with psychiatric wards more secure than those at the university, that provided twenty-four hour care. As if to placate Ms. Bateman, the order to detain April under the care of Ashford Mental Institution specifically added that April '*be granted full privileges and receive the highest possible care available at the facility*'. Within two weeks following the attack on Dr. Schuster, April was moved to Ashford.

CHAPTER 4

The smell of the sea carried on the hot August air and into the open interior of the convertible Jaguar. Dr. Elizabeth Hershey had received the car as a gift from her entrepreneurial father, in celebration of his retirement last year. It now meant she owned two convertibles, but she had no wish to offend her father by not using the jag, and besides, she had come to prefer it to her self-bought BMW.

She drove casually up the quiet Sea-to-Sky Highway towards Lions Bay and Brunswick Beach about ten miles north of West Vancouver. At Brunswick Beach she would be turning east, and up into the hills and mountains toward Brunswick Mountain. Two and half miles off the main highway, along a privately built road, set in two hundred acres of unspoilt parkland and forest, nestled at the foot of the mountains, stood Ashford Hospital.

The original building and now the main administrative unit, was almost one hundred years old and was originally built as an intelligence centre for the Canadian army. After the Second World War, the building was sold off and then purchased by the Provincial Health Authority and over several years converted into a Hospital. Additional buildings had been added over the years resulting in the three main care facilities, an administration centre, recreation buildings, and substantial gardens.

No one was admitted to Ashford unless they were considered a threat to themselves or other people. That said, the facility separated the men from the women, and the mildly violent from the seriously violent. The hospital is home to some of British Columbia's most dangerous individuals – those with severe personality disorders, behavioural problems and mental illness. The apparent irony of using this site to house these patients was not lost on Hershey.

Turning off the highway, she made the climb up towards the hospital's private and secure road. She knew she would be waved through at the main gate that would otherwise serve to stop any visitors that had not made prior appointments at least forty-eight hours ahead.

The main building was a substantial two-story with fifteen foot ceilings, and fronted by tall white stone columns, the architecture had been described to her as *Jefferson neoclassic*. Hershey just thought it was a large impressive, Roman looking building, that always managed to make her feel intimidated as she parked up and walked across the gravel to the main entrance. The newly developed wards, that were a brick-based eye-sore, could not be seen from the main entrance. Pushing the button to close the roof on the car, Hershey collected her case files and handbag from the passenger seat and made her way into the hospital.

After receiving a polite greeting from a receptionist, she signed in and collected her temporary badge.

"I'll tell him you're on your way up," the receptionist said.

Hershey proceeded up the large, ornate marble staircase. She had an appointment with Professor Charles McGill, Chief Executive at the hospital, concerning another recent suspected-suicide. Deaths at a high security institution were not uncommon, amongst the patients or the staff, although staff suicides were usually carried out away from the hospital. Peter Legwinski, a patient who was suffering from an acute personality disorder, had died yesterday from strangulation. As consultant senior psychiatrist, Dr. Hershey was required to follow up on all deaths or attempted deaths at the hospital, providing an independent review to the hospital's governing board.

She had been assigned to Ashford eighteen months ago and had established a good working relationship with Charles McGill. She knocked and entered his office.

"Hi Elizabeth, as well as ever, I see," McGill said, greeting her with a large generous smile. "Changed your hair again?"

"Charles, you always mention my hair, but you really have no idea if I have changed the style or not," Hershey replied playfully.

"So, have you changed it since we last met, or not?"

Hershey unconsciously felt the end of the brown curls which sat on her shoulders with her right hand. "I've not changed styles. Just added a few highlights."

McGill made her think of the kind of grandfather everyone was supposed to have - his large round slightly ruddy face with pale blue eyes surrounded by grey hair, thin on top, thick and bushy around the chin. His hand shake was firm but friendly. He was dressed as he always was while at work, in a white full-length cotton lab coat, black pants and casual black shoes. The shoes meant he spent the majority of his time at work walking around the hospital. The lab coat reflected the years of training and service before moving into senior management. Hershey didn't need to look to know what colour socks McGill would be wearing - always sky blue, matching his eyes and sufficiently unexpected, to let you know that under his aging skin, he possessed a sense of humour.

Despite the warm welcome, Hershey suspected he could be quite capable of being hard and cold if a situation required – a trait no doubt called upon in any role that involved responsibility for people's lives.

"So, how's that man of yours? Simon, if I remember rightly?" he asked.

"Oh he left, moved to Calgary, seems he couldn't share me with my work."

"I'm sorry, seemed like you liked him a lot."

"I did, just not enough." Hershey replied, with a short tight-lipped smile. "So, what's been going on?" she continued, moving toward the informal area of McGill's office. Away from his desk were three soft brown leather chairs. Two of the chairs placed together and the other across a knee-high glass and oak wood coffee table. Hershey knew to sit in one of the two and leave the lone seat for McGill. Hershey was wearing a black Chanel mid-length dress. Her shoes also black, leather pointed-toe pumps by Prada with a slender, not too high heel.

Hershey had built her relationship with McGill on trust, honesty, and by being good at her job. Her reviews had always been fair, and she shared them with him before sending them to the board to ensure he was never caught off-guard. She kept her opinions to a minimum, and stated the facts as she found them, which usually meant reasonable precautions had been taken by the hospital. Hershey was aware of reports of gross mismanagement and shocking security lapses at other so-called high security institutes, but she was also realistic enough to know that if someone wanted to kill themselves, there was not a great deal that could be done to stop them.

"Here you go," McGill said, as he picked up a pile of papers and files from his desk and placed them down on the coffee table. He then sat in the lone chair. "Peter Legwinski, suffering from an acute personality disorder, was discovered dead from strangulation in his room yesterday morning. He was only on our *caution* list, and so wasn't subject to close twenty-four-seven monitoring. He removed his vest and tied it around his neck. He stuck a pencil through the knot probably to ensure it wouldn't come lose, and then apparently just sat on his bed until he finally died from asphyxiation." McGill sat back in his chair, "We'll miss Legwinski. He thought he was a magician you know, performing in Las Vegas. He was brought here after cutting a woman in half during a now infamous performance seen by an audience of six. I guess they got to see a show they would not quickly forget. He wasn't actually in Vegas of course, but a small theatre in Edmonton where he was doing an audition. He could do a few card tricks that would keep people here entertained and for the most part he was no trouble. We didn't let him near a saw though."

"Nice," Hershey replied, "I bet his knife throwing act was really something."

McGill smiled, "Those are copies, so feel free to take them away." They both stood and McGill went to the door, "Take care of yourself Elizabeth, and when do I get a ride in that fancy car of yours?" he asked.

"When neither of us are too busy. Perhaps I'll take you to dinner one evening when I'm over."

* * * *

Hershey grabbed a coffee from the vending machine, sat down at a table in the staff lounge, and began reading through the file on Peter Legwinski. Born in 1966, Legwinski came to Canada in 1971 with his Polish parents. Originally settling in Montreal, Legwinski later left home and attended the University of Alberta, Edmonton, where he studied linguistics. He apparently had no problem graduating, but soon after his life took a downturn. With a string of drug and violent offences already behind him, Legwinski was introduced to the care and rehabilitation services. Only a year after being released he was arrested for the murder of a young women, a former girlfriend from the University introduced at the time of the audition as his assistant. Legwinski was later found to be judged insane and was transferred to a secure hospital. Following attacks on a fellow patient and a member of staff, he was finally transferred to Ashford with no institution now considered suitable within the Alberta province. After almost two years at Ashford without incident, Legwinski was downgraded in terms of risk, allowing him greater privileges and access, and reduced supervision. Recently, he had reportedly formed a friendship with a new patient, April Pritchard, a child who had transferred to the institute less than a month ago. From the staff interviews conducted so far, no one had noticed any sign that Legwinski might be prepared to take his own life.

The hospital comprised of four departments, Personality Disorder, Primary Care, Rehabilitation, and the Women's Directorate that catered specifically for women with varying illnesses and disorders. Until yesterday the Personality Disorder department was responsible for seventy-six males. Forty-eight women were currently under the care of the Women's Directorate with only twenty-three being kept on site, and only seven of those had severe personality disorders – *proof if any were needed, that most issues resided in men*, Hershey believed.

Over the eighteen months that she had been involved with the hospital, Hershey had come to know a few of the patients, but only as cases she was asked to report on. *What was a child doing here?* she thought. As she sat there a little longer she had decided she would introduce herself to April Pritchard.

Before leaving, Hershey called in on McGill.

"I'm going to call it a day. I'll come back tomorrow to finish off. Is there any chance I can meet April Pritchard? She seems to have seen a lot of Legwinski recently."

"How about you buy me lunch instead of dinner? Come get me for lunch tomorrow, I need to tell you a bit about Miss Pritchard before you meet our little princess."

Our little princess, huh? Hershey thought. "Yeah, sure, see you about one," Hershey replied, closing the door.

* * * *

Hershey and McGill took a table looking out across the Strait of Georgia. The day was warm and clear and the ferry from Horseshoe Bay could be seen making its way over to Hopkins carrying traffic heading for the Sunshine Coast. McGill ordered a cold beer to drink, Hershey a chilled fresh orange juice. After perusing the lunchtime menu they placed their food order.

"The board are expecting death by misadventure for Mr Legwinski," McGill started.

"I'm inclined to agree at this point. From the reports it doesn't look like anyone else could have been involved but there's not enough to confirm suicide was the intention." Hershey confirmed.

McGill scoffed, "Can't think why else he might tie his vest around his neck that tight."

Hershey smiled, "Yes you can. Anyhow, tell me about your 'little princess'."

"In thirty five years in this line of business," McGill responded, "I don't think I've known anything quite like this one. April Pritchard is eight years old." Hershey looked incredulous. Putting his hands up in defence, he continued, "She arrived here last month from UBC. She had been a guest of the psychiatric unit there until she attacked a member of staff. They recommended she be placed in a secure facility. We've had teenagers here, but no one this young. April suffers from aggressive somnambulism, but I doubt that's why the UBC took such an interest in her."

Hershey looked quizzical.

"She has an intelligence quotient off the scale. We know the IQ tests themselves differ, but they do all agree on one thing. April is exceptional. Anyway, it seems April may be getting a little tired of the countless tests given to her over the last few years."

"How did she end up at the university?" Hershey asked.

"She killed her parents. April got up in the middle of the night, took a knife from the kitchen, and stabbed them both. Her mom was seven months pregnant at the time and April removed the baby, thereby killing it. Carrying blood in her hands from the bedroom she went into the nursery and decided she was going to paint the room a different colour...red not blue."

"While sleepwalking?" Hershey asked. McGill nodded. "That's horrible," Hershey continued. "So, the university became her legal guardian?"

"Yes, apparently they have been aware of her since she was very young. Anyhow, she has a history of escalating episodes, but her conscious behaviour shows no signs of aggression at all. She's really a sweet kid."

"The attack at the university?" Hershey prompted.

"Sleepwalking again apparently, although this time there seemed to be some doubt. She attacked one of the staff with a broom," McGill confirmed, failing to hide his amusement, "I'm sorry," he added.

"She wasn't secured?"

McGill shook his head, the smirk now gone, "Seems she had struck up a friendship with the night warden, I don't know the details, but she somehow persuaded him to let her out of her room while still asleep."

The conversation paused while the waitress brought their food.

McGill continued, "We have a room for April with the women. She has full access during the day, enjoys games, the gardens and the pool, and we keep her monitored and secure at night. That's about all we can do. There's no point in medicating her. I hope for her sake she grows out of her habit sooner rather than later. She's on a six-month review and has been with us about a month now."

"Does she have any visitors?"

"Only one so far I think, Ms Jenny Bateman from Child Welfare. She had arranged the Pritchard's adoption of April."

"April was adopted?" Hershey said, surprise in her voice.

"Yes, rather sad. She was discovered just a few weeks old in Richmond Park, laying next to her mom, who had committed suicide," McGill explained. "Don't some folks have all the luck?" he added.

Hershey sat quiet as McGill tucked into his pizza.

"So, how'd April meet up with Legwinski?" Hershey asked.

"Legwinski had access to a lot of the recreational areas. Seems they enjoyed the gardens. Like I said, we've had no trouble from Legwinski, and besides, no one is ever really unsupervised. Apparently they got on well together, perhaps she liked his magic tricks, and he enjoyed the attention.'

"You mind if I meet April?"

"Not at all, I think it'd be good if you could spend some time with her. I just wanted to let you have the background first. She's the only minor we have at the hospital and I'm convinced it is not the kind of place where she should be growing up. See what you think, perhaps you could help return her to something more normal."

* * * *

That afternoon Dr.Elizabeth Hershey introduced herself to April Pritchard. April was playing checkers with one of the nurses in the women's recreational area. They took a walk through the gardens. Hershey had been told how landscaping had been used to help build a sensory rehabilitation garden. The gardens were based on Snoezeleon Therapy, where the design would draw on all the senses – scent, colour, different textures, sounds, and movement. Walking around, tears began to well in April's eyes as they talked about Legwinski. April had been told that Legwinski had killed himself. She would see him in the garden and he would show her magic tricks using different flowers and petal. He would join April in the meditations she had continued and expanded upon while staying at the university. April also revealed she was expecting a visit soon from Emily Jackson who, she explained, was both a student and a friend there.

As they talked, Hershey found April to be polite, respectful, and showing maturity well beyond her years. She was surprised that despite how brutal life had been for April, she displayed no sign of animosity or bitterness. She was a sweet child. Hershey asked April if it would be okay for her to visit again and spend more time with her. April said she'd like that.

Before leaving the hospital that day, Hershey spoke to several staff concerning Legwinski and the events surrounding his death. She inspected his ward, his room, and the security records for the night he died.

Hershey was introduced to Rowina Oledejo, a Nigerian nurse working at the hospital. Rowina had been on duty the night Legwinski died. After going over the procedures and Rowina's routine for that night, Hershey enquired as to how well she knew April Pritchard. She smiled brightly.

"Did you notice if April and Legwinski spent much time together?" Hershey enquired.

"Occasionally," Rowina replied, "I knew they would talk, sometimes they would meet up in the gardens."

"I understand that April may have been fond of his magic tricks. Why do you think Legwinski took an interest in April?"

"I take it you've seen her? She's a wonderful child. Seemed Legwinski was a little curious about how smart April is. But then who isn't? Have you seen what she can do? I just stick to checkers, that way she only knows of a dozen ways to beat me," Rowina chuckled.

Thanking Rowina for her time, Hershey left the hospital for the day. She had decided to drive home instead of returning to her office in downtown. Stopping at her local Chinese restaurant for take-out, it was after seven-thirty by the time she pulled up at home.

The house was a large detached property on quarter of an acre of some of Vancouver's most prestigious land in Upper Capilano. The garden backed onto the Capilano River Regional Park, between the Suspension Bridge and the Cleveland Dam.

Entering the house, Hershey took her phone from her bag and dropped the bag at the foot of the stairs. She then walked to the kitchen and grabbed a fork from a drawer and a bottle of water from the fridge. Walking to the lounge, she looked at her phone and noticed she had a voicemail. After placing the fork and bottle on the coffee table, she returned to the kitchen and made a start on the rice. She then checked her voicemail.

'Dr. Hershey, this is Detective Munroe from Vancouver Police Department. We haven't been introduced but I've been given your name with regard to assisting us with a profile for a case we are working. Please, could you return my call when you hear this? Thank you.' The voice was deep and smooth.

There were no further messages. As Hershey sat eating, she tried to recall where she had heard of Munroe's name. Then it came to her, she had seen his name in the paper, he was the detective on the 'Cannibal Killer' case. *What did he want?*

* * * *

In the evening, a nurse was collecting Legwinski's personal items from his room. Three small boxes were filled with books from his bookcase, a plastic crate contained clothing, and a further box was full of small trinkets and personal items. As the nurse collected the last of the small items from off the top of the bookcase, a small, gold-plated die dropped to the floor beside the bed. The nurse bent down to pick up the fallen item and noticed a folded piece of paper laying under the bed. She placed the die in the box with the other effects and picked up the paper. Unfolding the paper revealed a picture she had seen before but couldn't remember its name. The picture looked like it had been drawn in red crayon. The picture was of a Christian cross with a loop at the top. The nurse added it to the box.

CHAPTER 5

When Dorothy Kendall had left her home that morning to walk the short distance to her local grocer, her darkest nightmares could not have prepared her for the horror that had now befallen her. She was a short but trim lady with long silver hair that she would tie up in a bun before leaving her house. A spinster of sixty-two years, well known and loved in her local community, Dorothy was a grandmother to everyone.

Her head ached as she slowly came to. She remembered leaving her house and thinking how beautiful the day had started, the bright warm sunshine and still breeze. She remembered greeting Mr Reynolds before she decided to take the path along Froggers Creek. Some teenagers were sat on the grass with their bikes laying beside them, playing what she thought to be a card game. She saw a young woman walking a golden labrador and remembered almost saying hello to her before she realised the woman was talking into a cell phone.

She felt pain behind her eyes from a substance that she had been forced to breathe in. She recalled the strong hand that had pressed a damp cloth across her nose and mouth. She had woken up, disorientated, with her wrists and legs bound with nylon line to a chair. She heard no sound, only her own breath and the irregular beating of her own heart. As the pain eased she could see more clearly and she became aware of a putrid smell. She couldn't speak because of an object that had been jammed in her mouth and held in place by a cord that had been tied around her head. Her fear turned to terror as she saw what else was in the room with her.

On the floor lay the decaying remains of a black and white dog. A collie, Dorothy thought. Its head had been partially removed from its neck and its stomach had been sliced open with most of the contents spilled on to the floor. Metal cages were stacked against a wall, two appeared empty and one contained a brown and white floppy-eared rabbit. Stains of various colours covered the dark blue carpet and used tissues lay all around the room. A small clock on the mantelpiece gently went, *tick-tock-tick-tock*. The walls were covered in cream floral wallpaper stained with various splashes and colours. A necklace made from human teeth lay on a sideboard. There was a window to the room which had been almost entirely covered by thick purple curtains that had been pinned closed. A thin strip of sunlight crept into them room from across the top of the curtains. The white door to the room was ajar.

A tear ran down Dorothy's cheek and into the side of her mouth. She then realised that her bladder had not been able to hold, and despite her circumstances, she flushed with embarrassment. Breathing in the horrid smell made her want to vomit, but then she detected something else in the air – a smell coming from outside the room.

* * * *

In the relative privacy of his back yard, Edward Walker was preparing the gas barbeque. On a wooden table stood a cheap bottle of red wine, some chopped onion, salt and soft poppy-seeded bread rolls. Edward was no chef but he enjoyed his food.

* * * *

Hershey had returned Munroe's call and had arranged to meet him first thing at her office. Munroe was a large man with a bald head, standing at least six foot three she thought, broad across the shoulders and perhaps a little overweight despite his height. Hershey studied him for a few moments longer. There was a serenity to him, shallow wrinkles were forming around his soft, even sad, brown eyes, and his full brown cheeks were without blemish. Munroe was accompanied by another detective, Hale, who looked small next to Munroe, but was probably five-eleven and one-fifty pounds.

Hershey welcomed them into her office, where she had two leather captain's chairs waiting for them.

"Careful when you sit down," she said, looking at Munroe as she spoke. "The chairs are designed to lean back but I wouldn't want you to topple over," she added, while pulling her own chair around to the side of her desk. "Now gentlemen, how may help you?"

Munroe, rolling a toothpick between his teeth, glanced at Hale and then back at Hershey.

Munroe shifted in his seat before he started, "We understand you have some experience with profiling, forensic psychiatry, that sort of thing. You probably know that we don't get too many serial killers, so our experience in dealing with them is limited. Personally, I like it that way, but it puts us at a disadvantage when it comes to catching the real thing. We'd like you to take a look at a case, tell us what you think."

"The Cannibal Killer?" Hershey replied, almost a statement more than a question.

"Yeah. That's what the papers are calling him."

"Him? You sure it's a man?"

"Yeah. We took some teeth marks off one of the victims. The perp is male and we believe has had some fairly recent dental work. We know of at least three victims, and we'd like to get a better idea of the person we're trying to find. Perhaps you can help narrow the search?"

"Have you spoken to Seattle?" Hershey asked.

Munroe shifted in his seat again, "Yeah, this was their idea. It was actually Seattle that came up with your name."

Hershey allowed herself a little smile as she now understood why Munroe seemed uncomfortable. She decided against poking at it. She removed her smile and thought for a moment. She had lectured on the behaviours and motivations of serial killers many times and her work at mental institutions gave her access to some of them, allowing her to refine her findings and conclusions, but only once before had she been able to work alongside the Police in tracking one.

"I'll be happy to do what I can. I need to complete a report today, but I could start having a look tomorrow. Let you know what I think?"

"Please, we'd appreciate anything you might come up with. Here's the file we had compiled for you," Munroe said.

Hale passed over a thick file of papers, reports, and photographs, which Hershey placed on her desk.

"Not everything has been made public, so please, if you could, we'd much appreciate it if you would restrict this information to only yourself, thank you. You have my number. But I have also placed my card on the files there." Munroe said.

Hershey smiled at Munroe's subtle request to be called as soon as she had anything. "Yes, Detective Munroe, I have your number and I'll call you tomorrow evening and let you know where I'm at."

Nodding, Munroe left the office followed by Hale. Hershey closed the door and returned to the report she had started writing up on Peter Legwinski's death.

* * * *

The barbeque was ready and the anticipation had made Edward aroused. He tried to prolong the sensation by buttering the rolls and sprinkling on the chopped onion, but the desire was too strong.

As a boy, Edward had been told that Man was just an animal sharing the world with other animals. When he went to school, he was taught how life began by accident in the sea, and then eventually changed into all the life that now exists. Of course, this process would require many millions of years, which explains why we can't actually see it happening.

At nine years old, Edward remembered how the real meaning of life came to him. He was playing with another boy on the roof of an old, disused building when the boy found a gold necklace. Edward wanted the necklace for himself, but the boy wouldn't give it to him. That was when Edward pushed the boy from the roof. Edward saw the boy hit the concrete below with his leg snapping and head splitting open. Edward climbed down and took the necklace before returning home to tell of the accident – *Life is simply taking what you want while avoiding those that might take away what you have.*

Edward experimented with different pleasures. He had tried drugs, but they were expensive and took control. He played with sex, men, women, children, even animals on occasion. He had no desire for material possessions, for his status in the world was above all that. His greatest pleasure was food, and the best food was mature, healthy human organs.

Walking through the kitchen to the living room he picked up the large knife from off the countertop. He could smell the fear of the old woman before he entered the room. She had pissed herself, as they always do, a sign that they are ready.

* * * *

The line with which Dorothy had been bound burned as she attempted to free her hands. It was hopeless. Her muted cries would not be heard by anyone outside the house, and her throat had become dry, as saliva dripped from her mouth. Her thoughts turned to her friends and the bridge club, the cruise she had been on with her best friend, Colleen, then little Naomi who lived next door, whom she had come to love as her own.

Her thoughts were broken, as a man with short black, greasy-looking hair came into the room, smiling and holding a large knife.

"Ever wondered how the deer must feel as the tiger sinks its canines into its flesh? That burning feeling, and the terror of knowing it is about to be eaten?"

Dorothy felt her eyes bulging and her stomach turn as terror took its hold. She tried again to free her hands and move her legs, desperate to be free. The man slashed down the front of her floral dress, tearing it open revealing part of her bra, her ribs and stomach. Images of her parents when she was younger appeared in her mind. Then her brother, and then friends, flashed through her mind. Tears fell from her cheeks as she realised she would never see them again.

Looking into her eyes, still smiling, the man drove the blade into the top of her stomach and drew it down to her waist. Pain seared through her body as Dorothy felt the knife's violation. She could feel the sawing motion as it tugged and cut her skin, moving down, down through her stomach. She could feel the warm flow of blood as it escaped from her wounds. Her life ebbed. When it seemed she could bear no more pain, a calm numbness filled her body. The pain quenched and with it came a strange peace in the knowledge that she was about to die. Dorothy saw Naomi shining in a bright yellow dress, skipping in the garden, she was smiling and speaking but her words made no sound. Dorothy strained to listen as she felt movement inside her. She required her body no longer, her soul moving to a place where Death and Sorrow have no power.

* * * *

Evening had arrived, and Hershey was back at home having completed her report on Legwinski. She had grabbed herself a cup of hot chocolate and sat down to make a start on the file Munroe had given her. With her feet up on the coffee table, she opened the file.

The dates on the various papers and reports were all relatively recent. The earliest date was only several months ago following the discovery of the first victim, Anthony Hardwick. He was killed at age seventy-four, and his partial remains were discovered by a dog-walker in Bear Creek Park, Surrey, near to his home. Vital organs had been removed from the body – both kidneys, the liver and heart. Hershey examined the photographs taken at the scene and then before the autopsy. The cuts to the body were not entirely clean or straight suggesting a sharp but non-surgical implement; they were also not positioned for easiest extraction of the organs, meaning the perpetrator likely only possessed basic knowledge of anatomy.

The second victim was female; May Cooper, aged sixty-seven. As with Hardwick, her partial remains were also discovered in a park. There had been no apparent attempt to bury or hide the body in any real way. Like the first victim, the time of death was estimated to be less than twenty-four hours before the body had been discovered.

The third victim was male; Peter Caldwell aged sixty-four, discovered under very similar circumstances to the previous two victims. The victims had been discovered within the jurisdictions of different police forces. However, given the connection between the cases, it had fallen to the RCMP and in this case Vancouver Police Department to take the lead.

Hershey continued reading the various police and medical reports, sifting through the numerous photographs of the victims taken both before and after their deaths. Unaware of the time, she fell asleep on the sofa.

* * * *

Edward Walker was full. He wished he could eat like that every day, but he knew that would be too dangerous. He had not lived in Vancouver long, moving up from the States only eight months ago. He had needed to keep moving around while he experimented with different age groups and races. He had started, as everyone does, with animals. He had sampled hundreds of different animals from all around the world, but nine years after his search for the best meat had begun, he had finally found the very best – the organs of healthy elderly Caucasians.

He preyed on the single as they were the easiest to take. Edward couldn't abide complications in anything. He was a simple man with simple tastes. He would watch and follow potential food for a few weeks to ensure they were on their own. He would observe their routines, which all the elderly seemed to possess and value. It made things easy for him, uncomplicated. When he had decided on the time, he would follow them and take them easily. Although it was important his prey were still active, they were still too weak to provide any real resistance. Having eaten, he would simply return them to a quiet part of a park near their homes. He knew the bodies would be found, he expected it. He wouldn't be staying long. A few kills, then time to move on.

The body that was still tied to a chair in his room used to be Dorothy Kendall. He had watched her before taking her. He knew her routine, had seen some of those she cared for, and even enjoyed watching her spend time with the child from next door -the little Chinese kid.

As afternoon had turned to evening, Edward had finished cleaning the barbeque and went inside. The body still slumped there. To see the terror in his victim's eyes as he made the long cut down the chest and stomach was not the only reason he killed. The elderly were simply the best food and he had begun to miss the taste and the texture. He would occasionally bite them before removing their organs to ensure sufficient chemicals had been released by their terrified bodies, enhancing the flavour of the meat. He hadn't needed to bite Dorothy.

Dorothy had remained alive while the first few cuts were made and while his hands fumbled inside her body. He often wondered what that must feel like for them - *much more intimate than sex*, he imagined. He had tried the flesh, brain, eyes and other organs of previous kills, but none could match the flavour of the prized organs – the kidneys, liver and heart. Experience was a good teacher.

Edward bagged the remains of the dog he had killed a couple of days before and placed them out at the back of the house. Dorothy had bled over the chair he had tied her to and a large pool had stained the dark blue carpet. He normally purchased cheap rugs that he could simply roll the carcass in before discarding. But the dog had defecated on the carpet before he killed it. In his annoyance he killed the dog there and then, adding bloodstains to the mess. He knew he was going to have to replace the carpet anyway.

Edward cut a strip from the carpet and rolled up Dorothy's remains into it. Under the cover of the night, he returned to Froggers Creek and placed the remains of Dorothy's body near the foot of a large oak tree.

Tomorrow, Edward would clean the rest of the house, replacing the carpet and wallpaper in the so called 'living room'. He never really understood the term, but it made him smile nonetheless. He had already decided to rent a property close to a retired community and sample the delights of Seattle.

* * * *

Hershey woke crumpled on her sofa, and with stiffness in her neck, back and arms. She stood up, prepared the coffee pot and walked around for a few minutes to shake loose her muscles. The kitchen clock read six-fifteen. She went upstairs to shower.

Refreshed and more relaxed, Hershey returned to the sofa, and to the file that was now laid spread out across the floor and table. She had left a message at work saying she didn't intend coming into the office and that she did intend to work from home. Making herself comfortable with a cup of tea, she started making notes.

The key to any investigation, she had been told, was to make *connections*. It is the links between things that provide the real clues, anything else is simply evidence. Conclusions are drawn from the connections between the evidence, and it is those conclusions that would lead to the arrest. Without connections there can be no conclusion.

Hershey started to make a list of similarities between the victims and the circumstances in which they had been discovered. She made a separate list for differences. She started with the obvious – all elderly, all Caucasian, all had the same organs removed, and all were discovered in parks near to their homes. Then she looked deeper - all were elderly but reports from friends and family suggested they were still very active; they would go on walks, be regularly seen outside and were members of various clubs and associations. They lived in quiet locations, in areas people would still refer to as *middle class*. They were all healthy, non-smokers and at most could only be considered very mild drinkers. She added 'male' and 'female' to the differences list and the different areas around Vancouver that they had lived.

Hershey continued with her lists, extending them to include their known routines, backgrounds, friends and family members. The first victim, Anthony Hardwick, appeared never to have married. The second victim was divorced, and had remained single after that. The third victim's wife had died three years ago.

Hershey wondered how the killer might be choosing his victims. Clearly he preyed on the elderly. It seemed relevant that they were still active in the community. The location must have been a factor, but there must have been more to it than that. *Was it just coincidence that they were healthy,* she thought, *no real ailments, not on medication? If not, how might the killer have found that out? What else?*

A thought occurred to Hershey. She looked back through the photographs. She found a photo of each victim before they had been murdered, and others taken where the bodies had been discovered. She looked closely. Not sure of the relevance, she noticed that none of the victims wore wedding rings. *We* know they had relationships, she thought to herself, but to a stranger they might have appeared to be single, and for all intents they *were* single. She spent the afternoon reading through the forensic evidence to put together a view of how the crimes were being committed. Then she considered motive before working on the possible profile of the killer.

At eight-fifteen in the evening, Hershey felt she had something. Before she had chance to call Munroe, her phone rang…*Munroe.*

"Hi…Yes, I have some thoughts…No I've worked straight through…You're buying? Okay, give me twenty." Hershey hung up and went upstairs to change.

* * * *

They had driven to an Italian restaurant at Munroe's recommendation. Hershey had not been there before but she liked the look – *nice but still casual.*

"Are you going to eat with that toothpick in your mouth?" Hershey asked, as they were seated.

"Er? Oh yeah, sorry. It's a habit I picked up, thought it was better than biting my nails."

"You bite your nails?"

"Not anymore," Munroe replied, removing the toothpick from his mouth. "So, Doc, what can you tell me?"

"Here's what I'm thinking…the killer is probably a white male, between thirty-five and forty years old, and average intelligence. I believe he's a loner who watches his victims for some time before they are killed. He likes the elderly of course, prefers quiet neighbourhoods, and the fact that they are still active. I think he selects them because they are single."

Munroe raised his eyebrows, "But they're not single."

"I mean they were living on their own at the time they were killed," Hershey clarified. "I think that's how he selects them in the first place, *then* he watches them. He must scout a quiet location and select an elderly person who is out and about, and isn't wearing a wedding ring. He then watches them for a few days, learning their routine and making sure they are single, then he...does what he does."

Munroe nodded, "So I'll just do a search on old people who don't wear a wedding ring?"

"You called me, remember," Hershey said responding to the sarcasm.

"You're right, I'm sorry. Why isn't he too smart? I thought these types of killers were supposed to be above average intelligence."

"They are, usually. But this one is sloppy, obviously not concerned about the bodies being found. There's a whole load of forensics too – carpet fibres, marks on the bodies, human hairs presumably belonging to the killer. The cuts are not very precise, more approximate. He's either just started killing or he must be moving around all the time to avoid detection. It is possible he's been killing a long time."

"Which?" Munroe asked.

"Which what? New to killing or a shifter?"

Hershey thought for a moment, interrupted as their pasta arrived. The victims were selected, they had to match very specific criteria the killer was working to. The only explanations Hershey could think of were that the killer was selecting based on their look or because of who they were. There was nothing much to connect how the victims looked but the removal of the organs more than suggested the killer had developed a very specific appetite. *That* meant he had likely killed before, many times, each time refining his…taste. He would be compelled to move around as the specificity of his victims would soon alert the police to his presence.

"I think he's killed many times. He must have relocated to Vancouver from somewhere else. He's killed before and we are just seeing the first of our victims. I expect he'll move on very soon. You don't just start with what we are seeing here."

Munroe sighed, "We have another victim."

"Today?"

"This morning, Froggers Creek, Burnaby area. Dorothy Kendall aged sixty-two, and a spinster."

Hershey could sense real sadness in Munroe. Some detectives she knew were able to distance themselves from the crimes; some even said it was necessary in order to maintain objectivity and focus. But to Hershey, Munroe seemed…. weary.

"Why do you do this, Munroe?"

Munroe was about to take a drink of his coffee, but stopped when he heard the question. He looked at Hershey. Her long brown hair with loose curls gently resting on her shoulders; her manicured fingernails lightly gripping her wine glass. Her tanned skin was smooth, her hands elegant. Munroe thought that she was likely of Latin American or Spanish descent. The suede cream coloured jacket appeared fitted, reflecting her eye for style, an interest in quality, and just sufficient to advertise that she kept herself in shape. Her brown eyes and long eyelashes were framed under sculpted eyebrows. She was a beautiful woman.

Munroe shrugged. "I don't know. I'd be perfectly happy if there were no serious crimes or suicides, if my work simply consisted of burglaries and stolen cars. Most of the time things are fairly quiet. Vancouver's not exactly renowned for its high serious crime rates. When I was younger, becoming a cop just seemed like the right thing to do. Not even sure I'd be much good at anything else."

Hershey's face softened, she smiled but sensed a real sadness behind his dark brown, almost black eyes.

* * * *

That night Munroe returned home to his apartment in Burnaby Heights. He poured himself a small glass of orange juice and slumped into his favourite armchair -a snug, deep-red, Italian leather tub-chair that over the years had softened and twisted to match Munroe's frame. The curtains in the apartment were drawn and a solitary light bulb over the open-plan kitchenette cast an orange glow into the living area. Munroe sat with his back to the kitchen, in shadow. The distant sound of sirens bled into the apartment. Munroe took a sip of the juice, closed his eyes, and leant back his head. Without realising, he drifted off to sleep.

Munroe found himself driving on a deserted mountain road. It was night, and clouds moving across the face of a full moon cast spectral shadows on to the road in front. An old Phil Collins track was playing on the radio. The car looked familiar to Munroe. The seats were worn and the black dash was made from cheap plastics that rattled with loose fittings. There were scratches along the top of the dash and along the plastic door rims where he knew cassettes had been placed only to slide off at the first corner.

Munroe was sitting at the wheel, holding it, it was all familiar- a dream he'd had many times over the years. He looked up; just above his head was a burn mark in the roof lining that he knew would be there. The mark had been caused by one of his college friends putting a lighter to the roof to see if the fabric was fire retardant. Munroe smiled to himself when he heard himself say the only thing in the car that was retardant was his friend. Munroe was alone in the car – just him and Phil Collins.

The speedo read eighty-kilometres and the car was heading down the mountain road. Though shrouded, the road was familiar. Munroe felt the tension in his legs, in his arms. The road gently curved. A voice, Munroe's voice, sang quietly – *"I can feel it commin' in the air tonight"* – but his speech was slurred, and he knew he had been drinking. Eighty became a hundred. Munroe sat, holding the steering wheel tighter, as the trees on the side of the road flashed by the window. Munroe saw the sign advising caution – slow down, tight bend ahead. Munroe checked the speed again, his heart rate increased but he knew the car would break just in time for the bend. The car slowed slightly as it passed the sign. Munroe looked around; the car seemingly driving itself around the corner. A slight squeal from the tires. Munroe pulled his hands from the steering wheel but it made no difference. The car now passed the bend started to pick up speed again. More sweat gathered on Munroe's forehead. He pulled at the door handle – *nothing*. He pressed on the brake – *nothing*. Grabbing the steering wheel again, he moved it from side to side. But the car continued straight. It was hopeless. The voice, his voice, continued to sing. Munroe's heart raced. He looked to the trees, up ahead, movement in the moon light. He banged on the steering wheel, helpless, as the figure rushed from the trees. The car lurched forwards as the breaks gripped the wheels and the tires screamed against the pavement. The figure hadn't seemed to notice the car and made the short jump down on the roadside. The figure walked into the road and in front of the oncoming car. *Fifteen feet*, and the figure turns to look at Munroe. *Ten feet*, the figure raises its hands as if to shield it then freezes as if waiting for the inevitable. Munroe raises his arms in front of his own face. *Five feet*.

Munroe wakes, his breathing hard. The glass he had been holding now empty and on the floor; a small dark patch on the carpet. Sweat had formed across his forehead and on his shaven head. He wiped his head with his hand and shook the sweat onto the carpet. His neck ached. Munroe checked his watch - five-seventeen. Peeling himself from the chair Munroe showered and changed. He would be at work for six.

* * * *

Munroe, Hale and Hershey were at the Police Department reviewing the search criteria. Hershey was convinced their quarry had killed before, probably many times, he was a traveller and a loner, and would have been refining his kills. Forensics pointed to someone with short black hair. The lead on the dentals would provide a high degree of certainty, sufficient for an arrest, and the DNA would give a conviction – *if they had the killer to match them too.* Whoever the killer was, he wasn't known to any authorities.

Vancouver has one hundred and eighty-three parks and the elderly probably live near every one of them. The four bodies were discovered in different parks in different areas. Munroe needed more.

"Okay," Hershey said, she was thinking out loud, "we know the killer is probably a loner, and almost certainly a traveller. The number of kills he's probably committed would have led to his arrest unless it looked like he was changing his M.O or kept moving around. The carpet fibres and hair suggest the kills are carried out at his home. A home he probably rents if he's a shifter. He'd have to clean up after him or the mess he would be leaving behind would create a whole load of suspicion. That means redecorating at least the room he kills in. So, how many carpet stores in the city?"

Munroe shrugged, "hundred, two hundred."

"What if we get the profile to each store around the city, get them to contact us if anyone matching the profile comes into buy carpet large enough for at least a small room. If he pays cash get them to complete a receipt and ask for a name and address. He'll be buying a dark blue carpet if he replaces like for like. The killer is probably comfortable using his own name; he doesn't intend to stay long and I imagine probably wouldn't like the complications of obtaining and using false ID. From any names we get back we discount anyone already known to us with existing dental records. If that's not enough we can filter them further by taking out anyone owning their home or known to any of the authorities. We follow up on whomever else. What do you think?" Hershey asked, looking at Munroe.

Munroe glanced at Hale. "What if he's already bought the carpet?" Munro replied. "And if not, how long do we wait? What if he kills again before deciding to redecorate? What if the perp *works* in a carpet store?"

Hershey knew Munroe was right – it *was* a long shot. "Any better ideas detectives?" Hershey asked.

Within an hour, a profile was being emailed to carpet stores across the city. Hershey left to return to her work. She said she would call Munroe if anything else occurred to her. Munroe returned to his desk and replaced the worn toothpick in his mouth.

He sat back in his chair and looked at his desk - no pictures, no photos, *he* was a loner. The only personal item he kept, was in a drawer - a pocket book of daily thoughts written by Charles Haddon Spurgeon. Munroe never preached or sort to impose his views or beliefs on others, but he had believed in God since his late teens. His colleagues around the department all knew, but they respected him too much to poke fun. Besides, he was a good cop and a good man – and stood six foot four.

Putting his hands behind his large bald head, Munroe was thinking through the case, the way he had a hundred times before – the way the victims were chosen, the forensic evidence, the profile – all becoming heavier with the weight of additional evidence and information, but still nothing to point him to the killer. He hated waiting.

* * * *

The next day, the hot sun was attracting flies to the large green plastic bag that contained the remains of the rough collie bitch. Edward had forgotten about the bag. He had been meaning to dispose of the remains, but had left the house to purchase the materials he needed to redecorate the room.

Some children were playing next door when they took an interest in the horrid smell that carried on the warm breeze. With a lift from his friend, one of the children looked over the fence and saw flies swarming around a plastic bag. He saw a large gas barbeque that stood next to the fence just below him, and seeing a way back, curiosity won him over.

Moments later the boys came running into their house, shouting, calling for their Mom.

"What is it?" she asked.

"There's a dead dog in a bag next door, it's all cut up, it's really disgusting!"

The Mom went to look and was horrified to see the boys had left the bag open with the remains of the dog spilling out onto the neighbour's patio. She had not had anything to do with the man that was living next door, but she became alarmed at what he might think when he returned home. She also couldn't understand why he would be in possession of a mutilated dog. Concerned, she called the police.

* * * *

Edward knew he wasn't supposed to decorate the house he was renting. Before making any changes at all, the contract he had signed had stated he was supposed to inform the agents, who would then send somebody round to inspect the property. Edward had learned however, that letting them find out after he had decorated was never a problem, especially if it looked similar to how it had been before. He would simply tell them he had dropped something that had stained the carpet or splashed on to the wall, and thought it only right and proper for him to put things right – *he would tell them the truth.*

Looking around the store he found a similar carpet to the one in his room. Rented accommodation always came with cheap carpeting, and, if the walls were papered, it was always with the cheapest wallpaper. That was okay with Edward, as it meant replacement would also be inexpensive.

At the checkout he paid with cash. The spotty young man behind the till looked nervous, looking Edward up and down and he seemed to struggle to complete a receipt. The man asked for Edward's name to write onto the receipt which would also be his guarantee if he wanted to return anything. As Edward watched the man finish writing out the receipt, he thought to himself, *too tough and a little bitter.* Edward left the store.

* * * *

Munroe was at his desk going over statements taken from people at Froggers Creek when the new rookie detective, Agland, returned to his desk and asked, "Hey Munroe, your killer likely to fancy dog for lunch?"

Munroe frowned.

"Some lady has just called in reporting a mutilated dog in her neighbours back garden. She asked if someone would go check it out and smooth things over with the neighbour if it turns out to be just a misunderstanding."

"Is anyone going?" Munroe asked.

"Yeah, a uniform is heading over there now."

"Where?"

"Er…Richmond area," Agland replied, looking down at his notes.

Probably nothing, Munroe thought as he slumped over his desk. *What would the killer want with a dog?* He thought about phoning Hershey, but wondered if it was because he simply wanted to talk to her. As he sat there thinking, an officer working on his case came over, a little out of breath.

"We've had a call from a carpet store. Someone matching the profile we sent out, the carpet they bought was dark-blue. Name is Edward Walker but the cashier forgot to ask for an address. There's no criminal record, no DNA on file and no dentals."

"Where is the store?" Munroe asked, already getting up.

"Richmond."

Munroe was standing and putting his jacket on. He glanced at Hale, who was just rising from his seat. "Give me the store address. And get an address on Edward Walker."

"Yeah sure, here."

Hale snatched the store address from the officer and followed Munroe, running out of the door.

* * * *

Edward returned home and put the carpet he had just bought into the hallway. He had dumped the piece of carpet used to transport Dorothy Kendall's body in a dumpster at the back of some Chinese takeout the night before. The remainder now lay rolled up along the side of the house. He would dump that a little later. He placed the rolls of wallpaper he had bought on to the decorating table he had erected in the living room – he would complete the wallpapering before fitting the new carpet. As he went backwards and forwards, emptying the car, he noticed the two boys from next door watching him. The attention started to unsettle him - *not to worry I'll be out of here shortly*.

* * * *

In the car, they received confirmation of Edward Walker's address. He may not have had a criminal record or any of his DNA on record, but Edward Walker still paid his bills and even submitted a tax claim. The address Munroe and Hale had been given was the same address that had been reported in connection with the dog remains. Hale contacted the uniforms already on their way to the Richmond address, telling them to pull back - they were not to be seen. Munroe and Hale would go first. As they neared the address Munroe removed the flashing blue hat from off the top of the car, not wishing to attract any further attention.

Parking just down the street from the address, Hale instructed the responding officers to head around the back of the houses. The complex of townhouses were on a strata, side by side with small yards made semi-private by panelled fencing. Munroe and Hale got out of the car. Two young boys were playing next to the house Munroe and Hale were making their way over to. A concerned woman stood at a window. Munroe gestured to her to take the kids inside. Another police car drew up farther down the street. Officers got out of the car and readied their weapons. Munroe and Hale, keeping their weapons holstered, walked across the road to the house.

As they approached the front door, Hale sneaked a look into the front room through a crack in the blinds. A man, white with short black hair, stood in the room pasting wallpaper, his back to the window. Hale motioned to Munroe.

Munroe knocked at the door. Hale withdrew his gun and stood to the side ensuring he couldn't be seen from the window. Munroe knocked again. The door opened.

"Hello," the man said.

"I'm Detective Munroe, this is Detective Hale, do you mind if we come in?" Munroe asked, trying to control his breathing.

"I'm afraid you can't. What is it you want?"

Looking beyond the man, Munroe caught sight of a dark blue carpet rolled up and still wrapped in plastic. As Munroe considered his next move he was hit by a smell - *the smell of death.*

Munroe lunged forward grabbing the man with both powerful hands and dragged him forward out of the house and down onto the path. Hale stood surprised as Munroe drove the man face down to the ground and handcuffed the wrists behind the man's back.

"Okay! Okay!" the man shouted, "You've got your man, take it easy!"

* * * *

The wealth of evidence that had been compiled against Edward Walker proved unnecessary as he made a full unsolicited confession to the killings, and twenty-six more previous killings conducted across the States.

Munroe received national praise, TV coverage, and many letters of congratulations from fellow detectives and FBI Agents, but he felt embarrassed by the attention. Munroe also made sure the public were aware of Hershey's role in the arrest. Edward Walker, however, would not be standing trial. Psychiatric interviews and expert witnesses, and the very nature of the killings, ensured he would be kept in a high security institution for the criminally insane. Edward Walker was to become a resident at Ashford Mental Institution.

CHAPTER 6

September at Ashford had seen the closure of the Legwinski enquiry and the arrival of Edward Walker. Edward was kept in a room within the ward reserved for the most dangerous patients. The rooms were, in truth, cells, with whitewashed stones walls, a metal frame bed topped with a thin mattress, and a bookcase with a few chosen books. The fronts of the cells were transparent, made from acrylic four inches thick, reaching from the floor to ceiling, only obscured in the centre by the large steel plated security door and inset frame. The single corridor that stretched the length of the eight rooms in the ward was under continuous twenty-four hour surveillance.

April Pritchard heard about Edward's arrival from one of the staff. A newspaper left in the canteen had covered the killings in all their detail. April could not bear the thought of being held at the same place as *personalities* such as Edward Walker. Even though she was treated more as guest than a patient at the hospital, the association still made her feel sick and unclean. She wanted to get out.

Emily came to visit. It was her third visit, and she had managed to obtain agreement from the hospital to take April out. McGill was keen for April to lead a normal life, and he seemed genuinely pleased to authorise April's absence for three hours. A tracker fitted to April's wrist would ensure she could easily be found in the event she didn't return to the hospital at the appointed time.

Emily bought them both ice-creams as they walked to the shore down at Brunswick Beach. Rain was threatening as grey clouds gathered above, and the wind began to stir. Emily had been sharing her psychological studies with April. April's ability to understand complex concepts, emotions and behaviours astounded Emily. They would also discuss different philosophies and the relationships between circumstance, beliefs and motivations. Emily had even incorporated some of April's observations into her own studies and a recent paper she had written.

April told Emily of Peter Legwinski's death. She spoke of the magic tricks Legwinski would perform and then related his movements and actions and how they would deceive people's perception – but not hers. *Magic is a lie*, Legwinski had once told April, *the ability to convey a lie as the truth is what set people apart*. April shared with Emily that she considered Peter's inability to convince enough people of his deceptions as truth prompted his descent into madness. Emily theorised that one had to possess the propensity for such things, it lead Emily to believe that if through thought it was possible to go clinically insane, then a cure must be possible by reversing the process.

"Drugs only serve to dull the senses to contain behaviour by an artificial reduction in desire, but what if people's expectations and desire could be modified through thought?" Emily considered. "Let's say you're right and Peter had this overwhelming need to be recognised, appreciated, and this need drove him to try increasingly more daring or risky acts - in his case, magic tricks - in order to be recognised. Sadly, for him, such was the extent of this desire, the magic outstripped his abilities as an illusionist and he ended up killing people. Well, what if we could somehow retrain his thoughts? I don't know, make him see that recognition from others is not important. Perhaps he needed just one person to acknowledge him or find satisfaction from knowing he was doing his best and that was good enough."

"The mind rules the body," April replied.

"Exactly. The problem is that when someone becomes insane, you no longer have access to proper thought."

"Then you would need access to the mind another way."

"Yes, at a subconscious level. But that requires participation which is why modern techniques incorporate rapport."

"So it's easier if you're their friend?" April asked.

"Or at least if they believe that you're their friend. They become more trusting, listen more, and ultimately want to make you happy. Are you friendly with any of the patients at the hospital April?"

"Not really. I was friendly with Peter, but he's dead now. I'm friendly with most of the staff. Why?"

"Well, seeing as you are so interested, I have a little trick of my own I could show you. I use it to illustrate the power that the mind has over the body and how manipulating the senses and perception can be used to fool the mind. Want to see it?"

"Of course," April replied with enthusiasm.

* * * *

Rowina was having a coffee in the canteen when April and Emily walked over to her.

"Well, how are you my little April Shower? Have you had a good time?" Rowina asked.

"Yes, thank you. Emily took me to the beach where we walked around, I went paddling, and we ate ice-cream. Rowina, we have a favour to ask?"

"Oh yes? And how may I be of assistance?"

"We'd like to perform an experiment. You see Emily studies at the University, she studies the relationship between the brain and our behaviours, and she says she can perform some magic that demonstrates these relationships."

"Is that right?" Rowina replied, already confused.

"But we require your cooperation. Is that okay?" April asked.

"Its okay as long as you're not going to hypnotise me and make me think I'm a baboon or something, I've seen this kind of thing on TV."

"We won't," Emily assured.

Three other members of staff sitting close by turned to watch.

"Alright," Emily said, "turn and face me but stay sitting down for the moment. Tell me Rowina do you drink at all?"

"Occasionally."

"And what's your favourite drink?" Emily asked.

"I'm partial to white wine. Only on occasion you understand."

"And how does a fine white wine taste in your mouth?"

They continued, Emily asked Rowina to describe the sensation of how the wine would feel as it travelled through her body. As Rowina spoke, Emily gently touched key parts of Rowina's body – her suprasternal notch, solar plexus, lower stomach and thighs. April also noticed Emily would touch Rowina's right elbow occasionally. This process was repeated a few times until finally Emily whispered a word to Rowina, touched her elbow again and asked her to stand. As Rowina attempted to stand it was clear she was exhibiting all the signs of being intoxicated. Emily asked Rowina to try and walk in a straight line – Rowina failed, eventually sitting on the floor, laughing. Emily crouched down and instructed Rowina to look at her. As she did, Emily touched Rowina's elbow again and told her she was now feeling okay, and with that Rowina returned to her normal sober self. Everyone around was amazed.

Emily declared that even though Rowina had not had anything to drink it was possible to convince her brain that she had drunk and thereby induce her drunken behaviour. April applauded, while another of the staff asked if Emily could teach his wife how to do that as it would make his nights out so much cheaper. After a minute or so had passed, Emily walked over to Rowina, touched her right elbow and whispered again in her ear. Instantly, Rowina was drunk again. Everyone applauded. Again, Emily touched Rowina's elbow and instructed Rowina to look at her, telling Rowina she was now feeling fine, and with that she returned to normal.

"I couldn't stop myself from feeling drunk," Rowina laughed, "but then when you said I was okay, I really felt fine, no hangover, nothin'"

"Even better," the man called out, "I'd get into even less trouble!"

After, Emily walked with April back to her room in the Women's Directorate.

"Emily, do you think these techniques could help with my sleepwalking, help it stop?"

"I don't know, sweetheart, but there are those that think it could. The meditation I showed you might work. It's likely a long process. I'll tell you what, why don't we both do some study ourselves, and see what we can find out?"

Before leaving the hospital, Emily confirmed that she would be able to bring a few select books for April and that she would be visiting again the following week.

* * * * *

The following day, April was walking around the gardens in the light rain, unaware she was being watched by Donald McCoy. Donald was allowed out of his room for two hours a day, in addition to his twenty minute supervised exercise programme conducted on Mondays and Thursdays. This time was his rehabilitation time, a time for him to socialise, a time to venture out and regain confidence in a world that had rejected him.

Donald had been born to monsters. His father regularly beat him as an infant and throughout his childhood. His mother wanted a girl and was disgusted when Donald was born. She made the best of it by dressing Donald up in girls clothing, plaiting his hair and calling him Donna. As Donald became older, his father would abuse him while his mother had him dressed as a girl, and it was around that time, doctors concluded, when Donald started to escape to his own world. In Donald's world there lived only children, children who would play and sing happily and had no need to fear the big ones, for they couldn't see Donald's world.

As April walked slowly amongst the flowers and water features, Donald sang quietly to himself – *'April Shower come out to play, Donald has something he'd like to say.'* Donald had heard the nurses talking of a little girl that lived in a hospital, but here she was, playing in the garden at Donald's home.

April bent to smell some petals fused with deep orange and red colours. *'Bend over and smell the flower, my lovely little April Shower.'* Donald's heart beat faster, and colour flushed in his large rounded cheeks.

April continued to follow the path around to the Japanese area. According to the small information sign this style was based on the 'Katsura' with its large pond, use of white stone and wood to form natural looking structures and bridges. There were three small islands in the pond supposedly symbolising three of the five mythical islands off the coast of East Asia. Across the pond,

April could see a guard having a cigarette. A remote security camera twitched as it adjusted slightly to capture April in its view.

Donald followed slowly as the girl followed the path around his garden. The girl stopped to read the sign as she entered a new area. His heart raced but his gait was short and careful. Donald stooped a little as he walked as if it somehow made him harder to see. '*If April Shower will stop at the bend, Donald wants to be your friend.*' Donald followed. Then the girl stopped and sat on a swinging chair, a chair made for two. '*Donald be as quiet as mice if April Shower be nice.*'

As April drew a small book from her pocket, she noticed a rather short heavy man with glasses and short dark curly hair, slowly walking in her direction. She hadn't seen him before, but he was walking toward her, his eyes fixed on her. April glanced at the guard who was now watching her and stubbing out his cigarette but otherwise had not moved. April had heard of creepy men but hadn't considered that it might have referred to men who actually crept. Although the hospital was home to some of the most dangerous people, April was aware that only those considered low or no risk were allowed to walk in the gardens. As the man got closer, April noticed that the guard had put his radio to his ear and looking across the pond at them. The guard replaced his radio to its holder, he hadn't moved any closer.

"Hello, my name is Donald, are you the April girl?" Donald asked.

"Hello, Donald, I am April, nice to meet you?" April replied holding out her hand.

April had learnt that in order to build rapport it was important to reciprocate a person's body language. That would make them feel more comfortable and you appear less threatening. Donald appeared very nervous, but eventually shook April's hand, gently.

"Nice to meet you, April Shower."

That afternoon April and Donald talked until a nurse came to return Donald to his room. From their conversation, April had learned that the hospital was in fact Donald's home. Donald was aware that he had spent many days away lost, not knowing where he was and with no children to play with, until a big one showed him the way home. Donald was afraid of the big ones, they would hurt him and laugh at him, only sometimes did big ones bring him food and talk nicely to him. The big ones wouldn't let Donald play with his friends or make new ones, but that afternoon April and Donald had become friends.

* * * *

The following week, Emily visited again. They stayed at the hospital, sometimes in April's room but mostly in a corner of the canteen. Emily brought books with her on the work of people like, Milton Erickson, Fritz Perls, Richard Bandler, and various studies and papers. April took an instant interest in a study of autistic savants.

"There was a film made about that phenomenon," Emily said, "it was called 'RainMan'. An actor called Dustin Hoffman played the role of an autistic savant, someone with a social interaction impairment."

"Can they really do these sorts of things?" April asked, as she began reading the study.

Emily had one of the books open on her lap. She was browsing through some of the pages. "You mean specify the day of the week for any given date or memorise the entire US Highway system? Yes, some of them. We're not really sure what causes autism or what it is that enables some of them to perform extraordinary tasks. Some experts believe it's genetic."

"Is it true we use less than ten percent of our brains?"

Emily laughed, "Me perhaps but not you. No, we use the majority of our brains almost all the time. However, these studies do show what the human brain is capable of. Some people have amazing memory, some solve complex math quicker than the problem can be read aloud. The brain controls our bodies, interprets everything we interact with. It enables great works of art, the grace of a ballerina, the music of Mozart, or the construction of particle accelerators. Imagine, April, if the very best of human achievement existed all in the same person. Imagine if it were possible for every human to achieve that same level of excellence. Humans certainly don't reach anywhere near their potential, perhaps no one ever really has." Emily closed the book she had opened. "There are some cases," Emily continued, "of people who physically only have ten percent of their brain, say due to disease or massive trauma, but still have normal intelligence. The weird thing is though, it's common for a relatively minor injury to the brain to cause all sorts of problems. I think that's why I'm so fascinated by it – the possibilities and the complexity."

As they sat talking, April told Emily of the conversations she had been having with Donald.

"I think he's trapped as a young boy," April remarked.

"Do you know why he's in here? Are you sure he isn't dangerous?" Emily asked.

"I don't think they would let him walk around if he was dangerous to anyone, and Rowina says he hasn't harmed anyone. I'm not sure why he's here. I think he's just too scared to go outside, to live with people."

Emily smiled; she loved April's innocence and the simplicity with which she viewed the world.

"Has Edward been behaving himself?"

"He wouldn't be allowed out. You hear some of the staff talk about him occasionally. He gets letters from people apparently and doctors keep wanting to talk to him. Why are they so interested in him?"

"I think anything exceptional or different interests at least some people. You should know that," Emily said, roughing April's hair. "How has your sleeping been going?" Emily added, changing the subject.

"Nothing, not yet anyway. Apparently, I was talking in my sleep the other night, but I haven't even been out of bed since I arrived here. I don't think they're bothering to monitor me that closely now. Emily?" April asked, her tone more direct. April reached to take hold of Emily's hand. "I don't want to be in here, but even if they let me out, I have nowhere to go. No family, no home."

Emily gave April a hug. "You are always welcome to stay with me poppet, but you'd have to share with two other students, ignore underwear left on the floor, smelly socks, put up with potato chips all over the place, and dirty pots piled high in the sink."

"That's gross." April affirmed.

"Listen I've got to go, I'll come and see you again soon."

* * * *

"He's in there. You need anything else?" the guard asked.

"No, thank you," Hershey replied.

Hershey's responsibilities at the hospital included undertaking psychiatric evaluations, especially in the cases involving serious crime. She had read the reports from his interviews following his arrest and transfer to the hospital; from the transcripts Hershey was in no doubt Edward Walker was insane. Edward's profile was entirely typical of serial killers, although no conclusions had been made regarding a psychological explanation for his behaviour. Hershey had spent all her adult life studying human behaviour, all the serials she had interviewed showed no remorse for their victims, a complete lack of empathy, but something in Edward's statements didn't quite seem to fit with this expectation. Hershey entered the room.

"Hello, Edward, I'm Dr.Elizabeth Hershey, how are you this morning?"

Edward was sitting in the small, purpose built, interview room, his hands and legs chained and attached to the bolted chair that he was seated on. He didn't reply. Hershey smiled as she sat down opposite Edward. She placed a digital recorder on the table in front of her and switched it on. She stated her name, the date, and that this was her first interview with Edward Walker. Picking the recorder back up, she played back the recording to check the levels were adequate. Satisfied, she placed the recorder back on the desk, and pressed 'record'.

"I'd like to talk to you about your childhood if I may. Would that be okay?" Hershey asked.

Edward remained silent.

"I understand you were a popular child at school, lots of friends, enjoyed playing games. Did you enjoy school Edward?" Use of his first name was deliberate to help establish rapport more quickly.

Edward looked into his lap. Hershey knew Edward was considered shy, in his previous interviews it had taken a few minutes and several questions before he had spoken. In each of his previous statements, he had made references to survival of the fittest when asked about why he killed.

"So, do you think Charles Darwin was right or horribly mistaken?" Hershey asked.

Edward looked up. She had his attention. Hershey paused, giving him an opportunity to speak. He just looked at her, he seemed to be studying her.

"There are some people that think Hitler was simply helping evolution on its way, selective breeding programmes, creating a super-race. Personally, I think he was largely responsible for the deaths of millions of innocent people and demonstrated mankind's most tragic flaw. You see, I think people need each other, don't you?" Hershey said.

"Balance," Edward said, calmly.

"I'm not sure I understand. Hitler was providing balance?" Hershey replied.

"Nature demands balance. Didn't they teach you that at school Dr.Hershey? What is our goal if it is not to survive? And what lesson does Nature teach, if balance is not critical to survival? Tip the scales, lose the balance, and something doesn't survive."

"Is that what you do Edward, provide balance when you kill those people?"

"I only take what I need to survive. I use everything I take. No more, no less. You kill what you don't want, you waste more than the use, you take more than you need. That is not a sustainable way to live."

"Doesn't killing old people upset the balance?"

Edward smiled. "I'm sure you are aware that when you reach a certain age it's no longer possible to breed? Perhaps not too far away for you? Old people are takers, they can't work, they no longer contribute, but they continue to consume."

But they have been giving for the best part of their lives, asshole. She wasn't there to debate philosophy with someone who is insane. "How do you feel about your victims? Do you think about how they must feel, how their families and loved ones must feel?" Hershey asked.

"Does an animal stop to consider what its prey must be feeling? I doubt it. That doesn't mean it doesn't understand. When an animal strikes another, it knows how it feels, it knows it causes pain. It understands even though it changes nothing."

"Are you saying you understand the terror and anguish your actions must cause?"

"Of course. It doesn't change anything. You think the deer, or the antelope want to be killed? Or the chicken or the cow? Nothing wants to be killed except some pathetic humans. Killing is necessary. Perhaps if there weren't so many people walking around we could all be vegetarians, but then, perhaps plants also feel pain, who really knows?"

Hershey was surprised by Edward's response.

"You want to understand me," Edward continued, "but when you set aside your prejudices and hypocrisy, you will see we really are no different. I cause no harm to anyone or anything unless I need to. I harm nobody's property, I work hard. You think because we live in houses and watch cable TV that we're any different from anything else that lives on this planet, we're not. We just ignore the lessen of nature, convincing ourselves that we're civilised, better than anything else. It is not me that is deluded. I am certain if we lived as nature intended, a balance would be found, and we could all inhabit the Earth with everything else. We wouldn't need as many people, but then they are a sustainable food source."

"Is this something you have figured out yourself?" Hershey asked.

"Not really. Children are taught from an early age that we are just animals descended from apes, that were themselves descended from something else. We have invented all kinds of laws when none other than those provided by nature were required. Our laws stem from greed and nature doesn't tolerate greed."

"So, you think it's alright to murder people?" Hershey felt an increase in her breathing. She took a slow, longer breath.

"I'm sure you eat steak occasionally. You begrudge me the same every now and then."

Hershey closed the interview. From her studies, it had always been possible to see a cause, an emotion, that in killers was heightened, amplified and then twisted - hatred, power or any other desire that craved fulfilment, something. In serials, these emotions, the motivators, were not kept in check by in-built inhibitors - what we call a conscience or morals. As Hershey went to leave the room, she realised what it was that had been bugging her. Edward appeared to have control of his emotions, he seemed to understand what he was doing and why he was doing it. *But it isn't possible for Edward to just be a product of the education system. Was it?* she thought.

Hershey left the room, and had already decided to leave the hospital for the day. She knew more interviews would be needed to better understand Edward Walker, but she was in no hurry.

CHAPTER 7

Donald was having dinner at home. A big one had put mashed potato, peas and sausages on his plate. He had orange juice to drink, and a flexible red and white straw to drink from. He made shapes with the potato and let out a laugh when he fixed a sausage upright into the shapes he had made. Big ones were looking at him, and so he quickly destroyed the shapes with his fork and returned the sausage flat on the plate.

Donald finished his dinner by licking clean his plastic fork and placing it into a pocket. Looking down at his tray he noticed another fork, unused, that he couldn't remember picking up when he had collected his food. He placed the second fork into his pocket, then got up and went to return to his room for the night.

Donald was not classified as criminally insane. He had committed no crime. The real world had become a dark place for Donald. His mind had successfully constructed an alternate world for him, where Donald was happy and where adults, whom he referred to as 'Big Ones' only appeared as shadows - sometimes they would speak, sometimes they would leave things, but they were not able to harm him.

The reality of Donald's condition meant he was entirely incapable of living independently. Before being moved to Ashford he had become suicidal whenever confronted with even a semi-social situation. Since arriving at Ashford, he had come to understand it, or at least his version of it, as his home, a new home, where the experiences of the past were not present.

* * * *

Nurse Patterson escorted Donald back to his room. She was a stocky, overweight woman, with short brown hair that looked and felt like straw. As they turned into the ward, they walked toward the security office. The door to the office was open, inside black and white monitors flickered with images from the various cameras across the ward. Donald's ward, called the Cavendish Ward, contained nine rooms each with a wide-angled camera positioned in the corner. An image was displayed in twenty second intervals meaning that no one patient remained un-monitored for more than one minute.

Clement Shoal, the security guard, sat with his feet up at a desk and nodded as Donald and Nurse Patterson approached. The Cavendish Ward is used to house patients classified as having a propensity to harm themselves, but where they have not specifically committed any crime. The ward, and rooms, are painted with warm natural colours designed to develop a sense of peace, relaxing the patients. Classical music could be piped to each room independently, at the request of the patient.

"Donald!" called Shoal, as they passed the office door, "Sorry, I almost forgot, I have this note that was left for you. Have a good night now."

Donald took the folded slip of paper.

"Big One Shoal?" Donald asked.

"Yes, Donald?"

"May I have some music in my room please, the one that I like.'

"You certainly may, Donald. I'll put it on for you right away."

Donald continued past the office to his room. Nurse Patterson winked to Shoal as she went by, following Donald.

"You have yourself a good night, Donald," Nurse Patterson said as she closed the door to his room.

She toggled the lever underneath the handle, ensuring the door could now only be opened from the outside. Faure's *Pavane* began to play inside the room as Donald settled down on his bed.

Returning to the office, Nurse Patterson withdrew a small bundle of twenty-dollar bills from a pocket. She placed the money on the desk in front of Shoal.

"It's always a pleasure doing business with you, Nurse Patterson."

Shoal unlocked a draw in his desk and withdrew a metal container, eight inches long by two inches wide. Unlocking the container, Shoal picked up a transparent plastic pouch containing a fine white powder. He placed the packet on the desk and picked up the dollar bundle. Patterson picked up the packet and placed it in her pocket. This had been the twelfth time she had made a purchase from Clement Shoal, and he knew that within six weeks, she would be back for another.

* * * *

As Donald lay on his bed gently humming to the music, he remembered the note he had put in his pocket. He took out the note and unfolded it. He had now received several different notes. After he had read the few words on the slip of paper, he screwed the paper into a ball and placed it in his mouth. He chewed and then swallowed the paper. Donald lay back down and fell asleep.

Clement Shoal checked his watch. The ward was quiet, and all the patients were sleeping. The monotony of watching the alternating, repetitive images on the monitors would make him weary. To pass the time he would regularly read a book, or flick through a magazine, in preference to watching the screens. Tonight, he was reading a car magazine. He already owned three vehicles, but none were a utility vehicle.

Five staff at the hospital now depended on Shoal, and he would make thirty percent on each transaction. Working in a high security mental home brought with it high stress levels. Staff would either leave within two years of joining or find a way to last for twenty, or die trying. All of Shoal's customers were long term employees who had found their way of coping. He considered the operation more of a service, without it, staff attrition would be a lot higher.

Shoal lived a good life. Money held in various bank accounts, luxury items, and a client base that paid in tax efficient cash. Another spin-off from dealing in a hospital was that his clients were much less likely to overdose than the smack-heads on the streets. He had a steady client base built on long term relationships. The pay for his line of work wasn't much, but the perks more than made up for it.

As he browsed the car magazine, he didn't notice Donald sit up on his bed.

* * * *

A switch in Donald's mind flickered on. He had been sleeping precisely two hours when he sat up on his bed. The music had stopped playing and his room was quiet. A light bathed the room as though it were evening dusk and the tiny red LED on the camera flashed intermittently, but not strong enough to affect the soft light.

Donald swung his legs around and sat on the edge of his bed. He was still wearing his clothes. Reaching into his pocket, he pulled out the two plastic forks he had taken from the canteen. Placing a fork in each hand, Donald raised them to his eyes.

Slowly he pushed a fork into each eye. The blunted ends pressed deep into each eye before the cornea finally gave way and the fork travelled through the pupil and vitreous humour, penetrating under the optical nerve and into the temporal lobe of the brain, finally ending in the occipital lobe before Donald's hands ceased pressing. Donald remained seated, his body twitching as messages to his nervous system began misfiring.

* * * *

Shoal was making notes in pencil of various SUVs. When he had finished writing he glanced up at the monitors. When he saw the image on monitor two he had to look twice. He moved closer to the monitor, not quite believing what he was looking at.

Shoal hit a red button on the left side wall near his desk. Immediately an alarm was triggered in the staff lounge and the consultants' administration area. An indicator would flash on a map of the hospital showing where the alarm had been activated. No audible sound was made by the 'patient alarm system' as alarming the patients was not its purpose. This system alerted doctors to a patient related emergency, in the area indicated – the Cavendish Ward.

Shoal hit the button labelled 'Room 7' to force the image from the camera in Donald's room to be re-displayed on the monitor. Even though he stood looking at it, he still couldn't believe it. Quickly he ran down the corridor. As he pressed down on the handle to room the lever underneath toggled forward, releasing a catch and opening the door. The door opened toward him and Shoal took a step into the room. He heard a rush of footsteps coming up the ward.

Donald sat on the edge of his bed with forks embedded into his head through each eye, his body twitching nervously. Shoal stood, paralysed. Two doctors appeared at the door to the room, and one of them pulled Shoal out of the way.

"Find a gurney!" A doctor shouted.

The instruction took a moment to register before Shoal turned and ran back down the corridor. A doctor radioed for emergency surgery preparation. Shoal returned with a gurney.

"Help us get him up! You take his legs."

Shoal, still trying to grasp what was going on, did as he was told. He took hold of Donald's legs and helped lift him up.

"He's still alive!" the Doctor shouted, as they rushed the laden trolley down the corridor. "Clear everybody out of the way, we're taking him to surgery!"

Donald was still alive when surgery commenced but the removal of the forks and massive trauma to the brain had shut down his vital respiratory functions, and, although no one present said anything, the doctors considered it the best outcome.

* * * *

Hershey was working in her office when she received an encrypted email from the Administrator at Ashford. The email informed her of a death at the hospital to a patient named Donald McCoy. Hershey was requested to conduct the independent review. After reading the email, Hershey phoned the Administrator to arrange a meeting.

The next day, Hershey made the drive up the coast to Ashford. The summer weather had turned, and the days were darker, usually filled with swollen clouds in preparation for the coming season of rain.

Hershey and McGill greeted each other as usual, but Hershey could see the concern etched on to McGill's expression. They had talked briefly on the phone, but she hadn't noticed anything in his voice that suggested what his look was now reflecting.

McGill took a long deep breath and then gave a long sigh as he handed Hershey the file. Although less than forty-eight hours had passed since Donald was discovered, it was sufficient time for McGill and the hospital to have performed a review of their own.

"Is everything alright Charles?"

"Donald had one of those lives that no one should have to live. He was abused as an infant, abused as child, and abused when he got older. To the best of our knowledge, he never hurt a soul, and the best society had to offer was to put him here. And there's shit we seem to be able to do about it."

Hershey knew McGill rarely used profanity, preferring to use it sparingly which seemed to give it greater impact. Patient death however, was an all too familiar situation to them both. She paused for a moment, then asked, "Charles, what's *really* wrong? What's happened?"

McGill looked up, his sky-blue eyes piercing Hershey. "His nurse, Nurse Patterson with twenty-two years service, didn't respond to the call. She couldn't. When the alarm went out on Donald, she was slumped in a washroom stall as high as a kite."

"I'm sorry Charles. You know it's not the first time, and it's become routine at most other hospitals."

"Not at mine! I don't think she brought them in, which would mean someone is supplying. And if someone is supplying to her, then there'll be others too. Follow up on Donald, Elizabeth, but I want to know who's supplying drugs in my hospital."

"I'll find out what I can." Hershey left McGill's office.

Hershey sat in the canteen reading Donald's file. Hershey had online access to all the information the hospital kept on Donald, however her preference was to have much of it printed - the history, profile summary, routine schedules and medications, so she could read at her leisure with a drink, and usually some fruit to snack on. The file also contained prints of pictures taken from the camera feed in Donald's room on the night he died.

Donald's life had indeed been tragic. His file detailed several suicide attempts Donald had made during his teens and early adult life, but nothing since he had been admitted to the hospital, suggested he would take his own life.

Time stamp information in the file showed the times Donald was allowed out of his room, the time he ate, the time he returned to his room, in addition to the thirty-minute checks that confirmed his location. The information was kept for a minimum of three months for each resident patient. It was rarely used, but on the odd occasion it would be referenced in the trending of patient behaviour, and during therapy for certain patients. Hershey would use it to better understand a patient's patterns and routines.

Notes annotated to Donald's file and schedules, showed that he had almost no verbal contact with staff or other patients, only occasionally during each day would he appear to interact with anyone, and then only briefly.

Hershey looked through the remaining papers and at the stills taken from the security video tape. She immediately felt uncomfortable with the manner in which Donald had died. *How does someone do that? The camera clearly shows no one else was involved, and yet…*

She reached for her phone, and after searching for a number, she placed a call to an old colleague, a Medical Examiner. Hershey asked if it would be possible for someone to physically carry out what Donald had done to himself. After several minutes of discussion, they both arrived at the same conclusion – 'not consciously'. Although it might physically be possible to do, the level of pain, once the fork protruded the back of the eye, would make it practically impossible to do it as slowly as Donald had appeared to have done. 'It sounds like he was operating under hypnosis,' the M.E. had said.

That morning Hershey prepared a list of the staff she would want to see. She wanted to start with Clement Shoal, but he would not be arriving for the start of his shift until later in the afternoon. Nurse Rose Patterson had been suspended pending investigation. Her home address and number were listed in the file. Hershey made a further call and left shortly afterwards.

* * * *

Two girls dressed in their tight-fitting school uniforms walked across the deserted park to meet him. They wanted him, and he wanted them. They had put on their shortest skirts and black fish-net stockings. They knew it was what he liked. It turned him on. Their white blouses were loosely buttoned allowing their still forming breasts to show. Their underwear accentuated their shape. At thirteen they were ripe, and he would take them. Their parents obviously wanting him to take them, allowing them, encouraging them, encouraging him, and he was not about to disappoint.

He waited, anticipating, relishing what was going to happen. He knew how it felt. He would be their first and they would remember him for the remainder of their lives. They laughed and giggled as they approached. He was ready, aroused and ready.

The sound of a distant cell phone disturbed Alexander Jones from his thoughts as he stood at the small barred window in the washroom. Peering between the bars he could make out a woman with brown shoulder length hair, subtle use of colour, cut in what he imagined from this distance to be an expensive hairstyle. She wore an olive coloured tailored suit and wore tanned leather boots that stopped just short of her knees, meeting the hem of her skirt. She was tall, perhaps five feet ten without the heel. She was attractive even for an older woman, he thought, perhaps she was in her mid-thirties. As he watched, the woman on the phone walked across the car park and got into a convertible, one of those European models. The car reversed and he watched as it drove from the complex.

Though each room within the Orca Ward had its own sink and toilet, recent procedural changes now allowed the patients up to two visits a day to the Ward's new washroom. One patient was allowed access at a time. The chains were kept on and three taser-armed guards would provide escort. Alexander was in his seventh year at Ashford, but it was only in these last few months since the washroom visits, that he was able to glimpse at the outside world again.

Only the famous made it to the Orca Ward. In recent months the Orca Ward had seen a new patient added, Edward Walker. From conversations with the guards, Alexander had learned about Edward. Alexander considered him a worthy addition. Since the abolition of the death penalty in nineteen seventy-six, the Orca Ward had played host to Canada's most vicious killers. All that had come here had died here or were still here. Alexander was still very much alive and dreamed of getting out. He had no plans to die in this place. He had become famous in Toronto, reading about himself on an almost daily basis before further increasing his fame in British Columbia and his eventual arrest. Though he was found guilty for the death and torture of eleven girls, all teenagers, he was deemed to be mentally unstable, and not suitable for regular imprisonment.

Alexander had been committed to Ashford indefinitely, and had learned he was able to purchase certain favours and procure certain liberties. He had bought more frequent visits to the washroom, procured pornographic photos of young girls from the guards, even persuaded the guards to allow him to wander, escorted of course, around other areas within the high security facility. He would be physically chained to a security guard and limited to fifteen minutes but nevertheless, these concessions slowly and surely would improve his chances of escape.

He could also buy any information he wanted. He had recently bought information and pictures of the young girl that was now staying at the hospital, having heard about her from the guards, and he had already decided he would be buying information on the *cell-phone* woman with the fancy car. Before leaving the washroom, he returned to his thoughts.

CHAPTER 8

Interviews with Nurse Rose Patterson and Clement Shoal had established that Donald McCoy had sat up on his bed around two hours after first appearing to fall asleep. Shoal had mentioned giving a note to Donald, but no note was found, and Shoal stated that he hadn't read the note. Patterson confirmed the existence of the note prompting Hershey to review the security tape for Donald's room.

The recording showed Donald reading and then eating the note, just prior to falling asleep. The writing on the note was indistinguishable. The footage also showed Donald sitting up two hours later – precisely two hours later – then, taking two canteen forks from his pocket, he pushed them slowly into his eye sockets until only an inch of the forks remained visible – the whole time achieving this without any apparent flinching.

Hershey met with Rose Patterson at her home. Patterson was hopeful of being able to return to work with just a warning, but having seen McGill earlier, Hershey didn't share her optimism. Patterson claimed she had bought the drugs from off the street and only took them into work on rare occasions. She described herself as an occasional user seeking to escape the depressing reality of the institution. As Hershey sat there watching tears fall from a woman who looked like she had been hewn from granite, she couldn't help but feel some sympathy.

Later, Hershey met with Clement Shoal at the hospital. He was a very average man, average height, average build and weight, short black hair, brown eyes and black skin, he had been born in Sri Lanka. He possessed a cheap cocky, charm that might work on some women however, Hershey remained underwhelmed.

"Who did you receive the note from?" Hershey asked.

"It had been left on my desk. Anyone could have placed it there, just inside the door." Shoal responded.

"And you didn't look at the note?"

"No. Sorry, I didn't." Shoal confirmed.

"How did you know it was meant for Donald?"

"It's not the first time Donald has been left something like this. Sometimes the notes have his room number written on it, sometimes his name, on the outside folds."

"How many? How many notes has Donald received?"

"I dunno, five may be." Shoal replied.

"And you haven't looked at any?" Hershey pressed.

"At first yeah. Just pictures, more like symbols really. Just garbage, but then who knows, maybe they meant something to Donald?"

"And you've no idea where the notes may have come from?"

"No. What difference does it make? He wasn't killed by a note. They were just simple drawings, symbols like I said. Probably anyone could have drawn them." Shoal shifted in his seat and started tapping on the arm.

"Those are nice cuff links," Hershey remarked, changing the subject. "That a diamond in your ear?"

"Yeah," Shoal replied, smiling, "picked them up from Acapulco."

"Nice. That watch too. Couldn't have been cheap."

The smile dropped from Shoal's face.

Thankfully, the meeting with Shoal had been short. Other than the note, he had nothing else worth hearing. His accessories and perfectly white teeth betrayed an income greater than that paid by the hospital. *And trips to Acapulco,* Hershey thought.

It was early evening by the time Hershey returned to the canteen area to make a start on writing up her notes. To her surprise, McGill came over to her table.

"Hi Charles."

"How's it gone today Elizabeth?" McGill asked, pulling himself a chair.

"Well, McCoy's death doesn't make any sense ,and I agree with you about Patterson, I think she procured the drugs at the hospital. She said she would simply put them in her bra to get passed security. I take it she isn't aware of the chemical scanners you have installed?"

McGill shook his head," No. I'm aware it's still possible to smuggle things in, but a lot less likely if the staff don't know they need to take extra precautions."

Hershey nodded, she was aware of the full security measures in place at Ashford. "What are you going to do about Patterson?"

McGill made a deep sigh, brushing a hand through his willowy greying hair. McGill was a man of principles, a proud man that had invested heart and soul into turning Ashford into a well-respected award-winning institute. A good percentage of patients had been successfully reintroduced into society, leading honest trouble-free lives. McGill knew that many of the patients that passed through Ashford were those unfortunates that had been dealt all the wrong cards, and he understood enough about humanity to realise they could have been anyone. Seeing them return safely to society and being happy, was a source of great satisfaction to him.

"I should fire the bitch," McGill said with a hint of a smile, "but she's been a good and loyal worker for the most part of a long career. What do you think? Are you going to put it in the report?"

"Not if you don't want me too. What happened with Patterson has nothing to do with what happened to Donald. There was nothing she could have done, and like I said, you are not the only institution to have that particular challenge."

McGill nodded, "I shall probably just give her a caution, have her watched. I don't suppose I can force her to tell me who is supplying her."

"Charles, I know it's probably no consolation, but you are running one the best hospitals of its kind. The norm for these kinds of places is drug abuse, gambling, and petty corruption. At Ashford, it's the exception. You run a good ship here, it's a credit to you, and the majority of staff equally care and work hard for the benefit of the patients. One thing though…"

McGill looked up.

"Keep an eye on the guard, Clement Shoal, nothing specific, but I think something is a bit off with him." Pausing for a moment, Hershey said, "I'm concerned about Donald's death. According to the records Donald wasn't behaving in a way consistent with someone contemplating suicide…I realise a lot of his behaviour could not be considered normal, but even so. I believe he may have been asleep or a trance or something. It doesn't make sense though, he has no history of that kind, why remove the forks from the canteen? Unless it was premeditated."

"Isn't that the point? He took the forks *because* he was planning to kill himself." McGill replied.

"How can he plan to take the forks from the canteen to use later for his suicide when *asleep?*"

* * * *

The following day Hershey was back in her office. She was preparing for a lecture she had been invited to give at Toronto University, on the relationship of discoveries in the field of molecular psychiatry and possible treatments for mental disorders. In the thousands of person-years that had gone into understanding the brain and its relationship to behaviours and belief systems, science was still only scratching the surface of what everyone knew to be a very deep subject.

Many experts believe the brain to be an organic computer, pre-programmed with an operating system capable of self learning, determining who we are, what we can do, and how we will do it. Modern scientific research is based on the presupposition that the brain is the author, that everything that we are starts with the brain, to correct a disorder the solution must exist within the functions of the brain.

Hershey wasn't convinced. She had seen how injuries and trauma to the brain had affected people making placid men prone to violence or a violent man as sweet as candy, turning a confident athlete into a nervous wreck, and loved ones into total strangers. The evidence was substantial, and yet Hershey believed there was something else, a vital part that science could not see or wouldn't acknowledge. She didn't consider herself religious in anyway, but she believed life to be something more than chemical reactions, that life itself possessed something more, something metaphysical – a consciousness, a self, a *soul* – the body being a vessel into which this *something* is poured.

Hershey imagined what a cloned human being might be like; human in everyway but with no person inside, humourless, loveless, not capable of emotion. No machine is truly capable of random acts so for humans to exercise choice and express freewill there must be a further ingredient. Tests had shown that will the action of thought is preceded by brain activity- readying itself for action – if a person chooses not to act, the choice itself does not result in any brain activity. She wondered if the person inside a body ever really changed, if damage to the brain merely resulted in a dysfunctional body or problems with expression, and that the self-inside remained trapped until it eventually gave up the body in death.

She was finding it difficult to think about the lecture as storm clouds gathered outside the office window, and like the approaching weather, Donald McCoy's death seemed dark and foreboding. She had followed up on dozens of suicides and studied countless more, but Donald's was not like any she had come across before. Failing to progress her lecture notes, Hershey grabbed her bag and headed to Ashford Hospital.

* * * *

As Alexander Jones stood at the washroom window he was in for a real treat. First a pretty college girl pulled up in the car park in one of those small British cars. She was wearing black jeans and a UBC sweatshirt. She walked with the confidence of someone who had too much of a good thing, untouched by real terror. Moments after the girl had made her way into the hospital, Alexander recognised the now familiar Jaguar come into view. The car had cleared the security gate quicker than most, and then made its way down the meandering road to the parking lot. The woman soon exited the car with her tan handbag and a closed black umbrella. He knew who she was. He continued to watch, studying her as she walked a few steps before returning to the car. She reached in and grabbed what Alexander assumed to be a water bottle. She dropped it into her already bulging handbag and proceeded to walk across to the hospital administration building.

Alexander was wealthy, and not even multiple murder charges could alter that. Access to his money had proved difficult until he reached an agreement with the guard supervisor. Alexander had told the guard how to access some of his funds. In return for obtaining money and purchases, Alexander allowed the guard to withdraw a monthly fee. A consistent flow of information also became part of the deal, and what the guard didn't know, Alexander expected him to find out. He had warned the guard that if he ever took more than instructed he'd kill his family. Alexander realised he had no prospects of being released, but the warning still seemed to have the desired affect, the guard perhaps persuaded that Alexander had the ability to reach beyond his confinement to execute the threat.

He had learned that Hershey had been the one to help capture Edward Walker. Edward was now residing just two cells down from Alexander. Hershey had been mentioned by name in a local news article covering the capture at the time.

Alexander lifted his handcuffed arms and pressed down on the door handle. Frank Marshall, the long serving Orca Ward supervisor stood waiting. Frank didn't speak. Frank didn't like the fact that he had compromised himself for Alexander. He took money from him to help supplement his own income, but it also made life easier for the child killer, and it was eating Frank up. Alexander smiled as he walked past, back towards his cell.

Frank had moved Alexander to cell one almost two years ago, so he wouldn't have to walk Alexander passed the other cells when they let him out on his paid trips. The previous occupant died from being shot with a taser while trying to escape – Frank hoped the current incumbent might go the same way.

"Hey Frankie," Alexander said as he approached his cell. "I'd like some writing paper and a pen, I have a letter to write."

Frank turned the steel wheel to the cell door and opened it waiting for Alexander to enter.

"Don't you forget to bring me it now, Frankie boy."

Frank turned the wheel anticlockwise, locking the door, then signalled to the camera up on the ceiling. As he waited, he heard the deadlocks slide into place.

There were always at least three guards on duty in the Orca Ward, sometimes more depending on the number of inmates, which had never numbered more than six in the years Frank had worked there. Shifts were eight hours each with overtime limited to covering short-term absence - tiredness led to mistakes. Although part of the Ashford hospital complex, the Orca Ward was high security - automated systems, fail safes, single entry exit points, total camera coverage and armed guards, and that was merely inside the Ward. Outside, were high voltage fences, more armed guards, and a rapid response heat-seeking enabled helicopter. No high security inmate had ever made it out of the Ward.

Frank returned to the office, "Mr Jerk-off wants to write another letter."

"Well we'd better not keep the King of Creep waiting," replied Becker.

Becker turned his chair around to face a cabinet where he took out a notepad and pen. He was a middle-aged man, overweight, who used to wear glasses, but had to switch to contacts when taking this job. His hair was largely black though grey flecks had started to appear in increasing numbers. The chair strained as Becker turned the chair back around and handed Frank the pad and pen.

"Here you go old man."

"Thanks. I'll try not to shove it up his ass," Frank replied, in his usual deadpan way.

Returning to Alexander's cell, Frank lowered the hatch and pushed the items through.

"Much obliged!" Alexander called out.

* * * *

At reception Hershey signed in the Visitors book and noticed that a visitor for April Pritchard had just arrived, Emily Jackson. Walking from reception through the main administrative building Hershey saw April sitting at a table with someone in the guest lounge.

The lounge was an area for guests who were waiting for their appointments and a place where low-risk patients could meet and spend time with their visitors, in a less intimidating atmosphere than some of the more formal meeting areas. It was serviced by a small café selling hot drinks and pastries. Hershey walked over.

"Hello April, how are you?"

"Hi Dr.Hershey, this is my friend Emily she studies at the University. Emily this is Dr.Elizabeth Hershey, a forensic psychiatrist who helps out occasionally at the hospital."

"Pleased to meet you Emily," Hershey said as she held out her hand.

"Hi," Emily replied, shaking the extended hand.

"Do you mind if I join you for a moment?" Hershey asked.

"Please do," April said, "Emily has just got here. We were about to discuss some of the books I've been reading."

"I don't think we want to bore Dr.Hershey with that April. Let's talk about you, how are you?"

They talked for almost thirty minutes before Hershey got up and gave her apologies. While they had talked, Hershey had learned how Emily hoped to help April by teaching her to exercise greater control over her own mind and body. Emily had shown April how to induce a light trance, a state similar to that experienced under hypnosis, where it became possible to insert suggestions into the subconscious. Emily and April had been working on techniques that would associate sleeping with relaxing on a golden sandy beach, the sound of waves softly breaking and the sensation of a light warm breeze. April explained how every evening she would fall into this trance and remind herself that sleep was good. Hershey had glanced several times at Emily, whom she believed appeared a little nervous with how much April was sharing. This type of therapy was not without some controversy in the field of Psychology and even then, only practiced by fully qualified psychologists. Emily had also helped April acquire digital Cantonese lessons as well as material that Hershey recognised as complex math, but that April had corrected as *complex numbers.*

Hershey made her way to the Records Department to check on Donald's medication history. The Records Department keep the files and histories of all of Ashford's patients and staff up until they leave the care or employment of the hospital. Over the last six years temporary staff had been used to scan documents and transpose data on to the computer system to support easier access and enable computer analysis of the data stored. Subject to correct access levels and approvals this data could also be shared between hospitals and experts across the country.

Two banks of five computers sat on modern hardwood desks in the middle of the 'Enquiries' room. Two assistants sat behind a small reception area at the front of the room, and behind them half-way down the right hand side, an archway went through to 'Manual Records' where copies of archived files and records were stored on microfiche. The original files were now held in a separate building away from the main administration building. Two of the computers were occupied by members of staff, one a nurse and the other looked like a consultant Hershey vaguely recognised.

One of the receptionists acknowledged Hershey as she walked in and then over to a spare computer. The consultant looked up and nodded a greeting. Logging on, Hershey pulled up the records for Donald McCoy. The file that McGill had provided her didn't contain any medication history, it was also missing some of his daily timesheets over his last few days.

The computer system was based on a similar design to that used within law enforcement. A head shot was displayed in the right hand corner with a basic description and physical stats listed down the left-hand side. The similarities were deliberate, not because the law enforcement system was acknowledged as the best model, but simply to ease the integration of the two systems. The intention being to fully integrate the systems of all health service providers with those of law enforcement. Law enforcement depends on data, the more data available the greater their chances of catching criminals. It would mean that you would no longer have to commit a crime before the police had access to your DNA, dental records, and any sexual diseases you might have. A few years back Hershey had sat on a panel deliberating the potential benefits of such integration versus the perceived public concerns. In the end it had been decided that the public concerns were just that - simply concerns that had been acknowledged and ultimately ignored. The integration was going ahead.

Hershey hit the 'Medication' tab. Some patients suffering with anxiety or depression may receive daily doses of an agent such as buspirone or drugs such as fluoxetine, but Donald's recent history was blank. He hadn't even taken any aspirin or Tylenol. *Perhaps he wasn't at a risk of self-harm* she considered *or maybe the absence of anything being prescribed elevated the risk.*

Hershey hit the 'Timesheet' tab. The timesheet for the latest week was displayed. Other timesheets could be viewed by entering the date or selecting it from a calendar dialogue that would pop up. The timesheet provided a pattern of behaviour, the patient's routine. Occasionally notes would be added if anything happened that might be considered outside a patient's usual routine. Hershey noticed something unexpected. She searched previous timesheets going back over the last few weeks. Other similar notations had been made. On at least two occasions Donald had interacted with April Pritchard.

* * * *

"April it's probably not a good idea to talk too much about this stuff in front of Dr.Hershey," Emily said, after Hershey had left.

"Why do you say that?" April asked.

"Not all doctors approve of this kind of thing, they think its *mind-meddling*. It's hypocritical as they nearly all practice hypnosis and screw with peoples minds, but like most things, so called experts like to feel they are superior, that their years of expensive training actually mean something. They need to feel important and they don't appreciate those of us without letters after our name, interfering in things they think we don't properly understand."

"Dr.Hershey doesn't seem like that to me. And besides, aren't you studying to have letters after your name?"

"I have no intention of being like that. In fact, I am not intending to advertise my credentials after completing my studies. My interest is in helping others, not myself." Emily stressed.

"That's very noble," April replied, not able to contain her laugh. Emily started to laugh too. After composing herself, April continued. "I've read most the books and papers that you gave me. I can't say I've fully understood them, I needed to check on a few things to get a better explanation." April lifted her legs and tucked her feet underneath her as she attempted to make herself comfortable on the sofa. "It appears that there are at least three levels of consciousness, the conscious level which we experience when we are awake, the unconscious level which we experience when we are sleeping or knocked-out, and the sub-conscious level which seems to be always active but to varying degrees."

"Why do you say that?" Emily enquired.

"Because under hypnosis the subconscious appears very active, able to recall events that the conscious level cannot. When we are conscious, the subconscious is active gathering more information than that which we are actually paying attention too, which is why things like pattern interrupts or suggestion work." April shuffled in her seat as she continued, "You can make suggestions to someone who consciously doesn't recognise the suggestion but their subconscious does, like holding up your hands to someone and making a diamond shape, like a director or cameraman might do, and then asking the person later to pick a suit from a deck of cards. Expecting them to chose diamonds."

"What about the subconscious when we are sleeping?" Emily encouraged, her eyes widening.

"There are accounts in the papers where people have been able to recall events under hypnosis that had been conducted while they were asleep. This would mean that the subconscious had to be active even during sleep."

Emily clapped with excitement.

"Excellent April! You're so clever, it's wonderful. I believe we can use the subconscious to influence both our conscious *and* unconscious activities. When someone practices something over and over again the action requires less and less conscious effort, it becomes imprinted, we call it 'habit'. I think our habits lie at the subconscious level allowing our minds to focus on learning new things or working to progress the same skill further." April noticed Emily had started unconsciously to press the cuticles back on her fingers. "Although doctors still use medication to control behaviour and emotions, more and more results are being achieved through psychology. In the past a person who wanted to quit smoking might require months of therapy or those useless patches, but now results are being achieved in the first couple of sessions through hypnosis and suggestion. The sequence I wanted you to repeat is designed to teach your subconscious that sleep is good, to ensure you no longer sleepwalk with the assistance of your subconscious."

"I still don't really know what the subconscious is though Emily." April responded.

"I don't think anyone does, sweetheart. Maybe that is something for you to figure out when you're older.'

Emily pulled a comic book from her bag and placed it on the table. "Here, I picked this up for you. I know you like this one."

"Thank you Emily...Emily?" April asked. "Do you believe in God?"

Emily looked up from the comic she had placed on the table. "No I don't think so. I haven't thought about it much. I had a friend who did and an Aunt who would read me bible stories when I was a child. I think maybe we humans may have had some help along the way but an all-powerful, all seeing God, no, not for me, some form of extra-terrestrials are more likely."

"In one book I was reading someone says that Jesus was an illusionist. His miracles were just tricks that he in someway influenced or even controlled what people thought."

"Well it's possible. But if he did, it didn't do him much good. I think there's more chance the biblical writers were high on something. I think they were the illusionists, able to make people believe a lie."

They talked and laughed for another hour before Emily had to leave. April walked with Emily to the reception area, where Emily handed back her temporary pass and made her way back to the car park. After waving goodbye, April went to the canteen to see if she could find Lucas Vogel before he started his shift.

Lucas Vogel worked as a security guard within the Woman's Directorate, often on the Dolphin Ward which is where April's room is located. He was in his early forties, a lean man with short greying hair and light brown skin. He suffered with arthritis in his left knee and occasionally in his fingers during the colder rainy season.

April and Lucas often talked and had become friends. Lucas would bring in second hand console games and homemade cake for April. More recently, Lucas brought his own ten year old daughter Katie, in to visit April; they seemed to get on very well.

When April got to the canteen, she looked around but couldn't see Lucas. She checked her watch – *probably a few minutes early.* She went across to the far end and picked up a deck of cards to play with while waiting for Lucas to arrive.

CHAPTER 9

Lucas Vogel parked his aging Oldsmobile in the staff parking and made his way into the hospital via a secure side entrance. Swiping his card, a light blipped green and the door began to rotate. He didn't like these new doors. The rotating doors had been installed after someone had got into the building following a member of staff – 'tailgating'. No real harm had been done as the unauthorised stranger, dressed in an approximate nurse's uniform, was apprehended while trying to access the files of some of the hospital's more infamous guests. The new rotating doors were tailgate proof, but to Lucas seemed somehow less secure. Lucas shuffled through the entrance.

The canteen continued serving food until six p.m. Throughout the hospital the security shifts were staggered to ensure not all security staff were in the process of changing shifts at one time. Lucas' shift started at four in the afternoon and would see him through until midnight. The time was approaching three-thirty giving him enough time to fill his stomach with sausages, mashed potato and onion gravy. He grabbed a soda and piece of blueberry pie and added them to the tray with his meal. As he went to pay, April called out and waved him over. He was happy to accept the invitation.

"Hi April, how are you doin'? What you've been up to?"

"Emily came to see me again today, we talked and played. That Dr.Hershey also said hello, I think she must be looking into Donald's death."

"Strange one that one." Lucas said.

"What is? Donald or his death?" April asked.

"You are too young to know how he died but I can tell you it was strange, everybody's talking about it."

"Donald was my friend."

"I know Honey, but folks round here aren't all as normal as you and me, some do some pretty weird things, some do some real bad stuff.'

"You mean like the Cannibal Killer?"

"Yeah, he falls into the real bad stuff category. Anyway, I'm about to eat my lunch. Don't you worry about Donald, he's in a good place now, somewhere they take proper care of folks."

"You are referring to Heaven?" asked April.

"Yeah, Heaven. If we're good, we'll all get to go someday. No taxes, no dwindling pension plan, no growing old, no pain in your joints, only good food and no way to get fat. Like I said, Heaven."

April giggled, "You're funny Lucas."

"Fire'" April spoke quietly but deliberately, clearly pronouncing the word, but in a tone that contrasted their conversation.

"Pardon me?" Lucas asked, not sure if April had said something.

"Do you believe in Heaven, Lucas?"

"Of course, I believe in Heaven."

"Fire," April said quietly, while Lucas was continuing to talk.

"I've already booked my place," Lucas continued, not noticing.

"How do you book a place in Heaven?"

Lucas paused for a moment, "Well you've got to believe in Jesus...", *"Fire"*, and trust him to save your soul when you die. And He will. Anyways, how is your friend Emily?"

"She's good. One of the students that she shares a flat with said today she was going to leave. I think Emily is quite friendly with her, but I think she's more upset about having to pay more rent for awhile until someone else moves in. She asked about you. *Fire*"

"Asked about me? What does Emily want to know about me? I'm just simple old Lucas taking care of my two young ladies."

"She asked me to show you this picture, here."

April pulled a folded piece of paper from her pocket and handed it to Lucas. Lucas opened the paper and looked at the picture drawn in coloured pencil.

"What is it?" Lucas asked.

"What does it look like?"

"A yellow bell…", "*Fire*", "a bit like how I remember my old school bell when I was about your age, except that one was rusty from the weather."

"It is a bell. If you hold it up in front of your face and move it from side to side, you'll see that it rings. *Fire*'"

Lucas held the picture up and moved it as April instructed. As he concentrated on the picture the clapper did appear to move, hitting each side of the shell.

"Oh yeah. Hey that's pretty neat. I'll have to show that to Katie. Emily…", "*Fire*", "did this? Umm, they do make mean sausage and mash here," Lucas said, as he tucked into his food.

"Turn it around," April said.

Lucas turned the paper around revealing a picture with bright vivid reds, oranges and blues.

"Okay. What is this?" Lucas asked.

"It's just a picture of bright colours. It's one of those where you need to use your imagination. What do you see? *Fire.*"

Lucas stared at the picture, it looked familiar, but he couldn't place it.

"I'm not sure, you got me on that one I'm afraid."

"The trifle's good too." April stated.

"Sorry?" Lucas asked.

"The trifle is good too," April repeated.

"Yeah, had some of that the other day. So, anybody doing anything about getting you outta this place? They talk about your sleepwalking but I'm...", '*Fire*', "still waiting to see it. It's not that I want to see you go but you should not be in here. This is no place for you, especially you." Lucas stated, now pointing his knife toward April. Returning his knife to the food he continued, "My wife keeps threatening to come and break you out. I told you about her right? And Katie talks about you. Man, it bugs me that they keep you in here. Good job I'm also here. Keep an eye on you."

"Professor McGill came to see me the other day. He seems a kind man, he told me he's been talking to Health Service executives and Child Services about me. I think he wants to arrange for some testing in the hope I can at least, get transferred back to a normal care home. *Fire*. The Professor has also arranged for me to have some tutoring while I'm here, it seems they weren't set up to give a patient schooling, but it's sorted now." April was fingering the cards that were laying on the table. "I'll be meeting my tutor this Monday. *Fire*. I think we'll be doing Math, English, History and Geography. The Professor said I'll need to see someone else for sciences, but he's still working on that."

"I hope your teacher knows how smart you are, or you could be the one doing the teaching," Lucas smiled.

Lucas finished eating and invited April to finish off his soda.

"I've get to get to work. Don't you be back late now, I might just have a surprise waiting for you. Catch you later April."

"Lucas, don't be alarmed if I'm a little late."

Lucas frowned for a moment then smiled, "See you a bit later then." He got up and placed his tray into a trolley and headed off to start his shift. April smiled, picked up the cards she had been playing with and began to shuffle them.

* * * *

At four-thirty Hershey was finished in the Records Department and decided to return home. As she handed her temporary ID back at reception, the receptionist handed her a white envelope with 'Dr.Hershey' hand written in an elegant style on the front. She didn't recognise the writing, but it flowed with bold curves and straight lines. The writer was confident and possessed a creative streak, she thought. Hershey took the envelope and made her way to the car park.

* * * *

At six-thirty, April left the canteen and her playing cards. She had been teaching herself different shuffles and practicing a few of the tricks that Peter Legwinski had shown her before his death. The walk to her room from the canteen would take her back to the main building, across the large hall and into the Women's Directorate.

The Women's Directorate was a relatively new building connected to the main building by a short walkway. The building consisted of three separate wards each with its own security office, accessed from a small central reception area. All patients were given rooms within the Directorate. The women were placed according to the perceived level of risk they posed to either themselves, staff or other patients.

The Dolphin Ward kept the patients with the lowest level of risk, and the patients were usually referred to as 'guests'. These were women with very treatable and curable disorders such as, anxiety, depression and occasional drug users. Guests at the Dolphin Ward benefited from larger furnished rooms, with cable TV, ensuite toilets, and in April's case, a games console.

The Otter Ward housed female patients with mild aggressive tendencies and moderately violent or offensive behaviour, or long running addictions to strong hallucinogenic drugs. Many of these patients were considered high risk with respect to self-harm. The rooms in the Otter Ward were, through necessity, smaller and sparsely furnished.

The most secure ward within the Women's Directorate is the Seal Ward. Four patients are currently held on the Seal Ward and only one of those can claim to match all the criteria usually required for a long-term stay. Daniella Kitson, a classified *'schizophrenic with homicidal tendencies'*. These tendencies resulted in the deaths of nine newly born babies that had been under her care in the maternity ward where she worked. She was a fully trained paediatric nurse. She claimed she was following instructions given to her by God who wanted the children back. It was four months from the first suffocated infant, until she was caught in the process of suffocating her tenth. Daniella is the only woman currently residing at Ashford to have taken life.

At a little after six-thirty, April waved *hello* to Abigail who was sitting at the Women's reception. April pulled one of the large blue painted swing doors toward her and went through into the Dolphin Ward. Just a few feet down the corridor was the security office. Lucas was sat back in his chair watching clips on a tablet, when April stopped at the open office door. There were only two monitors in the office. The main display provided an uninterrupted view of the full length of the corridor. The second monitor was switched on but wasn't showing any images. This monitor was used to display night-time images from April's room only, specially installed shortly before April arrived.

Professor McGill had wanted a motion camera to be installed to April's room. The camera was activated automatically at eight p.m. or earlier by manual activation from within the security office. Once activated, the camera only transmitted images after being triggered by significant movement within her room. The idea was to maximise April's privacy while maintaining due diligence to her condition.

Lucas was now showing the build up to a hockey game on the tablet.

"Who's going to win?" April interrupted.

"Hi April, I think the Canucks will come good. I have this feeling about it," Lucas replied.

"Who are they playing?"

"The Leafs, it's an all Canadian match-up tonight."

"See you tomorrow, Lucas."

"Night Honey. Oh, by the way, I've left a game Katie asked me to give to you in your room, she said she hopes you like it. But don't stay up too late okay!"

April went to her room saying, "Say thank you to Katie for me!"

* * * *

At eight o'clock the camera in April's room blipped on. She was sitting down on her bed, in her pyjamas, playing the game Katie had lent her. The light in her room was on full and April could be clearly seen on the monitor in the security office, but Lucas wasn't taking any notice. He was well into the hockey match. After five minutes of no significant movement inside the room, the camera blipped off.

At eight thirty-seven the camera in April's room blipped on as April switched the TV off using the remote control and got to her feet to switch off the games console. She then turned off the light and got into bed. After a further five minutes, the camera blipped off.

At ten minutes before midnight, Leroy Correll came into the Security Office on the Dolphin Ward. Leroy often started a little earlier to allow Lucas to get away, '*Give my best wishes to the missus*', he would say. They chatted a little before Lucas collected his bag and made his way out.

At six minutes to midnight, April sat up in bed. Her movement was slow but deliberate, and would normally have been strenuous on her stomach muscles. The camera remained off as she sat up slowly in the darkness.

Two minutes later, Lucas stopped at the exit door and pulled out a cigarette from the packet in his pocket. He popped the cigarette into the corner of his mouth and felt around his shirt for his lighter. After trying each shirt pocket, he rummaged through the pockets of his jacket. In the inside pocket he carried a small box of matches, old but reliable technology. Failing to find his lighter, he lit one of the matches.

The flame from the match seemed to flare up in front of Lucas' face. He stood mesmerised. The flame seemed to grow in size and intensity. As the flame grew, it flickered with beautiful colours more vivid than he had ever seen before. The flame continued to grow, and his initial awe gave way to fear, and then panic. The spent match dropped on to the floor, but Lucas could still see the raging flame in front of him. He smashed the fire alarm, triggering an alarm.

The fire alarm system installed at Ashford is referred to as '*an intelligent system*'. The system is controlled by computer software linked to various sensors and triggers throughout the various hospital buildings. A sensor or trigger within a ward would only activate the alarm system within that ward, the remainder of the hospital would be unaffected. A sensor or trigger within the main building would activate the alarm system for the whole hospital, due to the main buildings greater potential for fire and the risk to all wards.

Whenever a fire sensor or trigger was activated, its location would be identified on the fire control system display, located within the main security office. Security personnel would be able to view camera footage from that area to help determine the next course of action. In any event, the deadlocks on any doors are released, leaving only the manual locks in place. The security to the external doors is deactivated. Fire procedures meant that all low-risk patients could be evacuated quickly, with medium and high-risk patients only being evacuated where the fire risk to those patients was considered high.

In his cell, Alexander heard the slight noise of the deadlock mechanism depressurising and the bolts slide smoothly back into the steel frame. He knew the system must be either faulty or a fire alarm had been triggered, though he could not hear an alarm. No matter, he thought, *standby*.

The large oversized guard at the main security office almost dropped his sandwich as the siren sounded, and the location of the trigger that had been activated was displayed on the systems monitor. Looking closely at the screen he could see another guard behaving strangely, as though he were trying to wave a swarm of bees from his face. It was Lucas Vogel. *What the hell is he doing?* None of the sensors in the area had been activated and there was no sign of smoke. The trigger on the wall at the staff exit near to where Lucas was swatting invisible bees, had been activated.

Doctors and nurses who were on their night-shifts started to appear in the main reception area, some wearing luminous yellow tops with 'Fire Marshall' written on the back. Low-risk patients also started to gather, escorted by nurses and more security guards.

April Pritchard unlocked her door from the inside, left her room and gathered with the other guests from the Dolphin Ward. The security guard at the main office got on his radio, but Lucas failed to respond. He called other guards and a nurse to the eastern staff exit where Lucas was still acting weird.

* * * *

Alexander lowered the hatch in the door to his cell and shouted, "Frankie! Hey Frankie boy, what's going down?"

Frank eventually appeared and said, "Alright, keep it down Alex. No need to get excited."

"You have no idea what I'm like when I'm excited Frankie boy. Come on, let us out."

"There's no need for you to be evacuated. You know the rules, you only get to move if the fire's about to burn your ass."

"Ahh come on, Frankie boy, at least let us out of these cells, let us stand in the hall, just in case. Fatso, can always point his gun in our faces."

"Hold on, let me check it out.'

Frank went slowly back to the office.

"What's he want?" said Becker

"He *says* we should let him out until we know what is going on."

"We should let the son of a bitch burn, that's what we should do. The radio's been going bananas, seems Lucas is in trouble. It sounds like he was the one that set the alarm going."

"Perhaps there is a fire then," Frank said.

Becker gave him a look…"Ahh what the hell. Let's get them out."

Becker pulled a long thick-linked chain from a drawer and passed it to Frank. From a locker on the wall, he took two small fire arms and handed one to Frank.

"Let's go round 'em up. Tanner is all dosed up, we'd better do him last, the other two can carry him if they have too. We'll do the Prince of Darkness first, then get Edward."

Frank and Becker approached Alexander's cell. The deadlocks had released automatically when the main alarm had been triggered. Becker held out his gun while Frankie turned the wheel on the door to open it. Alexander was pacing up and down as the door opened.

"Okay, Alexander don't give us any trouble now. Slip these on and we'll make our way down the hall. You know how much I'd like to put a bullet through that dirty head of yours," Becker said, as he aimed the gun at Alexander's face.

"You are *so* charming Michael. I bet you get all the boys."

Frank moved forward and carefully handed Alexander some hand and leg cuffs that he had added to the chain. Alexander put the cuffs on. Only after he heard the clicks, did Frank move closer and check they were properly attached.

"Now let's go collect Edward. Easy now," Michael said.

The three of them moved slowly from Alexander's cell and up the ward to where Edward was waiting in his cell. Alexander stood between Becker and Frankie as Frankie moved to open the cell door. As Frank began turning the wheel, Alexander moved slowly around, closer to Frank's back. A bead of sweat started to run down Becker's brow. Frank pulled open the door to Edward's cell.

"Okay Edward, here you go, put these on."

As Frank's arm reached across to hand Edward the cuffs, Alexander reached out and placing his hands over Frank's head pulled him back hard towards his chest. Frank grabbed at his neck as the chain links dug into his throat, he lost his balance as he was pulled back, his head falling onto Alexander's left shoulder.

"What cha' goin' do fatboy?" Alexander snarled, as he used Frank as a shield.

Frank was struggling for air.

"Let him go Alex, I'll put a bullet through your skull, let him go now damn it!"

As Becker aimed the gun at Alexander, Edward hit his wrists hard propelling the gun from Becker's hands. Edward then followed up with a punch to his jaw.

"Way to go Eddie boy!" Alexander shouted.

As Alexander pulled harder on the chain, Frank fumbled for his side arm. Knowing he had only seconds of consciousness Frank managed to hook his fingers around the gun. He fired towards Alexander's leg.

Pain exploded in Alexander's right leg as the gun went off. His grasp immediately weakened in shock and surprise. He yelled in pain and fell backwards as Frank managed to free himself.

Turning around Frank saw Becker bending slowly to the ground, reaching for his gun. Blood dripped to the floor from his Becker's broken lip. Frank looked up to see Edward running off down the corridor and out of the ward.

* * * *

On the security radio came shouting, "He's out, Walker is out! He's got out!!"

The guard in the main office hit the security alarm. The security alarm would normally seal all exits, unless in the event of a fire alarm. Even so, the guards at the main security gate and outside the buildings would still be alerted. No one would escape the grounds.

"Now what's going on?" asked Dr.Cheung, one of the hospital senior staff.

"Edward Walker is out of his cell!"

The doctor thought for a moment. "Can you see a fire on the monitors...? Come on man! Can you see a fire or any smoke?"

The guard was looking at the fire system's monitor again. "No. It doesn't look like there's a fire."

"Okay, get everyone back to their rooms. Shut down the fire alarm and secure the main doors. Do it!"

The guard reset the fire alarm system which would enable the main doors and exits to be secured. He sealed the exit doors, but left the other doors open to enable the patients to return to their wards. Dr.Cheung instructed the Fire Marshalls and nurses to get the patients back to their rooms quickly. Then he called some of the guards over.

"Edward Walker is out of his cell. We need to get him back there right away," Cheung said, trying to remain calm but still express urgency. "Bring up the main security cameras in the Orca Ward and the main building."

Frank and Becker returned the injured Alexander to his cell and locked him in. The fire alarm was deactivated, and the deadlocks were again activated. They headed out of the Ward to help with the search for Edward. "You can bleed," Becker said, as they left.

April Pritchard didn't speak to anyone as she returned with the rest of the patients back to their rooms.

* * * *

On arriving at the eastern staff exit, the two guards and a male nurse, Thomas Bessey, found Lucas Vogel almost hysterical. He was waving his arms around shouting "Fire! The building's on fire!"

The two guards grabbed Lucas' arms and wrestled him to the floor. The nurse scanned the area, there was no fire. A spent match and an untouched cigarette lay on the floor. Lucas began to settle down and seemed confused.

"What the hell are you doin' man!?" asked one of the guards.

"I...I don't know. I went to light a cigarette on the way out when I saw...a huge flame, like a fireball or something, here in the hall."

"Take him to Rehab and get someone to give him a sedative. Probably best to keep him here tonight until we know what's going on. Someone call his wife. I'll check around make sure it's nothing."

The two guards helped Lucas to his feet and escorted him to the Rehabilitation department. Thomas stood breathing in deep through his nose, smelling the air, unaware he was being watched.

Edward had made his way out of the Orca Ward and into the main building. The Orca Ward connected to the east-side of the main administration building, opening out to an area leading into another smaller open area near a small Rehabilitation unit and public washrooms. The area was hidden from the main security office by a supporting wall structure, but Edward could hear the commotion. Edward hid behind a vending machine, the absence of daylight through the windows and the small spot lighting affording him plenty of shadow.

As Edward watched, the man stood sniffing the air and checking the bin near the staff exit. He walked towards the vending machine and the corner

Edward watched from. Edward glanced back at the exit at the end of the corridor. The man, still walking toward the vending machine, was a bit shorter than Edward, skinny and on the wrong side of forty, still Edward knew he would need to be efficient.

The man came closer, closer. Edward leapt on to the man locking his head in his arm. As momentum carried Edward forward he maintained his grip on the man's head and twisted the neck sharply. The neck crunched as the spine twisted and snapped inside. The man's body went limp and dropped to the floor. Edward looked again down the corridor to the door with the Exit sign above. He ran to the door.

Pushing frantically at the pressure bar across the door, the door refused to open. *Come on, come on! Damn it!* Edward stopped and looked around the edges of the steel door...a security device, card reader. He looked back down the corridor and to the guard's body. He ran again.

* * * *

The camera of the Orca Ward showed the two security guards, Frank and Becker moving quickly down the connecting corridor. Dr.Cheung and the security guard watched the images being displayed from the south east security camera in the main building. Two guards had helped Lucas to his feet and moved out of the vision of the camera. Thomas Bessey could be seen moving slowly with his nose pointed in the air, he moved just out of shot. As Cheung watched the screen a little longer he couldn't believe what he saw next. The head and shoulders of Thomas Bessey fell into view as someone partially off camera appeared to knock Bessey to the ground. From the images, Dr.Cheung could tell Bessey's neck was broken. Bessey wasn't moving as he lay on the floor. Then someone came into full view of the camera before heading quickly down the corridor and toward the exit. Walker.

"He's just round there. Walker! He's over there!" Cheung shouted as he pointed across to the east-side of the building.

* * * *

Edward reached the body. He checked it hoping for an ID card. Nothing. He checked the shirt pockets. Nothing. He moved to check the pockets in the pants. Nothing, but some loose change in the front. As Edward shifted the body to reach at the back, he moved his hands over the holstered Taser, then a pair of cuffs. Then he felt a clip. He pulled, and the guard's ID card slid from a pocket at the rear. For the briefest of moments Edward anticipated freedom. Then he heard voices and the noise of running footsteps.

Edward knew he'd never make it back to the exit in time. He didn't want to have to go back. The stupid guards took him for some crazy guy. Alexander's presumption that they were same made his stomach turn. They were not the same – *I'm no child molesting sicko*. Edward unclipped the Taser and stood, aiming at the corner where the onrushing guards would surely momentarily appear.

They say just before death or perhaps even during, key memories replay through one's mind. Edward didn't believe it until now. He remembered as a boy, sat in class, listening to the teacher tell the class how humans had evolved from apes. TV documentaries stating with certainty, how animals needed to evolve and adapt to survive. Survival of the fittest. He remembered peeing himself as his father stood pointing and shouting at him, tears streaming down his face, *'There is no God. It's just this! Us. There is no fucking God!'*, his mother laying lifeless behind him on the hospital bed. He remembered thinking what's the point? Life is just too hard. He remembered the road traffic accident and the body skewered by a metal pole. He saw the horror etched on the onlookers faces – while Edward could only picture the lifeless body roasting on a spit...*round and around...round and around....the flesh beginning to cook.*

The guards rounded the corner and cautiously stepped into the corridor. Cheung stood behind them. Edward stood, staring back at them. A gun pointed at them.

"Put it down, Walker!" demanded one of the guards, "Drop the weapon! Now!"

Frank and Becker arrived, their weapons raised. "Easy now Edward," Frank said trying to remain calm. "Put the weapon down." Glancing to the ground to they saw the guard wasn't moving – purple bruising around the unnatural bulge on the neck. Frank's anger flared, Edward had been his responsibility. Frank shot into Edward's chest.

CHAPTER 10

Professor McGill had been notified automatically by the Hospital's security system. On seeing the notification sent to his phone, McGill phoned in to find out what was going on. Twenty minutes later, McGill had arrived at the Hospital. Three police cars had already arrived, hurriedly parked at the front of the main building, lights still flashing.

Inside, McGill got the good news and the bad. None of the patients had escaped and Walker, had been injured while trying to escape. Thomas Bessey however, had not survived an attack from Walker before his recapture.

McGill had been given some details when he had phoned in though they didn't make much sense. All the patients were in their rooms. Lucas Vogel was sedated and sleeping in the main rehabilitation unit on the first floor. His wife had been called. Thomas Bessey's body had not as yet been moved as crime scene investigators took photos and gathered forensics. McGill would be the one to have to inform Bessey's devoted wife and children.

The hospital had been returned to normal, but the events of that night had raised a whole series of questions. At a little after three a.m., McGill left the hospital, he would be back in just over four hours to make a start on the inquiry.

* * * *

At seven a.m. Hershey's cell phone began to sound. Hershey woke, stretched out an arm and grabbed the phone.

"Hershey…no, that's okay…What!..Yes, of course…yes, I'll come right away."

Putting the cell back on the bedside drawer, she pulled back the sheets and hopped in the shower.

* * * *

Hershey pulled up at the hospital just before eight a.m. still trying to make sense of what McGill had told her over the phone. *The fire alarm and the security alarm, now that must have been interesting*, she thought.

McGill had asked her to go to the Nightingale conference room on the first floor, normally reserved for the monthly executive meetings. When she arrived, all of the senior management team were present. McGill was stood at the front referring to a timeline of the previous night's events.

"At ten minutes before midnight, Leroy Correll started his shift, relieving Lucas Vogel, on the Dolphin Ward. They chatted for a few minutes before Lucas left to go home. Lucas went to the east staff exit where he stopped at the exit door." McGill was pointing to a crude floor plan of the building. "He took out a cigarette and moments later lit a match from a pack he was carrying. We're not sure what happened next, but Lucas dropped the match, still lit, and the cigarette, and started waving his arms around. He then smashed the fire alarm next to the exit door and started shouting

'Fire!'. Other than Lucas' behaviour everything seemed to be going according to procedure – the deadlock systems were deactivated and low-risk patients gathered in the their reception areas in preparation for evacuation. Dr.Cheung, please would you pick up from here?"

Dr.Cheung was used to long shifts and high pressure, but the events of this extended shift were showing on his face.

"During the fire alarm, guards Michael Becker and Frank Marshall who were on duty in the Orca Ward, decided to move the three patients in that ward from their cells to the holding area near the security office. This is contrary to procedure. High-risk patients should only be moved after specific instructions from Main Security. Guards Becker and Marshall acted without those instructions. While trying to move the patients, Alexander Jones attacked Frank Marshall. In the ensuing struggle, Edward Walker managed to escape the ward. Security at Main activated the security alarm following a radio call from Becker and under my instructions." Indicating the route from Main Security to the east staff exit, Dr.Cheung continued, "Thomas Bessey, assisted by two other guards, Miller and Li, attended to Lucas Vogel at the east exit. Then Miller and Li took Lucas to Rehab under Bessey's instructions. Thomas remained near the exit looking for any sign of a fire. There was no fire. Tragically, Thomas was attacked and killed by Edward Walker."

Dr.Cheung returned to his seat.

"Thank you, Michael. Okay, clearly, we need to understand what happened to Lucas Vogel. He was given a sedative and spent most of the night with his wife in Rehab. She took him home a short while ago. Elizabeth, please can I ask you to follow up on that?" Hershey nodded. "I also want to know what Becker and Frank Marshall thought they were trying to achieve opening the cells without having the fire risk confirmed. Beverley, please would you take that on. I want you to go back to your areas and check that everything was carried out in accordance with established procedures. A member of staff died here tonight because we got sloppy. Elizabeth, Beverley, please let me know when you have anything. All right, I'm done."

Beverley Cordell was the Personnel Director, a tall thin woman with dyed black hair and a narrow face that accentuated her already pointed features. The expensive makeup she wore couldn't keep the lines of encroaching age fully hidden. She had a true poker face, even when she smiled you were never really sure what she was thinking. McGill regarded her highly and would no doubt go with any recommendation she made regarding Becker and Marshall.

Hershey stayed behind, wanting to catch McGill in private. McGill looked up and saw Hershey waiting. Eventually the room cleared.

"Charles, a note was left for me at reception when I left yesterday, it was from Alexander Jones."

"A proposal for marriage?" McGill said dryly.

"He does want to see me. He says he has some information I might be interested in. He's on the Orca Ward right?" McGill nodded confirmation, his back now turned to Hershey as he stared out of a window.

"I've not been in that ward, how would he know who I am? And how does he get to leave notes at reception for people?"

"Alexander is wealthy. I've no doubt Alex is able to buy a few things within the hospital. His father won the lottery, his mother was then taken by cancer leaving Alex to inherit the lot. He may have heard someone talking about you or might possibly have seen you around the building. They do get access to a common room and the gymnasium." McGill then tapped on the window he had been looking out from. "And we do have windows," he added.

Hershey considered that a moment. The Sports Hall was located behind the Cavendish Ward and near the hospital gardens. The Orca Ward had its own pathway to the Sports Hall to avoid having to take the patients via the main building. Hershey wasn't entirely convinced, but she accepted Alexander might have seen her in the gardens.

"I guess it doesn't matter how he knows that I'm here. Can I arrange to see him?"

"He's just jerking you off Elizabeth…if you want to talk to him, fix it with Nichols, he's the Super over there. Probably best to arrange a time when Laurel and Hardy aren't on duty."

Hershey gave a clipped, but sympathetic smile at the reference to Becker and Marshall.

"Thanks Charles. I'll get back to you shortly on Vogel, but I should also tell you I'm still unsure what to make of Donald McCoy's death."

"Just tell them the facts, let the board decide."

Hershey nodded, "See you later Charles."

* * * *

Hershey decided she would leave it another hour or so before phoning the Vogel home. The time was a little after eight-thirty and Hershey had skipped breakfast in her rush to get to the meeting. She decided to drop by the canteen for cereal before seeing if she could find Nichols.

She was surprised by how busy the canteen was. Staff finishing their shifts as well as those about to start, were making good use of the facilities. A number of patients were lined up to get their breakfast. Hershey picked up a tray and a cereal bowl, she selected a packet of muesli and emptied the contents into the bowl. She added skimmed milk. Before making her way to the checkout, she picked up a carton of apple juice.

Hershey spent a few moments scanning the canteen for a free table at which to sit when she spotted a familiar face. As she walked over to the table, she noticed that everyone seemed to be talking about the events of the previous night.

"Hi April, how are you this morning?"

"I'm fine thank you, Dr.Hershey."

"April, it's fine for you to call me Elizabeth. Actually, I'd like that," Hershey replied, with a smile. "Were you woken by the events last night?"

"Yes, everyone must have been. Those alarms are very loud. Everyone has been talking about it. Apparently, someone set the fire alarm off by mistake."

"Were you okay?"

"I was okay, thank you for asking. I must have been asleep when the alarm went off. I remember waking up and there were a lot of people running around, quite a commotion. I was just getting up from my bed when one of the nurses came to check on me. I left my room with her and gathered here in the canteen with everyone else. Almost everyone else. I don't think they let the dangerous patients out of their rooms. We stayed in the canteen before one of the guards said it had been a false alarm and we were all to return to our rooms. Dr.Hershey…Elizabeth, are you married?" April asked.

Hershey was surprised by the question. "No. No, it seems all the men I meet don't want to share me with my work."

"Does that mean that you love your work?"

"Yes…I guess I must."

"So, you don't have any children?"

"No, none yet anyway. I still have time. A bit of time anyway. So perhaps one day I'll get around to having one."

"Does that mean you'd like to have children?"

"I'll tell you a secret." Hershey leaned in toward April and said quietly, "I'm very fond of children. The well behaved and polite sort anyway." Hershey reached across and playfully wiggled April's nose.

"You're nice Elizabeth, I think you would make a great mom."

"Why, thank you April. That's very nice of you to say. I just need to meet the right man."

"Have you come here for breakfast?" April asked, again changing the subject.

"I was asked to attend a meeting this morning to discuss what happened last night."

"A meeting because the fire alarm went off?"

"Well, it wasn't just the fire alarm, one of the dangerous patients managed to get out of their cell so there was a breach in security as well. And besides, we need to understand *why* the fire alarm went off. It wasn't exactly a false alarm, more of a mistake."

"How did the patient get out? I thought they were never allowed out." April enquired.

"They are allowed out sometimes, but it doesn't matter now, they're back where they belong. Don't worry yourself, sweetheart."

Hershey and April continued talking for almost an hour. April shared some of her past and more of her future hopes. April had tears in her eyes as she shared with Hershey how she had been adopted, and that she had been responsible for her adopted parent's deaths.

"I've never told anyone this," April said, "but I remember some things about that night. Mommy was going to have a baby. I was going to get a baby brother. I remember I so much wanted to do something for him, before he was born. Give him a present or something. I remember falling asleep that night thinking of the things that I might be able to do."

Hershey reached across and gently squeezed April's left arm.

"It was horrible. I woke up covered in their blood." April continued, her cheeks damp from the tears. "I don't understand why? Why would I do something like that? I loved my Mom. I wanted to be a big sister. Now I'm alone, in this place. I have no one, my real Mom is dead, she died, killed herself while I was still a baby. I don't know who my father is or if I even have any real family. It's not fair."

Hershey moved from her chair, crouching, she held April in her arms. "I don't know why these things happen April," Hershey said gently as she held April close, "Sometimes life is very unfair. But I want you to believe things will get better. I really believe that. Look at me." Hershey cupped her hands around April's damp face. "You are still very young, and I know it must seem like only bad things happen, but many good things happen too. Sometimes even wonderful things. You are smart and beautiful and I'm positive you will do something amazing when you are older." Hershey lightly kissed April on the head. "Listen, I'm going to make a promise. I promise I'm going to help. Let me see what I can do to help you, would that be okay?" Hershey wiped around April's eyes. "I don't want you to worry?"

April sniffed and nodded her head, "I'm sorry Elizabeth. I've never really had the chance to talk to anyone."

"It's okay, I understand," Hershey replied. She reached into her handbag and withdrew her purse and a pen. "Here, let me give you this." She took out a business card and wrote a number on the back. "This is my card and, on the back, here is my personal number. I only give that to my closest friends. If ever you want to talk, doesn't matter what time, I want you to call this number. I will do my best to pick up, but if I don't, you just leave me a quick message and I will contact you right back. How does that sound?"

April's tears had stopped, and she smiled. She hugged Hershey and said, "That sounds good. Thank you, Elizabeth."

Hershey squeezed April. As she left April that morning, she had become determined to improve April's situation.

* * * *

When Hershey phoned Lucas Vogel, his wife answered. She seemed upset, but Lucas soon came on the phone and said he would be happy for her to visit. Lucas lived just south of Sunset Beach. From Ashford it was back towards

Vancouver. The drive took less than twenty minutes. The weather was grey, and showers threatened. The rainy season had started, and grey would be the dominant colour in the sky until the following April.

Hershey was shown into the living room where Sandra, Lucas' wife, had already made some coffee. Sandra left them alone.

"How are you feeling now?" Hershey asked.

"I'm fine, all these people worrying about me. I was fine when I woke up this morning. I don't remember too much of what happened last night though to be honest."

"What can you tell me, Lucas?"

"I watched the hockey game, the Canucks beating the Leafs, then I found some old movie. I ran my checks as usual, and as usual nothing unusual happened. Leroy turned up a little before the end of my shift, we talked and then I left. I remember getting to the exit and taking out a cigarette." Lucas started to rub the palms of his hands together. "With no smoking rooms anywhere on the wards now, I'm gasping by the end of my shift. I couldn't find my lighter and so I used some matches I keep, you know, for emergencies. Last thing I remember is lighting the match. After that, I'm looking at Roger's face as we were sat on the floor near the exit. Roger and Matt took me up to Rehab where I spent most of the night. Sandra was there when I woke up and she drove me home. As I said, I'm feeling fine now." Lucas rubbed his forehead and added, "I just have this blank after lighting that match."

"Do you remember anything at all about the fire?"

Lucas shook his head, "Nothing, just lighting the match and then nothing. Weird I know right, but that's all. They said I had triggered the fire alarm in the main building. I hope it didn't cause too much trouble.'

"You normally use a lighter? Did you find your lighter?" Hershey asked.

"No. I was thinking that maybe it fell out of my pocket or something. I looked for it in the car when Sandra drove me home, but I didn't find it. We're not supposed to be carrying lighters, or matches, on the hospital grounds. But what are we supposed to do? I'm sorry Dr.Hershey, but the job can be stressful sometimes and the shifts long. It's not just me, most of the guards and a lot of the staff are smokers. They need to make some kind of provision for us, you know."

"Lucas, there was an incident last night," Hershey said, her tone soft but more serious. "One of the patients from the Orca ward got free, only for a short time. It was Walker. Becker and Marshall tried moving Walker and Alexander Jones from their cells. There was a scuffle and Walker tried to escape. I don't think he expected to get out of the hospital or anything, but he did get out of the ward."

"They got him, right? Before he did anything, right?" the concern showing on his face.

Hershey shook her head, "No, Lucas, Walker attacked Thomas Bessey. Bessey was looking the area over while the others took you to Rehab. Walker would have seen him as he made his way out of the Orca Ward. He took Thomas by surprise…Lucas, Thomas didn't survive."

Colour drained from Lucas' face. His head dropped as his hands came up to cover his face. Lucas closed his eyes.

"Lucas, it's not your fault. There's no way you could have known that would happen even if you had intended to set the fire alarm off. Becker and Marshall didn't get the okay to move them. They broke with procedure."

Lucas slowly shook his head in hands, then lifting his head he said, "Thomas was a good man. If the alarm hadn't gone off Becker and Marshall wouldn't have had a decision to get wrong. Why'd the hell did they try and move them?"

"They shouldn't have done. There was no fire, and procedure is to keep them in their cells unless main security instruct otherwise. They hadn't received those instructions. They took the decision to move them, no one else, Lucas."

Lucas took in a deep breath and expelled the air slowly. He then picked up his cup of coffee, his hands shaking. Hershey followed his cue.

"He didn't suffer. Not much consolation I know." Hershey said.

Lucas stared at Hershey. *But his family will!* Lucas thought, but didn't say. "So, what now?' Lucas asked.

"I'm not sure. I think they're happy for you to return to work if you feel up to it. But you should have a check-up, perhaps see Dr.Kutznova, before you do."

Kutznova is a therapist working at Ashford. In addition to spending time patients, she provides support and counselling to staff. Hershey liked her.

"What were you doing before your shift started?" Hershey asked.

"Nothing much, we'd been out doing a bit of shopping, groceries that sort of thing. I got to the hospital a little early, as usual, helped myself to sausage and the mashed potato before my shift started."

"Have you been suffering from any headaches, nausea at all, anything unusual at all?"

"No nothing. I'm fine. I've been fine."

"Everything alright at home?"

"Dr.Hershey, I'm fine, everything is fine, only Thomas is dead, and I have no idea why I triggered the alarm that ended up leading to him being killed."

"I'm sorry Lucas, but I had to ask. Have you eaten anything you don't normally eat?"

"What? You think someone spiked my potato?" Lucas replied sarcastically.

"I have to ask these questions," Hershey asserted. Lucas let out a sigh and nodded. Hershey continued, "Did you meet anyone, any strangers, did they give you anything?"

"No," Lucas replied, his frustration now evident. "Everything was as it should have been. I follow routines, I'm a routine man. We bought the same food, from the same shops, the way we like it. I drove to work around the same time I always do when I'm working that shift, in the same beaten up old car. I parked in the same spot, went to the canteen, ordered the sausage and mash a meal I must have had a hundred times. I sat down just before shift was due to start and chatted to April for a few minutes before starting. How many other ways can I say it. Everything was normal."

"You were talking with April before your shift started?"

"Yes, as I have done many times. She's a wonderful kid, I enjoy her company and feel for her stuck in that place. We just talked for a bit and I left to start my shift."

Hershey brought her cup to her lips. "How do you feel about returning to work?"

Lucas thought for a moment. Calming down he said, "I'm okay, I'll talk to Sandra. If it's alright, I'll skip tonight and start up again tomorrow. Is the hospital alright with me returning? You don't think I'm on drugs or anything?"

Hershey smiled, "No, I don't think you're on drugs. But you should go see Kutznova, I'll clear it with the hospital, but you should assume starting back tomorrow will be fine."

Hershey finished her coffee and got up to leave. As she got to the door she noticed a drawing on a sideboard,

"Did Katie do that?" Hershey asked, referring to Lucas' daughter.

"No, April gave it to me yesterday. Said it created an optical illusion if you look at it closely and move it side to side or something. Think she said her friend, Emily, had given it to her. I brought it home for Katie to try."

The picture was of a bright yellow bell with the clapper extending just off-centre from the base.

* * * *

Later, Hershey returned to the hospital. She dropped by to see Terry Nichols the Supervisor for the Orca Ward. He was playing cards with another member of staff in the small Orca common room. The patients in Orca were allowed to use the common room, under supervision, for up to three hours a day. Most of the time the patients would come into the room in the evenings, making sure they caught the news and stayed up to date with current affairs, and for a short time they would follow their own high-profile cases before public interest moved on.

While in the Ward, Hershey became aware that she had been tapping the index finger on her right hand against the thumb. Jones was also close by. Jones was a sexual predator, a rapist and a killer. *Why had he taken an interest in her?*

Nichols was a large man, six-five Hershey estimated, but not overly fat and probably confident of handling most of the patients that came his way. Hershey found him to be upbeat given recent events. He seemed more than happy to arrange her meeting with Alexander Jones. They agreed on two p.m. tomorrow.

From the Orca Ward, Hershey went to find April Pritchard. She was eventually directed to April who was sitting under cover in the gardens. The air was cool and damp with only a slight breeze. April was reading a book of poems.

"Hi April, I thought I'd come and see you while I was here. I wanted to ask you something. Would it be okay for me to talk to Professor McGill about your stay here? I mean, perhaps there is somewhere more suitable for you to stay, somewhere nicer, more of a home. What do you think?"

"I'd like that very much Elizabeth. I don't like it here. Not that the staff and even some of the patients aren't nice to me, they are, but…I miss having friends, I miss playing in the park." April looked at Hershey being sure to make eye contact, "I miss being in a family.'

"Let me talk to the Professor and see what we can do. April?"

"Yes?"

"That picture you gave to Lucas, the bell, did you draw it?"

"Yes. It was something Emily showed me how to draw, she said I should give it to Lucas."

"Does Emily know Lucas?"

"I don't think so, only what I have told her about him. She thinks he sounds like a nice man. He is a nice man Dr.Hershey, sorry Elizabeth.'

"Do you know it was Lucas that set off the fire alarm last night?"

"No." April replied, the upward inflection apparent in the word. "He won't get into any trouble, will he?"

"No, I don't think so. I think he'll be alright, it's just...Lucas doesn't remember setting the alarm off."

"That is strange. Why wouldn't he remember setting the alarm off?"

"I'm not sure," Hershey wondered. "Do you see Emily a lot?"

"She visits me most weeks. We chat online as well. She shares some of her studies with me. I don't understand all of it though. Is everything alright Elizabeth? Is there something wrong?"

"Yes, I'm sure everything is fine." Hershey smiled.

By the time Hershey had left April, McGill had already left for the day. Thinking through her options, Hershey decided on returning home. Grey clouds were forming as day gave way to night. Light rain had started to fall during the drive back to Vancouver.

At home, Hershey kicked off her shoes at the door, dropped her bag and placed her coat on the stand. She made her way to the kitchen and opened the fridge door before realising she hadn't made it out shopping in the last few days. A diet of fresh organic vegetables and meat demanded regular visits to the markets. There was little of either in the fridge. A dragon fruit sat on a shelf looking past its best. Hershey checked the clock but couldn't summon the desire for either shopping or cooking. Picking up her cell she scanned through her contacts. She dialled Munroe's number.

After calling Munroe, Hershey showered and changed. She stood for a moment looking at herself in the long mirror. She knew she was attractive. Tall enough for the catwalk, her full brown hair framed her large brown eyes, sculptured eyebrows, rounded cheeks with their slightly high set bones. Her nose narrow and her lips full. The casual green top she had thrown on sat at the edges of her smooth rounded shoulders, her skin looked tanned but in truth the colour stems from her South American heritage. She had a full bosom and her lines curved in at the waist before extending back out over her hips. Hershey placed a hand on her flat stomach and turned to the side, still looking at her profile in the mirror. From her hips, her long lean legs tapered down to her feet. The blue jeans she had put on felt comfortable and reassured her that the hours spent in the fitness room were worth it. *Why I am still single?* she thought. *Am I ready for a relationship?*

Refreshed, she headed out to meet Munroe at the Italian they had visited before. She put the Jaguar in the garage and drove the 3-series. By the time she arrived, Munroe was already sat at a table. Munroe stood to greet her and offered his hand. Instead, Hershey gave him a polite kiss to the cheek.

"You change your car?" Munroe asked.

"Er...no. This one is mine, the other one was a gift from my father. I thought, you know, it's a bit older and well, a bit plain."

Munroe smiled and nodded in understanding. "You wanted to appear normal but instead you have advertised that you actually own two luxury cars."

For a moment Hershey was quizzical, unsure how to respond. Munroe was still smiling. "If its any consolation and I meant it as a compliment, you are *not* normal," Munroe added.

Hershey gave a polite laugh, still unsure if she was being paid a compliment or being insulted. She gestured to the seats and sat down.

"Thank you for seeing me, and at such short notice," Hershey said.

"Well I don't have any serial killers to catch, so I'm enjoying only working twelve-hour days," Munroe replied.

The host took their drinks order while they perused the menu. Hershey couldn't tell if Munroe was trying to be amusing, sarcastic or serious, but there was an air of humility to him that she found rare in many of the men she had met. She had noticed before how relaxed she felt in his presence and it was the same now. She wondered if it was because he was a Detective or simply because his imposing frame made her feel secure. She thought it must be more...he's simple, easy, *even if a bit odd*. The waiter returned with their drinks and they placed their orders.

"There have been a couple of deaths in the last few days at Ashford. My role is to investigate the deaths and submit my findings to the board. I realise that's not exactly front-page news but the nature of what happened is very odd. Do you mind if go I over what I know? Get your take so to speak."

"Sure, shoot."

"Four days ago, a patient named Donald McCoy was found dead in his room, apparently having committed suicide. Donald was a patient classified as *at risk* meaning someone who might cause harm to themselves. But in the past weeks he displayed no sign at all that he might injure, let alone kill, himself. He was under no medication and staff had no concerns. His death was unexpected. But that's not what is really bothering me, it's the *way* he died."

"Should I eat first?" Munroe asked.

"Sorry, please go ahead and I'll try to spare the detail but suffice to say I don't believe he could have killed himself in the way he did without some form of pain control. I checked with a friend of a mine, an M.E., and she agrees. The pain inflicted would have prevented Donald from completing what he did to himself. Tests confirmed his medical reports, he hadn't taken anything that could have enabled him to do what he did. It doesn't make sense."

"Okay. Your friend, the Medical Examiner, she said it couldn't be done or that is was unlikely?" Munroe asked.

"Highly unlikely," Hershey confirmed.

"So, it is possible. Just unlikely."

"High unlikely," Hershey repeated.

"You said a couple of deaths." Munro said.

"Yes, another last night. The death itself is clear but the circumstances leading up to it certainly aren't. The fire alarm was activated by a guard who was behaving like he'd seen a blaze, but there was no fire and the guard can't remember anything about it. The fire alarm lead to a breach in security enabling our friend Edward Walker to get away from his cell. He ended up killing a nurse before being recaptured."

An image of Edward Walker as he stood at the doorway moments before his arrest, entered Munroe's mind, then followed images of the appalling photos taken from around the house and the mutilated remains of his victims that had been later discovered. Munroe swallowed and resisted the urge to ask how a fire alarm could lead to someone like Edward Walker getting free.

"The guard...drinking, drugs?" Munroe asked.

Hershey looked at him, "This was probably a bad idea. I'm sorry..."

"Hey no," Munroe interjected holding his hands upward, "I'm sorry. I'm too used to having to ask the dumb questions. Sorry please go on. I assume you have a theory?"

Munroe knew Hershey didn't get him here simply to tell a story or ask for his opinion. She wanted something.

"I'm not one for coincidences, but I think there may be a connection between the two deaths and the events surrounding them. This might sound a little crazy. There's a young girl at the hospital, she's very sweet, very likeable and *very* intelligent. I don't think she should be at the hospital, but she has had a difficult past and we still need to sort something out for her. Anyway, the girl, April..."

"Pritchard? April Pritchard?" Munroe interrupted again.

"Yes, you know her?"

"Yeah, killed her adopted parents in her sleep. How'd she end up at Ashford?'

"That's another story, she's not been there that long, just a few months. April had been talking to Donald on the day he died, and she had also been talking with the guard the night he set the fire alarm off."

Munroe moved his hands as if it say, '*So*'

"April gave the guard a drawing of a bell just hours before the alarm went off," Hershey continued.

"Are you trying to tell me you think April Pritchard is behind the deaths?' Munroe asked.

"I think she is somehow involved, but I don't think she realises it. April has a regular visitor from the university, a student named Emily Jackson. Emily is studying neuro-psychology and I know she has a keen interest in brain-behaviour relationships. I'm concerned that she could be using April to exert some form of control over people. I don't really know as none of this makes much sense."

"I'm not sure I'm following. You think that someone was able to convince one of the patients to kill themselves, and that the same person was behind the guard acting irrationally that then lead to another death? And you think this someone may be this Emily Jackson? Why would anyone do that? What's the motivation?"

"I realise it's a bizarre notion, but I've been playing this stuff through, over and over. I don't know why. Maybe it's some kind of experiment? I don't know. But what is the alternative?"

"If Donald was feeling down isn't it a little possible he could have killed himself?" Munroe asked.

Hershey leant forward, "He sat on the edge of his bed and calmly stuck two forks through his eyes and into the back of his head."

Munroe looked around the restaurant, they had attracted a few stares.

"Sorry." Hershey apologised. "No, I don't believe he could have done it without some form of pain control, nothing of which showed in his tox report."

"Could he have been on some form of drug that they didn't pick up? Not shown on his records." Munroe asked.

"Yes, that is possible, but to do what he did, Donald would have to have been feeling very suicidal, *and* taking pain control drugs, but still lucid enough to sneak two forks from the canteen to use on himself later. How does *that* make any sense?"

Munroe held his palms up, "Okay, so Donald didn't willing kill himself, so someone else was involved. But you say he couldn't have done it without pain meds?"

"Hypnosis has been used as an anaesthetic in surgery since the eighteen-hundreds - I think it may have been possible for Donald to have," Hershey glanced around, "done what he did, if he was under some form of hypnosis."

"Okay," Munroe responded, "The Security Guard, how does a picture of a bell make someone trigger a fire alarm?"

Hershey sighed, "I have no idea. Hypnosis can be used to implant suggestions, even instructions into someone's subconscious. It can be used to create relationships between an action or what is called an anchor, and the instruction. You must have seen the shows, put someone under, give them an instruction to remove their clothes when they see a specific word or something, bring them back up, show them the word and there you have it – a striptease."

"Yeah, but I don't really believe that stuff, and besides, I thought they at least had to be willing participants, highly suggestible or something," Munroe said.

Hershey nodded in agreement, "I think Donald and the guard may have been given to suggestion, but still, this would go way over anything I've heard of. I just think something is *off* and I am concerned that April may be in harm's way."

They sat in silence, looking down at their food, moving their forks around on the plate as if the answer would eventually be revealed.

"So, what can I do?" Munroe finally asked.

"I want to know more about Emily Jackson, what she does at the UBC, who she hangs-around with, what she does in her free time, that kind of thing."

"You really think she's involved?"

"There is nothing else to go on. No other scenarios make sense. If there is nothing, then at least I'll be able to sleep a bit easier. Please, could you take a look?" Hershey asked.

"You do know if we start looking into this Emily, and you are right, and she is involved, she could easily find out she's being investigated. That may point her to you. Are you comfortable with that?"

"I don't know what else to do. If I am right I can't see things ending here. She'll get bolder, try more things, try different things. And there's April to consider."

"Let me see what I can find out. I'll make a few enquiries," Munroe confirmed.

Hershey had got what she had wanted, and Munroe couldn't help feeling that he may have just been manipulated. They enjoyed the rest of the meal and lighter conversation before leaving the restaurant, in their separate cars.

CHAPTER 11

The following day, Hershey made the drive back to Ashford for her meeting with Alexander Jones. She arrived at the Orca Ward where she was greeted by Nichols.

"The room is just down here on the left," Nichols said. "Protocol is to wait until you are ready before bringing them out. Make yourself comfortable. We'll bring him in shortly. He'll be secured obviously, and a guard will remain in the room with you. He still insists on walking with a crutch while his leg heals, it'll be taken from him before entering the room. Please," Nichols opened the door and gestured for Hershey to go in, "we won't keep you a moment."

Hershey entered the room. Given the dozens of interviews she had conducted over the years, the routine was a familiar one. She briefly scanned the room; table bolted to the floor as was the chair nearest the door, the chair on the opposite side of the table was not secured. A water cooler stood in one corner with a stack of paper cups, above it a security camera twitched. The small green LED meant it was recording. Hershey sat on the chair farthest from the door. She had left her handbag at reception on the way in, preferring to keep it with the ladies rather than have any of the other guards keeping hold of it.

Hershey was very familiar with Alexander's history. He had a penchant for young and underage girls, a violent sexual predator driven by the urge to control and inflict his own will upon others. He had graduated from sexual assault, to rape, kidnapping and murder. His parents had divorced when Alexander was six years old. His mother was by all accounts a cruel woman. Alexander's wealth came from inheriting his father's lottery win, having died from a heart attack when Alexander was eighteen.

Alexander Jones soon became known to local Police. When the disappearances of younger girls started to occur, Police naturally investigated Alexander. When bodies started to be discovered, Alexander's alibi appeared water tight. At the time of at least two of the murders Alexander was said to have been with some older girls. Only as the number of bodies and disappearances piled up did the girls later retract their statements, saying Alexander had paid them to provide his alibi. Alexander brutally tortured, raped, and killed at least sixteen teenage girls.

The door opened, and Alexander Jones was escorted, chained and handcuffed, into the room. He was an inch over six feet tall with a lean muscular build and broad shoulders. His skin was white and unblemished, and he had piercing blue eyes, and fair shoulder length hair. His appearance was almost albino like were it not for the deep colour in his eyes and the yellow hue to his hair. His teeth were white and polished; the dollars spent on his grooming had not been wasted. In another world Hershey might have found him attractive, but in this one she was repulsed by him. Hershey felt herself shift her knees away from the side that Alexander approached.

"It's so nice to meet you Dr.Hershey," Alexander said as the guards secured him to the chair. The chains clinked as smiling he offered Hershey his hand. Not expecting a response, he looked Hershey up and down. "May I say dressing down is really not your style. Your hair is better down, loose, and jackets really do nothing for you. You should take it off, celebrate your female lines."

"I'm not here for advice on my appearance Mr Jones, what is it you wanted to discuss?" Hershey replied, her tone calm but firm.

"Alexander please. No one calls me Mr Jones unless they want money from me. Do you want money from me, Dr.Hershey?" Alexander paused before continuing, "I wanted to see you, see if there's anything I might be able to do for you. I'm hurt you haven't shown an interest me. I have many admirers, many of your professional colleagues visit me, I think they want to know where my charm comes from."

"I have no interest in you," Hershey replied.

"Oh, but you have, you're here now."

"What is it you want?" Hershey asked again.

"I have something I'd like to share with you, but we must be alone, he can't hear," Alexander pushed his nose at the guard.

Hershey looked at the guard stood in the corner of the room. Glancing at Alexander's chains she looked back at the guard and nodded. The guard shrugged his shoulders, as if to say, '*Your funeral*', and left the room. Hershey kept watching as the door closed, the guard remained, looking in through the window in the door.

"Okay, so what do you want to share with me?" Hershey asked, turning her attention back to Alexander.

"Ooooh...not so fast. These women in their fast cars and power suits, all work and no foreplay."

Hershey took a moment to calm her breathing. "I'm not here to play your games. Tell me something that isn't bullshit or I'm out of here."

Alexander sat staring at her. Hershey was about to get up when he said, "There's another one."

Hershey relaxed and turned her shoulders back toward Alexander. He had her attention. "Another what?" Hershey asked.

"There's another girl, a pretty little girl, although I can't imagine she looks too good now, but I'm sure her parents must be worried about her, wondering where their little girl has been all this time."

"You know of another girl?'

"I should do, she was one of mine," Alexander responded, grinning now.

"Not one of the sixteen?" Hershey asked.

"One of the seventeen actually. The police never asked and so I never said. I always thought the information might be useful for something, but I've had no real use for it, until now..."

"Are you saying you can point us to another victim?"

"Ebony Wilkes, beautiful Ebony Wilkes, a very fine little black girl."

Hershey paused before asking her next question. "And why are you telling me. What is it you want for this information?"

"I have two requests, one for a couple of friends of mine and one all of my own. I'll tell you where little Ebony is lying, and you have to arrange for me and my friends here to spend the day shooting pool, watching our own selection of movies, and drinking beer - that kind of thing. That's not too much to ask is it?" Alexander replied.

"And what is the other request?"

"Well, that's a little delicate, but I'm afraid essential to our deal. It's not negotiable. If you want to recover Ebony's little body and return her to her parents for a more traditional burial, *you* have to remove your clothes and let me look at you, naked, for say, thirty seconds. Can you do that Elizabeth? For little Ebony?"

"You're pathetic," she said as she got up. Raising her hand, the guard opened the door and entered the room. As soon as the guard was stood next to Alexander, Hershey walked around the table and left the room. As the door closed she could hear Alexander laughing behind her.

"Get him back in his cell," Hershey said, as she walked passed a guard stood just outside. Nichols came from the Common Room but was too slow to catch Hershey before she left the ward.

Hershey walked quickly, her flats making a noise as she walked despite the soft leather soles. She soon found herself pacing up and down in the gardens. A light rain was falling but she didn't seem to notice. *The bastard.* She was sure Alexander was just toying with her, but she couldn't take the chance. Taking out her cell phone, she called Munroe.

"It's Elizabeth…I have another favour I need to ask, I've just come from a meeting with Alexander Jones…yeah, the one and the same, he's given me the name of another victim, one unknown to the investigators…he said the victim's name was Ebony Wilkes…no, I didn't, I…I had to leave the room before I could ask him. Can you do a search for me, let me know what comes up? Thanks…Yeah, I'm fine…Munroe?...Thanks."

Hershey swiped her phone and continued pacing up and down, trying to calm herself down. *The asshole is jerking me around. McGill was right. But what if he wasn't? What if there was another?* Photos of some of Alexander's victims flashed through Hershey's mind. She used her hand to wipe a tear that had escaped her eye. She then noticed the slight trembling in her hand. She forced herself to stop pacing and took in deep breaths through her nostrils. She tried to clear her mind, think of something else. Her mind wandered. She was soon thinking of April, she had wanted to discuss April's situation with McGill, she wanted to help April. After another couple of minutes, she went back in and asked at reception if McGill was available.

* * * *

McGill wasn't free straight away, so Hershey had time to grab a coffee from the café. She also grabbed one for McGill together with a chocolate chip cookie she thought they could share. As she arrived at his office, Beverley Cordell was just leaving. Beverley smiled and held the door open as Hershey went in.

"Here you go two sugars and chocolate sprinkles just as you like it. Here, thought you might like this too," she said handing him the cookie, "I'll help you with it if you like."

"Thank you, Elizabeth, we were just deciding what to do with Rose Patterson, and Becker and Marshall. Feels like if we fire the lot of them I'll have no staff left. Beverley has arranged a support programme for Patterson, assuming she checks out alright she can return to work, but she'll be under close supervision. Becker and Marshall have received formal cautions. They said they acted in response to what they were hearing over the radio. We're not sure if Marshall will come back to work, he seems pretty shaken by it all. How is Lucas Vogel?"

"I met with Lucas yesterday. He has no recollection as to what happened. I don't believe he is taking drugs or medication of any kind and I don't think it's likely to happen again. I said we'd be happy for him to return to work, but suggested he see Dr.Kutznova. Lucas is feeling at least some of the guilt for Thomas Bessey's death."

"He couldn't have seen anything like that happening even if he knew what he was doing."

"That's what I said," Hershey replied.

McGill smiled, "So, did you get to see Alexander?"

"I did, but I want to talk to you about April Pritchard before we get into that."

McGill raised his eyebrows and looked over his glasses at Hershey. "Sure, what is it?" he finally said.

Hershey sat down. "I'm concerned for April. I think that keeping her here may be doing her more harm than good. I don't think this environment is right for her. Since arriving she has shown no sign of sleepwalking, and I'm wondering how long she should be kept here before an alternative is found."

McGill also sat down and dipping part of the cookie into his drink said, "Elizabeth, we do everything we can for her here. We treat her as a guest, but you are right, this isn't where she should be growing up. The problem is, it wasn't too long ago that she killed her parents and that unfortunate incident at the UBC is still recent by anyone's measure. The board are going to want more time."

"You've already enquired?" Hershey asked.

McGill nodded, "Last week. They've suggested a further two months and then an evaluation. Assuming no problems, they'll sanction a move."

"What if I told you she could be in danger? Being unduly influenced at least?"

"By someone at the hospital?" McGill asked, looking over his glasses again.

"Not exactly, she has a visitor, a student from the university."

"How would a move away from here make a difference to the visitor?" McGill asked.

Hershey had thought of that but hadn't come up with an answer.

McGill wanted to sound more supportive. "Listen, I'm looking into it. Perhaps if I threw in your support to the board they might bring things forward, but I think we need to offer them something. I find decisions are made much easier if options are provided. Where do we want April to go?"

Hershey's phone began to vibrate, "Sorry Charles, I'm expecting a call from the police department." It was Munroe.

"I have some information for you on Ebony Wilkes. It seems she disappeared almost eight years ago from the Richmond area, never been found despite an extensive search. Says here, it was unlikely she went missing voluntarily, good family relationships, well liked, a good student, no prior history. She had just turned fourteen at the time she went missing. It is possible Jones might be telling the truth. What we need is something from him that proves he must have been with her – get him to describe what she was wearing the day she disappeared for example. I looked for some things that most likely would not have been reported anywhere. Ebony had a small scar from where her appendix had been removed, and she was wearing a gold dolphin on a necklace that she had just been given as a birthday gift. I take it he didn't just choose to tell you this? He wants something?"

"Yeah, he wants something," Hershey replied.

Munroe didn't press the point any further. "Is he likely to talk to us?"

"I doubt it," she replied, *not unless you grow some breasts*, she thought.

"I recall the period, it was around the time bodies of some of his victims started turning up. Not my case, but you can imagine it dominated everything for a while back then. You need to get back in there, get confirmation, find out where he left the body."

"Right. Thanks," Hershey replied, her voice tailing off as she felt as if a hole had opened up inside her stomach.

Hershey ended the call and stared at McGill.

"What? Are you okay Elizabeth?" urged McGill.

"Alexander knows of another body, Ebony Wilkes, a seventeenth victim who went missing in Richmond just prior to his capture. Investigators didn't connect her disappearance to Jones."

McGill sat forward and ran his hand through his beard. "I take it he hasn't told you where the body is?"

"No. He has a couple of demands before he'll tell us."

Hershey then relayed Alexander's two requests.

"I can arrange the first request easy enough. What about the second?" McGill said. McGill stood, "That son of a bitch still tries to be the one in control. I'm sorry Elizabeth." McGill now ran his hand over his balding head. "He needs to prove he knows where she is before this goes any further." He let out an audible sigh. "What will you do?"

* * * *

Hershey took the afternoon off. Driving home she played things over in her mind trying to think of a way out. She was reminded of an incident at secondary school when she was fourteen years old when some boys from another school sprang upon her and took her clarinet. They demanded she unbutton her top and show her tits before they would return the instrument. She still felt ashamed how easily she did as they asked, and the thought of taking her clothes off for Alexander to simply look and gawk at her, like those adolescent boys, made her feel physically sick. *But how could I refuse? The Wilkes family, likely fearing that Ebony was dead, would still surely be clinging to the hope that they might one day see her alive. If she refused Alexander's request, could they tell the family Ebony was in fact dead, killed by that maniac, but then tell them they don't know where she's buried? Is removing her clothes really such a big deal?* At this moment, only she and McGill knew of the details of the request, and McGill had made it clear it was her choice, her decision. She had felt his sympathy – she didn't think he'd tell

Henebury

anyone if she chose not to go ahead with it. But *she* would still know. *And what if Alexander ended up revealing how he had offered to tell her?*

At home Hershey was without an appetite. Her home felt large, cold and suddenly a lonely place to be. She had hardened herself against any long-term relationships choosing instead to invest her time and energy into studying and the pursuit of her career. She went up stairs to run the bath.

Turning the taps off, Hershey sat wrapped in a white towel on the edge of the bath. Steam rose from the bath water and condensed upon reaching her exposed shoulders. She sat considering her life, her achievements, her loneliness. Tears welled within her eyes until eventually one tear broke free and fell to her thigh. The tear seemed to fall in slow-motion before exploding as it made contact with the skin below. Underneath the damp patch was a small almost forgotten scar. Thoughts flashed back to when she was nine years old. She had gone to the kitchen to pour her mom a glass of water. Her mother had been sitting in the back garden enjoying the early summer sun. Elizabeth took a glass from the cupboard and began pouring chilled water from a bottle she had taken from the fridge, when her mother let out a strained cry for her daughter. Elizabeth dropped the bottle of water and ran to the garden catching her thigh on a screw that protruded slightly from the patio door frame. But she hadn't noticed the small tear in her leg. Elizabeth arrived in the garden to see her mother collapse to the ground, clutching her chest, pain etched on her face, and her eyes expressing both fear and sorrow. Her father had been away on business and she recalled that deep sense of loneliness and helplessness as her mother was fading away. She remembered how fear gave way to action and Elizabeth rushed to dial 911 and ran to neighbours for more immediate help. Her actions saved her mothers life.

"You may *be* alone Elizabeth but you're not alone," she whispered to herself, wiping the tears. She allowed the towel to drop to the floor and entered the bath. As she lay there in the hot fragrant waters, part of her hoped Alexander was bluffing, that he knew nothing of Ebony's whereabouts, but then guilt returned – *of course I would want Ebony found.* She also knew Alexander wasn't lying, she sensed it. It seemed all her life she had been living with the aim of helping others, if not able to cure people then ensuring they received proper care, and here she was presented with an opportunity to help heal the open wounds of an entire family. She would not withdraw simply because of feelings for herself. She was not about to become selfish. That bastard Alexander was not in control. She could do what he wanted and if it meant getting some closure for the Wilkes family, she would choose to do it. It was her choice.

She imagined a fourteen-year old girl, *Ebony leaving school one afternoon with her friends. As the girl wandered home, a fancy car pulls up and offers her a ride home. It's an expensive sports car, and the young man inside is handsome and known to many of the girls at the school. The girl was flattered and curious. He spoke to her, told her she was beautiful, that when she got older he would really want to know her. She stands on the side of the road, debating within herself – he was too old, and she was too young, but he only wanted to talk – she got into the car. Police and volunteers searching the area, her parents putting posters in shops, on lampposts, photos in the newspapers. The years going by, no word, no contact, no news, just the thread of hope of being reunited with their daughter in someway, any way.*

Hershey's mind was set, her decision made. After her bath, the afternoon wearing on, and evening approaching, she phoned McGill – *"I'm going to do it, let's set it up. First, we have to know he's not lying, only then does he get what he wants."*

* * * *

The next day Hershey arrived at the Hospital forty minutes before her meeting with Alexander. McGill had made time, rearranging a couple of meetings, so he could have coffee with her. Hershey had earlier phoned Munroe to let him know she would be talking again to Alexander, but she still hadn't revealed to Munroe the conditions. Munroe wanted to send an officer to accompany her, but she thought she might lose Alexander's cooperation – *if that is what it could be called* – and besides they had nothing more as yet to suggest Alexander wasn't just lying to them.

"Please take him in, I'll be in momentarily," Hershey said to Nichols. Nichols expression straightened, but then he nodded. Hershey waited a moment after Nichols had left the office, then she opened the door and walked to the ladies washroom.

Hershey went over to one of the sinks, checking the mirrors to see if any of the stalls might be occupied. She was alone. She turned the cold tap and let it run a few seconds before taking a couple of paper towels. She damped the towels under the water and wiped her face. Dabbing her forehead and wiping down each side of her nose. She looked in the mirror at herself, breathing, one breath, then another, then a deeper, longer breath. Tossing the towels into the recycling she left the washroom.

Hershey entered the meeting room.

Grinning Alexander said, "I take it you have been considering my generous offer?"

"We need proof before you get anything?"

"Of course, you do, you don't trust me do you Elizabeth?"

"We know Ebony Wilkes went missing almost eight years ago from the Richmond area. We know you were in the area around that time, you were arrested at your home in Delta a few months later. So, what can you tell me that will make me believe you know where she is?"

Alexander smiled, then took a deep breath and expelled the air from his lungs. He tilted his head back and slowly closed his eyes. He stayed with his eyes closed and head back, held his breath for a few seconds, then slowly returned his head and opened his eyes. He stared at Hershey but his expression had changed, the smile gone and his eyes vacant.

"She was with two friends from her class, walking through the park near her school. I stood against a tree. As they approached I waved my keys and a CD I was holding. They laughed, I knew them. I had been with the two friends but not yet with Ebony, she remained untouched. Now it was her turn. I pointed to Ebony. She was wearing her school uniform, a white blouse and blue skirt. She was holding her books and a folder, and had a green bag hung over her shoulder. She walked towards me and took the CD from my hand. There's always a part of someone that communicates more than what is said, to tease, to give clues about one's real thoughts, but Ebony didn't get it, she wasn't listening. Ebony only saw an attractive slightly older man, who drove a car and enjoyed a good time. Do you read the signs Elizabeth?" Alexander paused but Hershey gave no response. Alexander continued, "We walked from the park to my car. She put the CD into the player and we drove off. We went to my home. I parked up on the driveway, switched the engine off. I gently stroked her thigh and kissed her on the cheek, but I could tell she was having second thoughts. *'It's* okay' I whispered, *'I'll take care of you'* I lied. I took her inside, she started to cry."

Alexander closed his eyes and breathed in deeply through his nostrils. "Ah the sweet smell of her hair." Still with his eyes closed, Alexander rubbed his thumb and index fingers together, "The softness, like silk."

Alexander suddenly opened his eyes, staring straight at Hershey, "My mother would wash herself, dry and brush her hair, even brush her teeth, before entering my room where I would be asleep. I was perhaps four, may be five, likely both. She'd come into my bedroom smelling of fresh scent, her hair soft and smooth. I would awaken with her touching me. If I cried I knew she would pinch me, scratch me, beat me, perhaps all three. You see my mother was what one might call a fucking bitch. She left before I could rip her eyes from her head."

Alexander closed his eyes again. "After I had finished with her little body, I drove off. The body on the passenger seat, covered of course.

"Where did you take her?" asked Hershey

"Not so fast Elizabeth, only proof, not the location until you carry out my requests."

"You've given me no proof, Alexander."

"Oh come, come. Ask the girls with her on that day. I'm somewhat surprised they never said anything. I must have made a lasting impression on them. Go ask Rachel I think one of them was called, Rachel Bridges that's it. Oh, and I guess I can tell you, that cute little golden dolphin she was wearing, I kept that with her body, it should still be around her neck, though I imagine it's a little loose for her now."

Hershey got up to leave.

"And Elizabeth," Hershey turned to see Alexander grinning, "please wear red, it's my favourite colour."

* * * *

Hershey relayed the details of the meeting to both Munroe and McGill. The reference to the dolphin necklace was almost as good as proof that Alexander had at least seen Ebony the day she disappeared. Hershey told Munroe of Alexander's request for the three Orca patients to be given leisure time but held back on Alexander's request for a private striptease. Munroe seemed surprised that was all Jones was asking for and asked McGill to make the arrangements. He offered assistance from the VPD to help with supervision. He also wanted to present when Jones gave up the location of Ebony Wilkes' body. In the meantime, Munroe said he would follow up on the Rachel Bridges lead. Later that day, McGill contacted both Munroe and Hershey to confirm arrangements had been made per Alexander's request. McGill asked Hershey if she was ready and still wanted to go through with Alexander's other request. 'I'm ready,' Hershey had confirmed.

Hershey treated herself to the next two days off. She called a friend who lived in Seattle and arranged to meet up for a meal before heading to see the

Ballet at the Paramount Theatre – only VIP tickets were left, but Hershey felt she needed the time away and she knew her friend would be delighted. Grabbing some items for an overnight bag, she grabbed the keys to the Jag and headed off.

* * * *

Frank Marshall sat alone in his living room, the large bottle of whiskey stood empty on his low pine coffee table, his firearm beside it. Though seemingly staring at the table, Frank could only see Thomas Bessey's body laying in a bloody mess on the hospital floor, his body twisted and lifeless. He could hear echoes of Alexander laughing at him – *'You got him killed Frankie boy! Should'a kept us in our cells. You really screwed up Frankie boy! Now whatcha goin' to do Frankie boy, you worthless piece of shit?'*

The vision blurred, and Frank was looking at the table once again. The empty bottle and then at the photo that stood in a cheap frame on the table. A picture of his wife and daughter – his ex-wife and the daughter he hadn't seen in years. In his mind Alexander was still talking – *'You're a useless spineless son of bitch, you might hold the keys, but you do what I say, you dance to my tune Frankie boy, no wonder your wife left ya, you're useless Frankie boy, good for nothin' Frankie Boy.'*

The next voice Frank heard was Beverly Cordell confirming he was cleared to return to work but that he would be receiving a caution for not following procedure. *'You are welcome back at the Hospital Frank, but get some rest, take the rest of the week off'*, she said. Frank wouldn't be returning to work. Picking up the gun, he opened his mouth and inserted the barrel. A tear for Thomas Bessey ran down his cheek, then he pulled the trigger.

CHAPTER 12

McGill's week had not started well. He received a call at the weekend informing him of Frank Marshall's death. On Monday morning he received a call from Bernard Golding, Chairman of the Board for the British Columbia Provincial Health Service. As soon as McGill knew it was Golding he knew it was bad news. Questions were being asked about what was going on at Ashford. '*The board are becoming concerned, Charles, we expect losses in this line of work but events at the hospital over the last few weeks are less than satisfactory. A meeting has been scheduled next month, the Board want you to attend. We need to understand what's been going on and what proposals you are going to be putting in place.*' Perhaps the discovery of Ebony Wilkes' remains would win him and the hospital a few points with the board, but as McGill sat alone in his office he knew he was losing his desire to carry on. *Why am I doing this?* he thought. *Perhaps it is time to pass on the reins, give someone else a chance.*

Munroe had been in touch regarding Alexander's claims on Ebony Wilkes – they checked out. Munroe wanted to proceed with Alexander's request. McGill guessed Munroe knew nothing of the other item and he wasn't about to break the news. McGill called Nichols into the office and brought him up to speed on what had been going on, leaving the request concerning Hershey out of the conversation, at least for now. Nichols was still upset over the news about Frank Marshall, as were most of the other guards and staff members, but McGill pointed out that now they had the opportunity to do some good. Nichols took responsibility for making the arrangements. Hershey had told

McGill that both requests should be fulfilled on the same day; McGill had agreed she would be the one to confirm the date. She confirmed Thursday, three days from now.

* * * *

On Wednesday afternoon, Hershey met up again with April. Hershey had noted that Emily had not been to visit again in the last few days. They discussed the possibilities and options for transferring April from the hospital. Something April had said had given Hershey an idea. They played board games and cards, but Hershey's mind was considering the hand that life had dealt to April – *left abandoned by her own mother with no idea as to her own identity, eventually adopted but clearly disturbed, suffering from a sleep disorder that lead to the horrific deaths of her adopted parents and their unborn child, a brother* Hershey thought. *Tested like some curiosity within a system that was supposed to be caring for her. And now here she was, still surrounded by death, no family, no one to love her, what chance does she have?* Then Hershey found herself smiling a little as she looked again at April, *young, beautiful, and brilliant. If only she had someone to help her, guide her, love her.* April was showing Hershey some card tricks she had learned.

"What's wrong? Your thoughts seem distant?" April asked.

"Sorry, yes sweetheart I guess they are?" Hershey replied.

"Is something worrying you?"

"No, it's okay. I have to do something tomorrow I really don't want to do, but sometimes you don't really have a choice."

"Perhaps I can help? Can I do it for you?" April asked.

Hershey gently held April's face, "I believe you would, but this is something I have to do. I'll be fine and hopefully some good will come of it. You needn't worry about me, I'll be alright."

"I think you are trying to convince yourself of that."

"April, sometimes it is best to keep answers to yourself, sometimes others need to get the answers themselves'" Hershey replied, gently squeezing April's nose. "You are right though. I really don't want to do the thing tomorrow. I'll tell you what, how about after, I arrange for you and I to head out somewhere, maybe go to the park, have a great meal somewhere and take in a show, a girl's day out. Would you like that?"

"Very much," April replied.

"Alright, I'll and come see you tomorrow, I shouldn't be too late. I'll come and find you before lunch so don't get anything before I arrive. Tomorrow we eat out, my treat.'

Hershey got up to leave.

"Elizabeth?"

"Yes April?"

"Don't worry about tomorrow."

Hershey smiled, "Thank you April, I've had a lovely afternoon."

*   *   *   *

At Hershey's request, Munroe had run background checks on Emily Jackson. Emily shared an apartment with other students on the University's campus. She was studying neuro-psychology and was expected to graduate with flying colours. She already held degrees in mathematics and computing and was known to possess '*a detailed understanding of astronomy*'.

Munroe had arranged for a junior detective to visit the University with an emphasis on being discrete. Munroe didn't want Emily finding out that she was being investigated but putting someone on the campus would provide better insight into her routines, the people she meets and the places she attends.

Munroe had called the University himself to make enquiries about the content of the studies that Emily Jackson was taking. Her courses covered the function and role of the different regions of the brain, the effects of trauma and disease, hypnosis, psycho-therapy, and the relationship to external environmental influences. The detective performing surveillance had also learned that Emily Jackson also studied magic, mentalism and 'NLP' – Neuro-Linguistic Programming, something neither the detective or Munroe had ever heard of.

*   *   *

Thursday morning and Hershey had been awake most of the night. She tried to calm herself by thinking of the Wilkes family in a few days time when they could finally say goodbye to their daughter. Munroe had phoned while she was having breakfast with an update on Emily Jackson, they had been carrying out some surveillance on campus after eventually obtaining approval from the Dean. They hadn't told the Dean *who* they were interested in, only that it was important to their ongoing investigations into a homicide and that they needed his full cooperation. Munroe felt they were getting about half of it. For a few minutes Munroe shared the information they had gathered, often having to refer to notes he had made. Hershey knew the real reason for his call, it wasn't a coincidence that he had called this morning. Munroe wanted to discuss what would be happening at the hospital, he had insisted Detective Hale be onsite but assured her that he would keep a low profile. Munroe lingered on the phone, his instinct telling him there was something else. Hershey could still not bring herself to tell him what she had to do in order to secure the information they were after.

Hershey returned to her bedroom, removed her dressing gown and found herself once again looking into the full-length mirror at herself. She had invested time, money and a firm will into keeping fit and eating healthy, retaining her natural beauty and yet now as she stood looking at herself, she almost wished it all away. *Why me Alexander?* she wondered to herself. She knew he was not driven by desire but by control. Even now having been locked up for years you still crave control, control over someone, over me. Well you can have your five minutes and we can add another murder conviction and give Ebony's family some possibility of closure. As she got dressed she put on white matching underwear under a silky cream blouse, and an olive-green knee length skirt and matching jacket. Hershey left the house and drove to Ashford.

* * * *

The three patients would be taken to the Common Room at the Cavendish Ward. The room was larger than that of the Orca Ward and already contained a number of the items and games Alexander had stated in his request. They would be escorted across to the room at ten-thirty a.m., after Alexander had seen Hershey. Many of the patients in the Cavendish Ward, possessing severe mental disorders but not considered a danger to others, would be going on a day trip. McGill had been able to make arrangements for a special visit to the Greater Vancouver Zoo, and additional staff had been drafted in to assist. McGill however would be remaining at the hospital, he was taking a personal interest in events there.

Detective Hale arrived and after an initial meeting with McGill and Nichols he looked over the room and the security measures that were in place. Hershey arrived later, ten minutes before her appointment with Alexander.

As Alexander was being moved from his cell to the secure room, Hershey came from the washroom connected to McGill's office. McGill escorted her to the Orca Ward. Still the Police were kept in the dark about Alexander's personal request.

"Usual procedure, Alexander will be chained and secured to the chair. He won't be able to touch you in anyway. A guard will be posted outside the room but as far as anyone is aware you're simply going in to talk to him. If Alexander talks about it, and he probably will, people will most likely think he's made it up, he is crazy after all." McGill tried to assure Hershey.

Hershey wondered about that. *What is crazy? Are we to believe he doesn't know what he's doing? Are we really smarter than he is? Who is controlling whom?*

"What about the camera?" Hershey asked.

"We should keep it on Elizabeth," McGill replied.

"What so the guards can get off on it later?"

"We can shut it off if you insist but I advise against it. I'll take possession of the file recording after the session if you like and I can keep anyone else from it."

Hershey gave McGill a look. She knew the guards would be aware of Alexander's personal request from the previous sessions. If they were given the opportunity, they would certainly view the session and probably make copies.

"Only you and Hale in the office, and after you get that recording, I'd like it please. You going to tell Detective Hale?" Hershey asked.

"Elizabeth, you know as well as I do, if Alexander gives up the information then the police will want to retain the original. You know policy requires me to keep a copy for the hospital records. You can have a copy of course and I promise the hospital copy will be kept secure," McGill responded, looking for Hershey's concession. "Yes, I'll advise Detective Hale of what is going on once we are in the office."

Detective Hale was with Nichols at the Security Office in the Orca Ward following his review of the preparations. McGill had asked them to meet him there. Once McGill and Hershey reached the office, McGill asked Nichols to leave the office for a moment while they discussed an item with Detective Hale. In the office, McGill closed the door and informed Hale of Alexander's personal request.

"He's a bastard," Hale stated, shaking his head. "Does Munroe know?"

Hershey shook her head.

"He needs to know. Perhaps you should tell him," Hale said. "And hey, for what it's worth...I think it's brave what you are doing."

Hershey gave a token smile and left the room. Nichols was just outside the office. "I'm ready, let's go, you'll be outside on this one?" Hershey asked, knowing the answer.

"Seems I'm always on the outside today," Nichols muttered.

Hershey entered the room.

* * * *

"Hello Elizabeth, so pleased to...see you. I'd offer my hand but it's a little awkward." Alexander rattled the chains around his hands.

Hershey looked him in the eye. "Please no need to get up," Hershey replied, walking without hesitation to her chair. She took of her jacket, placing it over the chair before sitting down. She held her chin up and tried to calm her breathing with gentle measured breaths, hoping Alexander would not be able to notice. She looked up at the clock on the wall. *He was going to give up vital information, incriminating information, I simply had to undress.*

"All right Alexander, you get your thirty seconds. You get what you want, you get to look and then you get some time with the boys. Then you tell us where Ebony is. You should be aware that failure to keep your end of the bargain will ensure you lose all your privileges, your access to the showers, your fan mail, news papers and your internet access, and all those other things you have been buying."

Alexander smiled, "Of course, but I'm a man of my word Elizabeth, you can trust me to…come good. Now if you don't mind, I believe we both understand, I believe you have something to show me."

Hershey could feel herself start to tremble as she stood and started to unbutton her blouse, her fingers stumbling at the buttons.

"Thirty seconds from when you've finished undressing Elizabeth, so take as *long* as you like."

McGill and Hale watched on the monitor as Hershey began undressing, Hershey's distress visible – "*Sick bastard!*" Hale shouted at the monitor.

The blouse dropped from her shoulders and on to the floor. Hershey then unzipped her skirt and let it fall. McGill looked away from the monitor.

"Very good Elizabeth, your body does you credit. Odd that you would take so much care with your body and yet you remain single. Seems a shame, almost a crime not be sharing yourself with someone Elizabeth."

Hershey stood in her underwear, her courage wavering.

"Your underwear Elizabeth, I want to see you all. And I note your reluctance to wear red, but I expected it. I didn't insist because I was curious. You see by not wearing red it clearly demonstrates my control, you see I gave you a choice but naturally you wanted to disappoint me. By wearing red, I might have been forced to think you were unperturbed by my request, simply being professional, but no, you had to seize the opportunity didn't you Elizabeth?"

"You are so full of shit. Your Phd tell you that?" Hershey replied feeling a slight quiver in her bottom lip. She turned her head away briefly and bit down on the lip. Turning back to face Alexander, she moved her chin up and unclasped her bra, letting it slip to the floor.

"Yes, that is better Elizabeth, much better. That wasn't…hard was it."

Hale now turned away from the monitor.

Hershey removed her panties and after letting them fall to her ankles, she looked up at the clock.

In the office, Hale and McGill heard Hershey say, "Thirty seconds."

Alexander sat staring at her, rubbing his crotch.

"I must say I am a little turned on by you Elizabeth. Sure, you're no spring chicken, but you are still lovely. Perhaps after I get out of here, you and me could get to know each other a little better, spend an evening together?"

"You are not getting out of here…ever," replied Hershey

Twenty seconds.

"How can you be so sure Elizabeth? I don't normally do older women. Unlike my good friend Eddie, I prefer them fresh, unspoilt, I want to be the first. But you're no virgin are you Elizabeth?"

Hershey remained standing, her arms straight by her sides. She glanced again at the clock. "Fifteen seconds."

"It's not too late, yet, for you to have children is it Elizabeth? Surely you have a few years left. You shouldn't leave it much longer though. I was thinking perhaps if or when you do have children, especially a girl, maybe I could get to know them."

"You will be rotting in hell before I'd let anyone near you. Five seconds." Hershey said.

"Thank you for your cooperation Elizabeth. I will be sure to keep you with me always," Alexander said, still grinning.

"Time's up." Hershey got dressed quickly and left the room.

"Okay, show's over," McGill said from within the office. Hale left the office and went to see if Hershey was alright. McGill stopped the recording and saved the last ten minutes to a file which he then stored on his own server. He then deleted the same length of time from the current recording before leaving the office.

* * * *

The three Orca patients were moved from the ward to the Cavendish Common Room. The patients from the Cavendish Ward had already left for their visit to the Zoo, they would be gone most of the day. Alexander, Edward and William Tanner were handcuffed and chained and then their chains linked together as they were taken from a side ward exit to the Cavendish Ward. McGill didn't want them paraded through the main building.

A temporary wet bar had been erected in the room together with a small selection of drinks. Tanner was usually kept under partial sedation due to his history of violent behaviour both in and outside of confinement. Tanner was only five feet nine inches tall but as muscular as an ox. He refused to have his hair cut in the five years he had been a resident at Ashford. His thick black hair was half-way down his back. Though he had tried to escape on several occasions he spoke very seldom – a man of action rather than words.

The patients were brought in and the chain that connected them was removed. Nichols, Becker and two other guards remained in the room with them. Nichols attended to the bar. They would be given a little over six hours which would include a full five course meal delivered from one of the restaurants down at Sunset Beach. The room already benefited from cable television and a variety of video games for the patient's amusement and therapy.

Hershey stood at the sink in the ladies washroom drying her face. The distant voices of those boys at her school echoing in her mind – *come on show us your tits*. Talking to herself in the mirror she said, "That bastard better tell us where Ebony is." Hershey let out a breath, straightened her blouse and brushed her jacket. Looking at herself again she said, "It's done, you did good Elizabeth." She left the washroom.

Hale was waiting outside the washroom. "Are you okay?" Hale asked.

"Yes, thank you, I'm fine." Hershey replied.

"Hey, if it's any consolation I think what you did took real courage. That guy is an asshole."

Hershey forced a smile. "Thank you. I'm going to head off. Could you or someone call me once you learn the whereabouts of Ebony's body?"

"Of course, yes, should be in just a few hours. They are in there now. McGill and I were going to grab some lunch. Did you want to...?" Hale replied.

"No, I'm good thanks. I have an appointment I want to keep." Hershey turn and left the Orca Ward.

The day wore on, Edward and Alexander played table games while Tanner watched cartoons. Alexander could stand okay but his movement was hampered from the gun shot wound he had received. After their meal, more drinks followed. It had turned late afternoon when Alexander and Edward insisted Tanner join them in a game of darts. The dartboard was electronic, and the darts had plastic shafts and blunted points. Tanner ignored them, but Alexander became insistent. They walked over and tried to get him up, that's when Tanner became violent.

Tanner suddenly stood and pushed Edward with both hands to the floor. Alexander took a blow to the face. Tanner shouted and rushed at Becker before he had a chance to pull his gun. Becker and Tanner fell to the floor and Tanner began pummelling Becker's face, there was a crack as blood from Becker's nose sprayed across the floor. Two tasers hit Tanner almost simultaneously, one from Nichols, the other from one of the other guards. Tanner's muscles went into spasm and he collapsed on top of Becker. Becker shouting from his injuries pushed Tanner to the floor. Two guards jumped onto Tanner and cuffed both his arms and legs.

"That's it, this charade is over!" Nichols shouted, now with his firearm drawn and pointed toward Alexander and Edward.

Hospital staff soon rushed into the room in response to the alarm call placed by one of the guards. They attended to Becker whose face was bleeding profusely, while the two remaining guards secured Alexander and Edward. Becker was helped to his feet and taken from the room.

"Get them back to the ward!" Nichols said, still shouting.

Guards secured Alexander and Edward who were then taken out and returned to their cells. Nurses checked Tanner. When Tanner spat at one of the nurses, Nichols drove his foot into Tanner's ribcage. One of the nurses gave Nichols a look and then said, "He's fine but he'll need assistance walking if you want to get him back to his cell right now." Nichols nodded to the remaining guards before taking his phone from his pocket. As Tanner was taken away, Nichols called McGill.

* * * *

McGill came to see Alexander in his cell.

"So Alexander, you've had your fun. Becker has a broken nose and cheekbone, Tanner will be having a headache for a few days, and you've had your own little peep show. Now you need to keep up your end of the deal, tell us where we can find the body."

Hale was watching from the security office.

"Did you record it all doc? Did you take a copy for yourself? Bet you told her you'd look after the recording for her didn't you, took it for yourself didn't you doc? Keep my copy right in here." Alexander said, tapping his temple.

"Alexander, your crap doesn't work with me. I've lived too long and seen too many creeps pass through here to give a shit about you. We've kept our part of the deal now you do yours, or perhaps your word is as worthless as you are?"

Alexander's smile dropped from his face.

"You'll find what's left of Ebony Wilkes near the Delta Disposal Site. I took her body there after I found no further use for her. That *is* after all where you dump garbage. She's in a grave about ten yards from the road and some thirty yards up from the north fence. Put her a few feet down, didn't want the wildlife digging her up. I remember resting against a tree after digging the grave – a silver birch or something. Perhaps the moist soil has been kind."

McGill nodded and stepped back towards the door.

"McGill!" Alexander shouted, as McGill left the cell, "Think I dropped my damn CD in that grave. I'd like it back."

Hale was already talking to Munroe when McGill returned to the security office.

"Let's get this show on the road." Hale said.

* * * *

Hershey sat alone in her car sipping black coffee from a paper cup, classical music playing. She checked the time again on the dashboard clock. She then got out of the car and grabbed a holdall bag from the trunk. Returning to the car she opened the bag where she had a change of clothes – soft pumps, a casual top and jeans. Hershey got changed while still in the car, putting the skirt and jacket on a hanger and laying them on the front passenger seat. She then placed a bag of candy she took from the glove box onto the centre rest, picked up her watch from the centre console and put it on. Leaving the car, she grabbed her handbag and the hanger from off the front seat. She popped the trunk and the lay the clothes flat on the clean inside. Closing the trunk, Hershey returned to the building.

It was almost eleven. Hershey was greeted at reception. "Dr.Hershey, right on time. April is just on her way out. She won't be a moment," the receptionist said.

"Thank you. Could you confirm for me the time April is expected back?" Hershey asked. She knew the time she had agreed with McGill but wanted to be sure reception had been advised of the same time. Hershey wanted to avoid any possibility of security officers descending on April while they were still out.

"Says here five pm. Will that be alright?" the receptionist asked.

"Perfect, thank you," Hershey replied.

The doors from the Women's Directorate opened and April who was being escorted by Lucas Vogel, ran to Hershey.

"Elizabeth! Thank you for coming and arranging this. I'm so excited, where are we going?" April asked, her arms open she grabbed Hershey around the waist.

Hershey felt herself flush a little. She glanced at Lucas, who smiled and nodded. Hershey stroked April's head, "the pleasure April is all mine." Looking to April's arm Hershey saw the tracking device – a rubber wrist band that in appearance was very similar to those wrist bands used in fitness. "I have a full day planned for us, I hope that's okay. We're going to drive toward Vancouver and stop close to where I live for some lunch. From there I thought we could visit the Suspension Bridge, then you get to decide if you'd like to take in a movie or we can head down to the quay and do some girl shopping, before we head back."

"Can I think about it on the way? I don't have much money to spend on shopping, but I do like the idea," April replied. April let go of Hershey's waist and then grabbed hold of left hand.

"Of course, you can. Come on, my car is out in the car park." Hershey said, with April leading the way out of the main building.

As they approached the car, April asked, "Is that your car, the red one?"

"Yes. It's the red one, a present from my father."

"Wow. It's a Jaguar correct? Just a two-seater. Am I okay to sit in the front?" April said.

"Yes. I did check, you are tall enough and heavy enough I think," Hershey laughed.

"You mean for the airbag? A friend of mine, Jenny Bateman, she had a car with airbags. But I was always riding in the back of the car when I was with Jenny."

As they approached the car, the indicators on the car flashed twice, acknowledging that the owner, or more precisely the key, was within proximity. Letting go of Hershey's hand, April ran to the passenger side. She had opened the door and jumped in as Hershey arrived at the car.

As Hershey got into the driver's seat, April said, "The car must sense you are here? I didn't see you use a key and yet the doors unlocked, and these lights are pulsing."

Hershey placed her hand into her handbag, opened her purse and withdrew the key. "It's just like a credit card, as long as I have it with me, there's no actual need to get it out. As I approach, the car will unlock and is ready to start. As I walk away the doors will lock."

"That's really cool. Are these for me?" April asked, reaching for the candy.

Hershey laughed again, "yes sweetheart, they are for you, but don't eat too much, you'll be having lunch shortly." Hershey pressed the button to start the engine.

The journey south toward Vancouver seemed to fly by. April was constantly asking questions, first about the car, then about where Hershey was living and her home, then about the islands she was seeing as the car wound its way toward the city. By twelve noon, they pulled into a parking space next to the Beachhouse restaurant at Dundarave park.

As April looked over the menu, Hershey noticed how often April would play with the necklace around her neck.

"Did someone special give that to you?" Hershey asked.

"Jenny Bateman, the lady I mentioned to you, she gave this to me. Though that's not why it's special to me. She said it belonged to my Mom. It's the only thing I have that connects me to my mom…to anyone really." April replied.

"Is that a V?" Hershey said, referring to the charm hanging on the necklace.

"Yes, at least I think so. I believe it's my mother's initial. I think of it as her first initial, but I suppose it could have been her family name or something entirely different." April said.

"I'm sure you're right April. People don't tend to use an initial for just their surname. And besides, if your mother was going to wear anyone else's initials I'm sure it would have been yours."

"My adopted parents gave me the name April, after the month in which I became their daughter. I don't know what name my mother would have given me. I suppose my name could have begun with a V."

"Perhaps you were called Victoria?" Hershey suggested, smiling.

"Or Veronica, eww!" April laughed

"Perhaps you were supposed to have been called Victor?" Hershey teased.

April laughed harder. "Don't be silly. I think we can be pretty sure my mommy knew I was a girl."

The waitress brought the drinks and took the order for the food. April ordered the gilled salmon burger while Hershey opted for the scallop and prawn linguine.

"Do you miss your parents April?" Hershey asked, after the waitress left.

"You mean my adopted parents?" April asked. Hershey nodded. "Yes, I miss them. They were the ones that found me. My mom, Maggie her name was, she was fun. We would play games, go for walks, and she'd help me with my studies, for a while at least. Then I think my Math became too hard for her. I loved them, though I'm not sure what love really is."

Hershey reached across the table to gently squeeze April's hand. "I'm sure they loved you April. April, can I ask…" Hershey hesitated, "it's perfectly okay if you don't want to answer, but do you remember anything of the night your parents died?"

"I know I killed them," April replied, a tear appearing in the corner of her eye.

"I'm so sorry April to ask. I'm just trying to understand." Hershey replied.

April wiped the tear away. "It's okay, I know you mean well. I don't understand why or how it happened. The University doctor's just put it down to my sleeping disorder and a tragic set of connected thoughts while sleeping. It wasn't the first time…that I cut something." Hershey squeezed April's hand tighter but remained silent, allowing April to continue, "Before that I had killed a cat that they had bought me. I think it was supposed to help with my sleeping, but I remember being curious how everything worked. I mean the cat…I just wondered how it moved, breathed, what happened to the food it ate, that kind of thing. I later read that Leonardo would go to the morgue to examine the dead. He would cut them open and then draw how the muscles and joints worked. But for my parents, I have no idea why. I was going to have a brother, he would have been nearly two now." April wiped away another tear.

Hershey got up from the table and gave April a hug. "I'm so sorry April, I won't ask again. We don't have to talk about it again unless you want to. I want you to know I'm here for you now. You never need to feel alone again," Hershey said, before returning to her seat.

The food arrived.

Hershey did her best to change the topic of conversation while they were eating. She got out her phone and opened a movie application. Offering her phone to April, she asked her to browse for any movies she might want to watch.

After finishing the entrée's, they decided to share a dessert, April chose the strawberry and rhubarb crumble, never having had it before.

After lunch, Hershey and April went back up to the highway for the short drive to Capilano and the suspension bridge. On the way, April confirmed she preferred to go shopping rather than catch a movie.

The rest of the day, as with the drive down, seemed to fly by. Hershey and April going over the suspension bridge, taking in the tree walk and trails. They then drove to Lonsdale Quay where they grabbed ice cream and explored the many boutique shops.

On the drive back to Ashford, light fading, Hershey couldn't help noticing April had become quiet.

"Is everything okay, April?" Hershey eventually asked.

April almost seemed startled by the question. "Yes, sorry, I have had a wonderful time, thank you Elizabeth. I was just thinking about what you had said earlier."

"What was that?" Hershey asked.

"About me not having to be alone, did you mean it?" April asked.

Hershey glanced away from the road to find April looking right at her. "Of course. Do you know when the last time was that you had an episode, April?"

"Just one since I've been at the Institute and that was shortly after I arrived, nothing since. Do you think I'm getting better?"

"You will very likely grow out of it and I expect the frequency, and probably the intensity, to diminish. It is possible you won't experience any more," Hershey said. "Listen, I've been talking to Doctor McGill, we both agree it would be better for you to be staying somewhere else. If it's okay with you, we will be asking the Board for permission to find you a new home, a proper home where you can hopefully start leading a normal life. How does that sound?"

"Do you think they will let me leave?" April asked.

"I think so yes, especially given you haven't had any episodes in the last few months." Hershey replied.

"But what would happen to me? Where would I go?"

"I've been thinking about that too April. I wanted to ask you…" Hershey reached across to hold April's hand, "I don't know if this is possible, but what would you think if you came to live with me?"

"With you!? Really!?"

"I don't know if it's possible April," Hershey was quick to repeat, "but yes, I'm thinking we could make it work. I'd have to hire a nanny, but I live alone and so have plenty of room in the house. I live near a good school and have money to pay for anything you may need. I won't pretend to be your Mom, but I would like to be your friend and I think we can look after each other. What do you think?"

April was smiling. She pulled at the seatbelt so she could reach up and kiss Hershey on the cheek. Sitting back in the seat she said, "That would be wonderful."

At that moment, Hershey's phone rang. The phone was connected to the car and Munroe's name came up on the dashboard. "Let me just take this sweetheart, it won't take a moment." Hershey grabbed an earpiece from the visor, placed it around her ear and hit a small button on the side. "Hi Munroe, what happened?...Yes, we're on our way back now, around ten minutes away. Did you get the location?...That's great news. You're heading over there now?...Er, sure, yes that would be fine. I can be ready in an hour. Ok, see you shortly." Hershey took the earpiece from her ear and clipped it back on the visor.

"Is he your boyfriend?" April asked.

"No sweetheart, he's a…more of a colleague really. This relates to that thing I mentioned that I didn't want to have to do. Well some good seems to have come of it. I need to drop you back and then go somewhere if that will be ok?" April nodded. "April, I had a really horrible morning, but you have made me forget all that and I've had a wonderful time. Thank you." Hershey added.

"Me too," April replied, reaching across the centre console to hold Hershey's hand. They held hands until they reached Ashford. Hershey hugged April before returning her to the Security officer on duty.

* * * *

Munroe had arranged to pick Hershey up from her home. Each of the cities in the lower mainland have their own municipal serviced by there own police force. Some cities outsourced policing to the RCMP others had their own. The Vancouver Police Department was financed from taxes paid by the residents of the City of Vancouver. Investigations for crimes committed across departmental lines had the potential to get held up while department execs postured for ownership. A set of agreed guidelines had been drawn up to make the whole process much faster. Alexander had taken victims from one city, killed them in another and moved the bodies to yet another. The VPD were the first to start connecting the dots, see the patterns and realise they were dealing with a Serial. They also had the greatest resources to bring to bear on the case. In Alexander's case, the other Police Departments seemed happy to defer to the VPD. Detective Inspector Martin had the lead. Alexander was eventually arrested and stood trial and faced fifty convictions including sixteen counts of pre-meditated murder. Over the next few years Alexander had managed to escape from one facility, only to be recaptured by D.I. Martin, and then cause sufficient disruption at another facility that Alexander secured a move to Ashford. D.I. Martin retired shortly after, his reputation secured as legend. The prospect of a seventeenth victim meant VPD remained as the lead Department. Having been mentored by D.I Martin, Munroe had asked and been granted the lead on the case.

"Hale has gone on ahead. A search and excavation team have been called in. I've asked them to simply cordon things off until we get there." Munroe said. Hershey looked across at Munroe. "Until I get there," Munroe corrected himself,

"Do you think we will find her, Munroe?" Hershey asked.

"Well it wouldn't be the first time the Police Department has been given the run around, and I don't imagine this would be the last. But yes, I think he's telling the truth. When people tell the truth, in my experience, what they say tends to be specific, it has detail. Alexander's directions have detail, the reference to the tree, the distances, and he mentions the north fence, not just *a* fence or *the* fence but the *north* fence. He's pulling the memories back...he was there."

They sat silent in the car, occasional updates being reported back to Munroe. The excavation team had arrived, then Hale who Munroe confirmed as the OIC – Officer In Charge - until he arrived, then confirmation the site had been secured.

"You know what you did today was pretty brave," Munroe eventually said.

"Thanks, but I didn't have much of choice. And besides all I did was take my clothes off." Hershey replied.

"You take your clothes off a lot doctor?" Munroe asked, maintaining his serious tone.

"At least once a day, sometimes more detective," Hershey replied smiling.

"Well I just wanted to say I think what you did was…pretty cool. If this leads to anything, the family doesn't need to know what you did but I'd like them to know it was because of you."

"Thanks Munroe, but it's not necessary. Let's just hope we can give some form of closure to the family and nail another conviction to that son of a bitch."

"Yes, ma'am," Munroe replied.

They arrived at the Disposal Site. An officer located at the entrance to the site signalled for Munroe to drive around the side. Munroe could see the police lights from at least three other vehicles a few hundred metres away. As they approached more units could be seen. Light rain had started to fall. Hale walked over to the car. Munroe glanced at the clock before getting out of the car. It was now after seven pm and night had fallen. "Probably best to stay in the car. This may take a while. I'll let you know as soon as we discover anything," Munroe suggested before closing his door.

"We've secured the surrounding area with uniforms at both ends as well as the site given by Alexander." Hale confirmed.

"There a tree?" Munroe asked.

"Yup, it's also a birch like he said." Hale said.

Munroe nodded. Hale turned and started to walk toward the site. Munroe followed.

As they approached the site that marked the area provided by Alexander, lights had been set up and a dog handler waited under an umbrella.

"Officer Li," Hale said, "this is Detective Munroe, Officer in charge."

Munroe nodded and gestured with his hand for the Officer to begin. Munroe reached into a side pocket and withdrew a toothpick from a small container. Within less than a minute the dog began circling a spot on the ground. Officer Li turned to Munroe. Munroe nodded, "Ok, let's get the dig team in."

Officer Li gave the dog a treat. She then unclipped a canister from her side and sprayed white paint on the ground identified by the dog. "Thank you," Munroe said, refraining from petting the dog. "That should be all for now but if you could if you could stay around just in case. No need to be out here though." Munroe said, looking up into the rain now beginning to fall harder from the black sky. Officer Li and the dog headed back toward the parked vehicles as three other people dressed in yellow overalls with 'Forensic' written on their back arrived. They began by erecting a shelter over the site and more lighting.

Munroe checked his watch. As the shelter was erected and the lights went up, Munroe crouched to get a closer look at the plants growing over the site.

"You see something?" Hale asked, standing behind Munroe.

"The plants, obviously the dog knows there's something there, sometimes the plants are taller, more of them. They can give an indication on the size of what's under there," Munroe replied. Munroe stood. "It looks like she's under there. I'm going back to the car. Come and get me when they find something."

"Sure," Hale replied, waiting for Munroe to leave the area before he crouched down on the same spot Munroe was in. Hale thought he could see it, the various plants visibly growing taller, making it seem as though they were sitting on a mound of soil below, though the ground was flat. Hale shifted a little to one side and tilted his head. The whole area of extra growth was may be five feet in length and perhaps two feet across.

Munroe returned to the car. He found Hershey sifting through various CDs she had found in various locations at the front the vehicle.

"You like classical?" Hershey asked, though it sounded more like a statement.

"I discovered it around ten years ago. Started listening to it after a friend made a CD for me. Thought I'd buy a few of my own. Helps me relax, that kind of thing." Munroe replied.

Munroe flicked the toothpick away as he got into the car.

"Pick one," Hershey said, holding several CDs as though they were playing cards.

Munroe quickly scanned the covers. "This one I think," Munroe replied, taking one of the CDs.

"Beethoven it is," Hershey said, as she took the disc from the case. "Number nine." Hershey placed the disc into the car's dash. They remained silent, staring out into the darkness as the rain continued to stream down the windshield.

Hale knocked on the car's window. Rain still falling. Munroe slid the window slightly as Hale confirmed, human remains had been found.

"The necklace?" Munroe asked.

"Not yet, just an arm so far," Hale replied, "let me see if I can ask them."

Munroe checked his watch again before reaching into a side pocket to retrieve another toothpick. The CD had gone back to the start.

"Mind if I?" Hershey asked.

"Sure, please go ahead." Munroe replied.

Hershey replaced Beethoven with Mahler.

"Why have you never married, Munroe?" Hershey eventually asked.

Munroe looked across at Hershey, making a point of raising his eyebrows. "Don't give me that, it's a perfectly reasonable question. What are you, early forties? You can be charming, occasionally and I think my mother would have found you attractive." Hershey said, smiling. "Why haven't you married?"

Munroe shrugged, "I'm not too sure. I've not really been one for relationships. The job doesn't make it easy for one thing." Munroe returned to staring out of the window. "It's not that I'm against it, just not sure I've met anyone that would be able to put up with me. I know I'm not easy to be around sometimes," Munroe replied, his voice tailing off.

Hershey gently squeezed his hand, pulling him back from wherever his thoughts had started to take him. "What is it?" Hershey asked, "a part of you always seems to be somewhere else. Who is it that has this hold on you?"

Munroe turned to look at Hershey, this time he was looking into her eyes. He gently squeezed her hand that had remained in his. He just looked at her, it seemed like minutes but what were probably just a few seconds. "It's not a *who*, it's more of a *what*. I don't sleep well. I keep having this recurring dream, the same dream, over and over. I'm sitting next to myself as I drive a car down a mountain road. Then…" Munroe shrugged again. "It's nothing, it just wakes me up sometimes, a lot of the time. Like I said, I'm not good company." Munroe moved his hand away.

Hershey was about to speak when Hale appeared at the window. Again, Munroe slid the window down. This time Hale held up an evidence bag that contained a necklace, a golden dolphin pendant attached. Munroe nodded. "There's something else." Hale said and then glanced at Hershey. Munroe looked at Hershey who then raised her eyebrows and moved her head forward. Munroe looked back at Hale, taking the toothpick between his fingers he pointed upward before returning it to his mouth.

Hale took a breath before saying, "They found the head...it's facing the wrong way around."

That night, Munroe drove to the home of Ebony Wilkes' parents. He had phoned ahead advising that they had important news on the case and wanted to confirm it would be okay for him to come over. But Munroe knew the phone call would help get them a little more prepared for what he would have to tell them...as much as any preparation is really possible. He didn't respond when asked on the phone if Ebony was alive.

Munroe had given the Hershey the option of getting a ride home or staying with him. She chose to remain with Munroe. They arrived at the Wilkes home just before ten pm.

As Munroe parked up on the single driveway to the duplex house, he saw the front door open. A couple perhaps in their late fifties stood in the doorway. They were staring intently at Munroe as he got out from the car. Munroe moved slowly and as he stood, he looked directly back at the couple, first the woman, then the man, then back to the woman. It was enough to convey to them why he was there.

Tears started to stream down Mrs Wilkes face. Then a wail, then her knees buckled. Mr Wilkes was quick to hold her and cushioned her collapse on the doorstep, her face in her hands, desperate moans coming from her soul.

Hershey had exited the car and quickly moved to the doorstep and sat down next to Mrs Wilkes. Putting a jacket around and holding her close, Hershey did what she could to comfort the woman.

Munroe reached the doorstep. A tear ran down Mr Wilkes cheek. They exchanged the slightest of nods before Munroe said, "I'm extremely sorry." Munroe reached for his badge, "I'm detective Munroe and this is Dr.Elizabeth Hershey. Dr.Hershey has been assisting us. Please may we come in?"

Munroe and Hershey stayed almost an hour at the Wilkes home. On occasions like these Munroe usually kept things as short as he could, relay the facts, inform them of next steps, give his sincere sympathies, then leave. Hershey however, chose to sit with Mrs and Mrs Wilkes, doing what she could to console Mrs Wilkes while Mr Wilkes attempted to take in what Munroe was telling them. Munroe showed them the evidence bag containing the necklace. They confirmed it as belonging to their daughter Ebony.

Eventually Mrs Wilkes found some composure and after some time asked about the nature of Hershey's involvement. Munroe replied only that Hershey had been critical to the discovery.

"We knew. I knew. I always knew," said Mrs Wilkes, drying her face. Looking at Munroe she said, "She wasn't going to run away or run off with some boyfriend. She was very happy, she knew we loved her, we'd remind her everyday. This was her home." Looking at Hershey she continued, "A mother knows. The day she disappeared I knew she hadn't gone voluntarily. As the time goes by, you realise whoever took her wasn't going to let her go." Mrs Wilkes took hold of both of Hershey's hands and turned to face her. "Thank you for helping. I know my heart will never be whole again but at least we get to put our baby to rest. I'll be able to go visit her. It would have been her birthday next month. I know she's with the good Lord now."

It would be three more days before the body of Ebony Wilkes was formally identified. Dental records were a match and DNA tests matched against samples taken by the Police shortly after Ebony had been reported missing. The funeral for Ebony Wilkes was held two weeks before her birthday. Munroe, Hale and Hershey all attended.

CHAPTER 13

In the days leading up to the funeral, Hershey spent what time she could researching the areas found to be of interest to Emily Jackson. She found herself frequently thinking of Munroe and wondered if she might be falling in love. Many times, she thought of April as she waited to hear back from the Institute and legal system on what options she might have open to her concerning April's welfare. Then her thoughts would come back to Ashford and the recent events that had occurred.

Hershey was well aware of the power of suggestion either from manipulation or hypnosis but the events at Ashford far exceeded anything she was aware of. *Where was Emily getting this from?*

Munroe had supplied her with a copy of notes that had been made and a recent photograph, though Hershey had told Munroe she had in fact met Emily Jackson at the Institute. Emily was slender, and like many students engaged in some form of medical study, she kept fit and ate well. She was five feet four inches tall and wore her straight dark brown hair in a slight bob. She was popular with other students though was not known to have developed any long-term relationships. She was respected as a hardworking, intelligent student by her teachers, but not exceptional.

Hershey did some research on Neuro-Linguistic Programming. NLP was developed in the early seventies by John Grinder and Richard Bandler. Bandler had realised that by merely mimicking the best gestalt therapists, he could achieve similar results. Bandler, along with Grinder, had developed NLP as a set of teachable practices that could be adopted giving inexperienced users a powerful toolset. Where many therapists and their practices might be employed for the benefit of the client, there are increasingly more practices, Hershey read, being employed for less noble pursuits such as improving sales persuasion, seduction techniques, and more recently to create an air of mysticism.

Hershey thought back to when she was seventeen and the first time she had hypnotised someone, putting them into a trance-like state. She could recall the tingle of excitement that she felt as the other student slowly descended into the trance. She remembers thinking how easy it was to do. In the years that passed, Hershey had learned a lot more on its potential uses however, the question of how hypnosis really worked or why still evades its practitioners.

She considered Donald McCoy's horrible death. Before the use of Chloroform or other medicinal anaesthesia James Esdaile, a Scottish surgeon working in India, found he could use hypnosis as a form of anaesthesia and thereby reduce the mortality rate from fifty percent to around just six percent. Hypnosis could be used to induce a state whereby the pain threshold was significantly increased. *Donald could have pierced his brain with the forks under some form of hypnotic suggestion. But how was he instructed to take the forks from the canteen and use them after awaking from his sleep?* Her thoughts turned to Lucas Vogel.

To her knowledge, all types of mind therapy and suggestion included some form of hypnosis, but what happened with Lucas Vogel appeared to have been achieved without hypnosis, as though his subconscious had been programmed some other way – *He believed he was seeing a fire. Did he trigger the fire alarm simply because he believed he was seeing a fire or did the drawing of the bell have any influence? Lucas said April had shown him the drawing.* As she replayed her conversation with Lucas and the accounts of what happened that night, she remembered what at first had seemed a minor detail. Lucas had stood at the exit and lit a match. *He did see a fire.* Perhaps the stunt was not quite as elaborate as she had been thinking, but nevertheless, it still required his subconscious to overreact significantly to the flame from the match for him to believe he was seeing a blazing fire. For any court to make a conviction, they would need to be convinced beyond reasonable doubt that someone could use an eight year old to convey subconscious programming into Lucas Vogel's mind, while he remained perfectly lucid, to create the illusion that a tiny flame from a match was in fact a blazing inferno.

On the morning of the funeral, Hershey was at her office. She checked for post and then her email. Still not having received anything with respect to April, she crafted another letter in the hope of forcing a decision. The letter was addressed to Bernard Golding, Chairman of the Board for the provincial health service with a copy to Charles McGill –

Dear Mr Golding,

As you know, I am the Independent Psychiatric Consultant assigned to Ashford Mental Institution. Around three months ago I became aware of a patient resident at the hospital, an eight year old girl named, April Pritchard.

During April's childhood she has been suffering from aggressive episodes of sleepwalking, culminating in the tragic death of her adopted parents at her own hand. April temporarily became a ward of the University before being moved to Ashford. In the several months she has now spent at the Hospital, no further episodes of sleepwalking have been recorded.

As I am sure you are aware, the overwhelming evidence suggests that the vast majority of children grow out of any sleeping disorders that they may express in their infant and junior years. Professor McGill and I are of the opinion that April may well no longer suffer from her sleeping disorder.

In addition, whilst I accept the severity of April's actions conducted under automatism, it remains highly unusual for an eight year old child to be kept at an institute such as Ashford.

With this letter I have enclosed a statement from the Vancouver Police Department confirming ongoing investigations relating to the deaths of patients Donald McCoy and Thomas Bessey. Thomas Bessey was killed by patient Edward Walker, but the circumstances leading up to his death are highly suspicious. It is my opinion and that of Professor McGill that April Pritchard may in fact be in danger while she remains in the custody of the Health Service due to circumstances connected to the deaths of Donald McCoy and Thomas Bessey.

I request that April Pritchard be given a full psychological evaluation and, subject to the findings of the review, be granted permission to seek foster care.

Yours sincerely,

Dr. Elizabeth Hershey.

Hershey knew any connection with the events at the Hospital with a Police investigation would be bad news for McGill, but Thomas Bessey's death was unquestionably murder, and Donald McCoy's death was difficult to accept as a suicide. To Hershey, it was possible that McCoy's death together with the events that lead to Thomas Bessey's murder were in someway connected. And if they were connected then something very disturbing was happening at Ashford.

McGill had assured Hershey he was happy to support any motion. Munroe had arranged for the statement to be made concerning Police interest in the events but would not go as far as including any connection with April Pritchard – Hershey would just have to rely on the Board's fear that she *might* be in danger.

She printed off two copies of the letter, signed both copies and put each one into an addressed envelope with a copy of the VPD statement. She also emailed an electronic copy to McGill. She placed the two envelopes in her 'Post Out' tray for her assistant. Then she wrote a message on a sticky note and stuck it on to her assistant's desk as she made her way out of the office. The note read –

Sam,

*I'm interested in getting a full-time
housekeeper, preferably with
experience of children from the age of
eight. Could you do me a favour and
look into it, perhaps come up with a
shortlist for me?*

Thank you, you're a star!
Elizabeth.

* * * *

The same morning as Hershey was writing her letter to the Board, McGill was sat in his office also writing to Bernard Golding. Although McGill hadn't reached the compulsory date for retirement, he felt he could no longer muster the spirit required to continue serving in his position. Over the years he had turned the Hospital around to become a place of distinction or so he thought. Recent events caused McGill to doubt himself, to doubt what he had achieved, and with the doubts, the joy of his work had diminished. He was ready to retire.

* * * *

After the funeral, Munroe and Hale needed to return to work. Hershey found herself alone and with no inclination to return home or to her office. She phoned McGill and asked if she could spend some time with April in the afternoon, away from the hospital. He agreed.

They picked up a takeout in Squamish and drove further north toward Whistler, stopping at Alice Lake. Though the temperature was dropping as fall approached, it remained warm during September. With children back at school after the summer break, only a few people could be seen around the lake. Hershey and April sat at a park table on the south shore.

As they unpacked the take-out Hershey said, "I was looking at your grades the other day. You are doing very well. Are you enjoying it?"

April nodded as she chewed on a crab cake. After swallowing, she said, "I have three tutors that visit me. When I first arrived I only had two but now I have three. The new tutor, Mrs Wong, she's nice, she focuses on science. Mr Dylan, my math tutor used to do some science with me, but he said I was becoming too much work for him. I also have a Language tutor, Miss Cameron, it's almost all English but with some French."

"Are you getting on okay with the tutors?" Hershey asked.

Again, April nodded before saying, "They give me lots of homework but that's okay, it's not like I have a lot of other things to be doing. Mr Dylan is funny, I think we are supposed to be working through the text book, but he often starts talking about other things and relating them to math. He says, 'Math is a language, simply a way of describing things.' I have not known Mrs Wong very long, but she seems very nice, we have started doing separate biology, physic and chemistry studies. Miss Cameron doesn't talk very much but that's okay. I don't think she particularly likes having to come to the Hospital."

"Wow these noodles are really good. Want to try some?" Hershey asked.

April shook her head, "No thank you," then, "Did you know I had a cat called Noodles?"

"No, I didn't, do you like cats?" Hershey replied.

"My Mom bought me the cat because she though it would help with my sleeping. I don't remember too much about the cat. We didn't have it for long as it died."

"Oh, I'm sorry April," Hershey said.

"That's okay, trouble is every time I see noodles I think of my cat."

"Children your age are in Grade 3 or 4 depending on their birth dates. Your birthday is in June, so you would be one of the youngest in Grade 4. Not that it matters when they are teaching the Grade 8 curriculum. Grade 10 for Math I understand."

"I do find much of what they teach to be quite simple. That's why I do my own studies. I have started learning about astronomy, I guess I'm just curious as to how things work or why they work the way they do." April said.

"Do you have any ideas on what you'd like to do when you get older?" Hershey asked.

"Not really. I haven't really thought about it yet. I enjoy learning about things, but I've only really thought about trying to find out who I really am. Who my parents were? What did they do? That sort of thing. There was a little bit of information on my real Mom but there's nothing about my Dad. I wonder why my Mom did what she did. She was obviously very upset but was it because of my Dad. Did he leave her? Was he nasty to my Mom? Did my Dad leave because of me, maybe he didn't want to have children?"

"I'm sure that was not the case April. I'm confident that you are not the reason you lost your Mom." Hershey replied.

"Why do you say that?" April asked.

Hershey paused for a moment, "I read about the circumstances. They are strange I'll admit but when they found you, you had a small mark, a very light scratch on your left wrist. I think it was made by the same knife that your Mom used on herself."

"You think my Mom wanted to kill me too?" April asked.

"I think perhaps yes, she may have had that thought. But look at it this way, she couldn't bring herself to do it. Something stopped her from harming you. My guess is what ever she was running away from or scared of, she must have thought you were in some kind of danger too. But when she came to place the knife to you, she couldn't do it, she couldn't bring herself to harm you April – she loved you. Instead, she took her own life and I'm sure left you hoping you would be found and taken care of by someone else. And free from whatever your Mom was running from."

A tear ran down April's cheek as she reached across the table to give Hershey a hug. "Thank you," April said, "I never knew about that. I think perhaps you are right. I always tried to believe my Mom did love me and now I think she really did. At first, I was angry at her for leaving me so alone. Then I knew it must have been something horrible for her to kill herself, I just hoped it was not because of me. Thank you, Elizabeth."

Hershey returned April's hug. "You are most welcome young lady. Come on finish up your food. I want to take a boat out onto the lake."

April returned to her seat and resumed eating. After a couple of minutes, she said, "It means that something or someone else is really responsible for my Mom's death."

Hershey looked up at April. "We likely will never know. I do know it must have been very hard for your mom and that she probably didn't feel like she had anyone to turn to for help. I'm so sorry April, but I want you to understand I am always here for you, regardless of what happens I want you to understand that. Think of me as family, an Aunt perhaps, a glamorous Aunt," Hershey said, with a swift shake of her head to waft her hair from the side of her face. They both smiled then started to laugh.

Hershey and April spent the rest of their time together in a dinghy they hired for a couple of hours before returning back to Ashford. Hershey briefly tried to find out more about Aprils relationship with Emily Jackson but chose not to share that she thought Emily might be manipulating her somehow. On returning to the hospital, April reached up to hug Hershey, giving her a kiss on the cheek, before heading back to her room and her homework. Before Hershey left she briefly went by McGill's office, she had a favour to ask.

* * * *

Two days later Emily Jackson pulled up at the hospital. Emily signed in and was told by one of the guards in the reception area that she would find April in the café lounge. April was reading a novel.

"Hi April, how are you?" Emily asked as she approached.

April looked over her tablet that she was using. Emily was carrying a few books and what seemed to be several folders. "I'm good. What are you carrying?" April asked.

"I've brought some more articles for you to have a look at. Some recent news on how developments have been used to create really positive changes in people." Emily responded. On reaching the table, Emily placed the books and folders down. "I thought these would be good for you."

April closed the tablet and placed it next to her on the table. "Emily?" she asked, 'All this mind control and mind over body, can any real good come from it?"

Emily was about to say something but then stopped, a frown forming on her face. Emily sat at the table. "Of course, that's what a lot of this stuff is. Why are you asking? People have learned to read better, improved their spelling, quit smoking, no longer fear heights or enclosed spaces or spiders. Lots of positive things, but you know that already. I brought you these because they discuss how people are using their minds to heal themselves. April, you said yourself you haven't been sleepwalking since we started the self-hypnosis. Why are you asking?"

"I've been thinking about it. I'd like to make a difference, a big difference, a real difference, cure cancer or Alzheimer's or something, but you just seem to be interested in the small things."

Emily's shoulders dropped. "That's not true. Of course, I'd like to be part of something significant. I was hoping we could work together, you have a tremendous curiosity April that enables you to see and question things most do not. I think that by sharing my studies with you, when you're older, you'll come up with something magical that will really make a difference. I just want to help. Why are you talking like this?"

"I don't mean anything by it, you've been a good friend to me Emily, but things have been happening and I'm not sure what to think any more." April said.

"What things? What's going on April? What do you mean I've *been* a good friend? I am your friend April. Is it that doctor? Is she putting things into your head?"

"No. She thinks *you* might be putting things into my head," April replied.

"April! That's not fair, I've only tried to be a friend to you, to help you. You know that. I was with you at the University. I stood up for you. I was your friend when you didn't have any. Why would this doctor be suggesting that I'm anything other than your friend? What the hell does anything have to do with her anyway?" Emily said.

"Elizabeth is trying to do what she can to get me out of here, to get me into a decent home, perhaps even her own."

"April, I don't know what is going on here or why you are talking like this. It would be wonderful if you were not locked up in here and had a better place to live and grow up in. Of course, it would. I don't know why this doctor would suggest I am trying to be anything other than helpful to you." Emily looked away and up toward the ceiling. She then took a deep breath.

Looking back at April she said, "Why would she tell you that I'm putting things into your head?"

April shrugged her shoulders, "I don't know. I don't think she thinks it's a good idea for me to be learning this material. I overheard some of the staff talking, they don't think the deaths that happened were an accident. There's going to be a police investigation. They think somebody might be causing the deaths to occur."

"Wait, are you saying people think I might be connected to what has been going on?" Emily asked. "What? That I am somehow involved? I thought the guard that died was killed by one of the patients?"

"He was. Edward killed him. But he got out because of the fire alarm going off." April replied.

"Okay, so how can that involve me in anyway?"

"I don't know, because there wasn't a real fire. Lucas set the fire alarm because he thought there was a fire. But there wasn't. There was no fire. He imagined it." April said.

Emily was quiet a moment. "So, the doctor thinks someone made him believe there was a fire. And she connects that to me because of the material we have been studying? How much does she know...of what we have been studying?" Emily asked.

"She asks me questions. She's browsed through some of the books and papers you brought me."

"April, I've had nothing to do with what has been going on. Okay I know how to improve the probability of getting someone to do something, but I wouldn't know how to get someone to trigger a fire alarm, especially if I'm not present. None of this makes any sense. May be the guard just had a seizure of sorts or something, maybe he's been smoking something or taking some meds that cause him to hallucinate. There could be a number of reasons. Thinking I could have had anything to do with it is crazy."

"Elizabeth thinks that the other deaths might also be connected." April said.

"What other deaths? Donald? The one you told me about?" Emily asked. April nodded. "I thought you said he killed himself?" Emily continued. "So what, now they think I somehow persuaded Donald to kill himself, is that it? And if I could do that, then I would obviously be capable of getting someone to trigger the fire alarm?" Emily stood, and brushed a hand through her hair. She turned her back on April then said, "This is madness. And what do you think April? Do you think I could have had anything to do with this?"

"I'm not sure you should keep coming to visit me Emily." April replied.

Emily turned and looked at April. "You are very special April. I've only wanted to help and support you." A tear escaped from Emily's eye. She reached into her handbag and withdrew a slip of paper and a pen. "Here, I want you to have this. Keep hold of it. You already have my email, and this is my cell number. Should you need me, just call this number," she said as she wrote her number on to the slip of paper and slid it toward April. "You can keep the

books. I don't want them, I brought them for you. Look after yourself April."
Emily turned and left.

* * * *

Emily returned to her first-floor apartment on the Campus. She took a set
of keys from her handbag but struggled to find the right key for the door. Her
hands shaking, the keys dropped to the floor. *Shit.* Picking the keys up from off
the floor Emily tried again at the door lock. This time she found the correct
key. She opened the door and let herself in.

As soon as she had kicked her shoes off, she heard a commotion. The door
opened into a small entrance with just enough space for a coat hanger, shoe
rack, and the stacked washer/dryer. The space then opened into a kitchen area
which lead to a small dining/lounge area. The commotion came from the couch
in the lounge where two men appeared to be hurriedly adjusting their clothes.

Rolling her eyes Emily said, "Billy, I thought we agreed not in the damn
apartment unless I'm away."

"Sorry Emily, I thought you said you would be out most of the day." Billy
responded, continuing to straighten his clothes and tighten his belt.
"Err…this is Dylan. Dylan this is my roommate Emily."

Dylan nodded. "Good to meet you Dylan. Now do you mind leaving, I
could do with the space?" Emily asked.

"Sure, we were just leaving." Billy confirmed. As Billy and Dylan pulled on their shoes and jackets, Billy asked, "Are you okay? You seem a bit…I dunno, upset."

"I'll be fine. I just need a bit of space." Emily replied.

As Billy opened the door to leave, he turned, "Oh I meant to message you. Some guy has been asking around the Campus about you. Pretty sure he's not a student and too dumb to be a teacher. I think he's a cop or something…an investigator may be. Are you sure everything is alright?"

Emily spilled the coffee she had begun to pour into a cup. "A cop? Yes, everything is fine. I'll be alright, thanks Billy. See you tonight eh?" she said.

Billy and Dylan left the apartment.

* * * *

Emily Jackson had spent the afternoon in silence, picking at the hard skin on her feet until the skin had started to bleed. The coffee machine remained on but the reservoir was empty. Scraps of paper lay across the table and floor, some torn into pieces others crumpled into balls. Afternoon had given way to the evening. Emily blew her nose once more and grabbing her laptop she began typing. Moments later, taking her laptop and phone, she threw on shoes and a jacket, grabbed her car keys and left the apartment.

An hour later and Emily was parked in her silver Toyota less than a hundred yards from Dr.Elizabeth Hershey's home in Capilano. Being a doctor Elizabeth Hershey was essentially self employed running her own business. Businesses have records – tax returns, directorships, legal filings, media and social items. Using her laptop and her phone as a hotspot, Emily located a picture of Dr.Hershey presumably in her office that also showed a photograph in the background. The photo was of a car, Hershey's jaguar that Emily had seen sometimes at the hospital. The car was parked in front of an expensive looking home. Sifting through other records had given Capilano as Hershey's general address. Emily had not had to drive around very long before she had located the property.

Emily had parked a short distance from the house and exited her car. There was a breeze, the air damp and salty as it blew in from off the sea. Emily zipped up her jacket and pulled the hood over her head. She walked to the front of the house, not sure what she had intended to do. *Look at her, fancy car, fancy house, fancy clothes. She must have been the one to throw suspicion onto me*, Emily thought. *What is her deal? Is she jealous of me, my relationship with April? Does she want April for herself is that it? Is she just so fucking poor at her job that the best she can do is blame me for what is going on at that place?*

Emily became aware that she had probably stood in front of the house too long. She had just started to walk away from the house when she heard a car pull into the crescent. The lights seemed to be following her and then the car pulled onto a driveway. Emily risked a look back. Hershey had returned home. Emily continued walking, following the road around and back to her own car. *If she has thrown suspicion on me and it is a cop asking about me on Campus, then the Dean must be aware. If the Dean is aware then at least some of the teachers will be aware and it's only a matter of time before the students know.*

The bitch is ruining my life. Emily sat in her car. A light rain began to fall. *What to do?* Emily thought.

Emily wasn't sure how long had passed when her thoughts were interrupted by the sound of a car engine starting. Emily looked up and out through the windshield. The jaguar was pulling back off the driveway and turning. Emily instinctively shrunk slightly in her seat as the jaguar drove past her. Emily started her car.

* * * *

Hershey had arranged to meet up with Munroe. He had requested eight-thirty that evening, and she had suggested Italian.

"You know if we keep meeting like this people will begin to talk," Munroe said as they sat down at a table.

"Let them talk." Hershey smiled. "I've sent the letter to the hospital board concerning April. I don't believe she should be being held there. And McGill and I believe she may be in some form of danger."

"You still believe she is being used?" Munroe asked.

"Occam's razor," Hershey replied, "it's the only thing that ticks all the boxes. So however unlikely it may sound, it remains the simplest explanation. And I don't believe in coincidence. Prior to April arriving at the hospital, Ashford experienced way less deaths than the national average for these types of institutions, less than two a year. Now in half that time we've had Legwinski, McCoy and Bessey's deaths, not to mention Frank Marshall taking his own life. And in ways we can't easily explain."

"Legwinski? I thought his was just a straight forward suicide?" Munroe asked.

"At first I thought it was. And probably still is but when I think about it more the circumstances were a bit odd. I mean there were no obvious signs he was a danger to himself. My point is, something out of the norm is going on there and neither McGill or I like the idea of April being in the centre of it."

"Okay, so if they approve her release, then what Elizabeth?" Munroe asked.

"Well, she'll be available for fostering, maybe adoption," she replied, feeling her head tilt slightly to one side.

"And I suppose you know someone that might want to foster a child like April Pritchard?"

"I might do…Come on Munroe don't be like that, she's a great kid, she's had a shitty time. She'll be good for me and I know I can be good for her," Hershey replied.

"Elizabeth," surprised to hear that he had used her name again and how comfortable it felt. "April Pritchard killed her parents. Even if there was no intent, she is at a secure hospital because a few people at least, including a judge, consider her to be a danger. And besides all of that, you may *only* work the hours of a doctor, but you are still not at home all that much."

"She's had no reoccurrence. What happened was awful and extremely rare but we all expect somnambulism to stop as she gets older. It probably already has. I don't need to work as much, and I can make arrangements for her, a housekeeper or something."

"Will they let you care for her? Be her guardian or whatever they call it these days?" Munroe asked.

"Why not? I have a good home, solid profession, I'm smart," Hershey started to smile as she spoke, "and I'm connected." Hershey picked up some bread and dipped into a mix of olive oil, balsamic and black pepper.

Munroe shook his head.

"What? You never cared for anyone?" Hershey asked, crumbs escaping her mouth as she spoke.

Munroe looked into her green eyes, for a moment he almost said what he was thinking, but then said, "You know for a classy lady you have some very *un-classy* habits."

"A bit like that toothpick you keep in your mouth?" Hershey replied.

Munroe smiled. "Yeah, I guess, though I've never been accused of being classy." Munroe said, taking the toothpick out his mouth to look at it and then return it to the corner of his mouth and between his teeth.

"So, Munroe, when is Munroe going to divulge his first name?" Hershey asked

"Munroe does just fine, only my Mom uses my first name and then only when she wants to tell me off."

"And does she? Tell you off?" Hershey asked, taking a sip of wine.

Munroe hesitated, and looked into her eyes again. "I thought we were talking about you and April."

"We were but you changed the subject."

"I did?"

"Yes, you said I was a classy lady."

"Ahh yeah, I did, after you shot breadcrumbs all over the table." Munroe said, taking a drink of water.

"What happened to you Munroe?" Hershey asked. Munroe almost spilled his water. Before he could respond, Hershey continued, "I mean, you don't drink, you don't smoke, I've never heard you swear. You seem somehow reluctant in your work and you said you have trouble sleeping."

"Reluctant?" Munroe repeated, "Why do you say that?"

"I'm not sure. I know you work very hard and are by all accounts very good at your job, I'm not questioning your ability or commitment, it's just…sometimes it seems like you do it because someone told you to do it, I don't know, like a penance or something. What happened?"

Munroe was silent, staring into Hershey's eyes. He had never shared his secret, not with anyone. He wondered if she would be the one. Then his thoughts were interrupted, "Sorry what?" Munroe said.

"I said, I brought you here to go over the deaths at Ashford again with you." Hershey repeated.

"You still think Emily Jackson is involved?" Munroe asked.

"Yes, I do. She's using some sort of hypnotic suggestion. She's able to use a trigger that kicks off a programming she has placed within a person's subconscious. With Donald the program kept him in a state where he would not feel the pain of forcing…of killing himself. I think he subconsciously took the forks out of the canteen. What I'm unclear on is what she used as the trigger. With Lucas Vogel the trigger was a match. She must have known he was likely to light a match before leaving the building, *that* triggered the program – the program made Vogel believe the flame from the match was some huge fire and the drawing of the bell must have been another trigger for Vogel to set the fire alarm off."

"What about the nurse, Bessey, who was killed?" Munroe asked.

"I don't think Emily could have meant for that. It's like she's playing some sort of game to see what can be achieved. She probably viewed Donald as expendable."

"Elizabeth, we've been over this. We have a man on the Campus, who incidentally, I'm going to need to put on to something else. What *else* can I do? You may have something but short of camera footage and recorded conversations this is all going to be more than a little difficult to prove."

"I know, but let's just assume for the moment I'm right. How would you go about catching someone like that?" Hershey asked.

"We would probably set up a sting of sorts, a trap. We could try running surveillance but that's not going to be possible inside the hospital without putting someone on the inside. And there's just not enough here. Bessey's murder will be added to Walker's list of convictions and the others..." Munroe opened his palms, "are suspicious at best."

Hershey reached across the table and squeezed Munroe's hand. "Thank you for the help. I must be starting to sound a bit cranky myself." Hershey said.

Munroe gently reciprocated the squeeze. "You care about the hospital and especially the child. She matters to you. We can interview Emily Jackson as part of the follow up on Bessey's death. If she is involved in anyway the Police presence will probably be enough to spook her or anyone else that might be involved. I don't see her trying anything else." Munroe assured.

Hershey smiled. She kept her hand on Munroe's just a little longer than necessary before withdrawing her hand. They returned to their food.

A couple of minutes of silence had passed before Hershey said, "Munroe?" Munroe looked up. "I have to go away for a few days. I'm giving a lecture in Toronto. When I get back, do you think we can go for dinner and keep work off the agenda?" Hershey asked.

Munroe stopped chewing then swallowed. "You mean like a date?" he said.

Hershey smiled, "Yes I suppose, like a date. Would that be okay?"

Munroe was smiling. "Yes, that would be just fine."

After the dinner, Hershey gave Munroe a polite kiss to the cheek before getting into her car. Hershey said she would call Munroe once she got back to fix a time with him. Munroe was first to drive away. Hershey lingered in the parking lot, checking her appearance in the rearview. As she pulled out of the lot, she hadn't noticed the silver Toyota pull out behind her.

CHAPTER 14

At ten thirty-six on Friday morning Hershey's office phone rang. After one ring, the call was automatically forwarded to her assistant's phone. Sam picked up.

"Good Morning, this is Samantha, Dr. Hershey's assistant, how may I help?"

"Is Dr. Hershey there please?" said a voice.

"No, I'm sorry Dr. Hershey will not be back in the office until Thursday next week. Am I able to help? Can I give her a message?"

"It's really quite important I talk to her, could you tell me where she is?"

"I'm sorry Dr. Hershey is lecturing in Toronto today, she won't be back in Vancouver until Wednesday afternoon. I will be talking with her later today and can pass on a message and your contact details. Can I ask who it is that is calling?"

The caller hung up.

Almost an hour later, the phone rang again.

"Good Morning, this is Samantha, Dr. Hershey's assistant, how may I help you?"

"Hi Sam, it's Professor McGill, is Dr. Hershey available please? I called her on her cell, but she doesn't appear to be picking up."

"No, I'm sorry Dr. Hershey will not be back in the office until Thursday now. Can I take a message for her?"

"Oh yes, sorry I had forgotten. No, it's nothing urgent. She had asked me to make her aware if something came up. Could you tell her that Emily Jackson came to the hospital today? She came to visit Edward Walker. Please ask could she call me when convenient. Thank you." McGill hung up.

That evening after the lecture and the compulsory social drinks, Hershey checked in with her assistant. Sam confirmed a reservation at Diva's for two on Wednesday evening, provided an update on short-listing potential housekeepers, shared a request from the Nature Publishing Group asking if Hershey would like to contribute to the Molecular Psychiatry journal, and went over the messages that she had taken that day.

"Are you sure Professor McGill said Edward Walker, Sam" Hershey asked.

"He definitely said Emily Jackson had been at the hospital and had visited Edward Walker. Why? Is that strange? I'm certain I noted it correctly." Sam asked.

"Yes, very," Hershey confirmed. "Sorry Sam I didn't mean to imply…it's just that I was expecting Emily would visit, but to see Edward Walker makes no sense at all. And besides why would Charles allow it?"

"Well he had forgotten you were away with these lectures. Perhaps he did make a mistake." Sam said.

"Yes," Hershey replied, the doubt clear in her voice. "Okay thanks Sam, thanks for making the reservation, I'll confirm with Munroe now. Don't worry about the message from Charles, I'll try and call him tonight. Speak to you tomorrow."

After ending the call, Hershey remained sat on the edge of her hotel bed. She glanced at her watch…just after six. Returning to her phone she called Munroe. After the third ring she was taken to his voicemail…*Detective Munroe is unavailable at this time*…Hershey waited for the beep before saying, "Hi Munroe, it's Elizabeth. Just calling to say I've made a reservation for us at Diva for Weds evening, 8pm, hope that works for you. I can come by and pick you up if you'd like though you'll need to let me have your street address, Burnaby Heights right. Anyway, call me when you get the chance. Bye."

Hershey glanced at her watch again. It would be after nine in Vancouver and she debated phoning McGill. They had enjoyed a long, trusted relationship that Hershey believed was anchored on a healthy mutual respect for each other, that respect extended to not troubling each other at unsociable hours unless necessary. Hershey fingered with her phone, scrolling McGill's contact info up and down. She pressed the call button. McGill picked up.

"Charles McGill, hey Elizabeth," McGill said.

"Hi Charles, sorry to disturb you, I just got off the phone with Sam she said you called earlier today. She said you mentioned that Emily Jackson had been to the hospital and visited Edward Walker?"

"Yes, that's right. This morning in fact," McGill confirmed.

"I'm sorry Charles, I don't understand, why would Emily be visiting Edward?"

"I've no idea. I only found out about it myself after the visit." McGill said.

"Aren't you supposed to approve visits to the higher risk patients?" Hershey asked, knowing the answer.

"Yes, I know. It was Nichols that had okayed it. I did speak to Nichols who said that she had told him she was doing some research on your behalf as input to a book you were looking to write. He said as he had seen you two together at the hospital he assumed it was okay for a supervised visit." McGill replied. He could hear Hershey sigh.

"So, what did she want with Edward?" Hershey asked.

"Nichols said she repeated that she was doing some research for a potential book and asked Edward if she could ask him a few questions. He agreed. She asked about his background, where he grew up and his education. She then asked some questions relating to his convictions and seemed to want to explore why he killed. I realise she isn't working for you but perhaps this was her way of getting input for her own material, would be quite a coup for a student to be able to include a first-hand account of this sort. Of course, I'm not pleased with the breach in protocol but its nothing more than an inventive prank."

"Charles, there must have been more to it than that. Something is going on at Ashford and Emily Jackson is at the heart of whatever it is. I believe she may in some twisted way be using her access to the Hospital to conduct experiments, manipulation, suggestion, even hypnosis. I am concerned for April because I think Emily might be involving her, that's why I want April out of there. I mean, shit Charles, now what is Emily up to?"

"It's likely nothing Elizabeth. Listen, because of the breach I have blocked Jackson's access at the hospital entirely. Any visits she tries to make will be declined and if she turns up at the hospital again, she will be asked to leave. She didn't meet with April, nothing happened with her talk with Walker, and she won't be allowed back. She'll get her five minutes of fame in whatever paper she's writing and then that will be it. Nichols realises his mistake." McGill replied.

"Was there anything else, anything else that Emily may have said to Edward? Did they talk about anything that Nichols may have thought strange or did Emily attempt to pass Edward anything? A piece of paper perhaps?" Hershey asked.

"I went over the meeting. It was recorded so you can view it for yourself. It all appears very routine," then McGill hesitated.

"What Charles? Was there something else?" Hershey pressed.

"Only at the end, just before the meeting ended, Jackson did lean forward and appeared to say something to Walker, though you can't hear what was said on the recording."

"Did Edward respond?" Hershey asked.

"He did say something. You can see his lips move on the video but again it's not possible to hear what was being said. Elizabeth, I'll keep the recording, you are welcome to view it of course, but it's really nothing to be alarmed about. And listen, I have something else. Golding has booked a video conference with me for Wednesday morning. I expect they have decided on whether to support April's release or not."

Hershey remained silent for a moment. "Thank you, Charles for your support with that. It means a lot. I'm back in Vancouver on Wednesday. I'll call you as soon as I land." Hershey ended the call.

Hershey got up from the bed and walked over to the window. To the west was the Theatre district where Hershey had seen several shows over the years. She knew the city well having studied both biology and psychiatry at the University. She thought back to some of the friends, many of whom she had allowed herself to lose contact with. She considered some of the relationships, some very casual, a few meaningful ones over the years. But as she looked out from the fifteenth-floor window, she wondered what was next for her. If the Board agreed to April's release, what then? Hershey tried to imagine April as a teenager, then as a young woman, taking her to the theatre, sharing her life with April, watching her grow up. For many years Hershey had been focussed only on herself, her education, her career – the years studying, time at Kings College, London, at Pennsylvania as well as here in Toronto. Like her father she considered herself successful. *But what now?*

Hershey's cell phone began to vibrate on the bed. She picked up the phone...*Munroe*.

"Hi Munroe," Hershey said as she picked up the call.

"Hey. I got your voice message. Yes, Wednesday evening should be fine assuming nothing comes up of course. How are you doing? Lectures, right?" Munroe asked.

"Err good thanks. Thanks for calling me back." Hershey said.

"Is everything alright?" Munro asked.

"Yes, I'm fine. McGill called earlier. I had asked him if he would call me if Emily Jackson visited the hospital. He told me she had gone there today but to meet Edward Walker."

"Can she do that? I mean, can people just turn up and visit people like that?" said Munroe.

"No, not really. Patients are allowed visitors of course, they are still technically patients, and not prisoners. But for the higher risk patients there are procedures. I just don't understand why she should want to." Hershey replied.

"What did McGill say? I assume she must have been supervised?"

"She said she was doing research on my behalf, asked Edward some pretty standard type questions. But at the end she apparently whispered some things to him. McGill doesn't know what was said."

"And you think she's up to something again?" Munroe asked.

"She *is* up to something Munroe. But what I have no idea."

"I have to attend something," Munroe said, "Did you want me to call you back a bit later?"

"No, I'm fine thanks. I'm going to soak in the bath and then get some sleep. I'm fine."

"Okay, well, have a good night. Elizabeth?" Munroe said.

"Yes?"

"You can call me any time you know that? I can't always pick up, but I will always call you back as soon as I get the chance."

"Yeah, I know, thanks Munroe. Go do what you need to do, and I'll call you when I get back into Vancouver on Wednesday. Okay, bye."

The flight back to Vancouver had been uneventful. Hershey had tried to catch some rest in her business class seat but had found sleep hard to come by. She scanned the various movies and programs on offer. Not finding anything of interest she settled into an old paperback she had been carrying around for just such occasions.

The plane landed just after three pm. Hershey switched her phone back on and waited for it to connect to the subscriber. She had a message waiting, McGill. She knew McGill would not leave the Board's decision to voicemail, he would simply have asked her to call him. Hershey had managed to avoid checking baggage and the domestic flight meant no Customs to go through. She was soon out of the arrivals terminal and into a cab.

From the backseat of the cab she sat staring at her phone, McGill's contact details staring back at her. Earlier in the week she had Sam set up interviews for three of the short-listed housekeepers. *Was she going to need one? Even if they decline her release, they will have to let her go at some point. There's no reason for April to remain at Ashford*, Hershey thought. Hershey called McGill

"Charles, it's Elizabeth, you have the decision?" Hershey asked.

"Yes, Elizabeth, it's good news. They have approved her release. I've arranged for her to have a final psych evaluation in the morning and then she is clear as far as the hospital is concerned to leave whenever. You said you would make the arrangements with Child Services, it's then really up to you guys as to when she leaves."

"Charles that's wonderful news. Thank you, thank you for your support on this." Hershey said.

"You are most welcome. I'll assume you will want to let April know?" McGill asked.

"Yes, for sure. Let me finalise things with Child Services and then once we've agreed a date for her, I'd like to be the one to tell her." Hershey said.

"Okay then. Elizabeth, are you certain about this?" McGill said.

"Yes, Charles," Hershey replied almost laughing. "Yes, I am. I'm very much looking forward to it. I completed the application for guardianship. I do need to make sure I have proper cover at home for her but that is all in hand. She can attend Handsworth High school which is near my home, as well as continue getting her private tuition. I'm going to take some extended time off to help her get settled and likely cut back on my hours until she's a bit older."

"Well, good luck with Child Services. Are you still coming in tomorrow?" McGill asked.

"Yes, I'd still like to view Emily's meeting with Edward. I'll be there around ten am. Perhaps I can take April out for lunch?"

"Of course, enjoy the rest of your day," McGill said before hanging up.

Hershey wiped a tear from her cheek but the smile remained.

* * * *

Hershey placed her flight case on the doorstep while she searched her handbag for the house key. Finding her keys, she unlocked the front door and pushed it open before picking up the case. She stepped into the foyer.

Hershey closed the front door behind her and simply stood on the shoe rug, still holding her case. The porch light shone through the window in the door casting both light and shadow into the hallway. For a moment Hershey imagined opening the front door to find April running up to her to give her a welcome hug, and the smell of coffee and homemade bread drifting from the kitchen, and a housekeeper smiling like the Cheshire cat – a sure indication that a great dinner was ready to be served. Hershey placed the case on the floor, two of the wheels connected with the hardwood and the noise brought Hershey back to the empty house. She was still alone but not for much longer she thought.

Hershey kicked off her shoes and checked her watch. The afternoon would shortly turn to evening. She hung up her jacket and dropped her handbag to the floor. Grabbing her phone, she dialled Sam as she headed upstairs.

Almost two hours later, Hershey came down the stairs, her hair down but gripped back, she was wearing an emerald necklace and matching earrings, and a black satin backless dress. She opened a closet near the foot of the staircase that housed many pairs of shoes, different coloured clutch bags, scarves and gloves. Hershey reached down and took a pair of black Armani shoes from a box and slipped them onto her feet. She grabbed a black leather clutch bag and transferred some mints, perfume, purse and makeup from her handbag. She grabbed her phone from off the bottom step and a Chanel vintage jacket from the closet, opened the front door and left the house.

The car automatically sensed the key that Hershey kept in her purse, the doors unlocked. As she slid into the driver's seat, the engine start button pulsed azure blue. She provided Munroe's post code to the car which brought up the route to his apartment. She started the car and pulled off her driveway onto Patterdale Drive. As she drove down Capilano Road and onto Highway 1, she was unaware of the car following behind.

Traffic on the Highway was heavy but moving. Hershey knew Munroe was attracted to her. His pupils would widen, his shoulders would open up just a little more when he saw her, while his posture appeared to tighten before relaxing again. The Edward Walker case had brought them together and unlikely as it seemed Alexander Jones had brought them even closer. She pictured Munroe, tall, broad shoulders, his shaven milk chocolate coloured head, brown soft eyes, the five o'clock shadow around his chin and mouth. She smiled as she recalled his voice, deep and smooth. And then that smile of his. She hadn't seen it often enough but when he did smile, it had an immediate effect on her.

As she made her way over the second narrows bridge, she asked the car to call Munroe. Through the car speaker system, she could hear his phone ringing…*three…four…fiv,*

"Munroe," he said, sounding a little out of breath.

"Are you okay?" Hershey asked.

"Hi Elizabeth, yeah I'm almost ready."

"Good, I'm just pulling onto Hastings, I'll be outside in a couple of minutes."

She pulled up opposite Munroe's apartment. She noticed that it overlooked a small park. The drizzle had turned to rain. A car turned into the road, and drove passed, parking up further down the road. Hershey waited. Eventually, she saw Munroe dressed in a light tan suit and brown shoes make his way across the road with his shoulders hunched like it made a difference to the rain. He was carrying something.

"Hi, sorry I'm a little late. I'm not used to powdering my nose. Here this is for you."

Munroe handed her a single red rose. Taking the flower, she kissed him gently on the cheek.

"Thank you, it's lovely."

She placed the flower flat on the dashboard in front of her.

The Jaguar pulled off and took the first right down Ingleton and then right onto Hastings. They were heading back into town. The rain helped obscure the Toyota that followed behind.

Diva's was one of Hershey's favourite restaurants. She enjoyed the variety of menu and watching the horde of chefs busying their way around the large open view kitchen. She picked up her rose from the dash as they made their way from the adjoining underground car park to the restaurant. A sharply dressed man sat at a piano playing a tune Hershey recognised but hadn't heard in a long time – *Say Hello Wave Goodbye*

"A drink first at the bar?" the host asked.

Hershey looked at Munroe.

"No. Thanks," Munroe replied.

The host took them to their table as a waiter arrived to take their drinks order.

"I'll have a glass of champagne, we have something to celebrate. The 2002 Bollinger will be fine, thank you." Hershey said.

"We do?" Munroe asked, "I guess I'd better have a fresh orange juice please.'

Munroe made a point of getting Hershey seated before removing his jacket and getting seated himself. "What are we celebrating?" he asked.

"McGill called me yesterday to say the Board will agree to April's release. She had a psych evaluation today which they have verbally confirmed is fine. April can leave as soon as she has an approved place to go to. Now I just need approval from Child Services to become her legal guardian and she'll be able to come live with me."

"Wow, I realise this has been on your mind for some time now but it still all seems a bit... well, quick"

"I'm not getting any younger and while the career has been very good to me, I'm after something more. I think I'm finally ready to settle down a bit."

"Well good for you," Munroe said, "Does April know?"

"Not yet, I'll tell her tomorrow."

"What about the housekeeper?"

"Sam has been working on getting me a shortlist. I should be able to start interviewing this week."

The waiter returned with their drinks.

Taking his glass of orange juice Munroe said, "Well I'm really pleased for you," and chinked glasses.

Hershey smiled. "Yes, I'm certain it's the right thing to do."

The waiter took their meal order. Munroe ordered the smooth liver pate to start, and the filet steak, medium. Hershey chose the tomato soup to start and the salmon to follow.

"Has there ever been a Mrs Munroe or a nearly Mrs Munroe?"

Munroe pulled the toothpick from his mouth. "Not really. I've kind of been married to the job. I think most women find it hard to live with someone that can't really be relied upon for all that normal life stuff. Most other detectives I know have been through several marriages, expensive business or so I'm told. I've had relationships, don't get me wrong, I enjoy a woman's company, it's just…well, difficult. What about you?"

"I've had relationships, but nothing ever really got serious. I think I was too wound up in my work to really put the time or effort into anything else." Hershey replied.

"And now?" asked Munroe.

She looked into his soft brown eyes. "Now? Well, I'm a little older, a little wiser, and a little lonelier. I think your priorities change, mine are definitely changing. I've always pushed my self so hard, the education, qualifications, the years of practicing, the hours. I'm starting a little too late for the whole family thing but yes, I think I'm ready to settle down, kick back a little on the career."

They sat staring at each other for a moment. "So how did your lecture go?" Munroe eventually asked.

"Well. Advancements are being made all the time, we're able to treat more disorders, more diseases and disabilities, improve people's quality of life."

"What was the subject again?"

"Molecular Psychiatry," Hershey confirmed

"Oh, right."

They both laughed.

The food arrived. Over the course of the meal they made light conversation covering the weather, politics, and recent news events. They decided to share dessert, a chocolate praline.

"Are you a religious man?" Hershey asked.

"What makes you ask?" Munroe replied.

"I don't know, the usual. You don't drink or use profanity and I've noticed the other officers seem a bit different around you, they seem to swear less," Hershey said smiling. "I was wondering if that might be your motivation, for doing what you do."

"I don't think I'm a religious man, but I do believe in God if that's what you mean. And no, that's not why I chose the Police."

"So, what is it? I thought you were going to tell me something, that night we were in the car waiting at the site. I said you seemed reluctant as though you had to do this line of work, like you had no choice."

"Are you always like this?" Munroe asked.

"Of course," Hershey replied. She reached across the table and held Munroe's hand. "I care about you Munroe, but I can't help feeling that you are holding onto sadness, what is it?"

Munroe took a deep breath and glanced around. He cleared his throat. "When I was younger, in my teens, there was a party." Munroe swallowed hard before continuing, "some students had organised one summer up on Cypress. You know I've never shared this with anyone," Munroe said.

Hershey squeezed his hand, "Please go on."

Munroe swallowed. "I had been at the party, drinking, dancing, having a good time but it was getting late, I was getting tired and I had to drive home. I got in my car and started to drive back down the mountain. It had begun to rain, and I was having trouble seeing the road." Munroe swallowed again. "I...err...was just part way down when." Munroe could feel his bottom lip wobble. "Do we have to do this now?"

"Please Munroe, it's okay, tell me," Hershey said, quietly.

"Well er, I was driving down the road when someone, one of the students ran from the slope and on to the road in front of me." Munroe quickly wiped a tear that had escaped from his eye. "I had no time to turn or stop. I just hit him." Munroe covered his mouth with his hand. "I...err...didn't really know what to do. I had been drinking so I figured the Police weren't going to believe it was an accident. I got out of course, the guy wasn't moving but he was making some noise. So, I...got back in the car, drove on a little farther and then called for an ambulance. I didn't want to hang around for them to get there so I carried on driving. I was on the highway when I saw the ambulance and fire truck coming the other way. They took the student to the hospital." Munroe wiped another tear from the corner of his eye before it could drop. "I thought he was going to be okay."

Hershey took Munroe's hand in both of hers. "It's okay, there was nothing else you could have done Munroe. I'm sorry, I shouldn't have pressed you, I'm sorry."

Munroe cleared his throat again. "When I learned that he hadn't made it, I was devastated, I didn't know what to do. The Police knew he'd been hit by a car of course and questioned the other students, but none of them were able to connect the dots. When the Police came to talk to me, I didn't see any point in confessing. It couldn't change anything, and they wouldn't have believed it was an accident, so I told them I hadn't seen anything, that it must have happened after I left."

"So, you joined the Police because you felt the guilt?" Hershey asked.

"No, I became a Christian because of the guilt," Munroe replied, forcing a smile. "I joined the Police because I felt I needed to do something useful. Maybe I felt the need to pay something back, I don't know. But here I am, some twenty years later, still feeling like I have something to pay back."

Hershey was stroking Munroe's hand. "There was nothing you could have done. From the sound of it, even if you were fully sober it wouldn't have made any difference. Was the guy sober?"

Munroe shook his head, "Nah, he was pretty gone. I can still remember the smell of weed and alcohol on his breath. I thought he was going to make it."

Hershey, still holding Munroe's hand said, "It *wasn't* your fault Munroe, it was just…a horrible accident. And for what it's worth I think you're a fine detective and done a great deal for the community."

They talked late into the evening until Hershey said that they should think about returning Munroe home. Munroe was quick to help Hershey with her chair as she got up from the table. He then helped her with her jacket before putting on his own. As the exited the restaurant Munroe stopped her. Hershey looked at him.

"I've been wanting to say how beautiful you look tonight. I've really enjoyed tonight, thank you." Munroe said.

Hershey placed her hand against his cheek. "Thank you, me too. I'm sorry again for pressing you but thank you for sharing that with me, it means a lot." She kissed him on his cheek but close enough to his lips to give the kiss greater meaning."

The driver of the Toyota watched them as they left the restaurant. Rage burned within the driver. The driver had sat for hours outside Hershey's home trying to control the anger that welled within, debating the next course of action, but the lack of action merely stirred the anger to rage. *When to act? What if she spends the night with the man? Must act.*

The driver watched as the large man turned back after they had walked part-way down the exit ramp of the underground car park. He returned to the restaurant and after quickly stopping to talk to a host, he disappeared further into the restaurant. The bitch stood for a moment on the ramp and then continued down toward her car. The driver paused...*Must act, act now...*

The driver grabbed the wrench from the front seat and quickly exited the Toyota. With a glance at the restaurant, the driver ran across the road and down the ramp. Across the lot Hershey was still walking toward the Jaguar, her back to the on rushing figure.

Hershey reached her car and opened the driver's side door. Before getting into the car she stopped to search inside her clutch bag. She was unaware of the figure that moved quickly between the concrete pillars and the high-sided vehicles that were parked. She withdrew her hand and quickly used a facial wipe before pulling a small aerosol breath freshener from the bag. Before spraying Hershey glanced over the car's roof toward the exit ramp, but didn't see Munroe. As she went to press the small canister she felt a flash of pain from the back of her head, her legs buckled, and her eyesight blurred. As she slid down the car, a blurred figure stood over her. Unsure where her bag had fallen, Hershey's hand scrambled for the bag as the figure appeared to swing again. Hershey's hand found the bag on the floor next to her. She reached into the bag as something came down towards to her head. She pressed what she hoped was the car's panic alarm.

Munroe returned from the washroom, feeling a little embarrassed at having to go back to use the washroom. Though he had drunk a bit during the evening, he knew it was the nerves that had caused him to really need to go, as he thought of what might happen after they had left the restaurant. *Gangbangers, rapists, even serial killers could not make him as anxious as he was feeling right now*, Munroe thought. He nodded to the host as he left and walked briskly down the ramp. It was then that he heard a car alarm sounding from within the parkade. His walk quickly turned into a jog and then to running as he realised it was the Jaguar, but he couldn't see Hershey. As his eyes scanned the area, he saw a figure walking quickly behind the vehicles on the opposite side to him, heading towards an exit ramp. The figure looked short and was wearing a black three-quarter length rain coat with its collar up and a black woollen hat.

The figure hesitated momentarily than ran for the exit. Munroe was caught in two minds – *where was Elizabeth?* He ran after the figure. He was a good runner with the power of a seasoned sprinter. He didn't think it would be long before he caught up with the figure, this would be no long-distance chase. He followed the figure up the ramp and into the rain. The figure ran across the street, narrowly being missed by an oncoming vehicle. Munroe pursued. The figure opened the door to a silver car as Munroe jumped. He slid across the rain-soaked roof of the car and into the figure. They landed on the floor with Munroe easily overpowering the figure. The figure let out a scream as Munroe was about to land a punch, when he realised the figure was a woman. Grabbing hold of the raincoat, Munroe got to his feet, dragging the woman to her feet and pulling off the hat. It was Emily Jackson.

He removed handcuffs from his back pocket and placed Emily's hand in one. He then pulled her across to the passenger side of the car and secured the other cuff to the handle on the car door. Without saying anything, Munroe ran back across the road and down into the parkade.

He found Elizabeth slumped on the floor, unconscious and blood running from a wound to her head. The alarm stopped sounding. He checked her pulse, *she should be okay* he thought. He hesitated a moment, he wanted to lift her, but he wasn't sure of her injuries. He reached into his jacket, pulled his phone and called for an ambulance and assistance.

* * * *

It was sixteen hours later before Hershey came around and opened her eyes. She lay in a room with pale green walls. The bed was firm but comfortable. Her head ached, and her eyes and face felt swollen. Her vision was blurred at first before more of her surroundings came into focus, she was in a hospital. She was alive. A sharp pain seared through her head as she lifted her head slightly to view more of the room. Her head dropped back to the pillow. She was about to close her eyes as a shadow came over her – it was Munroe.

"Hi," Munroe said gently.

Hershey gave a slight smile only to discover the movement was painful, still she wanted to speak.

She whispered, "Did we…spend the night…together?"

Munroe smiled, "Yes we did. And I didn't leave in the morning either.'

"Did…you get them?"

Munroe nodded. "Emily Jackson, she hit you from behind. You have a fracture to the back of your head, it will take some time to heal but you should be fine, unless you are planning to take up hockey. Your shoulder is badly bruised, we're thinking you managed to dodge a blow. Probably just as well. The pain should clear in a few days."

"My face?"

"Swollen from the blow to your head, a bit blue but otherwise fine," Munroe replied. He put his hand carefully to the side of her face, "You are still beautiful."

Hershey gave another slight smile as she moved her hand up from the bed. Munroe moved his hand from her face to hold her hand.

"Thank you. Wh…where is she?" Hershey asked.

"She's enjoying a room at the station. Hale is on it, she's been booked on aggravated assault, it should keep her off the streets a while."

"Do we know…anything? Why?"

Munroe squeezed her hand, "We'll take care of it. You need rest. The doctor is going to want to come in and run some tests now you've woken up. I need to get to the station but if it's alright with you I'd like to come back tonight."

Hershey tried to smile again, "I'd like that…very much."

CHAPTER 15

Munroe and Hale worked out of the VPD's headquarter building on Cambie and 2nd. Their desks were located on the 4th floor near, but not next, to each other. Munroe's desk was somewhat isolated from the other detectives. Hale was typing up interview notes as he saw Munroe approach.

"How is she?" Hale asked.

"She's sore but the doctor expects her to make a full recovery, likely to be kept in a few days. She has a fracture to the back of her head that will take a few weeks to heal." Munro replied taking off his jacket and dropping it to the back of his chair. Munroe sat down and started to type at his keyboard. "Anything from Jackson?" he asked.

Hale shook his head, "Nothing. I'm just doing the last of notes now. The rest are there if you want to review them, along with the recordings." Hale knew Munroe preferred to go over material himself rather than have Hale, or anyone else for that matter, summarise things for him. Hale didn't mind, it was another of Munroe's *things*, and besides Hale considered Munroe to be the most respected cop in the Division, Munroe's results spoke the loudest.

Munroe put his headphones on and began by viewing the video recordings of each of the interviews. There were currently three in total. He knew there would be more before Jackson is transferred to a correctional facility to await trial. While listening more than watching the first interview, Munroe read over Hale's notes and arrest sheet. Before the recording of the initial interview had finished Munroe paused it and took off his headphones.

"Elizabeth believes Jackson is behind the deaths that occurred up at Ashford." Munroe said.

Hale looked up from his desk. "You never said why."

"She thinks Donald McCoy killed himself because he had been programmed to do it. And the situation that ended up with Thomas Bessey being murdered by our good friend, Edward Walker, had also somehow been orchestrated by Jackson. Lucas Vogel the guard on duty, lights up a match on his way out then decides to set off the fire alarm." Munroe paused, looking out of the window next to his desk rather than at Hale. "Don't you think it's kinda scary?" Munroe said, sounding like more of a statement than a question.

"What…having that kind of control? You think she's right?" Hale asked.

"Can't think of any other explanation," Munroe admitted. Still looking out of the window, across the intersection and out at the Olympic village, Munroe's mind began to wander. Munroe replaced his toothpick.

"The thing I find strange is…if Emily Jackson did do those things then why just attack Elizabeth straight out like that? She obviously found out about our investigation into her which might give her motive, but if you can get people to kill themselves or get someone else to do the killing for you, why would you just come out and attack someone?" Munroe said.

Hale was holding a coffee cup in his hand. "Maybe she got so pissed about the investigation she just decided to vent her anger by attacking Elizabeth? We both know how an emotional response can override a rational one."

Munroe was shaking his head. "I don't know the two things don't quite add up."

Hale placed his cup on his desk. "Donald McCoy sticks two forks into his eyes and some guard who's probably had too much to sniff, sets a fire alarm off. Then Jackson becomes too disgruntled about the investigation and decides that Elizabeth is the one behind it. The things don't have to be connected." Hale said.

"You can't just stick forks into your eyes, not slowly like Donald McCoy did. I verified what Elizabeth had said, you would need to be on some form of strong medication or operating under hypnosis or something like that. McCoy wasn't on any strong meds. The guard's tox report was clean, he hadn't even been drinking. So, if you *could* somehow convince someone to kill themselves by sticking forks into their head, and get someone to think they are seeing a blaze just by lighting a match, does it sound likely that you would just come out and hit someone you didn't like over the head?"

"Munroe you just want me to agree that it's unlikely that the two things can go together. Okay, it would be odd but weird shit happens all the time, people do…frigging stupid things all the time, one minute methodical the next reckless. We can't always know why but we can put the psycho's away."

"If Emily Jackson was behind the events at the hospital and hadn't have attacked Elizabeth, she'd still be out there without a hope of us catching her."

Hale muttered something to himself.

Munroe was quiet for a moment then, "What did she say when you asked her why she went to see Edward?"

"Work it out for yourself." Hale replied.

"Cute." Munroe said.

Munroe's mind was whirring. Hershey had said Jackson had mentioned Alexander Jones and Ebony Wilke's names during the meeting with Walker.

"She had said, *work it out for yourself.*" Munroe said.

Hale nodded.

"What do you think she meant by that?" Munroe asked.

"That she isn't going to tell us why she met with Edward Walker." Hale replied.

"Jackson told the Supervisor that she was doing some research. He assumed that because he had seen her with Elizabeth that the research was on behalf of Elizabeth, that's how she got access. What is there to work out unless that isn't the real reason for her visit?" Munroe asked.

Hale sighed, "Even for a Detective you ask too many questions. Perp's do what they do because they're evil bastards or lunatics, there isn't always something to understand."

"Cute," Munroe replied.

They were silent again, and Hale returned his attention to his keyboard and computer monitor. Munroe was still thinking and returned his gaze to the window. The cogs of his mind well oiled, serviced much more regularly than he would have liked by senseless acts of violence, scenes of death, cruelty and neglect without apparent motive. Puzzles are at first pieces, pieces to be assembled, one by one until gradually something takes form.

"You know that April Pritchard is up at Ashford?" Munroe said. "That's the same little girl that cut up her parents several months back that Agland and I went to. Killed them in her sleep."

Hale looked up again. "The same kid that was found those years back in Richmond Park? She was adopted?"

"Yeah, she killed her adopted parents."

"I remember the killings. Did it in her sleep or something like that? Wow, that's a pretty shitty start to life. Found as a baby lying next to her dead mother in Richmond Park, catching a break by being adopted only to end up responsible for causing their deaths. What is she…eight years old and already in a place like Ashford. Geez," Hale said shaking his head.

*Eight years old...discovered in Richmond Park...eight years old...eight years ago...Richmond...the hair...those eyes...*Munroe's mind was churning, data were the pieces, the pieces turning in his mind, seeking connections. Then,

"I know why Emily Jackson went to see Edward Walker."

"Go on, why?' Hale asked, leaning back in his chair.

"She thinks April Pritchard is Alexander's."

"How the *hell* did you get to that?"

"April is eight years old, found as a baby in Richmond Park. Ebony Wilkes as far as we know was Alexander's last victim. He picked her up near her school in Richmond nearly eight years ago. Alexander was in the Richmond area at the time April would have been conceived."

"And so were seventy-thousand other men. And besides, April could have been conceived anywhere, you don't have to go to Richmond to conceive, come on Munroe that's a huge stretch even for you."

"May be, but it would sure explain why her Mom killed herself and they do share traits. Anyway, I think Emily Jackson believed it."

"So why go to see Edward, why just not ask Alexander?"

Munroe shrugged, "I guess she thought Alexander wouldn't tell her. Perhaps she thought Edward might know or at least might find out. Maybe she didn't want Alexander to know in case she was right. But there's a much better way to be sure." Munroe was already starting to get up from his desk.

"Well it just gets better for that one. Discovered in a park laying next to her dead Mom, having to be kept in a secure facility because you're a danger to others when asleep, and your Dad turns out to be the King of Creeps. Where are you going?" Hale said.

"Ashford," Munroe replied, putting on his jacket as he walked passed Hale's desk. "It's okay finish the paperwork. I'll call you."

* * * *

When Munroe arrived at Ashford Hospital, Professor McGill was not around. He was referred to Dr.Cheung and asked to wait in Reception. It was several minutes until Dr.Cheung appeared. Munroe introduced himself and explained he was investigating a series of events and needed the assistance of the Hospital. Munroe asked they move somewhere more private.

Having moved into one of the offices close by, Dr.Cheung asked, "How can we help detective?"

"I need to prove paternity. Not for myself. I think Alexander Jones may have fathered a child. I don't expect he will be aware and so I'd like to keep that confidential. If I want to prove paternity I can only do that via DNA correct?"

"Correct," Dr.Cheung confirmed. "Blood types can sometimes be used to quickly disprove someone, but they can't be used to establish proof. DNA proves paternity beyond doubt. So, what do you want from us detective?"

"I'm going to need DNA from Alexander Jones and another of your patients." Munroe said.

"Detective, I'm sure you are aware we are not authorised to release the DNA of any of our patients without an appropriate instruction. Either a consent or court warrant. But you said two? Do you mean there is another possible father here at the hospital?"

Munroe turned away unconsciously tapping his thumb against his forehead. "I mean the samples I wish to compare are both currently patients here," he said.

"You're talking about April Pritchard. She's the only patient we have young enough. You think Jones could be her father?" replied Dr.Cheung. "Then you don't need a warrant." Munroe looked back at Dr.Cheung and frowned. "I mean, we record and retain the DNA profile of all our patients."

"So you already know they are not related?" Munroe asked.

"Not at all," Dr.Cheung replied, "the computer isn't asked to check for matches. We're not a forensic lab."

"But you can check for matches?" Munroe pressed.

"Of course, I'll take you there now."

Munroe followed Dr. Cheung passed main reception and around to the Records Department. Inside, they walked down to a bank of computer terminals where Dr. Cheung signed-in. From a menu he selected 'Profiles' and then entered another ID and password.

"We keep records of their fingerprints, blood sample and a patient's DNA profile," Dr. Cheung explained. "I believe the intention is for DNA to be collected for all births, following accidents and admissions, as well as crimes of course. Give it a few years and there'll be no such thing as a John or Jane Doe."

After a few clicks of the mouse and a moment to retrieve the data, Alexander Jones' DNA print was displayed, a series of black and white marks varying in width across a wide band. Once retrieved, Dr. Cheung selected "Compare" and browsed the database for April Pritchard.

"This'll only take a moment."

Within seconds, the two DNA bands were being displayed. Alexander Jones at the top, April Pritchard's underneath. The word 'MATCH' was displayed at the bottom of the screen.

"Well, I'll be…who would have thought that?" Dr. Cheung said quietly.

"Thank you for your help Dr. Cheung. Please can I ask that you keep this to yourself, at least for now? It is related to an ongoing investigation."

"I'll need to make Professor McGill aware." Dr. Cheung said.

"Okay, but no one else, please."

* * * *

McGill arrived at St Paul's within an hour after Munroe had left the hospital. McGill's secretary had given him the floor and department where Hershey was recovering. He made his way to Hershey's private room, he wasn't alone.

Hershey was a mix of black, purples and blue around the eyes, with bandages to her shoulder and forearm. She was sat up in bed as McGill and his guest entered the room.

"Hi sweetheart, how are you?' Looking at McGill she whispered, 'thank you.'

April placed flowers on the bed, and gently kissed Hershey on the cheek.

"These are for you, daffodils and roses, they're supposed to help with bruising though I'm not quite sure how," April said.

"Thank you, they're lovely."

"The Professor told me that you had fallen and hurt your head. He said you'd look a bit bruised but that you should be fully recovered within a few weeks. Those bruises look really sore. Are you going to have to stay here for a few weeks?" April asked.

"I should only have to stay in hospital a few days, no more than a week. And yes, I am a bit sore." Hershey replied. With a glance toward McGill she continued, "The bruising and swelling is mostly from where I hit the back of my head. I needed a few stitches back there. The doctors have given me some medicine to help with the pain, at the moment it's not too bad. And seeing you is a wonderful surprise."

McGill gave a nod and April seemed impressed.

"Well even with the swelling and all those bruises, you're still beautiful to me." April said.

"I'm going to leave you two alone for a bit. I'll be back in say, thirty minutes?" McGill interrupted.

"Thank you, Charles," Hershey replied. "So, what have you been up to?" Hershey asked April.

"I've been wanting to see you. The Professor said you were away for a few days doing a lecture. He said you're a sought after lady."

"Did he now?"

"Emily came to see me. I had been thinking about what you said and that maybe she wasn't everything she appeared to be, that maybe she wasn't *really* my friend. I asked her not to come and visit me anymore at the hospital, but she got a bit angry."

Hershey touched April's face with her right hand, "It's alright baby I think you did the right thing. I wouldn't worry about Emily, she'll be okay. And so, will *you*. Listen I have something really important to tell you."

April jumped up and sat on the bed.

"You know that Professor McGill and I have been discussing your stay at the Hospital. We both think it's not good for you to be there, that you no longer need to be there. You've not had any episodes for a few months now and even if you had, we don't think Ashford is the right place for you. Well, we discussed it with the Board and they have agreed. You no longer have to stay at the Hospital."

"Really? Honestly? Does that mean I can come live with you?" April asked. "I know you didn't want me to get my hopes up, but ever since you mentioned it I've been thinking about it all the time."

"Yes sweetheart, you will be able to come and stay with me, just as soon as I get out of here." Hershey replied.

April leaned over and hugged Hershey around the neck. Pain shot down Hershey's shoulder, but it was quickly dismissed in favour of the show of affection. They both started to cry and just held each other.

"Thank you, Elizabeth," April said releasing her grip. "Was that what that test was for?"

Hershey wiped the tears from her face.

"Did I hurt you? I'm so sorry I just forgot everything when you told me." April asked.

"No, it's okay. These are happy tears. Like yours," Hershey said, reaching to wipe April's tears from her face. "Yes, that was what the test was for. It was hospital procedure. They just want to make sure they don't let anyone go that might still be a danger to themselves or someone else."

"What about your work? Is there anyone else at your home?" April asked.

"No, no one else, not yet anyway. I was planning to get a housekeeper. She would stay with us, cook, help look after you. I have a few people I wanted to interview. Perhaps you could help me? And besides, I'd like to cut back on my hours so that I can spend more time with you. I'll take a break from work."

"Will I have to do any of those tests?"

"No sweetheart. I'm not going to make you do anything that you don't want to do, except may be ask you to clean your room every now and again. There's a good school near my home and if you want you'll be able retain your tutors that have been coming to the hospital. The high school is good, but I don't think it will be long before you will have learned enough to graduate. School will allow you to meet other kids, hopefully make some friends, live a somewhat normal life."

Tears started to run down April's cheeks again. "I don't know what to say, why would you do this for me?"

"Because you are a very special person April, you deserve better things. And I enjoy your company very much. It would be my pleasure to look after you if you'll let me." Hershey replied.

"That would be wonderful, really thank you Elizabeth thank you. Do I still stay at the hospital for now?"

"Yes. I need to get a bit better and we need to find a housekeeper. It shouldn't take any more than a couple of weeks." Hershey said.

"I will be at your home for Christmas!"

"Yes, I hadn't thought of that. You will need to let me know what you would like for Christmas." Hershey said.

"You have already given me more than I could have wished for," April replied.

The held each other again, though this time April was more careful.

* * * *

By the time Professor McGill and April were leaving St. Paul's Hospital, Munroe was leaving the Ashford Institution. Munroe didn't know what his discovery meant. *So, Alexander Jones was the father of April Pritchard, so what?* Any paternal rights he may claim to have had were all but severed the first time he seduced and killed a thirteen year old girl. *Did Alexander know? What had Emily told Edward? Would Edward have talked to Alexander?*

Munroe's thoughts turned to Hershey. Alexander had made Elizabeth take her clothes off. Sure, he no doubt got off on seeing her naked but Munroe knew Alexander simply wanted control, to experience control even in a place where he doesn't possess any, to experience control over someone he had never met. Alexander was both evil and smart and that combination made him really dangerous. Elizabeth wanted to take care of April Pritchard, take her into her home, become her guardian. *Could Alexander possibly know?* Elizabeth needed to know.

As he arrived at the hospital, Munroe found Hershey sitting up and finishing a bowl of soup.

"You must be feeling better than you did this morning." Munroe said as he entered.

Smiling, Hershey replied, "Hi Munroe, yes, I am thank you. The meds definitely help."

"And someone else has brought you flowers."

"McGill stopped by earlier. He brought April with him. It was lovely to see them."

Hershey looked into Munroe's eyes; she saw concern. "What is it?" she asked.

Munroe let out a deep breath. He helped Hershey place the tray down before he sat on the edge of the bed. "Emily's little visit to Edward had me thinking," he said.

"Me too, I've been wondering about that."

"Elizabeth, there's something you need know, it concerns April."

"What?"

"I've found out who her father is. Her biological father."

"Wh…Who?' Hershey asked, sitting up straighter.

Munroe looked into Hershey's eyes not sure how she might take the news or the wisdom of sharing it with her at this time. "April's father is Alexander Jones."

"Wh…No it can't be…how can that be? Munroe you must have made a mistake. It's not possible. Munroe?"

Munroe gently shook his head.

"Elizabeth, I've had it checked out. I've seen the DNA results. It was just something Hale said this morning about the timing and location of Ebony

Wilkes. It places Jones around the same location around the same time that April must have been conceived."

"You are being ridiculous. How can you have any idea where her natural mother was when she conceived? And even if it was in or near the same area, there must still be thousands of possible fathers." Hershey replied.

"I know, I know. I don't like coincidence. I go from time to location to their features, the blue eyes, that blond hair. I just get these ideas and then I have to check them out. I thought this may be an easy thing to check. So, I did. I checked." Munroe said. "The hospital has every patient's DNA on record. All it needed was a comparison. It's a match Elizabeth, I'm sorry."

Hershey seemed stunned. Munroe held her hand. He looked at her and could see the movements in her eyes, she was playing it all out. A tear ran down her cheek.

"Does April know?" Hershey asked.

"I don't think so. I mean the hospital didn't know and as far as the hospital is concerned there's been no contact of any kind between them. I don't see how she could know. Or him for that matter." Munroe replied.

"The poor child. Her mother was raped by Jones and fell pregnant. Rather than abort she gave birth to a baby girl. She couldn't cope with the situation. She must have intended to take the baby's life as well as her own, but couldn't bring herself to harm the child. She must have loved and hated the child at the same time. Every time being reminded of Jones and what he did, when she looked at the child? My God."

"I'm sorry." Munroe said again, as he saw the realisation etched onto Elizabeth's face.

"The bastard has done the same to me." Hershey said, her voice tailing off. "Are you are certain he doesn't know? You don't think me wanting to adopt April has anything to do with what he made me do?"

Munroe shook his head, "How could he know? He did what he did because he needed control, control over you, control over us, to experience control over the situation. April is entirely…"

"Coincidence?" Hershey added.

"I was going to say separate. The odds appear remote but think about it. This is Vancouver, how many care facilities like Ashford do we have. It's the only place to house lunatics like Jones. And for someone like April, she ended up there because of her sleep issues." Munroe said.

Hershey fell silent again, then said, "I'm going to be there for her. It makes no difference to me. April is innocent in all of this. She didn't ask for any of it. It makes no difference to me Munroe. I shared the news with her this morning that she could come home with me. It was wonderful, I'm not sure I've ever felt so happy as I was this morning. That bastard is not going to take that from me or from April. It doesn't change anything?"

Munroe got off the bed and moved closer to Hershey. He held her, gently, and she could feel his warmth, his love.

"I still want her," she said quietly.

After a few minutes of silently holding each other, Hershey said, "I think I may know why Emily attacked me."

* * * *

Munroe found himself dressed in strange clothes, walking through dense forest and foliage, and down a steep slope. Music was blasting in his ears, but no music he had ever heard before– *Rap*. He reached to his ears and found he was wearing small, but comfortable headphones. A voice in the headphones was screaming violence and profanity to a synthesized rhythm of drums and bass. Munroe tried to remove the headphones, but they wouldn't move. He continued down the slope. It was dark with only occasional light from the moon breaking the eerie darkness. There was a chill to the air. Munroe looked again at his clothes. He was wearing a red sport jacket and stonewashed jeans. He couldn't remember ever owning a red jacket. He tried to stop his movement down the slope. He couldn't stop. He realised he wasn't in control. He continued down between the tall trees, sounds of hate and anger continuing to pump into his head. Munroe looked at his hands as he steadied himself as he descended – *his skin was white!*

The realisation of where, or rather whom, he was struck like lightening, in an instant and with terrific force. Munroe found himself trapped in another's body. Shock gave way to terror as he realised in who's body he must be trapped. Munroe started to panic as the body continued down the slope. Munroe looked down and across trying to see through the trees and to the road he believed was below. Glimpses of what he knew to be headlights could be seen but still the body continued down the slope, seemingly oblivious to the danger. Closer and closer, he was taken to the road below. Munroe could only sense himself screaming '*No!*' as the body stepped from the trees and jumped down onto the road. *The headlights, the car, his car!* Munroe stared as the vehicle sped towards him. He tried to jump back out of the way, but the body remain transfixed. '*Move!*' Munroe felt himself shout, but he heard nothing but the sound of screeching tires. The vehicle lurched forward, the rear end rising as the brakes must have been applied and fought to rein in the car's velocity. It would be no good; the car was travelling too fast and not enough time to react. Munroe could only stare as the inevitability of what was going to happen took hold.

The vehicle hit, and Munroe felt himself floating. He looked down to see the blacktop passing underneath. Munroe had expected to feel the impact and crippling pain, but there was nothing. Time seemed to slow to almost nothing and only the weightlessness of floating above the road could be felt. Then, with a sudden jolt, the floating stopped, and Munroe lay still looking up at the moonlit night. He thought he heard a car door open and then footsteps, rushing, getting closer. The he heard a voice – "Shit, no!" The voice sounded familiar. As he lay there quite still, he could sense the cool tarmac below but still he felt no pain. Munroe tried to turn his head and look toward the footsteps and the voice, but his head wouldn't move. Then the scattered grey clouds and moonlight were obscured by a figure that stood over him and peered down. The face in front of him came closer, looking into Munroe's eyes. A black hand came into view and a thumb and finger moved towards his eyes. The last thing Munroe saw as his eyelids were closed by the approaching hand was *himself.*

Munroe awoke breathing heavily, slumped in his arm chair with a light sweat across his brow. He wiped the beads of sweat away from his eyes and considered the dream. But he knew it was more than a dream. It was a *Regret.*

Forgiveness from God for the death of the young man was not enough for Munroe; he would perform his penance and try to pay back what he could.

* * * *

The following day, Munroe and Hale interviewed Emily Jackson again, so far, she had said nothing of why she attacked Dr. Hershey. Emily would shortly be transferred to the Women's Correctional Centre in Maple Ridge, a forty minute drive from Vancouver, where she would be remanded awaiting trial for aggravated assault. Munroe wanted information. Munroe started.

"Emily, what's the nature of your relationship with April Pritchard?"

Emily looked at Munroe. "What's the nature of your relationship with that doctor?" she replied.

"You're a student at UBC with good grades and by all accounts a great deal of potential. You were asked to act as guardian for April Pritchard, a child prodigy who the University had taken under its wing. After the incident at the University you continued to visit April at Ashford. Would you describe yourself as a friend?" Munroe paused though he was not expecting an answer.

Emily was still looking down at the table they were seated at. Munroe continued, "I know why you went to see Edward," Munroe said leaning in toward Emily. She looked up. He had her attention. "You believe Alexander Jones might be the biological father of April Pritchard. But what was it you expected Edward to do? Go ask him to confirm it? Do you think he'd know? Emily." Munroe leaned back and again paused. This time Emily held her stare at him.

"So, is it true? Is she, his child?" Emily asked.

"It doesn't matter. You believe it is and that's why you went back to Ashford. But why Edward? Why not ask Alexander directly?"

Emily continued to look at Munroe but remained silent.

"You'll be aware there have been a few odd situations occurring at the hospital. We are looking into the death of a patient there, Donald McCoy, and another incident that lead to the death of a member of staff. Do you know anything about those events?" Munroe asked. "I understand your studies include Neuro-psychology, you study the brain and how it affects how we function, how we behave. One of the security officers at the hospital believed that he saw a blazing fire when all he did was light a match. How might that be explained, can you tell me?"

Still Emily said nothing.

Munroe pressed harder, "Donald McCoy somehow managed to press two forks into his head through his eyes. Lucas Vogel triggered a fire alarm because he thought he was seeing a fire in the hospital. The ensuing procedural problems led to the death of a member of staff at the hands of your friend Edward Walker."

"He's not my friend," Emily interrupted, "Edward Walker is not my friend."

"You went to see him. Tricked your way in, had your little interview. What did you want Emily?" Munroe said. "You see I think you are involved. I think that you are carrying out an experiment of some kind, manipulating people at the hospital."

"That's why you were investigating me?" Emily said. "Your guy made a piss poor job of trying to conceal it. Do you realise how you sound detective? Emily looked away for a moment, looking at nothing in particular, but it was a look that Munroe recognised. Munroe gave her a moment to process. "You think the patient was somehow persuaded to kill himself what, through hypnosis or something? And you think something similar was used on the guard. Is that how you think I'm involved? This is absurd on so many levels. I've never met these people. Why would you think I have anything to do with it?"

"Because until you arrived nothing weird had been going on," Munroe replied. "And you gave Lucas Vogel a picture just a few hours before he set that alarm off, a picture of a bell ringing."

"I don't know Lucas Vogel. Of course, I didn't give him a picture."

"But you do know to which picture I'm referring?" pressed Munroe.

Emily stared at Munroe. After a moment Emily let out a deep breath. "Detective, I have no idea what you are talking about. I would visit the hospital to see April, whom I consider a friend and feel some responsibility for. Yes, I shared some of my research with her and yes, I showed her how to draw a picture that created the illusion of a bell ringing. April must have given it to the guard. But that doesn't mean anything, there's no way that could have any affect on anyone. I attacked that bitch because she was turning April against me. The last time I met April, she told me she didn't think I should keep going to visit her. I knew that doctor must have been manipulating her, putting ideas into her head. April and I are good friends. She may only be eight years old but she's so much more than that. I just want to be there for her, to help her realise her potential."

Munroe looked across to see Hale wipe a hand across his chin. Munroe felt Hale's frustration. Jackson had admitted the attack on Elizabeth but seemed confused about the events at the hospital.

"She pointed you at me," Emily said. Munroe looked up. "That doctor of yours. She told you I must be involved in those things at the hospital." Pushing her chin up she said, "You two couldn't have come up with that. And because I'm the neuro-grad it must be me. There must a number of explanations for what happened, the patients do have illnesses, and most are on strong behavioural inhibiting drugs I bet. The guard could have been on anything, did you check what he was smoking? And why me, there must be a bunch of psychologists up at that place including your girlfriend, maybe it's her experiment."

Munroe stood and turned toward the door, his hands on his hips.

"Why did you want to see Edward Walker?" Hale asked.

Emily turned to look at Hale. "Oh, you do speak. April shared with me her desire to try and find out who she is, who her parents were, that kind of thing. So, I did some digging. Pictures are available of her mother, but no one has been able to identify her. I got to thinking why a new mother would take her own life, shitty life, abusive husband, acute post partum depression, rape. Like you, I worked out that her mother was in the age range of Alexander's known victims, she was found not too far from his known hunting grounds, and I don't know, she looked like his type. Anyway, I found a newspaper article of Alexander's conviction. There were some photographs taken outside the courtroom after the trial. I saw a familiar face among the public spectators."

"April Pritchard's mother," Hale said.

Emily nodded. "So, if I confronted Alexander about it and he didn't know about April, me asking questions might lead him to April. I don't want that creep making that connection. I asked Edward if Alexander had said anything to him, and in return for publicizing Edward's case, Edward was going to ask Alexander if he one of his victims matched April mother's description."

"Where were you going to publicize Edward's case?" Hale asked.

"No where," replied Munroe, turning back around and returning to his chair.

"Edward Walker isn't crazy. Okay he's a little crazy, but he doesn't kill for the sake of killing. He's nothing like Alexander. Edward is just…mixed up. We're all animals and he doesn't see anything wrong with preying on the weak. Edward doesn't want to be adored or famous, he just wants to be understood. I offered him that in exchange for his assistance."

"Do you have anything else to tell us?" Munroe asked.

"I didn't mean to hurt your girlfriend. I just wanted to…scare her. I knew she was saying things about me, turning April against me. When that cop turned up on campus I knew she must have been behind that. I was screwed, and I hadn't done anything. I followed her, then when I saw you and her together I got even more angry. I was just going to confront her, tell her she had it all wrong."

"You hit her with a jack wrench," Munroe said.

"I was angry. Anyway, she's going to be alright, isn't she?" Emily asked.

Munroe rose from his chair. "You are going to be transferred to the Women's Correctional Centre at Maple Ridge this evening, while you await sentencing, assuming you are pleading guilty. If not, you'll be waiting there until your trial. Your parents have contacted us. It seems they were advised of your situation by one of your friends. They have arranged a lawyer for you. We'll let the prosecutor know you have been cooperative." Munroe glanced at the wall clock, "Interview complete. It's now two forty-seven pm."

After Emily had been returned to her holding cell, Hale turned to Munroe and said, "She seems to think that you and Elizabeth are more than just good friends."

"It's what I told you. That was the first time we went out. Yes, I'm fond of her but nothing has happened between us." Munroe replied.

"Yet," Hale said smiling, "nothing yet."

* * * *

The next day Munroe returned to Ashford. McGill agreed to Munroe taking April offsite for a while, after reassurances from Munroe that nothing would be recorded, and their time would be strictly off the record. The formal approval from the board regarding April's release meant it was no longer necessary for April to be electronically tagged. Munroe found April playing a game of chess with a member of staff. April was wearing a blind-fold. As he approached, April turned her head toward him,

April turned her head toward Munroe as he approached her from the side. "Hello Detective Munroe," April said, starting to untie the blindfold.

"Hello April," Munroe replied frowning. "How did you know it was me?"

"You came to my house, you and detective…Agland." April replied.

"I'll leave you two alone, she was beating me anyway, I was just trying to provide some practice," said the nurse, as she got up to leave.

Munroe sat down where the Nurse had been sitting. "So, you remember me?" Munroe asked.

"You are a large black police officer in a city where people with any African ethnicity remain a minority. And you were kind."

"I see, well, thank you. I'm sorry that we had to meet under such circumstances."

"That's okay. Why are you here now?" April asked.

"I wondered if you and I could talk for a bit. Professor McGill said it would be alright if you'd like to go out. I understand you are all set to be released from here?" Munroe said.

April smiled. "Yes. I'm expecting to leave in the next few weeks. I hope to go to a normal home to live."

"That's great," Munroe said. "Mind if we head out?"

April jumped from her chair.

Munroe tried to keep the conversation casual as they drove to Sunset Beach; asking how April was and what it was like at the hospital. April talked of her different friends, staff and patients, and the things she would do to occupy her time. Munroe pulled into a café.

"Room for pancakes?" Munroe asked.

"Always," April replied.

They entered the café and took a seat looking out across the bay. They ordered sweet pancakes, April's filled with vanilla ice-cream and chocolate sauce, Munroe's vanilla ice-cream and banana.

"Dr. Hershey tells me you're no longer suffering from any sleeping problems."

"Not for a few months now. I've been teaching myself that sleep is good for me. I've been trying to remove any anxiety before I sleep and to remain relaxed. That way my body shouldn't want to keep getting up. Seems to be working."

"I understand one of your friends is Emily Jackson, from the university."

"Yes, Emily is my friend. She was good to me while I was at the university. I didn't like it there. The university has been generous, but they just want to test me all the time. I think Emily understood how I was feeling. When I came to the hospital, Emily was the one that still came to visit."

"What's Emily like?" Munroe asked.

"She's nice. She studies psychology and would share some of her studies with me. She's convinced I'll make some kind of great discovery when I'm older.'

"Did she ever ask you to do anything you didn't want too?" Munroe asked.

"Emily? No, she did seem a bit obsessive, and I've seen her get angry on occasion, but no nothing like that."

"Has she ever hurt you or made you feel like should could hurt you?"

"No," April replied, starting to giggle, "I did think she was going to hit this kid this one time. We were out walking around campus and another student fell into me knocking me over. I was a bit shaken but okay. When I turned around Emily had hold of this guy, she was shouting some unpleasant things to him and I thought she was going hit him, but she let him go in the end. Sorry I probably shouldn't be laughing."

Munroe smiled and nodded.

"Why do you want to talk to me Detective Munroe?" April said.

"Munroe is fine, you can call me Munroe. It was Emily that attacked Dr.Hershey. I think she may have done it because she was jealous."

April looked out of the window at the boats on the water. The clouds were overcast, and the wind was up.

"It was probably my fault," April said.

"What was your fault?"

"I told Emily I didn't think she should keep coming to see me at the hospital. Elizabeth had told me she was concerned about Emily. Emily got very angry, she must have taken it out on Dr.Hershey."

"I don't think you could have known Emily was going to do that." Munroe said.

April returned her gaze to the boats.

Munroe said, "I understand you're going to live with Dr.Hershey."

April smiled, and looking at Munroe, said, "Yes, isn't it great? I'll be able to go to school, live a normal life. She must have told you. You're fond of her, aren't you?"

"Why do you say that?"

"Because your eyelids widen slightly when you mention her name. They don't make the same movement with Emily's name. So, you feel differently about them and I don't think you are fond of Emily."

"That's quite...remarkable. Yes, I am fond of Dr.Hershey, she's a good friend and a very capable lady, and I'm sure you'll be very happy."

Now Munroe found himself looking out of the window.

"April, how did you know it was me, back at the hospital?" Munroe asked.

"I was beginning to think you weren't going to ask," April said, smiling. "I was blindfolded. I find I can focus better when I remove one or more of my senses. Your footsteps are different, your shoes are hard wearing, the tone made by those shoes suggests you are heavy, and the time between steps suggested your stride was larger than average. So, a big, tall man with shoes not made for working in a hospital. And besides, you are the only person I have met that wears that Chanel aftershave from the blue bottle."

Munroe found himself smiling at April's observations. He paused before asking his next question. "Do you think it's possible to control someone?" he asked.

"Do you do that a lot?" April replied.

"What?"

"Just change subjects like that."

"Sorry, old police habit. So, do you, think someone can control another person?"

"Of course, if you love someone you'll probably do almost anything for that person, so if the person you love chose to, they could probably get you to do most things that you wouldn't normally do or do for anyone else. I'm sure you get a lot of success getting people to do what you want, when you stick a gun in their face."

Munroe knew April was exceptional but listening to her began to unsettle him.

"I don't have any money to pay for the bill." April stated.

"It's okay, I have it covered," Munroe said.

"There you see."

"Sorry, what?" Munroe asked, confused.

"I just said I couldn't pay and you said you would cover it. We were talking about control and I said something out of context. You should have asked why was I changing the subject, but you didn't. You just went with it and said you'd cover it. The reason you did that is because you are so used to reacting that way, you are programmed that way, something I did or rather said prompted a specific, predictable response from you...*programming*.'

"I see," Munroe replied, although not sure that he did.

"That's why we feel guilty sometimes..." April continued, "Because we realise after the event that we could have predicted the response to something we had done. We feel like we were the cause even though we hadn't carried out the act. Like me feeling guilty about the attack on Elizabeth. We see now what happened when I told Emily to stay away from me, but the truth is it could have been worked out before I said anything and therefore, in theory, possible for me to have planned the attack by using Emily."

"And did you?" Munroe asked.

"What?"

"Plan the attack on Dr.Hershey."

"Of course not, it's our emotions that keep us in check. I'm very fond of Elizabeth, if I could have predicted Emily's actions then I wouldn't have said anything to her, thereby possibly avoiding the attack on Elizabeth. And I wouldn't be sitting here feeling guilty for what happened."

Munroe cut across his pancake. "Maybe when you're older you'll explain all that to me."

April laughed, "You're funny, Munroe."

CHAPTER 16

Hershey had completed eight days in the Hospital before her attending doctor agreed to her release. The bruising on her face from the blow to the back of her head had almost disappeared, only a small pale-yellow patch below each eye remained. The stitches in her head would dissolve with time. The tissue around her shoulder was still tender but the majority of movement had returned. The shock of the attack had been replaced by optimism for the future and of making memories with April.

Munroe had offered a police car to return Hershey home, but she chose instead to arrange her own taxi. Despite the weather being cloudy and raining, Hershey wore her oversized sunglasses. During the ride back, she remembered she had several messages waiting on her voicemail. The traffic was heavy as they made their way across downtown, Hershey adjusted the volume on her phone. Of the messages that had been left only one was of interest to Hershey, Sam had called to say she had short-listed some housekeepers for her to review, she had emailed the details. Hershey looked at the list of names, but their resumes were not easily read on her phone.

Hershey arrived home a little after twelve and after making a start on her laundry and checking what groceries she had in the house, she logged on to her computer and printed off the resumes. With some hot tomato soup and a coffee, Hershey started to read over the resumes.

Hershey noticed that Sam had selected from two agencies based in the City. None of the candidates were below thirty years of age and all were female, but otherwise the list was quite diverse. Hershey had a preference for two of the candidates and phoned Sam asking her to make interview arrangements.

After Sam called back confirming dates and times, Hershey called McGill to confirm he was agreeable to allowing April to be present at the interviews. He approved.

The next day Hershey followed up with Child Services who had arranged for her to receive an interim order for guardianship. Sam had arranged for Hershey's background checks to be completed while Hershey was recovering in hospital. The full court order could take a couple of months before processing, Hershey didn't want to have to wait that long. Over the course of the next few days Hershey and April conducted the interviews and had made plans for a celebratory dinner to include McGill, Munroe, Lucas Vogel and his daughter Katie, Rowina and Jenny Bateman. At April's request, Hershey and April would be arriving by limousine.

"Did you settle on a Nanny?" asked Jenny as they were all seated.

Hershey looked to April to answer. "Yes," April said, "we have decided on Angelina Flores. She was born in Portugal and moved to Canada after marrying a Canadian. She is a mother of two, a boy Robert and a girl Francesca, who are now both adults and living in different parts of the US. Sadly, Angelina's husband died three years ago. Excellent references, Angelina has over twenty years caring for people, ten of which as a full-time Nanny. She's fluent in Spanish as well as English and Portuguese."

"Why did you choose her?" asked Katie.

"Because she was the only one that brought a sample of her cooking with her to the interview, chocolate and pear scones, yummy," April laughed.

Munroe reached across and gently squeezed Hershey's hand, "I'm really happy for you. I hope everything works out," he said.

"Of course, it will," Hershey replied, returning the squeeze.

"Well, I'd like to make a toast," said McGill raising his glass toward the centre of the table. The others followed. "Wishing you health, happiness and good fortune in your future together. To no more care facilities for you young lady, and an easier less stressful career for you Elizabeth. May Angelina prove to be a great housekeeper and a wonderful cook, and may I be invited round often. All the very best."

"All the best," they all said as their glasses chinked.

* * * *

The following Thursday afternoon Hershey went to pick up April from Ashford Hospital for the last time. It seemed most of the staff and low-risk patients had all gathered to ensure April received a good send-off. A number of the nurses shed tears as April said her goodbyes. McGill was the last person April said goodbye to – she hugged and gave him a kiss to his cheek, saying she wouldn't forget his kindness and that he was to come to the house and sample Angelina's scones.

April's few possessions and numerous presents were loaded into the BMW filling the trunk and back seats. As they drove off waving to those left behind,

Hershey was unaware that she and April were being watched from a window in the Orca ward.

* * * *

Angelina arrived as promised at nine a.m. on Friday morning. She had arrived by taxi having been told at the interview she would have access to a car. Hershey had made arrangements for Angelina to be added to the insurance for the BMW.

During the day Angelina made extensive notes covering both Hershey's and April's preferences and dislikes. Hershey is particular about eating organic fresh fruit and vegetables and has a preference for certain stores. In the afternoon, Hershey and April went shopping for clothes and any additional bedroom furniture April wanted. After dinner April was helping Angelina unpack some of her things, they were sitting in Angelina's bedroom.

"Does Angelina have a meaning?" April asked.

"Yes," replied Angelina, "it means little Angel, I guess my Mama must have thought I was her little Angel. And Flores means Flowers in Portuguese but I prefer the Spanish, which means Blossoms."

"That's nice, Little Angel Blossom."

"I assume you were born in the month of April." Angelina asked.

"No, actually I was born in June."

"Then isn't April a bit of an odd name for someone born in June?"

"I was adopted when I was still a baby. My new parents called me April because it was in April that I became their child."

"Do you know what April means?" Angelina asked.

"It's the fourth month of the year," April replied.

"It is, but it comes from the word aprilis which means 'to open', also a reference to flowers. Some people think April comes from Apru which is short for Aphrodite. Do you know who Aphrodite is?"

"Isn't she the Greek goddess of love?"

"And beauty, yes she is. Which do you prefer?"

"…I prefer 'to open' it makes me think of new beginnings."

"That's nice, love and beauty are all well and good, but a new start is filled with hope and possibilities, yes?"

"How do you know so much about names?" April asked.

"Well, where I was born names are important. In many countries and different cultures, names are often associated with blessings where parents name a child in the hope of the child receiving a blessing relating to the name they have given. Perhaps you just got your blessing a little later than some. From the look of you, maybe you will be getting both blessings – love and beauty, and a life where you grow to blossom with new possibilities."

April smiled.

That weekend Hershey watched as Angelina and April quickly established a bond that made her think of her own childhood and the time she would spend with her grandmother. Hershey's thoughts moved to her parents, she hadn't told them of the changes in her life, she wondered how they might feel – would they accept April as a grandchild? As Hershey lay alone in bed on Sunday night she thought only one thing now remained missing in her life – a man. She thought of Munroe.

* * * *

Hershey had decided to take a further two weeks off work. She didn't feel fully ready to return to work following her attack and she was keen to spend as much time as she could with April. She did however, need to submit her conclusions and recommendations to the Hospital Board on the events that had occurred there over the past few months. With respect to the events surrounding Donald McCoy's death she left out any opinions or conclusions and simply reported what had happened, her findings were inconclusive. Thomas Bessey's death stemmed from a false fire alarm and a subsequent break down in procedure. Bessey's death would in time be added to those already committed by Edward Walker but in truth it had little impact except on the family of Thomas Bessey. In Frank Marshall's case, she added that in her opinion he had committed suicide suffering from the guilt arising from Thomas Bessey's tragic death and the mental strain of having worked in excess of ten years on the Orca Ward. She recommended that going forward, staff should not be required to work longer than two years on the high security ward without working less stressful duties for a minimum period of six months.

Hershey and Munroe met for lunch during the week. They agreed not to discuss the events at Ashford only that Emily Jackson was now awaiting trial while retained in custody. Munroe asked how April and the new housekeeper were settling in. Hershey replied, but her mind wandered as Munroe went on to talk about some of the changes the new Chief of Police, the first woman to secure the position in the VPD, was looking to introduce. *What would it really be like being married to a detective? Would our relationship cope with the stress of him being called away at any time?* She tried to imagine life with Munroe. She thought she knew what to expect, she thought she would be able to manage. She felt comfortable in his presence, secure, calm, happy, when she was with him. Though she would no doubt want more of his time than he would be able to give, she decided part of a life with Munroe was better than a whole life without him.

"Do you think you will eventually get married Munroe?" Hershey asked.

Munroe stopped talking and then Hershey realised she had interrupted him. He looked into Hershey's eyes.

"My life is…difficult. I'm a detective. I'm on call twenty-four seven. If I'm working a case, and I usually am, even my leave is spent working. I'm not a regular guy Elizabeth. I don't drink, I don't party, I don't much care for socialising, I'm a Christian, and I've been known to study tire marks in my spare time."

Hershey was smiling. "Different isn't the right word for you Munroe. You are special." She reached for his hand. "Would it be alright if we spent more time together, get to know each other more?"

"I'm very fond of you Elizabeth, I'm just not sure I'm any good for you. You're a doctor with a Phd, educated, a consultant, you've travelled, you're…" Munroe was reaching for the right word.

"Classy?" Hershey suggested.

"I was going to say, you're out of my league. You can do much better than me. Any man would be honoured to be at your side." Munroe replied.

"Don't be silly, Munroe. And it would be my choice anyway. Are we agreed?" Hershey asked.

"Yes. That would make me very happy." Munroe reached across the table to kiss Hershey on her cheek. As he was about to kiss her she turned her head and the kiss went to the lips. The kiss lasted longer than Munroe had intended before he sat back down.

"And you were thinking of classy," Hershey said, laughing.

"Yes. I did think of classy but thought it would have been an unclassy thing to have said."

* * * *

More than four weeks had passed since April had moved in to live with Hershey. Although Angelina owned her own apartment she had come to spend increasingly more time with Hershey and April, often staying over in the guest bedroom. Hershey had returned to working but tried to keep her hours more relaxed, often making a point of getting home in time for dinner with April and Angelina. April would always provide a recap of her day, where she was at with her school studies and any news events that had caught her interest. April shared that she had started to learn some Portuguese from Angelina. Hershey had also noticed links to learning Cantonese websites on April's computer search history.

In the evenings Hershey and April would cuddle up on the couch and watch TV shows, or sometimes play board games. On occasion when Hershey had work to clear in the evening, she noticed April and Angelina would often play with playing cards. It was a Friday evening when Angelina offered to put April to bed. Hershey still had notes to write up from several consult sessions she had had during the week. She was happy for Angelina's help. April kissed Hershey good night.

"Is there something troubling you child?" Angelina asked as she sat on the edge of April's bed brushing her long straight hair.

"Why do you ask?" April asked.

"Because my dear child, I am a woman of experience and I can see that you have not been your usual self today. In fact, you have not been your usual self for a few days unless I am mistaken. What is the matter?"

"You know Elizabeth is seeing that detective, Munroe." April started. "Well, I don't think he likes me."

"And why would you say something like that?" Angelina asked.

"When I was younger, I suffered with sleepwalking. At first it just started off as regular sleepwalking, getting out of bed, sometimes getting dressed and leaving the house."

"Good gracious. You are not old now little one. What were you doing leaving the house at night when you were even younger?"

"I was sleepwalking. I wasn't really in control of what I was doing. My parents added an alarm to wake them, but at first, they didn't know to expect it. I knew how to unlock the door. Anyway, my episodes became more aggressive."

"That doesn't sound good. More aggressive how?" Angelina said.

"We had a cat, his name was Noodles. I killed Noodles while I was sleepwalking."

"Oh, that's horrible. Why would you do such a thing April?"

"It wasn't my fault. I understand now why I did it. I have always been curious how things work. How the body works. What happens to the food we eat, how our bones and muscles enable us to move, how the organs work together to allow us to live. I don't believe I intended to kill Noodles but somehow while I was sleeping I must have been thinking about how

Noodles worked. Our behavioural inhibitors don't function normally while we are asleep. I went down to the kitchen, took one of the knives, returned to my room and while Noodles was apparently sleeping on my lap, I cut into his stomach."

"Oh, my poor child. I'm sorry. Is that how you ended up at the hospital?" Angelina said.

"Things got worse." Tears started to run down April's cheeks.

Angelina stopped brushing and held April, "Oh my little Angel, it's okay you don't have to tell me. It wasn't your fault, you are just a child."

"I killed my parents. I didn't mean to. I was asleep and just wanted to paint my baby brother's room red." April was crying.

"Oh, my dear child, it's over now. It wasn't your fault. Sometimes terrible things happen, sometimes terrible accidents happen and there is nothing we can do about them. Sometimes we just have to accept that the world and people are not perfect. Here, come, stop your crying. You're safe now and with people that love you. There, there," Angelina said holding April and wiping her face. After a few moments Angelina asked, "How does any of this relate to the detective?"

"He was the one that came to my house back then. I don't think he believes it wasn't my fault. I mean, I was tested by doctors and with my history, no one tried to say I did it on purpose, but I don't think he believed it."

"I'm sure he did my Angel. Why would anyone think a child would want to kill their parents? I haven't noticed anything. He seems fine with you." Angelina said.

"They weren't my real parents. I was adopted. My real mother killed herself when I was a baby. The police never identified who she was, so I don't know if I have any other real family. I can see it when he looks at me. He at least thinks I may have been capable of killing them." Angelina continued to comfort April. "I'm scared Angelina," April said.

"What on earth of?"

"I'm scared if Elizabeth and Munroe do get together then he will find a way to come between me and Elizabeth. I'm scared they will send me back."

"Oh come, come. I'm sure it won't come to that," Angelina assured.

"Elizabeth is very fond of him and I can see he is very fond of her." April started to cry again, and now she held on to Angelina. "I don't want to go back. I'm happy here with Elizabeth, with you."

"Don't you worry about anything my angel. There are many things that could happen. I'm sure you are probably wrong but even if you were right, they may never get together, and Elizabeth cares for you very much that I do know. If that detective did try to come between you, I'm certain Elizabeth would not allow it. And I will always be here for you my little child, you have nothing to worry yourself about."

April stopped crying and as she held on to Angelina, a smile broke on April's face.

* * * *

Munroe and Hale got up to stretch their legs. Their day had started with introductions and a walkthrough of the agenda for the next two days. They had now been sat for two hours as the second morning session came to a close. They had both been selected to attend a seminar covering several high profile serial killers, their habit and behaviours and the techniques used by law enforcement agencies to eventually capture them. The purpose of the seminar was to introduce a controversial technique, based on police provocation, that was gaining popularity within the agencies for its rate of success. The hall was filled with police and law enforcement officers from all around North America, Munroe estimated some four thousand years of experience was gathered in the same conference room. *An excellent terrorist target if ever there was one.*

Munroe and Hale made their way to the coffee and Danish pastries situated at the back of the room during a break in *'provocative pursuit'*. Hale picked up a raspberry doughnut. Munroe stuck with a coffee and shortbread biscuit.

"Alexander didn't make it to the list or Eddie Walker," Hale said, referring to the names of celebrity killers that had been listed on the Agenda.

"At least those guys leave evidence, something to go on so that when they're caught it can be proven."

Hale frowned. "You still churning the stuff from Ashford over in that head of yours? Walker killed the guard. Emily Jackson admitted the attack on Elizabeth. What else is there?"

"Donald McCoy's death," Munroe replied. "And yes, Walker killed the guard but who initiated the events that lead to the killing?"

"You don't think it was Jackson?" Hale asked.

"I don't know that it matters. My point is how would we ever prove it? If someone were capable of...programming someone, how would you prove it? And no, Jackson is smart but she's also erratic. She went route one with the attack on Elizabeth, it doesn't square with planning or programming or whatever the hell it was. If someone convinced McCoy to kill himself, then we have an unsolved murder on our patch. Jackson is going to be tried for McCoy's murder."

"Jackson didn't know anything about McCoy's death," Hale said.

"That's what she said, but she would say that."

"No, I mean, I *know* she didn't know anything about the death?" Now Munroe was frowning. Hale continued, "After that first interview I did with her. I stopped recording and was about to leave the room when she asked me how McCoy died. I had asked her earlier in the interview about it but hadn't said how he had died. As I left, she asked me how he died. I really don't think she knew. I don't think she had anything to do with it," Hale said confidently, taking another bite out of the doughnut.

Munroe stood silent, thoughtful, as Hale devoured the remainder of the doughnut. Just as Hale placed the final piece in his mouth, Munroe placed his cup back on the table.

"I'm getting out of here. I have got work to do." Munroe said.

"Munroe?...Wait a second!" responded Hale.

Hale took a quick swig of his coffee and grabbing another doughnut from the table quickly squeezed passed other delegates and out the double doors after Munroe.

* * * *

It was late on Friday afternoon by the time Munroe and Hale arrived at Ashford. They had driven straight from the conference in Seattle, up Interstate 5 catching delays at the border crossing before hitting Vancouver downtown traffic and out over the Lions Gate bridge. Munroe recalled the time when Hershey first brought the death of Donald McCoy to his attention, he heard himself saying – *'Ok, so Donald didn't kill himself, so someone else was involved.'* That is what had been bothering him all these weeks. – *if the someone else wasn't Emily, then who was it? And then the same person would become the prime suspect for the false alarm that lead to Bessey's death.*

At the hospital, Munroe asked for Professor McGill but he was unavailable, McGill had left early for the weekend. They were directed to Dr. Michael Cheung.

"Detective Hale and I would like to review any footage you may have leading up to and including the death of Donald McCoy and the false fire alarm incident that involved Lucas Vogel." Munroe said.

"Detective, Donald McCoy's death is not under police investigation. As you know, the hospital conducts its own investigations into all deaths that occur on the premises. Only those considered to be suspicious are referred to the police." Cheung replied.

"Please. We believe it may be connected to incidents we are investigating. I could arrange for a warrant but I'm failing to see why the hospital wouldn't cooperate without a warrant."

Cheung nodded. "Professor McGill has left for the weekend. He's heading away and asked not to be disturbed unless it was urgent. I don't think he'd mind you taking a look. Here, this way."

Munroe and Hale followed Cheung down a corridor and into a small office. A security officer sat at one desk that had a bank of monitors slowly switching between cameras positioned throughout the hospital. Another desk also had a pair of monitors and computer on it. Cheung told the officer why they were there. The three men stood while the officer wheeled his chair over to the other desk, powered up the computer and the two monitors came to life.

"I'll be just a minute while I find the footage," the officer said. "What's the date?" the officer asked as a list of files filtered by ward and then date appeared on one of the screens. Cheung leaned over the officer and pointed to a file, "this one," Cheung said.

As the footage came on to the screen, Munroe asked if he might take the seat while he reviewed the footage. Chung left the office briefly while the officer showed Munroe how to pause, fast forward, and rewind the footage. Cheung returned with another chair which the officer was quick to accept.

"There has to be something here, something that points to someone?" Munroe muttered.

"That's the McCoy footage? You know there was that drawing that Lucas Vogel was carrying with him when he set the alarm off." Hale said, standing beside Munroe.

"Hey, now that you mention it, you should go and pick that up. I think Elizabeth said Lucas had it at his home."

Hale stood there, not sure if Munroe was being serious.

"Go on," Munroe said with a short wave of his hand. "I'm sure Dr.Cheung will tell you where Lucas lives. Isn't he down at Lions Bay or somewhere close? I'm going to be here a while so there's no harm in seeing if you can get hold of it."

Hale looked at Munroe, who continued to view the footage, and then looked at Cheung. Hale and Cheung left the office. Munroe watched as Donald McCoy came into view. He appeared to be talking to someone as he returned to his room. Munroe watched. McCoy's movements weren't fluid but looked a little stiff to Munroe's eye, as if McCoy suffered from arthritis. McCoy removed two forks that had been wrapped in a paper napkin from a pocket. Sitting on the edge of his bed, his movements looked odd, *almost robotic*

Munroe thought. McCoy looked straight ahead as he lifted one of the forks level with his right eye. McCoy's expression was blank, no tears, no sign of anxiety, and no hesitation as the fork punctured the right eye. Munroe had to force himself to watch, he needed to see. Just as Elizabeth had explained, McCoy simply continued to press the fork into the eye, deeper and deeper, until his head twitched, and he stopped pushing the fork, leaving a little over an inch remaining. McCoy was still alive. He raised the second fork to his left eye and with identical speed and precision, pressed the fork into the eye. As the second fork went deeper, McCoy's body jolted and shook. His arm dropped to his side, his head and shoulders slumped forward.

Munroe played the footage forward and then all the way back, then forward again. *Nothing*. With help from the officer he loaded up the footage from the false alarm. The officer loaded several files, each file providing footage of the same date and time but from different cameras around the hospital. The officer was clearly familiar with the files. Once loaded, each file ran in its own window. The officer rearranged the windows and suggested Munroe focus on a particular group he had arranged. Munroe watched the various clips that reflected what looked to him to be the regular workings of a hospital – staff moving up and down hallways, in and out of wards and rooms, patients coming and going. Eventually it became clear to Munroe some staff were preparing for the shift change, gathering their bags and leaving the hospital. Lucas Vogel came into view. Munroe followed him as he left one camera and appeared on the next. Munroe leaned closer to the monitor.

"Can we make this one bigger?" Munroe asked the officer.

"Sure," the officer replied, wheeling his chair over beside Munroe. With a couple of clicks, the footage Munroe had referred to was enlarged on the screen.

"Thanks," Munroe said.

"No problem. You're welcome."

Munroe watched closely. Lucas was checking his pockets. *The cigarette...where's the lighter?...Can't find the lighter...looks for the matches...there you go...everything normal...oh, what was that?* Munroe paused and slowly rewound the footage, then forward again. Munroe paused the footage. Lucas Vogel's face could be seen in profile. Frame by frame, forward, then back, then forward again. Munroe couldn't be sure what he was seeing. Lucas lit the match and for a split second, the length of one frame, he appeared to have the same blank expression that he had just seen on the McCoy footage. Then it all changed, Lucas expression quickly changing to one of astonishment then panic. *Normal...blank...surprise...panic* Munroe said to himself as he clicked through each frame.

An hour had passed before Hale returned clutching the piece of paper. Late afternoon was giving way to evening.

"Vogel wasn't in when I arrived, but his wife went and found the picture. She said she knew where it was because little Katie had it tacked to her bedroom wall." Hale said.

Looking at the picture Hale was holding Munroe said, "That's not the one."

"Yeah, it is," Hale replied, turning the paper over to reveal the bell drawing.

Munroe took the paper from Hale and turned it back over. Munroe was looking at a colourful drawing on the other side from the bell. The page was divided into several layers of colour, the top of each layer looking like a mountain range with varying jagged edges. At one end of the page, which Munroe assumed to be the bottom of the picture, the layer was coloured red, the next orange, the next yellow, then green, blue, a bluish-violet and then violet. At the very top, between the violet mountain range and the top of the page was an area of white then a thick black straight line. Munroe was staring at the picture.

"Nobody mentioned this picture on the back," Munroe eventually said.

"It doesn't look like much," Hale replied.

"Did Emily say anything about this?"

Hale shook his head. "Not to my knowledge, nothing to me for sure."

Munroe held the picture up to Hale, "What do you think it is?"

"Well I would have said it looks a bit like a rainbow, except the colours aren't right and the lines are jagged." Hale replied.

Munroe looked up at Hale. "I don't think it's a rainbow. And I think these colours are right."

Munroe got up out of his seat, video footage still running.

"Detective there's still some video remaining," the officer said.

"That's okay thanks. I don't think we're going to find anything we don't already know about. Doctor Cheung?" Munroe asked the officer.

The officer glanced down at a monitor, "Out of the door to the right, down the corridor, fifth door on the left."

Munroe left the office. Hale soon followed.

On entering Dr.Cheung's office, Munroe said, "Do you know when April Pritchard was actually transferred to the hospital?"

"Around the end of July, I believe, one moment let me check."

Dr.Cheung pulled up April's records on the computer. "Here…the twenty-eighth of July."

Munroe's mind was running. Hale was standing with both hands on his hips.

"Dr.Cheung, have there been any other incidents of note between the twenty-eighth of July and Donald McCoy's death. Has anyone else died or been hurt, anything odd? What about a patient Peter Legwinski?" Munroe asked, more in hope than belief.

"Frank Marshall took his own life following the events with the fire alarm and Thomas Bessey. Peter Legwinski, a patient here, died on the twenty-sixth of August. I remember the date because it's my birthday," Cheung replied.

"How did he die?" Munroe asked.

"Confirmed strangulation, suicide. No one else involved. Tied clothing around his neck and fixed it there using a pen if I recall," Cheung replied.

"So, nothing odd found with his body? Pictures or drawings or any kind?" Munroe asked.

"Not that I am aware of. His personal affects are probably still in storage unless a family member collected them, though I don't recall any family visiting Peter. You can have a look for yourself. When a patient dies the room is cleared of any items and stored until collected by family members or disposed of after two years. This way." Cheung rose from his seat and left his office, with Munroe and Hale in tandem.

Dr.Cheung led them upstairs and into a room containing dozens of metal lockers lining two walls. The room reminded Munroe of a sports changing room except for the red carpet flooring.

"The patients name should be written on the front of the locker. Legwinski should be just…here."

Cheung stopped at a locker and punched in a four digit code. "Sorry, it's not very secure, all the lockers have the same code."

He opened the door to the locker and reached in, withdrawing a box big enough for a large pair of shoes.

"Is that it?" Hale asked.

"That's it." Cheung replied, handing the box to Munroe.

Munroe sat at a bench in the middle of the room, presumably for this purpose. He opened the box. Immediately his eyes were drawn to a folded piece of paper that lay tucked down one side. He unravelled the paper, no more than a few inches across, to reveal a drawing of a crucifix with an oval loop at its top. The cross had been coloured yellow and Munroe noticed two thin faintly drawn lines extending from the base of the loop.

"I've seen that before," Hale said.

"It's an Ankh," Cheung stated.

"A what?" Hale asked.

"An Ankh, an Egyptian symbol I believe, represents Life or something like that. I've known surgeons to wear them, for good luck I suppose."

"Not for Peter Leg Win Ski," Hale replied.

"One last thing please doctor, you still keep a handwritten Visitor log?" Munroe asked.

"Well yes and no. Yes, we do ask that visitor sign in, but they are also logged on computer. You want to see the log?" Cheung replied.

"Yes please." Munroe replied, "Perhaps I should just look at the manual log first?"

"I'll take you to main reception. You can check both from there," Cheung said.

"Come on," Munroe said to Hale, "I want to show these drawings to someone. Thanks for your help Dr.Cheung."

At main reception, Munroe started paging through the Visitors log. Hale watched as Munroe went back through the book to July twenty-eighth, and then slowly forward from that date.

"Er, thank you Doctor Cheung, that's been most helpful," Munroe said, not moving his attention from the log.

"Well if that's all, I will leave, I promised the family I'd try to get home in time for the hockey," Cheung said.

Munroe scanned down the names on each page as he paged forward. "Excuse me," Munroe said to the receptionist sitting near by. "This is Detective Hale, I'm Detective Munroe. Could you show my colleague the computer visitor log please, starting from July twenty-eighth, thank you?"

The receptionist looked at Munroe, then at Hale then started to type on her keyboard. Hale moved around the reception desk, so he could see the computer screen.

Eventually Munroe reached August twenty-seventh, his finger stopped a third of the way down the page at *Emily Jackson*. He returned the open page back to today's date.

"Any entry for Emily Jackson prior to August twenty-six?" Munroe asked.

The receptionist slowly scrolled down using the computer mouse. It wasn't long before both Hale and the receptionist shook their heads.

Outside, rain had started to fall. "Let's go," Munroe said to Hale. As he turned and walked toward the exit he said, "thank you."

As they stepped out of the hospital and into the rain, Hale said, "Where are we going? And what's going on?" Hale asked, his frustration showing.

Munroe checked his watch, "Nowhere. It can wait until tomorrow," he said.

"What can wait?"

"Emily Jackson." Munroe replied.

"Munroe help me out here," Hale said.

"Why didn't Emily mention anything about the drawing on the other side? She was happy to tell us about the bell," Munroe asked.

"She didn't say she'd drawn *that* bell only that she had shown April how to draw *a* bell. May be this wasn't drawn by her in which case she wouldn't know what was on the back," Hale replied.

"Right, so April would have drawn this other picture too."

"So?"

"I think it means something," Munroe said.

"It means she knows how to draw a poor rainbow," Hale replied.

"And what's this other picture mean, this Ankh?" Munroe asked.

"Oh, come on Munroe, really? Now you want to add Legwinski's death as suspicious? That's why you were checking the entries in the book?"

Munroe stopped walking and turned to face Hale. "After seeing the footage of McCoy's death, I'm inclined to agree with Elizabeth. I don't think he could have done what he did without significant pain medication, or," Munroe was searching for the words, "it was like he was hypnotised or something. You said yourself you didn't think Jackson had anything to do with McCoy's death. All we have is this childish drawing. Peter Legwinski strangles himself and we find another drawing that could have been drawn by a child, with his belongings. Emily Jackson's first visit to the hospital was the day *after* Legwinski killed himself. She hadn't even been to the hospital. Coffee?"

"Sure," replied Hale.

They were quiet in the car as Munroe drove them back toward Vancouver. Munroe took his phone from his jacket pocket and plugged a cable into it. Moments later Mahler was playing in the car.

They stopped at a Starbucks on Robson. Rain was still falling. Hale placed the *cherry* as he liked to refer to the emergency vehicle light, on the roof of the car so they wouldn't be disturbed because of where they had left the car. He stopped saying he was going to '*pop the cherry*' shortly after partnering Munroe, after Munroe threatened to taser him.

"You know this could easily just be all bullshit," Hale said, once inside.

"Possibly but unlikely," Munroe responded. "I mean, something made Lucas react that way when he set the alarm off. I saw his face, he was perfectly normal one moment, then he lights the match, then his expression just goes blank for a moment, and then he starts to panic. Like the match flicked a switch or something. If that was planned by someone then that might also explain McCoy's death. If both those events were planned, then why not Legwinski's?"

"And you don't think Emily's involved," Hale said.

Munroe nodded agreement.

Hale took a drink of his latte. "You think an eight year old girl is capable of doing this?" he said.

"You should see this kid, she's like no other kid you've ever met. Sure, she can be sweet but she's so smart. She may be eight years old but she's no eight year old."

"What are you going to do? You are saying Elizabeth could now be living with the psycho child from hell."

Munroe nodded again. "Now you are where my head is at."

"So, what now? The pictures aren't worth nothin'. No one is going to believe a child can do what you're suggesting, or anyone else for that matter. We've got nothing except some dead bodies where she wasn't even present. Is it even murder even if you could persuade someone to kill their self?"

Munroe replaced his toothpick after it broke in his mouth. "It's incitement at least. And if I hold a gun to your daughter to force you to kill yourself, that *is* murder. If someone really can do what we're suggesting, then they are committing murder." Munroe stated.

"That's great Judge Munroe, but how do the detectives get any proof?" Hale replied.

Munroe sat quiet, drinking more of his coffee. Hale looked out of the window on to the street. Despite the cold and the rain, Robson remained filled with people jumping in and out of restaurants, cafes and side shops.

"Provocative pursuit," Munroe said.

"What? You mean from the seminar we are supposed to be at by the way?" Hale replied, drawn away from looking out of the window.

"Where you are certain a suspect is involved in something, but you just don't have the evidence, you have to turn the screw, apply some pressure, get them to act and be there when they do." Munroe said.

Hale found himself nodding.

Munroe looked at Hale. That morning at the seminar they had been told that provocative pursuit depended on no one being aware it was happening. The police did sometimes bait a suspect to draw out an attacker, but that required knowledge of what constituted bait, a brunette wasn't bait if the killer preferred blonds. Entrapment involved the crafting of a plan in order to set the bait. Provocative Pursuit meant engaging with the suspect directly, making them nervous, getting them to alter their patterns or routines, perhaps getting them to change their modus operandi, make a mistake or even a confession. The technique was controversial as it could easily be interpreted as harassment by the criminal friendly justice system, but developments in criminal psychology had opened up opportunities to apply just the right amount of pressure to provoke an action, rather than too much and have the suspect hibernate or retaliate through the legal system.

"You do realise that if you are right about the kid, Elizabeth is in the firing line," Hale said.

Munroe nodded. "But I'm going to be there."

"You going to tell the Captain? He's expecting us back tomorrow."

"Maybe, later. But first I want to see what Emily Jackson makes of these drawings."

* * * *

The next morning Munroe and Hale drove to where Emily Jackson was being detained in Maple Ridge. They asked to see Emily Jackson privately in a room. After fifteen minutes and several phone calls a member of staff took them through. Emily was already in the small interview room. Munroe and Hale entered.

"I thought it must be you," Emily said.

"Good morning Emily," Munroe replied. "I have a couple of drawings I'd like to show you, thought perhaps I could get your opinion on them."

Munroe sat at the chair opposite Emily while Hale stood in a corner of the room, arms folded. Munroe unfolded the first piece of paper and placed the drawing of the Ankh on the table.

"Nice, you draw that?" Emily asked.

"I assume you know what it is?" Munroe said.

"It's an Ankh, an Egyptian symbol or hieroglyph that is supposed to represent Life and some think love and reincarnation. But you could have asked anyone who wasn't a cop and found that out."

"It was found in Peter Legwinski's room. Legwinski apparently killed himself up at Ashford, near the end of August."

"And this means something?"

Munroe took the second paper from his pocket deliberately only showing the *bell-side*.

Emily said, "That's a drawing of the bell I told you of, that I showed April how to draw."

"But this one isn't the one you drew correct?" Munroe asked.

"That's why I said 'a' and not 'the' detective."

"This one was given to Lucas Vogel by April Pritchard the day he set the fire alarm off."

"Yes, you said. And your point is what Detective Munroe?"

Munroe turned the page over, revealing the coloured drawing on the reverse. Emily sat looking at it for a moment, studying it.

"Do you know what it is, if it means anything?" Munroe asked.

"It's the heat spectrum. The colours represent those made in flames as the temperature rises. It's possible to create thousands of different colours by mixing various elements, like they do with fireworks, but these colours represent the standard escalation. I'd say the presence of white and then black really distinguishes it from say…' Emily stopped hesitant. A smile crept on to Emily's face. "I don't believe it," she said.

"What? What don't you believe?" Munroe pressed.

"April drew this didn't she? She drew the bell on the one side and the flames on the other." Emily leaned back in her chair. "She knew all along."

"What did she know Emily?"

Emily sat shaking her head in disbelief. "When you told me, April had drawn the bell I had showed her I thought it was probably just coincidence, the bell on its own couldn't have been enough, Lucas would have had to have seen a real fire, but this," she pointed to the drawing, "could have been used to somehow heighten what he saw, amplify it, make it seem more intense. But you'd still need a trigger."

"Like a flame from a match?" Munroe asked.

"Yes, possibly. If Lucas went to light say a cigarette, his subconscious could have been programmed to make him think he was seeing a much larger fire. She knew, she knew all along. I thought I was teaching her, maybe I was, but this…I couldn't do this."

"And what about this Emily? What about this Ankh, could that have been used to get someone to kill himself?" Munroe asked.

Emily picked up the drawing of the Ankh, she then noticed the two faint horizontal lines extending from the base of the loop. She smiled.

"These drawings could be used as *Anchors*, something to attach feelings or thoughts, or even actions too. Under say, hypnosis, it's possible to reduce the craving someone might have for smoking a cigarette by attaching a feeling of satisfaction to an action, such as pressing two fingers together. Then later, the patient simply needs to press the fingers together to help reduce the urge." Emily continues to stare at the picture. "This is a good one."

"Why is it a good one, Emily?" Munroe asked.

"It looks very innocent, but these two faint lines are probably more noticeable to the subconscious. They make the picture appear a bit like a knot. So, you have the loop of the ankh and the subconscious would see a knot. The person tied something around his neck, didn't they? My God, did April draw this as well?"

Emily looked at Munroe, then at Hale, then back at Munroe she then slumped into her chair. "She knew all along," more to herself than those in the room, "April knew. She used me. All the time she was just using me."

Munroe got up and he and Hale left the room.

CHAPTER 17

It was Sunday and Angelina had returned from church. She was preparing lunch in the kitchen while April sat drawing at the table. Hershey was at her computer in the study.

"Why do people go to church Angelina?" April asked, continuing to draw.

"Some people go to make friends, some people go because it makes them feel good, and some go because it makes them feel important."

"Why do you go?"

"Because I, like some, believe there is a God to whom we will all have to answer, one day."

"So, do you go to church because you fear God?"

"Perhaps, the Bible tells us that the fear of God is the beginning of wisdom. And I believe one should take time away from day to day things to think on God, and to thank Him for our lives," Angelina said.

"But who is God?" April asked.

"God is the Creator, he created everything and put everything in its place and, how do you say, laws to govern it."

"Can you see God?"

"The Bible tells us no man has seen God but that those that see Jesus see God. God is a spirit."

"You believe in spirits?" April asked.

"Of course, God is spirit and there are lots of other spirits too."

"Like what?"

"The Bible speaks of Cherubim and Seraphim, of Angels and Demons."

"Angels and Demons, they are spirits?"

"Yes, I think so, they can appear, how do you say…materialise. They can appear and then seem to disappear. I don't think they really disappear, but just change into a form we can no longer see."

"So, there are good and bad spirits?" April asked, no longer drawing.

"Yes. God's spirit is good, but there are many demons, they are bad spirits. You never heard of Jesus casting out demons?"

"Elizabeth doesn't believe they were demons, she says they are people with fractured personalities, chemical imbalances or brain disorders." April replied.

Angelina didn't respond, choosing instead to continue preparing the vegetables.

"Are these spirits among us?" April asked.

"Why all these questions Little Flower?"

"It seems to me that if you are right then science is looking for answers in the wrong place."

"Now what does that mean?" Angelina asked, now finding herself asking the questions.

"Doctors attempt to help and cure people, but a real cure is only possible if the root cause is treated and removed, or else we are only treating the symptoms and the problem is set to recur," April stated.

"Is that right?"

"Yes, so if you are right and Jesus did cast out actual demons, then demons would be the cause of the problem and drugs or therapies would only be masking the problem, treating the symptoms so to speak."

"You should not worry yourself about such things. Sometimes the body does get damaged and it can't function properly for the person. It doesn't mean a demon is the cause. There's room for your Mom and me to both be correct. You have your whole life to live and enjoy. And someone with your brain and pretty looks should enjoy life to the full. You have had such a difficult start to life, now you must learn to enjoy it and enjoy what you have. Lunch is almost ready, go get your Mom."

April sat a moment. "She is, isn't she?"

"What?" Angelina asked.

"Elizabeth, she is my Mom," April replied, smiling.

While they were eating lunch, April asked if she could call Hershey 'Mom'. The question caught Hershey off guard and April waited for her response. To Hershey somehow being called Mom would make everything permanent. As she sat there looking at April she saw a child that didn't know who her real mother was and probably never would, a child that had no one else in the world, a child born illegitimately, whose father was a mistake of nature, a monster. For a moment the thought of being a mother scared Hershey but she replied, "Of course, Princess, if that's what you want, it would make me very happy."

* * * *

On Sunday evening, Hershey lay across the sofa in the living room. She was alone watching a movie on television. April had gone to her bedroom to play before sleep and Angelina said she was going up to her room to read. The heat from the open fire warmed the room. Hershey checked her watched, ten minutes after nine, still no sign of Munroe. She knew he had been attending a seminar south of the border and wondered if he would simply turn up at the house. She had thought of phoning him, but she didn't want to sound like the housewife keeping a tab on her husband's whereabouts. She got up to make herself a cocoa.

As she approached the living room door a figure appeared the other side, seen through the decorative glass panes in the door. For a moment Hershey was startled, still not entirely used to no longer living on her own. She opened the door toward her and April stood there, standing still, dressed in her pyjamas.

"April?" Hershey asked. "Is everything alright?"

"Sorry Mommy, I'm having trouble sleeping, do you mind if I sit with you for a little bit?"

"Yes darling. I'm just going to have a cocoa, why don't you have one with me and see if that makes you feel any better?"

"That would be nice."

April went and sat down on the sofa in the living room while Hershey made two cups of warm cocoa in the kitchen.

"Here you go baby," Hershey said, as she passed a cup to April.

Hershey checked her watch again.

"Is there something else you want to watch?" April asked.

"No, it's…I thought perhaps someone might be coming around."

April sipped some cocoa from her cup. "You mean Detective Munroe?"

Hershey looked at April. "It's okay for you to call him Munroe. He's been away for a few days and I thought maybe he would come around tonight. What do you think of Munroe?"

"I think he almost loves you. I think he thinks he could love you. And I think you want to love him," April replied.

Hershey slid along the sofa and cuddled up against April. "And what do you think? If I fall in love with Munroe, would that be okay?"

"He'll make me leave, he won't want me to be here," April replied.

Hershey sat up. "No Honey, that's not true, he's very fond of you. Why do you say that?"

"He thinks I had something to do with the fire alarm. He thinks I had something to do with Emily attacking you. He doesn't like me, I can see it when he talks to me, even when he just looks at me."

"Wh…that's not true April. You were being used by Emily. She attacked me because she was jealous, she was using you and I think Emily is a little well, fragile. *It wasn't your fault*, Munroe understands that, he likes you."

"He came to see me," April said

"Munroe?"

"While you were still in hospital, he came to see me, asked me about Emily and the attack on you." April stared at Hershey, then said, "He didn't tell you, did he?"

Hershey fell silent.

April continued, "All my life I have only ever wanted someone to love me. If you go with him, I'll be alone again."

"No April that's not true. I love you April,' she heard herself say. "I won't leave you. Yes, I am fond of Munroe, but *you* are my priority."

April smiled and hugged Hershey tight and kissed her on the cheek. "I love you to Mommy."

* * * *

By Monday morning, Munroe had still not been around to the house neither had he phoned to see how things were or say how the seminar had gone. Hershey got dressed for work and for a moment recalled what April had said the night before - *he'll make me leave, he won't want me to be here.* Before heading out Hershey checked her phone again for any messages or email. By the time Hershey left for work, Angelina was busy helping April get ready for school. Hershey kissed April goodbye as she left the house. As she drove off to work, she thought of phoning Munroe but decided against it, *he must have been called onto something, he'll phone when he's free*, she thought. She didn't notice the car parked in a side street with Munroe sat at the wheel.

Munroe stayed in the car as Hershey drove off in the Jaguar. He had debated whether to phone her, tell her what he had found out, how he felt. Munroe dropped another tooth pick to the floor. How could he tell her, she was never going to just accept April was behind the events just because he said so. It would drive a wedge between them, something he desperately wanted to avoid. For one of only a few times in Munroe's life, he didn't know what to do. As he sat there he watched as Angelina opened the front door and left the house, holding Aprils' hand. *School* he thought.

* * * *

Munroe was feeling guilty. His police instincts told him to approach April, apply some pressure to her, and make his suspicions known to her to see how she would react. He guessed she would almost certainly make Elizabeth aware and then he'd find himself having to explain himself to Elizabeth. Munroe phoned Elizabeth and asked if she could meet him for lunch. She sounded happy to.

They met at a café downtown for coffee and a sandwich. After getting seated they caught up on each others last few days. Munroe made no mention that he and Hale had left the seminar early to further investigate the events at the hospital. He didn't mention his meeting with Emily Jackson.

"My parents called," Hershey said, "I finally plucked up the courage to tell them about April. I told them they had a new granddaughter."

"A granddaughter? Must have been a surprise," Munroe replied.

"Yes, I think it was a bit of a shock for them. I hadn't given them any idea. I told them a bit about her background, how she became orphaned and then placed into the care system,"

"How she killed her adopted parents?" Munroe added.

Hershey gave him a disparaging look. "I didn't mention that she had been adopted. I don't see how that is important at this stage. She suffered from a disorder, terrible things happened as a result, and now she is fine and free from that disorder. Anyway, they called to say they are coming to stay over for a few days. They want to get to know April."

"Well that's good," Munroe replied, trying to sound sincere and hide his concerns.

"I thought it would be good for you to meet them too? Perhaps come over for dinner, stay a while, if you are not too busy," Hershey said.

Munroe reached out and took Hershey's hand, "That would be great, of course I'd love to meet them."

They enjoyed the rest of the lunch and time together. Munroe's phone rang, and he made his apologies then kissed Elizabeth before leaving.

"Tomorrow for dinner then!" Hershey called out after him.

Munroe didn't turn around but raised an arm and signalled a *thumbs up* as he left.

* * * *

That evening, Hershey was again at her computer. She closed her files and email, she then opened an online diary that she had been keeping since April had arrived. In it she would right details about the day they had had, the seemingly trivial things of everyday life, and she would capture anything that she especially wanted to remember. She looked at the previous day's entry and how April had asked to call her Mom. Before starting on today's, she closed off yesterday writing in April's response to her question about Munroe - *He'll make me leave, he won't want me to be here.* She then wrote – *you are my priority.* Under today, she wrote how she was disappointed that Munroe had not called her but that they had met for lunch. Munroe had given no explanation for not having called her earlier. Hershey wrote how she had been offended by Munroe's remark about April killing her parents. She looked again at what April had said yesterday - *He'll make me leave, he won't want me to be here.* Hershey paused in thought, then wrote, *Munroe thinks April has something to do with the events at the hospital?* Hershey checked her watch. Before closing her diary for the evening, she added – *Parents called. They are coming to stay for a few days. Maybe should ask Angelina to take a few days off, enable Mom and Dad to spend more time with April.*

April was doing homework while sat with Angelina in the kitchen. The school were obviously well aware of April's ability but the homework they continued to give her was from grade eight. April was finishing forty minutes of homework in less than ten. Angelina asked if she might take April out for a short drive and perhaps grab a dessert from somewhere, after April had completed her homework. Hershey found herself wanting to join them but something in Angelina's tone made her think she only meant for her and April to go. Hershey checked her watch again, hoping Munroe would call. She agreed. Hershey felt alone.

Outside, across from the house and tucked into a side street, Munroe was again sat in a car watching the house. Munroe was on his own time, if there was such a thing for a city detective. Hale had offered to help but Munroe refused, preferring to be alone. If Elizabeth were to need him he wanted to be close by. He watched as the garage door opened and the BMW pulled out of the driveway. He could only make out Angelina and April. *Elizabeth must be alone in the house. Where were they going?* Munroe ducked down as the headlights swept over his car. Munroe let the car drive passed before sitting back up. He chose not to follow them but instead, content that Hershey was at least safe for now, he suddenly felt very hungry. Munroe reached for his phone and called Hershey.

"Hey, sorry I couldn't call earlier. I know you mentioned dinner tomorrow, but I wondered if you'd be free for dinner tonight, you know, before I get to meet the parents." Munroe said.

"I was beginning to wonder if you were going to call tonight. Dinner would be great. Angelina and April have just left the house, so I'm home alone. When can you be here?" Hershey asked.

"Actually, I'm close. Say ten minutes?"

"Sure. I'll be waiting."

Munroe hung up. As he looked across at the house he noticed the condensation from his breath misting the windows. Munroe started the car and turned the heat up. Checking the dashboard clock, he drove off.

Ten minutes later Munroe pulled up onto the driveway, car suitably warmed up. He sat there for a moment and noticed the curtains move. He still decided to get out of the car expecting to get to the passenger side before Hershey.

The front door to the house opened and Hershey appeared, dressed in black jeans and a pullover. She locked the door as Munroe stopped and opened the passenger door. Hershey thanked him with a polite kiss, as she got into the car.

"Where is your car?" Hershey asked

"Oh yeah, I had to borrow an unmarked one earlier today. Didn't get around to swapping it back. I wanted to see you," Munroe replied, looking to see if Hershey accepted his explanation.

Hershey smiled. "Where to?" she said.

"You good with Milestones?" Munroe asked.

"Perfect, let's go."

The evening wore on accompanied by the seemingly ever present Vancouver rain. Hershey and Munroe enjoyed both the meal and conversation. Hershey choosing to steer clear of telling Munroe she had been offended by his remark yesterday concerning April. Munroe choosing to steer clear of raising his suspicions that April was involved in the events at the hospital. Instead they kept the conversation light and optimistic. At eight thirty Hershey received a text, *back at home, will put April to bed at nine, Angelina.*

Instead of returning Hershey home, Munroe drove to the nearby Cleveland Dam, where they walked for a bit under the cover of an umbrella. As they returned to the car, Hershey stopped and held Munroe's face in her hands. They kissed, a long passionate kiss.

"My parents will be here tomorrow," Hershey said, looking up into Munroe's eyes.

"Yes, you said, we're all going to have dinner tomorrow," Munroe replied.

"I mean, I'd like you to take me home. Stay with me tonight," Hershey said.

They returned to the house. Hershey taking care not to make a noise as she entered. After closing the front door, they kissed again…longer, more intense, more urgent. They kicked off their shoes. As Hershey led Munroe up the stairs he noticed the light flickering in a room downstairs.

"It's okay. We have a real fireplace in the lounge. They know to keep it covered. Come with me," Hershey said, taking hold of Munroe's tie.

As they entered the bedroom, Munroe was feeling conflicted. He had been intimate with very few women. His Christian belief meant he viewed intimacy as marriage, and intimacy with more than one woman was adultery – *till death do you part.* But he knew this moment would arrive. He hoped for it, even prayed for it. He wanted to commit himself to Hershey. Hershey removed her pullover and let her jeans drop to the floor. She turned to face him dressed only in her underwear. Munroe looked at her. She was kind, intelligent, and beautiful. Munroe gave thanks and took Hershey in his arms.

After their lovemaking, Munroe slept through the night, no waking up, no bad dream. A little after six a.m. Munroe's phone started to vibrate. It was Hale. Rather than pick up, Munroe got up from the bed and washed quickly in the ensuite. He got dressed and gently kissed Hershey on the forehead. Hershey stirred and opened her eyes. She smiled.

"I need to go. I'll call you a little later," Munroe said, kissing her again, "thank you," he added.

As Munroe left the bedroom his phone vibrated, a text from Hale – *bus stop at Richards and Davie*. Munroe left the house. As he drove off he didn't notice the blinds move at an upstairs window.

At breakfast, April could not help notice the contrasting moods of the two ladies that accompanied her at the table. It seemed Hershey could not stop smiling, whereas Angelina seemed upset and not conversing in her typically positive tone. Hershey hadn't seemed to notice, but April didn't think Angelina's mood was directed at herself.

Hershey told them both that her parents were expected this evening and were planning to stay at least a week, probably more. She asked Angelina if she would prepare the bedroom and plan a dinner for the five of them plus one.

Hershey left the house a little later than usual. Shortly after, Angelina and April left the house and started the walk to school.

"What is up with you this morning?" April said, holding Angelina's hand.

Angelina's looked down at April. What makes you think there's anything wrong?"

"Well, you didn't say good morning to Elizabeth. You didn't speak while you cooked breakfast and you put the plates down on the table a lot firmer than you usually do. You seemed to be okay with eye contact with both me and Elizabeth, so I don't think you are upset with either of us." April replied.

"You are an observant little thing aren't you," Angelina replied.

"So, what's wrong?" April pressed.

Angelina returned to looking ahead. "I was going to tell you later, but I guess now is a good a time as any. Elizabeth keeps a diary. I was cleaning up a bit last night when I noticed she had left her computer on. Of course, I am not one to pry, but I couldn't help read some of what she had written."

"What had she written?" April asked.

"Seems her parents will be coming over to spend some time with you," Angelina said.

"Why is that upsetting you?"

"It's not, well not really. She's going to ask me to stay away for a few days I think. To give you and your new grandparents some time to bond. It's a good thing I suppose but I, anyways, it doesn't matter, that isn't why I am being upset." Angelina paused, and April chose not to press her. "You are right about that Detective Munroe. It seems he does think you have something to hide. Elizabeth wrote that Munroe thinks you are involved in the events that occurred at the hospital."

"Did Elizabeth say anything about what those events were?" asked April.

"No and I don't want to know. But even I have enough sense to know they can't have been good," Angelina replied. "Anyway, what are we going to do?"

April stopped walking and looked at Angelina. "What do you mean?" April asked.

"Well those two seem to be awfully close. How is it going to work with him being a detective and thinking you are some kind of criminal? What is the world coming to when they think it's okay to blame an eight year old for anything?"

April resumed walking, still holding on to Angelina's hand.

"I'm pretty certain he was at the house last night, I heard things if you know what I mean," Angelina said.

"He was. He stayed the night. I saw him leave this morning, that's why Elizabeth was smiling all the time at breakfast."

"Yes, I noticed that too," said Angelina.

They were quiet as they turned off Capilano road and into Edgewood road. Then Angelina stopped walking and turned April to face her.

"Listen to me, April. I want you to take this, if anything should go wrong I want you to go to this address and I will meet you there. There is a key under a pot near the door."

April looked at the paper, "This isn't your address," she said.

"I know. My son sometimes uses this home. He isn't using it for the time being and I haven't gotten around to renting the property out yet. If you have to leave Elizabeth's house, they will likely look for you at my address, so that is going to be no good. I doubt the police know anything about my son's place."

"I don't want to leave Elizabeth. She's good to me. She won't believe him." April said.

"I know my child. I am sure you are right, but I want you to have this option. If something happens and you think you need to get away, you go to this address. And here take this, don't spend it, you will need some money if it comes to it," Angelina said, handing April a small purse.

A tear ran down April's cheek. "You're scaring me, Angelina."

Angelina gave April a tight hug. "I'm sorry my darling. I don't mean to, but I don't want you going back into that good-for-nothing care system. It's no good for you. I can look after you until you are old enough to look after yourself. If needed, you can live in a different country if you want, I have friends and family in Portugal and in Span. I just want you to know, you have a choice."

April hugged Angelina back. "Thank you," she said.

"I'm sure this will all get sorted out and you and I, and Elizabeth will carry on being very happy together. This detective will lose interest or Elizabeth will, and we will be back to how things were. Come on, now let's get you to school."

* * * *

Munroe arrived at the location Hale had provided. An ambulance crew were attending to someone lying on the pavement. The person, a young male Munroe thought, was covered in blood and wearing a neck brace. As Hale walked over, Munroe noticed two males sat in the back of one of the police vehicles.

"Probable homicide," Hale said as he approached. "The two in the vehicle there are brothers. Appears they took exception to the quality of some drugs they procured from the dealer over there," pointing to a man being attended to. The brothers said their sister collapsed last night after taking heroin they had bought from this guy. She died this morning from a fentanyl overdose. The brothers here decided to exact their own form of justice. The guy here, identified as one Stuart Carston, is likely in critical condition after the beating he received. Mr Carston's acquaintance, a Mr

Bobby Pitchwell, didn't fair so well, his body has already been taken away."

Munroe looked around. Uniformed police were in the process of putting up a cordon. The fire crew had parked their truck to prevent traffic from turning into the scene and now stood watching and talking next to the truck.

"Where have you been?" Hale asked, now smiling.

"What do you mean?" Munroe replied.

"Dude, you are wearing your clothes from yesterday. I don't think you've ever done that since I've known you. You still staking out Elizabeth's house?"

"Err, yeah. Fell asleep. Didn't have the chance to change," Munroe said.

"Munroe, you're going to have to let that go. There's no hard proof that the girl was able to orchestrate any of the things that happened. Look I know you and Elizabeth are close, I get it, but you either have to put it aside and just be content that you are there should anything else happen, or you are going to have to walk away, find another woman."

Munroe looked at Hale and said, "Too late. Now shut up and let's get to work on this."

* * * *

Hershey's parents would be arriving from Kelowna. They had phoned ahead to confirm they should be there within the hour. Preparations had been made. April was washed, a blue bow in her hair and wearing a sailor collar dress by Chloe. Dinner was a traditional roast beef. Hershey received a text from Munroe, he was running late but thought he would still be there in time for dinner.

Hershey was standing at the window when her parents pulled up onto the driveway. "Quickly April, they're here," she said.

April ran to hold Elizabeth's hand and together they went to the front door. They waited until her parents rang the door bell before opening.

Munroe arrived twenty minutes later and just as Angelina had started to plate the main course. Hershey went to the door.

"I bought these, hope they're okay?" Munroe said, handing a small bouquet to Hershey.

"They are lovely thank you. You ready?" she said, opening the door wider for him to step in. Munroe nodded.

Dinner went better than Hershey had expected, everyone seemed happy and her parents seemed to take to April very easily. Munroe seemed awkward at first but was soon made to feel welcome. Only Angelina seemed quieter than usual, but it was time for family and she had been busy with most of the preparations.

Hershey's parents insisted on cleaning up after dinner. Angelina excused herself and retired to her room. April was showing Munroe card tricks at the

table. Hershey got up from the table to help with the clearing up. Munroe
watched as Hershey left the table.

"You're very good at this," Munroe said to April

"It's not too hard, just a little practice needed," April replied, and she
spread the cards on the table and invited Munroe to pick one. "What would
be more impressive, shall I return the card you selected to the deck, shuffle
the cards, then counting through the cards tell you which one you selected.
Or, shall I leave the card you chose there on the table, flick through the
remainder of the pack not taking any more than two seconds and then tell
you what the card is?"

They looked at each other. "You can do that?" asked Munroe

"I can do both. But which one would you be most impressed with?" said
April.

"Leave the card on the table."

April picked up the remaining cards and kept them face down. She then
turned the deck over and very quickly flicked through the deck, taking less
than the two seconds. She returned the deck face down again to the table.

"Okay, I know what card you selected?" she said.

Munroe moved back a little in his chair and smiled. "You trying to tell me,
you know which card is missing from the deck simply by flicking through
them like that?"

April nodded, "If I get it right, how will it make you feel?"

Munroe moved again in his seat and unconsciously loosened his collar and tie. Munroe let out a nervous laugh.

"The reason you asked me to do it this way is because you know there's no trick. It's simply me, looking and memorising each card as I flick through them in order to know which card is not present. The other way, and you are not sure if it is a trick or not, you assume it is trick so it's easier to believe. Perhaps a marked card or me deliberately placing it back in the pack at a specific point. That would be true, it's something anyone can do with a little practice. But this way, there's not many that could do that. No one you know, perhaps no one in Vancouver," April said.

"Or Canada," Munroe added.

Without having touched the card that Munroe had selected, April said, "It's the four of spades."

Munroe glanced to see that Hershey was still helping with the clearing up. He looked back at April who was staring back at him. He leaned forward and quietly said, "I know who you are. I know what you have been doing. You manipulate people."

April also leaned forward, "If I can do the things you think I can, then shouldn't you be more careful. Elizabeth will never believe you. She'll choose me over you." She then smiled and got up from the table.

Munroe remained at the table, alone, looking at the card face down in front of him. He didn't need to look at the card.

"Everything alright," Hershey said, returning to the table.

"Yes. She's quite exceptional isn't she," Munroe said.

Hershey smiled, "Yes she is." She leaned over to collect the deck of cards from off the table, then seeing the card in front of Munroe she also picked it up. Before adding it to the pack she turned it over to look at it."

"Four of spades," Munroe said.

"That's pretty good Munroe, I didn't see you look at it," Hershey said.

"Didn't need to," Munroe replied.

After tidying up, they all moved into the lounge Munroe was drinking black tea and Hershey joined her parents with a glass of wine. April joined them and was keen to share what she had been learning at school, and explained how her class friends, though much older, had become used to her being in the class.

Munroe watched and listened as April weaved her spells. Hershey's parents were enthralled. Hershey was both delighted and clearly proud. Munroe sipped on his tea. He looked at Hershey, April was right, if she did have to choose, he was sure Hershey would side with April. He had tried to dismiss his suspicions at first, but April had baited him, just like tonight. She knew that he knew, and it didn't matter. Hale was right, unless April screwed up and did something that everyone could see, there was no way he could remain in a relationship with Elizabeth.

Munroe was interrupted from his thoughts when he heard April say 'goodnight' to everyone. She gave everyone, including Munroe, a hug and kiss before leaving the room.

"April, perhaps I might escort you to your room young lady?" Munroe suggested.

"A police escort, of course you may. Goodnight everyone," April said.

Munroe followed April up the staircase and then to her room.

"You said that I was nice that first time we met," Munroe said.

"You were. My parents had died, my baby brother had died. I had no one left. You came to the house, doing your job, but you seemed sensitive to the situation. You didn't accuse me. You might even have felt sorrow for me."

"I believe you convinced, I don't know how, Donald McCoy to kill himself," Munroe said, "but what I don't understand is why would you do that?"

"Mr Munroe, if I did convince Donald to kill himself then it would most likely have been done to prove that it can be done. Nothing more, nothing less. An experiment if you like."

"No, I don't like. That stunt you pulled with the fire alarm resulted in a man's death," Munroe said.

"How could I be blamed for the death? Those stupid guards didn't follow procedure, that killer got loose, and someone ended up losing his life as a result. It really had nothing to do with me."

"One of those guards took his own life because of what happened. All of it would have been avoided if you hadn't tricked Lucas Vogel in thinking he was seeing a fire. The actions we take and the choices we make have consequences. You might be as smart as everyone says, but you have no regard for the consequences of your experiments."

"You think I don't care about people, but I do. I care about Elizabeth, Angelina, my friends at the hospital, my friends at school, I cared about my parents."

"Then why did you kill them?" Munroe pressed, trying to keep from raising his voice.

"I couldn't help it. It wasn't my fault. I'm not a monster."

"But you did persuade Donald McCoy to take his own life?"

April nodded, "Donald was a boy trapped inside a man's body. He had been abused and tortured by people who were supposed to take care of him, to the point where he couldn't function. I had been developing my own techniques from material Emily had been sharing with me. I didn't expect it to work, Emily had said that kind of thing wasn't possible, but it did work."

They both heard a door creak. Munroe opened April's door wider then he reached into a trouser pocket and withdrew a digital recorder. He held it up to show April before pressing the stop button.

"Everything alright, April?" Angelina said, appearing at the door in a dressing gown. Her gaze moved from April to Munroe.

"Yes, thank you, April," Munroe said, tapping the pocket to which he had returned the recorder. "Have a good night now, I'm sure I'll see you again soon," Munroe said, squeezing past Angelina at the door.

Angelina watched as Munroe made his way back down the stairs.

"Are you okay?" Angelina asked again.

"He's not going to give up Angelina. He thinks I'm a bad person, he's going to find a way to convince Elizabeth. He wants Elizabeth for himself. He's going to make Elizabeth take me back. I think we will need to leave Angelina," April said, starting to cry.

Angelina sat on the edge of the bed and held April close. "Don't you worry my little flower. Elizabeth is a good woman, but she has poor choice in men I'm afraid. I thought he was up to no good when I heard his voice."

"Did you hear what he was saying?" April asked.

"No poppet, only that it didn't sound very friendly. Here let me tuck you into bed. I don't want you to worry about things, your Auntie Angelina will keep you safe. Don't you worry."

Munroe returned to the lounge. Hershey tapped the space on the love seat next to her.

"Everything alright?" Hershey asked.

"Yes, everything is good," Munroe confirmed, smiling and settling in beside Hershey.

Two hours later, Hershey's parents excused themselves and made their way up to bed, leaving Hershey and Munroe alone. Munroe got up and placed another log on to the fire.

"You were up there a while with April? Is everything okay?" Hershey asked.

Munroe smiled, "We were just talking for a bit. Yes, I think we understand each other better now," he said.

They sat there on the love-seat in front of the fire. The colours of yellow, orange and red reminding Munroe of the drawing April had given to Lucas Vogel. As they both sat watching the flames take hold of the new log, Munroe was wondering how to best share his recording with Elizabeth, and when. He decided it could wait a few days.

At two a.m. April sat up in her bed. Her room was dark but for a slight orange tint that seeped from the streetlight through the blinds in the window. She switched on the reading light that was next to her bed. Quietly she replaced her pyjamas with winter clothing, and placed some more clothes and belongings into her backpack. She switched off the lamp and slowly opened her door. She listened. She could hear Angelina's occasional snoring, nothing else. She walked slowly towards the staircase, passed Angelina's bedroom, and then passed the bedroom Hershey's parents were sleeping in. She reached the stairs where she stopped to look at Hershey's bedroom door, on the other side of the landing. April listened again. *Nothing.*

April slowly made her way down the staircase, the wooden floor creaking despite April's light steps. Tears began to run down April's face. She went into the kitchen and picked up the money from a drawer that was kept there for housekeeping. From another drawer, April took a small knife and placed it into a side pocket of her backpack. She then took two apples and a banana from the fruit basket and placed them in her pack. April returned to the hallway and the bottom of the staircase.

"April, what are you doing?" came a voice from the top of the stairs. The figure started to come down the stairs.

"Elizabeth, it's okay, I'm okay, no need to come down. I was just a bit hungry," April replied, holding up an apple and turning, hoping to hide her backpack.

"Then why are you dressed? What's going on?" Hershey asked, now half way down the stairs.

April turned and unlocked the front door. She had managed to open the door when she felt Hershey's hand on her shoulder.

"Stop, what are you doing? April, what's going on?" Hershey said, pulling April back into the house.

April struggled but lost her footing as she tripped on the door sill. She fell back into the house. Hershey moved around in front of her blocking the way out of the house.

"April, please, tell me what's wrong. Why are you doing this? I don't understand what's going on," Hershey said again, crouching to help April to her feet.

April got back to her feet then took a step back away from Hershey and toward the lounge. The door to the lounge swung open as April's backpack pushed against it.

"It's your boyfriend. He wants you to himself. He told me he means to get rid of me and Angelina. He's going to make you take me back, put me back into care. He says that is where I belong."

"What? He told you this? He told you this tonight? Is that why he was with you so long?"

"I'm not going back into care. I'm tired of everyone else deciding what I should do or where I should go. From now on, I decide. Please get out of my way, Elizabeth," April said.

"Don't be silly April. You're eight years old. Where on earth do you think you are going to go? It's two in the morning. Why are we even talking like this, you don't have to go anywhere. This is your home. I don't know what Munroe is talking about, but we can work it out. April, you don't have to go anywhere. Please, stop this, let's just sit down and sort this out."

April took another couple of steps back, further into the lounge. She could feel the heat emanating from the fireplace, the remaining embers casting an orange glow onto the side of her face.

"He knows," April said, "he knows what I did at the hospital."

"Knows what April? What are you talking about?"

"I was responsible for Donald's death. Emily had been giving me these books. Emily said it couldn't be done, but I wanted to try it. I didn't expect it to work, but it did. Donald killed himself because of what I did. It was my fault!"

"April, I don't understand. How could you have possibly caused his death? Please, April sit down, calm down and let us talk this through. We can work it out. It doesn't matter what happened, I am here for you. This is your home now. I won't let anything happen to you."

April took another step back into the room and toward the fireplace. "It's too late Elizabeth," April replied, glancing down toward the fireplace. "You need to let me go. You should let me go."

Hershey took a step toward April, "I'm not letting you go anywhere, April. I've promised to look after you and I keep my promises."

"Then I am sorry to have to do this," April said, as she grabbed the poker from the fireplace and swung it at Hershey's head.

The brass poker connected. Hershey felt a flash of pain then slumped to the floor in front of the fireplace. April dropped the poker and stepped around Hershey and out of the lounge. April looked back into the lounge and saw that Hershey remained on the floor, but was moving her arms around. April returned to the front door satisfied Hershey would be okay to find Angelina half way down the stairs.

"Good Lord, what has been going on?" Angelina asked.

"I'm leaving. I'll go to the address you gave me. You will be able to find me there. Munroe has set a trap for me, I can't wait Angelina," April replied.

"Then let me come with you now. I'll take you. Let me just put on some clothes and we'll take the car. I can return it before the morning. Go wait for me in the car. I won't be long."

April made her way through the house and into the garage. She grabbed the keys to the BMW that were hanging up on a key chain. Angelina made her way back up the stairs.

In the lounge, blood dripped from Hershey's head. Her vision was blurred. She moved her arms around, disorientated. The room seemed to be spinning. Hershey grabbed the fire guard, knocking it over and partially on to herself. She could feel the heat from the guard through her dressing gown. She started to panic, struggling to push the guard aside.

Angelina returned down the stairs. She went into the kitchen and then into Hershey's study. As she returned from the study she thought she could smell burning. She peered into the lounge. Hershey was on the floor moving her arms around. The fire guard was on the floor beside her and a log from the fire had fallen onto the rug. The rug was starting to burn. Angelina dropped the bag she had been carrying and went into the kitchen. She returned with a wet towel, but smoke was starting to fill the room and the rug was now in flame. Hershey was still on the floor, but had managed to move herself from off the rug and away from the fire.

Angelina threw the towel on the flaming rug. She tried to stamp the fire out, but it was not good. Smoke continued to fill the room. Angelina went over to where Hershey was now lying and grabbed her by the ankles. She struggled to drag Hershey across the room, trying to keep her away from the encroaching fire. They made it to the hallway, just as the fire alarm at the top of the stairs went off.

Angelina scrambled to find her cell phone. She dialled nine-one-one and told them there was a fire in the house. After giving them the address, she remembered April would be in the garage. Angelina made her way into the garage, clicked the button to open the garage and then she started the car.

Something had disturbed Munroe from his sleep. He looked out of the windshield and across at Hershey's house. He thought he could see movement inside. As he watched, the light in the lounge grew brighter, and then larger, before he realised what he was looking at. Munroe grabbed his phone and called for an ambulance and fire service. As he got out of his car, he saw the garage door open and the BMW pull out. Munroe was running. The BMW stopped. Angelina and then April, got out of the car. April saw Munroe running towards them. Angelina had left the driver's door open as she went to the front door. As Munroe arrived, Angelina's was pushing at the door, but it wouldn't open.

"Where's Elizabeth!?" Munroe shouted. He could hear the fire alarm inside the house.

Even in the dark, Munroe could see Angelina was visibly shaking. "Where is she? Where is Elizabeth?" he repeated

"She must be behind the door. Its not opening properly, Elizabeth must still be behind it. I pulled her from the lounge and asked April to help me get her out of the house," Angelina replied.

Munroe looked across at April, "What have you done?" he said.

Munroe didn't wait for an answer. He tried the front door. It opened about six inches before bumping up against something. Smoke was now coming from inside the house. "Elizabeth! Elizabeth!" he called. Munroe quickly looked around. To the left of the front door, the fire seemed to be raging now in the lounge. To the right was a smaller window, the study, but still large enough for him to get through. He took off his jacket, took a couple of paces back, and using his jacket to cover his head, he ran and jumped through the study window.

"Get in the car!" April shouted to Angelina, "We need to get out of here."

Angelina looked at April and then back toward the house.

"It'll be okay. Munroe will get Elizabeth. Come on, we have to go before more police arrive. Munroe will think I did this. He'll make sure they take me away," April said, "Come on Angelina, we have to go."

Angelina returned to the car as April jumped back into the passenger side. The car pulled off the driveway as Munroe came from the front door carrying Hershey in his arms. As Munroe jogged across the street, he saw the BMW drive away.

Munroe gently placed Hershey on the neighbour's lawn. Hershey was trying to speak. Munroe bent lower to hear.

"My parents, my parents are still in there," she said.

Munroe got up, "I'll get them, don't try to come back into the house. Stay here."

Munroe ran across the road. In the distance he could hear sirens. Munroe reached the house. Despite the incessant rainfall, the wood structure homes quickly succumbed to the heat. Smoke was billowing from the front door. Crouching Munroe stepped into the hallway. He could feel the heat from the lounge, flames now licking the door frame. Dark patches were forming on the hallway ceiling near the lounge. Munroe reached the staircase, the smoke filling his lungs and forcing him to choke. Not sure if the smoke would be even thicker as he climbed the stairs, he decided he was going to risk it anyway. Covering his mouth as best he could, Munroe ran up the stairs and turned right at the top to where he thought the parents must have been sleeping. *Why the hell weren't they awake?*

Munroe opened the bedroom door to find Hershey's parents just standing there.

"We sleep with these in our ears," Mrs Hershey said, holding some rubber earplugs. "The alarm woke us up. Then we could smell the smoke. We were just getting our gowns on to see what was going on."

"We have to get out of here right now. Let's go!" Munroe shouted.

He grabbed Mrs Hershey by the arm and still holding her arm, walked her briskly out of the bedroom onto the landing. He risked switching the landing light on. Thick smoke was pouring up from the stairs. He didn't know if they would make it out. He grabbed Mrs Hershey, picking her up and putting her over his shoulder. "Follow me down!" he shouted to Mr Hershey.

Munroe used his jacket to cover Mrs Hershey as much as possible. He took a deep breath before descending the stairs. He moved quickly. The heat was intense, the smoke thick making visibility impossible. He could hear Mrs Hershey groan. Munroe rushed from the house before taking his next breath. He hoped Mr Hershey was right behind. Munroe continued to the end of the driveway before placing Mrs Hershey onto the ground. As he stood, he saw the fire trucks turn into the road. Munroe turned back to the house, expecting to see Mr Hershey leaving the house. *Where was he?*

Munroe rushed back to the front door, but the heat pushed him back. He wasn't getting in there. Behind him the fire crew were getting prepared. Munroe stepped back from the house.

"Please sir, move back away from house!" a fireman shouted through a mask. "Get to the other side of the street and away from the house. We'll take it from here."

"There's one more! He was following me down the stairs!" Munroe shouted back, before moving away.

Munroe returned to Mrs Hershey, she was coughing and still lying on the ground. A fireman came over and placed an oxygen mask to her face.

"Will you stay with her?" Munroe asked. The fireman nodded. Suddenly the windows from the lounge blew out.

Munroe looked back at the house, still no sign of Mr Hershey. Munroe jogged across the street to Hershey. She was regaining consciousness. He crouched and held her close. He then noticed the blood coming from her head. More sirens. An ambulance arrived and then a marked police vehicle. Munroe stood and waved one of the paramedics over. Munroe crouched back down and held Hershey as the paramedic arrived. He showed the medic the wound but continued to hold her as the medic treated the wound.

"April?" Hershey said.

"She's gone Elizabeth, I'm sorry," Munroe replied.

"My parents, are they okay?"

Munroe looked across the street to the house. Mrs Hershey was now being escorted to the back of an ambulance. As Munroe watched, a fireman emerged from the house carrying Mr Hershey over his shoulder. One of the medics rushed over with a stretcher. The fireman placed him down on the stretcher. Munroe could see the body was limp, lifeless. The fireman removed his helmet and breathing apparatus. The fireman looked at the medic and signalled with his thumb across his neck. The medic started CPR but Munroe could see from the fireman's reaction that he didn't think he was going to make it. Munroe's head sunk.

"Munroe, my parents? Are they ok?" Hershey repeated.

Munroe looked down at Hershey, "Your Mom is going to be fine," he replied.

"And Dad? Is Dad okay?" Tears welling in her eyes. "Munroe?"

Munroe shook his head very slightly, "I'm so sorry."

End of Part One...

Acknowledgements

I would like to express my sincere thanks and appreciation to the following people for helping to make this book become a reality:

My wife, Mandy, for her encouragement and support, and for all those hours taking great care of the kids while Dad was locked away.

My mother for her support, feedback and assistance with the artwork, also to Paul Weichel for providing his talent on this revised front cover.

And to, Leah Girvitz and my sister Sandra for their invaluable input.